The hard years on th
the Greek. He had
married various wive
the delightful excesse
them for long. His c
of the pea and the thr
Votan set off to try to
had lost: the Deed of .... Gold in Ireland.

The long shadow of the Roman Army still lay over the misty island of Britain. The underground world through which Photinus made his way westwards to the Summer Country was one of treachery and intrigue, where the kings and the druids fanned the last dying flames of resistance to Roman rule. The conquerors were interested in Britain now only as a source of silver. And the eyes of the Eagles, like those of Photinus, turned to the west and the Gold Rivers of Wicklow. Through the bloody battlefield of Tara and the smouldering ruin of Ireland, Photinus came at last to the rivers, and there he learned what he had come so far for — the Secret of the Gold of Ireland.

Also by John James

VOTAN

and published by Bantam Books

NOT FOR ALL THE GOLD IN IRELAND

John James

BANTAM BOOKS
TORONTO · NEW YORK · LONDON · SYDNEY · AUCKLAND

NOT FOR ALL THE GOLD IN IRELAND

A BANTAM BOOK   0 553 17359 6

Originally published in Great Britain by Cassell & Company Ltd.

PRINTING HISTORY

Cassell edition published 1968
Universal-Tandem edition published 1971
Bantam edition published 1988

This book is set in 10/11pt Paladium

Bantam Books are published by Transworld Publishers Ltd.,
61-63 Uxbridge Road, Ealing, London W5 5SA, in Australia by
Transworld Publishers (Australia) Pty. Ltd., 15-23 Helles
Avenue, Moorebank, NSW 2170, and in New Zealand by Transworld
Publishers (N.Z.) Ltd., Cnr. Moselle and Waipareira Avenues,
Henderson, Auckland.

Printed and bound in Great Britain by
Cox & Wyman Ltd, Reading

Gaul

CHAPTER ONE

Well, if you really want to know how it was I came to be in that lugger, on a fine reach south-west in a north-west gale, with the north coast of Ireland on my left hand, in company with a Druid, a Colonel of Thracian Cavalry (misemployed), the King and Queen of the Silurians, a Priestess of the Gods Below, to whom I may or may not have been married, and a handful of Brits who alleged they were sailors, then I will tell you.

It all started in my Uncle Euthyphro's house in Ostia, at dinner on a warm spring evening. It began with my Uncle Euthyphro saying:

'Someone will have to get it back. And he may even have to go to Britain to do it.'

I made a face at him. Go to Britain? He might as well have said go to the waters of Lethe. After all, what did any of us know about Britain in those days? It was difficult enough for the ordinary citizen to go there, almost as difficult as getting ashore in Egypt, though of course it was simple to arrange for members of a wealthy family of merchant-priests like mine. But so far nobody in the family had wanted to go there, although we did some trade, in dogs and wool and oysters and mussel pearls. We had an agent in Londinium, and so we didn't need to go ourselves.

Well, what did we know? It was an island where it rained a great deal of the time. A hundred years ago, now, His Sacred Majesty the Emperor Claudius had conquered the fertile southern quarter of the island, where the Brits live, and had left the Northern Desert, as huge as Africa, to the painted Picts, building a wall to keep them out. The Brits, we knew, were the same people as the Gauls, speaking the same language, and the Irish beyond the Empire were the same people also, Many of the nations of the Celts had been broken up long ago, and parts of them lived in both provinces. For instance, the Parisii lived around Lutetia in the north of Gaul, but another branch of them were spread all around the fortress at Eboracum.

The Brits were a strange people, we had heard. Of course we all knew that every third Briton was a magician, and that they had strange things to do with the dead, though quite what nobody was sure. Yet there were plenty of men in Rome who in their youth had served their time as tribunes in the legions in Britain, and they would always tell you how fond they were of their little Brits. You often find this among men who have to go and live among primitive races — they fall in love with their charges. Literally, too. There had even been a few who had talked wistfully of how they would like to live in the island permanently, farming for wool. Going native almost, if only they could find the daughter of some great landowner, once a noble and now a Citizen of Rome, as some were by great and rare good fortune, to marry.

But go to Britain myself? I thought, that evening, in Ostia. Not if I could help it. Somebody else could do that. But there, if you could learn to stand the taste of butter, you could stand anything, and I could eat it without turning a hair. Not that butter would have stood very long, in my uncle's house in Ostia that evening. Nor that it was really very hot, even for the first of May, but it was the last really comfortable evening I was going to have for a long time, though I didn't know it. So it wasn't the heat that made my cousin Philebus sweat. It was the talking-to that his father Euthyphro and I had just given him. All the names in my family follow the same pattern. It all started with my grandfather who had an obsession with philosophy, and believed that a thing partook of its name, that was part of its character. So he called all his sons and grandsons after dialogues of Plato, and I had uncles called

8

Phaedo and Crito too. And if it had not been for my mother, who came from up in the hills and was half Galatian and so had a will of her own, and for the North Wind for whom she had a particular veneration and who therefore kept both my father and my grandfather mewed up in Alexandria for three weeks, I might well have been called Laws or Republic, or even Banquet. But even that might have been better than the name she gave me, Photinus. Neither good Greek nor good Latin, that name, and perhaps Grandfather may have been right in holding that the name governs the character of the thing. I seem to have spent half my life looking for better names. Votan I've been called, and Mannanan, and so many others, and each new name has brought me some kind of profit and some kind of loss, some gain in knowledge, some loss of innocence.

Well, it was quite hot that evening, and the dinner had been quite good, all except the goose liver which had been spoilt, and that was quite easily remedied: we just sold the cook and bought another which improved the general efficiency of the kitchen. I mean, it's not everybody who *wants* to go and work in the sulphur mines, is it? But my cousin Philebus wasn't thinking too much about the food: he had other torments on his mind. I had brought one of the family's ships in that morning, it being the easiest way from the Old City to Rome, where I had a good deal of business to discuss with my uncle. Clearing the port authorities and dealing with all the documents relating to the cargo had taken me well into the afternoon, and I had only got into the house just in time for dinner. I was very tired, and then I had been thrown into the middle of this first-class family quarrel. I felt that before I made any suggestions about future action, I wanted to hear it all again, quietly, this time. My uncle was one of those men who can never forget they aren't at sea.

'Now, Philebus, as I understand it, you bought some kind of monopoly from the Emperor, or rather from one of his Sacred Majesty's Chamberlains.'

'Yes. From Faustinus.'

'And you paid?' I knew it must have been expensive.

'Twenty-five thousand sestertia.' But not as expensive as that, twenty-five million copper sesterces.

'How much . . .' I began to ask, and then thought, it was no use now asking how much of that was for Faustinus himself. 'You lost the deed gambling.'

'Three cups and a pea,' nodded Philebus miserably.

'The method is immaterial,' I said consolingly. 'I could take any man alive by that game if I held the cups, and even if I didn't I would never lose a game if only I could count my thumbs. But if you aren't up to my standard, you shouldn't play. Never stake anything of value unless you can cheat, or have enough influence to buy your way out again. But do you remember who it was you were playing with?'

'It was Gwawl. Everybody knows him, even though he's only been around the tables in Rome for a month. He'll play with anybody.'

'That's a strange name. Is he a Greek?'

'Sometimes he says he is, and sometimes he says he's not. Some people think he comes from a Lugdunum Greek family, and you know how Greek *they* are, been there for a couple of hundred years, and intermarried with the Gauls all the time. But if he is from Lugdunum, there's nobody here who knows his family. He might be anything, Gaul, Syrian, Spanish, anything.'

'But look here,' I protested, 'a Monopoly Deed like this isn't a bearer document, not usually. *He* can't use it.'

'He made me sign a transfer deed. He had it all written out ready, and the witnesses as well, waiting. The deed itself was in my name, personal to me. Now it's personal to him.'

'A lawyer, then, is he?'

'No. He lives by his wits, gambling on the Games, mostly.'

From this point on I ignored Philebus. He was grateful for that. I asked his father:

'You've tried to buy it back?'

'He wanted two hundred thousand sestertia.'

'And the monopoly is worth . . .?'

'I don't know.'

'What do you mean, Uncle, you don't know? You've spent enough of the family's money on it.' I felt I could speak like that to Uncle Euthyphro, I was on equal terms with him, not like Philebus. 'What about the man you took it over from?'

'Well, the truth of the matter is, we weren't taking it over from anybody.'

'Not from anybody? But someone must have had a monopoly of the Gold trade with Britain.'

'Not Britain.' My uncle was almost squirming. 'There's Gold in Ireland. That's what the monopoly was for. Everybody knows there's Gold in Ireland, whatever else they don't know about it.'

I looked so astonished at this that even my uncle noticed it and stopped talking while I got my breath back. I tried to remember what I did know about Ireland, and there wasn't much anybody knew. It is an island, not much smaller than Britain, and it lies thirty miles, or less, from the coast of Britain. It exports hunting dogs, now, and nothing more. Nothing at all. Certainly not Gold. And I had never met anybody who had ever been there. When I got my breath back, visibly, my uncle went on:

'Of course, any Gold you get from there will have to go through Britain, and it will have to come in legally, as there'll be too much to hide. There's no difficulty there. But there's been no Gold coming from Ireland that I can trace since the conquest of Britain. Even what used to come in was all worked up, and very old-fashioned too.'

'So you mean to re-open the trade with Ireland?'

'Well, I was chatting with Faustinus, and I thought it would be good for the lad.' He jerked his head at Philebus, who was trying to corner the world supply of Falernian into his own gullet, that being his best idea of a commercial operation. 'Every boy ought to have a chance to *do* something when he's young: it sets the tone to his own life. I

11

had that long trip south of Leptis Magna, that set the tone for me. I've been thirsty all my life since, and I've passed that on to Philebus. And how long was it . . . three years . . . four . . . you were away up on the Amber Coast? I know it made me, and look what it did for you.'

'Yes, look what it did for me,' I agreed, as he passed me the wine jar in a hurry while there was still some left. 'It turned my hair white in a night, and it took years for it to come back black again. And it gouged my eye out, and nothing will ever bring that back.'

'Nevertheless,' said my uncle, growing a little pompous as the wine jar emptied, 'you will not deny that it gave you a certain confidence in your manner, a certain *élan* in your dealing with the world . . .'

'If you mean that I seem to think that the worst has happened to me, then I agree: I think it has. No calamity I precipitate on myself from now on can be as catastrophic as those I have gone through already . . .'

'Not merely that. Surely you admit that you learned a great deal from what you experienced?'

'Well, yes. I admit, I did marry two queens, and seduce one, and that taught me to be very wary about Barbarian women. I'll never bother with another one as long as I live. I did reorganise a trading firm, and I sent half Germany money-mad. I made one king and I killed another, and that has taught me to be sceptical about the basis of authority. I led an army in battle, and won, and I made up at least four hundred songs about it that you may hear in any barracks in the Empire where there are German auxiliary cavalry. That taught me to be very wary of what the poets tell us. But on the whole, I think the effect was on the North, and not on me: I remained a Greek, nothing more, nothing less. You think it would have done Philebus some good?'

'Well, I did. I don't think so now. He could never stand the pace, you can see that. Here we are, only two hours at table, and he's out to the vomitorium already. Look what he's got to do now. He's got to get the Deed of

12

Monopoly back first, and that's only the beginning. Some-one will have to go to Ireland, and set up a system for getting the Gold over that we can leave an agent to work. The man we've got in Londinium now, for instance, he can do all that, once it's started, but as for the spadework — why, Leo Rufus couldn't organise an orgy in a wholesale slave warehouse. Someone responsible will have to go there.'

'But when you go,' I warned my uncle, 'you will have to leave someone just as responsible here in Rome. I wouldn't like to think of Philebus in charge.'

'Oh, I'm not going. I thought you might.'

I looked at him as bleakly as I could.

'I've done enough travelling up there. I've got a bigamous wife among the Picts, waiting for a chance to eat me the first step I take outside the Empire. And I've a real wife at home in the Old City, and a baby coming in the autumn.'

'You'll be back home by then.' My uncle was a good salesman.

'Well, I suppose . . . I might as well have a last fling while I have the chance.'

'You've had four last flings to my certain knowledge. This will have to be the very last.'

He blinked at me in a benign way, the look he used when he was selling winded horses as racers. Philebus came back, his face the colour of the sea on a dull day. I asked him:

'Do you feel like going to Faustinus and asking him to cancel that deed and to issue another one?'

The green of his cheeks turned a little paler. He shook his head miserably.

'All right,' I told him, trying to sound kind. 'You can take the ship back instead of me. Have you been to sea before?'

'No.'

'Then there's no way to learn like being in command. The mate is a Galatian, and he's a good sailor, remember that. The supercargo knows what's what, he'll see you through. Then you can tell my father what's happened.'

'Oh no! I couldn't face him.'

'It's him or Faustinus, take your choice. When you've

13

done your sea time, then perhaps we can let you loose on land.'

'But what shall I tell him?'

'Anything you like. Say it was a whim of mine, to go back to the North just once more. The whole voyage is fixed up. Troops to Byblos, cedarwood to Alexandria, corn to Corinth and statuary back here. And if you see my wife, smack her on the backside for me and tell her it had better be a boy, this time. Now, about my business. How's this Gwawl travelling?'

'There's a draft of Illyrians going up to join the Second Augusta in Isca. He's going with them as mule-train boss with the baggage as far as Bonnonia.'

'A man who has to work his passage across Gaul and you gamble with him for all the Gold in Ireland? What on earth was he staking against it — don't answer that! You thought it looked so easy there wasn't a chance of losing, and he probably put down an embroidered cloak or something. Now, Philebus, just you lose my ship like that, and I'll gut you alive, I will. *And* your father will sharpen the knife for me.' I never gave Philebus time to remember that he was only two years younger than I was. However, he might as well feel he could do something useful. I went on:

'You know Rome, you can help to get me started. First of all, send off a courier to our agents in Londinium and Bonnonia, and in all the towns on the way, to say I'm coming. Don't say why, just say I'm on my way, and they're to give me all the credit the family name will bear.

'Next, we'll have a night out in Rome. I want to see this Gwawl so that I recognise him in future, and so that he won't recognise me.

'Last of all, I want a litter and carriers arranged all the way from here to Bonnonia, starting, let's say, next Wednesday, and a bunch of reliable men as escort.'

'Wednesday? But he'll have two days' start then. You'll never catch him before he gets into the Province!'

'I don't want to. If you fancy tackling the baggage-master

14

of a legionary draft when the troops are all around him, go ahead. Let *him* keep the Deed safe. If I can get to Bonnonia before him, I can catch him at sea — alone. Besides, I can have a few days in Lutetia on the way. People keep on telling me about the girls there. And that reminds me . . .' a sudden thought had struck me. 'There's another last thing you can do. I want you, Philebus, to go and buy me a girl for the journey, as a parting gift. I bet you know where to go.'

'He does,' said Uncle Euthyphro coldly. 'And he'll pay out of his own money, not out of the family's. Will any woman do?'

'Of course not. Listen carefully, Philebus. I want a woman who doesn't weigh more than a hundred pounds, if she's going to come in the litter with me. For the same reason, she's got to be clean and decent and not too stupid. And the less Latin she speaks the better. You see, I want a Brit.'

That would be difficult, I thought. Nobody in their senses will buy a British slave. There are too many magicians in that island: you don't want to be bewitched overnight and wake up in an ass's head or something. I went on. 'She's got to be miserable and want to go home. If she does what I want, then I'll set her free in Britain when I get there. So make the bill of sale out to me, and put her age down as thirty-five, whatever it really is, or the manumission won't be legal.'

Philebus didn't object to this. He answered:

'I know the very thing. It's what Gwawl was wagering against the Monopoly Deed. And whatever he asks, it will be worth it if you can make him pay for what he did for me.'

CHAPTER TWO

I had my night out in Rome, and another three after that, before I had my good look at Gwawl in a fashionable bath-house, not at all the kind of place to expect to see the baggage-master, of a legionary mule train. If I'd been Gwawl, I thought, I'd have been a little more careful about the consistency of my disguises. Myself, I decided, I wasn't going to bother about any disguises or fancy dress in Britain.

No, I thought, time and again in those few days, I was going to be just Photinus and nobody else. No more was I going to do anything myself, either. I would have enough agents among the Brits for that. I would just stand aside and plan, and tell the others what to do. And least of all would I have anything more than necessary to do with British women. That was how I had got into trouble in Germany. First I had married a native, and then I had done other things, distilled drink, and organised trade, and even raised an army of my own. No, that personal dealing was over. What others wouldn't or couldn't do for me would remain undone.

My Uncle Euthyphro agreed.

'Just leave it in the hands of the Gods,' he told me. 'But what worries me, my boy, is what Gods? I know that the Unconquered Sun dismissed you from his service. Who do you worship now? The Moon and Stars?'

'No,' I replied, quietly, because it wasn't something I liked discussing. 'As far as I worship anything, I worship the Gods Below. Wherever you go, you find different Gods for this and that. But the Gods Below are the same everywhere.'

By dawn on that Wednesday morning I was glad enough to settle into the nice comfortable litter, and jog off with the curtains drawn against the sun. I hadn't been to bed on Tuesday night at all, and so I was glad of five hours' sleep. We moved at a steady trot, most soothing, with the litter bearers changing every quarter of an hour, so smooth I never noticed it. Our escort came close behind. Big hard men, they were, mule-drivers for the family most of the year, freedmen or freedmen's sons, and their leader was a nasty customer called Marco with a scar from eye to throat. I was glad he was on my side.

When I woke up, I had a good look at the girl Philebus had bought from Gwawl for me. She wasn't very young, she must have been eighteen at least, but she was small built and plump, nearly down to the limit I'd set, though she got fatter as we went. She couldn't have been anything but British with that dark brown hair, nearly black, and those blue eyes, not ice blue like the Germans so often have, but the blue of woodsmoke, soft, lazy but with the fire behind it all the time. She reminded me of my first bigamous wife, Bithig, who had been a queen among the Picts, and who was probably still looking for me. To get away from her, I remembered, we had had to steal a ship belonging to a crusty old man called Caw, whom we sold to Starkadder Eightarms the Pirate. Still I thought, I'll be quite safe, I won't be going within a hundred miles of the Wall.

I looked at the girl in my litter, who didn't really look like Bithig on closer inspection, and asked her what her name was.

'They call me Candida around here.'

'But your real name?'

'Cicva.'

'All right, Cicva. After this morning, we speak not one word of Latin together. Then, if when we land in Britain we find I can pass for a Brit, I shall set you free.'

She didn't like the word Brit, I could see it in her face: they none of them do. To outsiders they call themselves

17

Britons, in full, but to themselves they call themselves Comrades, Cymry. But Brit is the old Army word and I used it when I wanted to. I was paying, wasn't I?

The best way to learn a language is in bed. That was the way I learnt German. I learnt the language of the Brits in a litter, which was almost as good, if not better. We watched the long coast swing by, and I learnt the words for sea and ship and for all the fishes and shell-fish. We turned away from the sea, and I learnt the words for ox and plough and for all the plants that grew.

We turned north at Marseilles and up the Rhone. Coming south, it's much faster and more comfortable to take a boat, but not going north. This is a surprising thing. I saw a map once, hanging on a wall in Alexandria, and it showed quite clearly that Rome is in the centre of the world, and that Africa is at the top, and that Britain and the Land of Norroway are at the bottom, and that is why the greatest rivers of the world, the Nile and Rhine, flow downhill to the north. So going north ought to have been easier than it was, but if the Rhone flows in the face of nature, then perhaps the road does the same thing.

A little way before Lugdunum we caught up with the legionary draft. Of course they got off the road to let us through. It's wonderful what a show of money will do when you're travelling. I walked by the litter with Marco, and Cicva peeped out through the curtains. I pointed Gwawl out to them. Marco asked:

'Shall we kill him tonight?'

'No, no! I want him alive as far as Bonnonia. He's got something I want, and we'll let him worry about looking after it. We'll pass them and have a few days in Lutetia.'

I got back into the litter. I asked Cicva:

'Did you see him?'

'Of course. Why *can't* we kill him tonight? We could take all night over it.'

'You sound as if you want to kill him personally.'

'I do. If it weren't for him I wouldn't have been kidnapped and sold down here.' She wouldn't tell me anything more about it. She wouldn't say what part of the island she came from, or who her people were. This was unusual. Most of these girls are only too eager to assure you that they would be princesses if only they had their rights. But she wouldn't say a thing.

We stopped a little way further up, to have a midday snack at a tavern, and the handful of officers going up with the draft, and riding ahead of it to keep out of the dust, stopped there as well. I called them over to join us. We had various mutual acquaintances. I asked after Aristarchos the son of Demons. Last I heard of him, I told them, he'd been commanding a regiment of cavalry at Carnuntum.

'All Brits they were, too,' I remembered. 'What were they called? Hadrian's Own Danube Rangers?'

'Oh, the Wall-eyed Warriors,' said one of the centurions. The legions are always glad to make fun of the cavalry. 'But he's left those now. I don't know where, but I think it was a promotion.'

They asked after Philebus — I hadn't realised he was such a rake.

'He's well at sea by now,' I told them, and they all laughed again — they could afford to, I was paying for the wine.

'Better to travel like you with all home comforts,' someone said waving at Cicva, who had brought us some cheese she had been bargaining for in the village. Like all the Brits she was a connoisseur of cheese, and Gaulish was near enough to British, as even I could tell by now, to let her hold her own in the market.

'I've got to have someone to watch my blind side,' I told them — I had a quite tasteful false eye in that day, of jet, carved in concentric circles — and the officers hooted with laughter and tried to pinch her bottom without my seeing it, and they were in great good humour when the mule train came swinging up the road and Cicva ran off to hide her blushes in the kitchen.

I pointed to Gwawl. I said:

'Now there's a real old-fashioned mule-driver for you. Where did you find him?'

'Oh, that one,' they all said at once. 'He's a bad one, he is. Even his own family wouldn't own him, wherever they are. A Brit, you know, and one of the nastier ones. Good little fellows, but every now and again you find one like him. Usually, though, they have red hair. You've got to watch out for the red-haired ones.'

I looked again at Gwawl. His hair was black, and tight curled, and it bristled on his thick forearms, with the sinews knotted and corded under the skin. When I had seen him in the baths, I had only thought him gross, the kind of man who sits down in a tavern and then picks up his belly in his hands and puts it on the table. But now he had fined down with the long march, and he just looked big. He was as tall as I am, but he weighed at least half as much again, I'm sure. I looked down at myself, and I took the hint.

After that, I used to get out of the litter for a part of each day and walk with Marco, much to the relief of the bearers. By the time we got to Lutetia I could walk the whole twelve hours of daylight, and that in the early summer, with my bag over my shoulder, and never want to stop once for a rest. We passed beneath the ruined walls of Alesia, that great fortress of the Gauls. Caesar had tumbled the ramparts and hacked the gates from their hinges. And the Lord of Alesia, that great king, who might have reigned as Emperor over all the Gauls of the world from Britain to Galatia, great Vercingetorix, long dead now, dead and thrown into the sewer. But there was no weeping, even for Cicva, over that old dream, no singing that old song again. There was no stopping till we reached Lutetia.

We had a few splendid days in Lutetia. We quartered ourselves on the family's agent, a man called Julius Macrinus, who had a very pleasant house on the south side of the island, looking on to the river. It was a really delightful time, and even today I occasionally meet people

who remember it. The girls . . . the drink . . . the food
. . . surprising when you consider the reputation the place
has for being a sad and strict town. There's no culture in
Lutetia to speak of, no art or anything else to turn an
honest penny over, which may be one reason why it's
getting so prosperous.

Then one morning, while everyone else, muleteers
and all, were sleeping off the last and most outrageous
party, Marco and Cicva and I took horses and rode off
to Bonnonia.

CHAPTER THREE

We moved in on our agent in Bonnonia. He was even more embarrassed to see us than Macrinus had been. He was expecting an important Greek businessman, somebody used to dealing in millions and bargaining with the Governors of Provinces, and that of course he got. But he didn't expect me, with a variety of false eyes to suit my moods and hair all over — I had let it grow, beard and all, on the way up from Rome. And he got Marco, who had a scar across his face that turned his eye outwards, so that the milder he was feeling the more brutal he looked. Cicva was the most respectable of the three of us, to look at. I'd given her some money to get dressed up with in Lugdunum, and you know what Lugdunum fashions are. Then she'd had them altered to her own taste in Lutetia, and we all know the Parisii have no sense of how to dress. She ended up looking like an only moderately successful whore.

Marco was quite happy. He was anchor man, which suited him. He was to see that everyone was contented in Bonnonia after I left. He knew perfectly his place in my plan. The only trouble was that I hadn't got a plan. I had a vague idea that nothing would come right till I had a ship. I had to go and find one.

On the second night in Bonnonia I took out of my baggage an old grey cloak with a hood. I put it on, and went out. Marco followed me. He kept a few yards behind me, and when I went into a tavern he would stand by the door, just inside, making it clear that I wasn't alone.

The first tavern I went into — I was choosing the less reputable ones, the ones down by the quay, where the

22

clientele would be sailors, and not the most respectable sailors either — well, the first one I went into, I called for drinks all round. While everybody was drinking my health — and after the long journey, and the nights in Lutetia, I needed some attention to my health — I stood by the bar counter, and I drew idly in the sawdust of the floor with my toe. I drew a face, at least a circle with eyes and a mouth, and eight lines sticking out of it like arms, and to each arm I gave a hand holding some kind of weapon, an axe or a sword. Nobody took the slightest notice. I finished my beer and moved on.

I did precisely the same in the next tavern I came to. Again nobody seemed to take the slightest notice, except for the man next to me. He dipped his finger in a puddle of beer and drew a fish on the bar counter. He looked at me meaningly, which was difficult with the squint he had, and then quickly rubbed it out again. I didn't know anything about that, so I just said:

'And mackerel to you, brother,' in Gaulish, and moved on to the next tavern.

But when I got into the third tavern, I only had time to draw the circle, when someone took me by the elbow, and drew me away. I looked at him. He seemed familiar, somehow. Perhaps he had been in the other taverns and had run on in front of me. Perhaps I had met him before, sometime, on the Amber Road. He was a big man and yellow-haired, his face smeared with pig fat against the salt wind. He steered me across to a booth at the back of the room. Marco stayed by the door and watched.

The men at the back of the room were all sailors, and all dressed as Friesians. I turned back the edge of my hood, and let them see the patch over my eye. Nobody said anything. They put a big horn of beer in front of me, the kind of vessel you use in drinking matches. The beer was strong, dark and sweetish. I drained it at one long, slow draught. It nearly killed me. I was out of practice. Then one of the sailors asked in the Germans' tongue — he must have been a Dane from his dialect:

23

'You are looking for Starkadder Eightarms?'

'And if I were?' I lifted the eyepatch and let him have the full benefit of the emerald I was wearing in the empty socket. I had it carved by a man I know in the Piraeus. I will give you his name if you like. It showed, tiny but clear, the wolves dancing around a tree, a tree with a man in it. I listened to his reply.

'Then I would tell you, that he is at the other end of the Shallow Sea, harrying the Fenni.'

'And Alfhilda Vikarsdaughter, his wife?'

'With him. Where else should she be but with him?'

'And Caw? Where is Caw?'

'Gone, long gone. Who knows where?'

'Smuggling lead,' I told them. 'Let's have some more beer, and no half measures this time.'

And we did. Everybody got quite talkative in a secretive way. They were all painting ludicrous pictures of Caw swimming the Channel to Britain with a pig of lead under each arm in case he sank, and the whole atmosphere of the tavern became a good deal easier. We drank a good deal more. More Germans came in: soon there were about a score of them. By the time we started singing 'Sweyn, the Bastard King of Scania', the few respectable customers left. The landlord didn't object: he was singing too.

The Germans were all sorts. About half of them *were* Friesians or Batavians, but the rest were Saxons and Thuringians by their accents, and Goths, and even a Lombard. This last was rather stupid. He couldn't understand the subtleties of travelling incognito as quickly as the others, and once he called me 'All father' quite openly, and all the others shushed him. But every man was a sailor, just the kind you would expect with Starkadder.

I got into a corner with a few of the most prominent. The others were trying to make Marco drunk, and I could have told them they had little chance of succeeding. I asked the leader, who had first taken my arm, his name. He did his best to play the Friesian, but if his accent was anything to go by, he was a Goth. He said:

'Call me Bert.'

I asked the next man.

'I'm Bert too.'

'Just the same as him?'

'Just the same. We're all Bert, just call us Bert.'

Well, perhaps it's better not to have a name anyone can tell you by if you're in their trade. None of them asked my real name. They thought they knew it. Why should I know theirs? They only wanted to know my business that night, and whether it was the same as theirs was every night.

I was right. They *were* some of Starkadder's men, who had brought a prize down from the Shallow Sea, and now they were waiting for Starkadder to come back for them. Meanwhile, they were willing to try anything which would turn a profit and not make Roman ports too dangerous for them. After all, Starkadder had to have somewhere safe to winter in, and refit, and sell what he stole in the North. This was what I was looking for.

'There's a man coming here soon,' I told them. 'I want him—'

'Dead?' interrupted Lombard Bert, hopefully.

'No!' I answered, a little crossly. 'He wants to go to Britain. I want him to go to Britain — but on my ship. And with me in it. And I want him to have a nice quiet game of dice or something on the way. But I haven't got a ship.'

'Anybody we know?' asked Goth Bert.

'A man called Gwawl.'

'Oh, him,' said Lombard Bert: I said he was rather stupid, and his talents, though considerable in their way, were limited in their scope. 'I can kill him easy. I haven't killed anybody for weeks.'

'If you don't keep quiet,' Goth Bert grumbled at him, 'I'll take that flaming axe of yours and throw it in the dock.' He turned back to me. 'So you want a ship?'

'And a crew I can rely on.'

'And one that Gwawl can't rely on.' Goth Bert followed

my drift perfectly. A Batavian Bert came in with the crucial question:

'How much are you offering?'

'How much do you want? What's the regular rate around here?'

After that, it was only a matter of haggling. Hard cash for the crew; for the ship, I guaranteed a cargo both ways at four times the usual rates, wine out and hides back. That was to Londinium, but of course, I myself would leave the vessel when she cleared the customs at Rutupiae.

The Berts had two ships, prizes they'd not yet sold, and I went to look at them next day. One was very fine, a Gothship, sleek and beautiful and fast, twenty rowers a side. And the finish, wonderful! It made you open your eyes at the very thought of the kind of craftsmen they had up there in the North, doing everything, as I knew, with axe and adze and no other tools, no saws or chisels for them. I'd always wanted to have one of those ships under me. I didn't take her, quite unsuitable.

The other was a Friesian, comfortable and roomy, as broad as she was long, or at least she looked it. She was decked, and under the poop where there was enough head-room for a man to stand she had quite a cosy cabin. She set the one big square sail, and there were sweeps for the times when there was no wind, and that was rare enough up in the North. I took her, but that was the next day.

That first night, we had a real party. We had lots of singing and embracing and rubbing of cuts together to mix blood, and I got Marco to join in that. One of the hardest things I had to do was to keep Marco feeling happy, since he couldn't understand a thing I said to the Germans. And then before the feast got too unruly, I bawled out:

'I'll give ten gold pieces for a sword!'

'Not on shore,' said Goth Bert. 'It's a hanging matter here to carry a sword, unless you have a licence, and I've never met a man yet who has.'

'Well I have,' I told him. 'A general licence, from the Emperor's Chancery, to carry a sword anywhere in the

Empire, in defence of my goods.' And that's what a bit of influence does for you, that and a name for quite fair dealing all across the Mediterranean Sea.

'Even so,' went on Goth Bert, 'they're strict here. The Port Captain, he winks at what we've got in the ships, but we mustn't bring any weapons ashore. If you wait till we get aboard, I dare say we can fit you out.'

'I doubt it,' I told him. 'I want a Sax, a good one, well shaped, curved no more than the bow of a ship. A back edge thick as my thumb, the bone-breaker. The fore edge like a razor, the mailsplitter. Point like a needle, the heart-piecer. And I want an Ingelri.'

For Ingelri was the greatest swordsmith of all Germany, and his blades were like no others. They were all silent for a few moments, and one murmured, a fat man he was, that ten gold pieces wouldn't do it, no, nor twenty either, seeing it meant going across the Rhine. But in seven days he himself came to me with a Sax, a splendid one, but for one thing — he couldn't get an Ingelri in the time, he had had to make do with an Elfbert. Of course, to those who know their iron, this was almost as good, for Elfbert was Ingelri's apprentice, and if his swords had a fault it was that he tended to make them a little heavier towards the point than need be.

There was no hilt to this sword, of course, just the blade and the tang with the iron pommel at the end. We took it to a swordsmith in the town, who did a lot of work for Officers of the Garrison. First he had to be satisfied I had a right to own the weapon, and then he looked at the quality of the iron, and his eyes glistened. He asked me if I had any preference in the form of the hilt. I said no, provided he made a showy job of it. And if he knew of a goldsmith, then he could melt down these coins, and set in it — and I took them out of my wallet — these stones, garnets and emeralds and a blue sapphire, and here was a big ball of crystal.

It took him some days. He beat out the tang into ridges in the shape of an X, and instead of beechwood or horn, as is usual, he made the grip of walrus ivory, carved and weighted to fit my hand. Then, with the Gold, he ornamented the arms of the X to look like a man, spreadeagled, and the gems set in to point off his clothes, and the great ball of crystal where the head should be. A sword it was now fit for any of the great Kings of ancient Gaul, for Vercingetorix or for Dumnorix, or for Brennus himself to throw in a balance and make the insolent Romans pay.

But as for a scabbard, he told me to keep it in the plain wooden sheath, covered in leather, that Fat Bert brought it to me in. He insisted that he was the finest hilt-maker in the world — but his equal in the company of scabbard-makers lived in Londinium, and even if I were not going there, it would be worth the journey to have a scabbard made to match the hilt. He gave me the name.

I put the bill in to the family. So far this chase had cost about eleven thousand sestertia, what with buying Cicva (because I couldn't let Philebus pay for that, after all), the journey up, hiring the ship and crew, and all the expense of making sure that when Gwawl arrived in Bonnonia he would find no ship but mine willing to take him. This wasn't so expensive as you might think, because he had been in the town before, and everybody he had met on that occasion seemed to bear him a hearty dislike, though why I could not find out. Still, all this was a little cheaper than the two hundred thousand Gwawl had asked for in the first place. Or it would be, if I could catch him.

I asked Goth Bert where people usually went to ask about Channel passages, and he told me about a tavern called the Capricorn. We went there and arranged to take the whole place over the night Gwawl arrived in Bonnonia. At least, we told the landlord we were taking it over.

'And if you object,' Lombard Bert told him, 'I'll bash your bloody head in with my axe. I haven't killed anybody for days.' Even he had his moments of usefulness. The landlord agreed.

I spent a long time letting Cicva know exactly what she had to do.

28

'When he gets here, I want you to be ready and dressed up in the Capricorn. You'll want some of those clothes I bought you in Lutetia, that's just the right touch, ornate and flashy but a year or two behind the fashion. Now with your hair piled up on top and dyed yellow . . . No? All right, then, dress as you please as long as you think he won't know you. The most favourable thing is that he won't expect to see you. Are you quite sure, then, that you can handle Gwawl?'

'Yes, as long as I don't have to sleep with him. I don't *have* to sleep with him, do I?'

'That's up to you, dear. If you can manage without, so much the better. Don't let him have any profit or pleasure out of this that we can avoid.'

'I don't want to. I don't like him. I mean, as well as hating him. I don't like him either. I like you, Photinus. Why don't you try to sleep with me?'

'Because I don't do that sort of thing with every pretty girl I get hold of.'

'What will you do when you finish the hyena hair?' And that was a clever question. As you know, all you need do if you are a rake and worried about it is to take some hair of a hyena, and burn it to ash, and mix the ash with grease to form an ointment. Then you rub it in . . . that is . . . you rub it well in, anyway, and immediately your whole conduct changes. You stop running after women, you work harder, and get awfully staid, and everybody says what a reliable and respectable citizen you are now. Well, it may be good for trade, but who wants to live like that? And besides, the smell of the ointment — no wonder you can't get anyone to sleep with you in that state. So I said to Cicva:

'And why should I sleep with a pretty girl like you, with a wife and a baby at home?'

And that was more like the truth of it, that and my determination not to sleep with any more barbarian women, or even to speak to them more than was absolutely necessary, not like the last time I was in the North. It only gets you into the most appalling trouble.

Phryne was enough for me, I thought. I had come home from the Amber Road to find that my grandmother had arranged it all. I must admit she was not very exciting in her mild, submissive, Mediterranean way. And she had no mind at all, really, almost illiterate, and not the slightest inkling of what was going on anywhere outside her own kitchen. It made no difference to her whether I said I was off to Rhodes or to Gades or to Ultima Thule, they were all just the same to her, all vaguely somewhere 'away'. Still, she let me hold the little girl sometimes, and that was more than anyone had let me do before. And now there was another child on the way, in the early autumn, and this ought to be a boy — I had done all the right things, sprinkled the bed with the pollen of the male date flower, and turned it with the head to the North, and made Phryne eat parsnips and myself gorged on orchid roots till we were both sick.

Besides, though I flattered Cicva, she was not really very attractive to me, except in the face, for she was short, and heavy hipped. I like women that are tall and slender.

Anyway, I thought then, I ought to be back home by the autumn. The summer ought to see me into Ireland, to arrange terms of trade with whatever king controlled the Gold mines, and then at once back through Gaul to Ostia and a ship back home to the Old City. That's what I thought then. But first of all, I had to get the Deed of Monopoly back from Gwawl, and pass it on to the family's agent in Londinium.

Settling with Gwawl was all worked out in my mind now. It's fascinating how these problems solve themselves once you start to think about what resources you have and how they can be used. Now we had covered every possible variant. We knew how to deal with Gwawl loitering, Gwawl in a hurry, Gwawl early, Gwawl late, Gwawl drunk, Gwawl sober, Gwawl angry, Gwawl pleased. Marco and Goth Bert and I planned and planned, while Cicva looked for hours at a time into a mirror and tried on her wigs and painted her face in a thousand different ways. It kept us all happy while we waited for the draft to arrive.

One of Marco's Spaniards came into Bonnonia two hours ahead of Gwawl. There was another man following him, in case he changed his mind and went to another port. The legionaries had gone into a camp outside the town and cooled their feet a while. The mule-drivers cooled their throats, scorched raw by the language they had been using all the way from Rome on their treacherous beasts. But Gwawl came on into the town. You could spot him a mile off in his black and white shirt, striped from neck to hem. It was a Gaulish shirt. They like bright colours, and the more colours, and the more complex the pattern of stripes and checks, the better. And the Brits wear their shirts the same way, hanging down over their trousers loose to the buttocks, not down to the knees as a civilised man wears his tunic over his bare legs, or tucked short into the trousers at the waist as all the Germans do.

Gwawl just came straight into the Capricorn. It was the easiest thing and the simplest you could imagine. It was obvious he wasn't expecting to meet any danger at all, not as long as I kept out of sight. I wasn't in the bar, I watched from the kitchen — when you have only one eye, a very narrow crack is enough to look through.

In the bar, Gwawl found only a crowd of sailors very obviously having one for the Channel, and a blowsy woman with an empty basket. Cicva had done well with her face painting, and her wig — she could have passed for thirty easily, and did so in the dim lamplight. But you can never trust a woman — instead of the fine Roman dress I had got her in Lutetia, she wore a scarlet blouse in the British manner. And beneath that, she wore the ten or twelve petticoats the women up there delight in, each one a different colour and, if possible, a different material for each, cotton if you could afford it, and linen, and wool. Over the top one she had a linen apron, with lace frills at the edges, and over that a broad belt of red wool, embroidered with flowers, and fastened with a big bronze

31

brooch. Her shawl, over her shoulders, had also cost a good deal of money, for it had a fringe of red tassels, and I thought then, from the little I knew, that Cicva had ideas about rank that were quite beyond her — only noblewomen among the Brits wore such elaborate shawls. And little, indeed, I knew. But if all this finery, justified or not, caught Gwawl's eye, it was worth the expense.

Gwawl bought something to drink, and then looked round. It was obvious that Goth Bert was the Captain: he was drinking two to his crew's one. Gwawl began to haggle for a passage. When they were nearly settled, Cicva put her arm around Gwawl's shoulder and said beerily:

'That's right, boy, you come in my little boat with me!'

'Clear off!' Gwawl shouted at her. 'Find your own bunk and someone else to pay for it!'

It was clear that he sensed some subtle double meaning in her words, that a respectable woman would never have intended. And Cicva resented that.

'You Syrian by-blow,' she told him, not loud or shrill, just quietly nasty. 'You big slob. Who do you think you're talking to?'

Cicva had a good vocabulary now in both Greek and Latin, as well as British and Gaulish, and a few choice phrases of doubtful provenance that Goth Bert had taught her, in every dialect of German from the Alps to the ends of the Shallow Sea. She used them all.

Here she was, she said between the profanity, sold her embroidery and trouble enough it was buying it up on her other side of the water to bring it across to peddle here, and not much profit she made on it either, not more than three or four hundred per cent, after all her expenses were paid, and now home it was she was going, with her passage paid and a purse full of money in her apron, and if Gwawl didn't appreciate her company he might as well wait for another boat, and the Gods only knew when that would be, the way trade was going in these days. And Gwawl heard Fat Bert say that that was right, and who did he think he was, talking like that to a decent woman who travelled with them every month punctual as the moon, and why should he bother about a casual stranger who had insulted an old-established customer. Lombard Bert said he hadn't killed anybody for weeks, and nobody told him to keep quiet.

Just as I began to think they might be overdoing it, Gwawl swallowed what was left of his beer and his words together, and bought three rounds, one after the other, for everyone in the place, Cicva included. Goth Bert put the passage money up by another half, and Gwawl agreed to it without any further argument, seeing himself at a distinct disadvantage and him in a hurry, too.

Lombard Bert picked up Gwawl's bag to take it down to the ship at once. I slipped out the back way and followed him. We whiled away the time of waiting by sitting on the forecastle and going through the bag, but there was nothing there of any interest to me, though the Berts earmarked several things for future distribution. When we finished I repacked the bag in something like the same order, and began rubbing pig fat in my face as a protection against the salt wind, which burns it otherwise. Lion fat is much better, but I couldn't find any in Bonnonia.

After we had arranged Gwawl's belongings to our satisfaction, I strolled on the quayside and looked at the ship. There is nothing as beautiful as a ship, even a clumsy broad-beamed tub like the *Gannet*, as the Berts had renamed her. When she was in the North I suppose she had been called something like 'Fleet Wind from the Ice', rather on my grandfather's principle that she would partake of the qualities of her name. She was a good ship, nothing remarkable, but reliable and sturdy. We would have to sweep her out of the harbour, but once we were clear of the land there was a wind from the south-west, just right for Britain.

Gwawl was a long time in coming. I went back into the ship, and I looked at Bonnonia. The full round moon flooded the shore with a bright pale light, so that the patches of shadow were as dark as a bottomless pit. I thought that it was like the good hard noonday sun of the South, that has no half measures. Either a thing is in the dark and cannot be known, or it is out in the pitless light and cannot be hidden. I sat on the bulwark with my legs dangling and looked at Gaul, a familiar land of wine and olive, where everything was what it was, where a mule-driver was a mule-driver and a pirate was a pirate, and a slave girl only a slave girl. That was the last I knew for many a day of clarity and single-mindedness and fixity of meaning. For the wind was right for the misty island of Britain.

CHAPTER FOUR

It was an hour or so after sunset, then, on that evening at the end of May, when Goth Bert and Cicva brought Gwawl down to the quay — or, to be more accurate, before Cicva and Gwawl carried Goth Bert down to the quay. The delay had done us no harm, because we had to wait for the tide, but as it was we barely had time to take the three aboard and cast off. Gwawl and Cicva went into the cabin under the poop. I squatted on the deck above their heads, next to the steersman, and the crew rigged the sweeps. Goth Bert joined me. When I realised how much beer he had drunk I persuaded him to lie down while I took the ship out myself. It was a good thing the steersman knew the channel.

After a little while, when we were nearly clear, Goth Bert came to his senses again and I let him have his ship back. I lay down myself on the deck, with my ear to a knot-hole, and I could hear most of what went on in the cabin. I heard Cicva:

'It's a long trip. I always get bored. How about a little game to pass the time away?'

I didn't hear Gwawl answer for a while. He was still a bit drunk, and I hoped that he wouldn't be sea-sick: there wasn't much wind, really, and the ship was now doing that horrible motion like a screw. Then there was a slight scuffle in the cabin — that showed he wasn't *too* sick — and a bit of giggling and squeaking.

'Not *that* kind of game!' Cicva told him sharply, but not too sharply, not wishing to cut him short altogether. 'There are too many people about.'

There were, too. We had twenty-eight men in that ship,

besides the two in the cabin, and it was a problem where to put them all. But at least they were sailors and didn't get in each others' way. Fat Bert suggested towing Lombard Bert behind on a line. This provoked a good deal of horse-play between the men who weren't at the sweeps, and when I could listen again Gwawl was saying:

'. . . and then you guess which cup the pea is under.'

'Oh yes,' said Cicva, 'I have heard of it. Find-the-Lady, they do call it where I was brought up.'

Now, I never heard it called that before, which shows how limited even a Master's knowledge can be, and myself the greatest Lady-finder of them all. Gwawl added, deceptively offhand:

'Of course, you have to bet something on it to make it worth the while playing . . .'

And then I couldn't hear for quite a time, because Goth Bert had them ship the sweeps and set the sail, bringing her round into the breeze, which was beginning to freshen a little. When all the shouting and running had stopped, I could hear Cicva sounding clumsily coy and not being very good at it.

'We call it "Strip-Glyn-Naked". Every time you lose a turn, you take another garment off.'

Gwawl was very clever and played hard to persuade, but I could hear the prurient lust bubbling in his voice. For myself, I was getting a little worried, because I had planned for Cicva to do it all in one or two passes. But you can never trust a woman to stick to a plan. It was Gwawl, I thought, who needed the Hyena hair, and Cicva played him like a fish when he thought he was playing her.

First of all, of course, he let her win. She had his cloak. Then, though he didn't realise it, she let him win. He won her apron, and her shawl, and her cap, a flat padded cap that the women there wear to carry tubs of shellfish on their heads. I was a little worried in case she took her wig off with her cap, but it all went well. She let him take all these with little squeaks of protest. Then she went to work.

All those weeks in the litter, Cicva had studied the game

of the pea and the three cups with the greatest Master of
the Art alive, the greatest Master of all time, that is to say,
with myself. I had also got her to a fair stage of dexterity
with the finger game, and she could palm and switch dice
as if she were a magician born, and by this time I was
beginning to wonder if that were not what she was. Now
this was the first time that Cicva had played against anyone
but myself: it was, in fact, the first time she had played
against anyone of inferior natural talent to herself.

She just cleaned him out. On each turn, she had him
staking another garment against the ones he had already
lost. By the local rules where Cicva came from, and to
which she insisted on playing, talking Gwawl down in a
shrill torrent, she nominated the garment. First of all she
regained her own clothes. Then one by one she took tunic
and shirt and trousers and shoes. When she pointed to his
belt, which had a big pouch on it, I heard him cry in an
anguished voice:

'No, no, you can't take that. A belt is not a garment.
Who will recognise me without my belt? You can't make
me gamble on that!'

We were prepared for trouble at this stage, and Bert
Longnose, who had looked in to see if they wanted any
more beer, said:

'Do what the lady says. You started it.'

Bert Longnose was a very long thin man with a long thin
evil face, and he had Lombard Bert's axe in his hand, by
accident, it seemed. So Gwawl put the belt on the table,
and did what he could with the look of a drowning man.
When Cicva had won it — she was working the cups now
— she flicked it onto the deck of the cabin, and Bert
Longnose heeled it out behind him through the leather
curtain that served as a door. In a moment I was looking
through the great wad of vellum by the light of the
forecastle lamp.

I had to read through the whole of the Monopoly Deed
to make certain that all the pages were there, six of them,
and to be sure there was no delicate knife-work and no

clever alterations and improvements. The Deed of Transfer was on one sheet, with my cousin Philebus' signature at the bottom. There were also a number of other documents of interest, letters of introduction from bankers in Rome to bankers in London, and, quite intriguing, some to the Commander of the Second Legion, who seemed to be in debt all over the place.

I took the Deed of Transfer into the waist, where one of the lesser Berts had a brazier alight on a sand tray, and we fried eggs and bacon over the parchment towards dawn. The moon had gone now, and so had the stars, and there was thick mist rolling around us. I was glad I had put on a pair of the Gaulish trousers I had bought in Lutetia: tunic and bare legs may be civilised and gentlemanly, but they're not for the sea in the North. Gaulish trousers — and British ones are the same — have wide bottoms to the legs, and they are easy to roll up when you're walking through the swamps of that rained-on land: in fact, in the far West, you may even see the old men, who do not care about fashion, walking about in trousers cut off a little below, or even above, the knee. German trousers, of course, you will know, are tapered to fit tight and snug around the ankle, and in my opinion are quite unsuited to a maritime life: but the Berts all wore them, however impractical.

When it was really light, Cicva came out of the cabin and sat with us eating, and peering through the mist trying to see the coast of Britain. Several times the Berts all agreed that they saw it, though I could have sworn it was just more mist. Gwawl didn't join us.

'Oooh! That *was* a night,' said Cicva, when she had finished her breakfast, licking the fat off her fingers in a lady-like way. She stretched and blinked. 'I hope that was what you wanted.'

'Perfect. I trust you didn't leave him anything.'

'Not a sausage. And I didn't give him what he was looking for, either. But I did give him an old apron to make him look decent. It was white, once, and I drew a black stripe on it with pitch, both sides, so he ought to be satisfied.'

'Can I kill him now?' asked Lombard Bert. 'I haven't killed anybody for — Hey! Come back! Bring it back!'

Goth Bert went up on the forecastle, and threw the axe with a splash into the water. Lombard Bert screamed things after him that even Cicva knew to be obscene.

'Waste of a good axe,' I observed.

'Oh, no,' Fat Bert assured me. 'It's on a line. We'll haul it out by dinner-time and sell it back. We often have to do it.'

Lombard Bert's curses were interrupted by some even more horrible cursing, and in a wider variety of languages. Gwawl had come out on to the poop, and was standing looking down at us in the waist. He was only wearing the apron for a breech clout, but he was by no means cold in the clammy air. He was aglow with rage.

'I ought to have known that your family was behind all this,' he shouted at me. 'Where's my clothes? Where's the money? Give me back my clothes! Give me back my letters!'

'Not likely!' Cicva was happy, taking off her wig and wiping the paint from her face with Gwawl's best shirt. 'I won it all, fair enough.'

'How much did she get?' asked Fat Bert in an innocent interested way.

'Every penny. She's cheated me out of every penny I had.'

'In that case,' ruled Goth Bert, who tried to sound like the captain sometimes, 'you can't pay your fare, can you? Chuck him over the side!'

And so they would have done, but Cicva asked, being soft-hearted, like all women:

'Have you got a spare boat? Cheap?'

Of course, they had, a round skin boat like the Picts use.

'How much?' she asked them.

'How much had he got?' they chorused. Cicva counted out all Gwawl's money, which only came to three denarii in silver and a few coppers.

'Just right,' they said, 'but a paddle is extra.'

So for a paddle she gave them his clothes to share out,

39

and that was worth having, because he had bought a lot of good tunics in Rome, and he had also picked up several pairs of Gaulish trousers in Lutetia. His best cloak they very generously put aside to take back for Marco, Goth Bert insisting on that. Those two scoundrels were already on very intimate terms of understanding, and I was afraid it might eventually turn out to their mutual advantage, as long as neither of them was hanged.

We put Gwawl into the skin boat, and passed him down the paddle. Someone wanted to give him a knife, too, to cut his throat with, but when I pointed out that he couldn't pay for it they all remembered what a dreadfully unlucky thing it is to give a knife as a gift: a free gift of a knife always cuts friendship, they told him.

But we did give him a jar of beer, and a loaf of bread, and we left him the salmon mallet to scare the birds with. We gave him a lot of good advice, too, like, 'Britain's that way', or, 'A fortnight to Jutland if you paddled hard.'

We weren't so far from that elusive shore either. The Berts kept on pointing it out, but it all looked like mist to me, even though Cicva suddenly said that she could see a man holding a white shield. At that we pushed him off, and sailed away, leaving Gwawl sitting in his little boat, cursing us to the ends of all the world till we lost his voice far off in the mist.

CHAPTER FIVE

In fog there is no wind, or very little wind, and it was the drift of the waves and Gwawl's paddling that carried him out of sight of us. It got thicker. It is hard to tell at sea, but I do not think we could have seen anything fifty paces away, if there had been anything to see, or anything to pace on. We just sat there in the damp, soaking mist and waited for it to clear. We kept quiet. You never know who may not be about in fog.

About the middle of the morning we heard a ship. It went by close, but not close enough to be seen. It was a big one, I should have said by the noise, thirty oars a side. They were paddling and listening by turns, you know how. A long stroke, and then lie back on your oars while you count up to eight . . . nine . . . ten . . . and then the hammer falls for the next stroke. And in between the strokes the only noise is the hiss of the water under your forefoot, and you have time to listen for other oars in the mist, or men talking or laughing.

No one in the other ship talked or laughed. We only heard the oars. It might have been a Roman warship out looking for pirates, but Goth Bert thought it unlikely, and he ought to know. Cicva slipped into the cabin, and an awful lot of swords appeared from unlikely places. Someone gave Lombard Bert his axe back, free. We were safe enough, really. With twenty-nine of us altogether, counting Cicva with her cooking knife, in the old tub, there wasn't really room enough for a boarder to get on to the deck, let alone do any mischief. However I was glad nobody had tried it.

By the time the long-spaced oar-beats had died away into the wet mist, I had had enough.

'All right!' I shouted. 'Get the sweeps rigged.'

'Oh, no, not that again,' everyone said in horror, and someone suggested, 'Why don't *you* whistle for a wind?'

'That I won't. It's more trouble than it's worth, and I'm out of whistle. We'll sweep her — that is, you'll sweep her.' They still argued till I bellowed, loud as any wind, 'Who's chartered this barge, anyway?'

Then they got out the long sweeps, two a side, three men to an oar, and worked in ten-minute relays, grumbling that this wasn't what they had turned pirate for in the first place, and this was the penalty for descending to honest charter work. But they worked, all the same. We took a free vote on which way was north-east, and in that direction we made, I suppose, about half a Roman mile in the hour. I stood on the poop and gossiped with Goth Bert, who had made a study of his profession, about the general superiority of oars over sail, if only you can find enough men willing to row.

'But that's the trouble,' he told me. 'You can't get free men to do it, not in merchant ships. Has anyone tried using slaves? You must have done it, down there in the Mediterranean. You can always teach us a thing or two about the use of manpower.'

'It's not worth it,' I assured him. 'I've not seen it done in ships, but when you have a gang on a mill, pushing the windlass around all day, you have to keep them chained night and day, and you have the most dreadful trouble with sanitation. If you do that in a ship, you'll have the slaves dying off like flies.'

He agreed, and added: 'Besides, if you're boarded, with slaves you have fifty or sixty men you can't arm. Real rowers fight.' He changed his tone. 'Look! It's getting a bit thinner up there.'

It was, too. In another half-hour, it was quite clear and there we were, not half a mile out of Rutupiae. There was enough breeze to hoist the sail and start unshipping the sweeps — we had been rowing due south, as it happened — and so we slid in past the guardship. They shouted that we had been lucky to get in, that Starkadder Eightarms was cruising in the fog. The Berts murmured to each other that it wasn't him, that they knew the sound of his oars, they'd pulled them themselves often enough, he never took anything off this coast, he wanted always to be safe inside the Empire, this would be some Black Dane masquerading. One of the Berts said it had smelt more like Irishmen to him, but the others all laughed at him and asked who had ever heard of Irishmen so far east as this.

At least the guardship didn't think we were pirates.

'They know us well enough,' Fat Bert told me. 'There's many a time we've brought in merchant ships that we've rescued from wicked pirates that boarded them at sea, and an act of valour that is: half the value of ship and cargo is what the Port Captain's authorised to pay. Course, you have to be careful in the retaking that nobody gets hurt, and you've got to make sure that the merchant men don't capture any pirates in their enthusiasm, and you have to have two ships before you think of it, but a very virtuous way of dealing it is.'

We had the sweeps rigged again, to pull us round between Rutupiae Island and the mainland, so that we could lie off the jetty. The customs came off to us in a small boat, and had a cursory walk around. They were expecting me — there had been a clerk from our family's agent in London waiting for me for some days. They were very willing to take me ashore in their boat, while the Berts worked the *Gannet* round and into Londinium. I said a tearful farewell to them — they couldn't think how they would ever get such an enjoyable and profitable and wholly legal commission again.

Cicva and I took our bags and left. I don't know if you've ever been to Rutupiae. There's nothing to see on the island, only the customs post. Every ship going up into the Thames, or farther north up the east coast, had to come in there for clearance, otherwise they're not allowed to unload. There's no real town, except for the usual little cluster of small houses and a tavern or two outside the walls. Nothing to see? Yes, there is. Over everything is the great monument to the Emperor Claudius, marking where He first slept the night on British soil. His Sacred Majesty, three times life-size, stands on an eighty-foot arch of white marble, and out from under it leads the road that passes through Eboracum to the Wall. It is a beautiful gleaming sight. There's not a square foot of marble that is left plain. It is all covered with the most exquisite carving. There are episodes from the Conquest, and from the Triumph, with supplicant Britons and chariots and camels and troops in campaign dress on one side. The other side has the full regimental titles and badges of all the units taking part, each with a group of various ranks in their dress uniforms. There's none of this monotonous white wall for you there, that's old-fashioned stuff. Just think, in two thousand years it will still be there, dominating the sea just as it does today.

I would have liked to spend an hour examining the details, even though Cicva obviously didn't like to see what to her must have been a symbol of national humiliation. However, the little clerk who had met us wanted to get us through the formalities of entering the province as quickly as possible. Of course, with him to vouch that I was who I was, and being who I was, it only took a few minutes to get past all the officials, and the main sensation was caused by the fact that I had a sword, and that I actually had a permit with me. The clerk was just explaining to me and to the officials that he had rooms ready for us in the village, when there was a sudden commotion in the doorway of the office, and there stood Gwawl, swearing in a mixture of Latin and Gaulish and British in a way which put me off wondering how he had got there so quickly. And there was the Port Duty Police Officer standing there listening to him as though he were being told the essential and total truth about the nature of the universe. Well, I know there's a lot to be said for equality under the Law, but there are limits, especially for people of my importance.

Gwawl swore at us so much that the Duty Police Officer told him to moderate his language. It's never good tactics to antagonise the Police over trifles. A serious offence it's easy to get away with, once you've established a price, but with a little disorderly conduct, where you can't easily conceal it, why, they have you at once.

Gwawl let off with a stream of accusations of how we'd tricked him into going on our ship, and then stolen all he had, clothes, money, everything, and set him adrift naked — 'No, not naked,' said Cicva. 'You had my apron on' — and that quite spoilt his flow. Anyway, he said, he'd been set adrift, in a skin boat, to die of thirst or be eaten by sharks or whales or sea-serpents. Was it our fault (and I agreed, privately, no it wasn't) that he had got ashore and been able to sell his boat for rags to cover his nakedness and then begged his way all along the road from Dubris to Rutupiae?

At this point he paused for breath, and I managed to start talking. I assured the Duty Police Officer that this fellow had been only the usual kind of trickster, with all his capital in flashy clothes. He had wiled his way into our ship with a promise to pay later, and then settled down to cheat the poor sailors out of all they had by indescribable manoeuvres with the dice. But in that he had failed, and unable to pay for his losses he had stolen a boat, a good one, and made off with it in the fog. So I demanded that the Port Authorities should immediately undertake criminal proceedings against him for boat stealing, and in any case, with such an important and valuable cargo clearing, and with one of the most important merchants of the Empire passing through, why weren't the Port Captain and the Officer Commanding the Garrison here as well?

The clerk wanted to go off to Durovernum, and warn our agent, who had a villa there and would be waiting for us, and bring *him* back to Rutupiae (in the morning, probably, I thought) to bail us out of jail where we would by then probably have spent the night. I told the clerk pretty sharply that he ought to be quiet, because if anyone was going to spend the night in a cell it was to be him as a surety for our answering any charges, and there was no likelihood I would hesitate to sacrifice my bail. In any case, why wasn't the legendary Leo Rufus here waiting for us, instead of wasting his time at Durovernum?

In any case, I insisted on the two officers being brought, and when they came, I saw that my luck was in. I would not even have to use family influence. Most of these officials at the ports are officers from regiments of native cavalry, themselves coming from outside the Empire, and now, too old to command a squadron any more, they are granted Citizenship and a peaceful retirement in a post like this. Of course, the really stupid ones don't get these jobs.

I'd begun to guess when I heard the Duty Officer speaking Latin, and when the two senior officers arrived I saw that I had been right. They were both Germans, born somewhere beyond the Rhine, Thuringians I should say, and I took it as a direct sign from Apollo that the Garrison Commander had his arm in a sling and a bandage about his wrist.

A gift from Apollo? But I no longer served the Unconquered Sun. Long, long ago now He had released me from His service, and I no longer practised the healing art, the art that I had learnt in the Temple in the days when I was a whole man and still had both my eyes. No, I had left His service, and in the years since I had healed no one. But here I stood to face the two senior officers, in my grey cloak with the hood thrown back a little to show my hair all crusted white with the salt, and my good eye flashing, and my bad one covered with a patch, as I always had it at sea, or on the road. I had little option, dressed thus, but to play the part I was cast for: but it was a great mistake, I know now, to deal thus in healing after I had been dismissed from Apollo's service, and I am sure that it was the cause of all the trouble I had later.

Gwawl stepped forward and began to make his complaints again, and Cicva interrupted and offered to buy

46

his horse-blanket — at least, she said that if he had five more like it she would give him a copper sestertius for the half-dozen, and in any case where was the rest of the money he must have got for that valuable and well-built boat, made to last a thousand storms on the Western Sea, or had he been cheated out of it?

Meanwhile, I walked over to the two senior officers, and I undid the bandage on the Garrison Commander's wrist. When I felt that the bone was only pulled out and not broken, I tried to remember which way to jerk, and I said the charm I had so often said in the North long ago:

> Blood to blood,
> Bone to bone,
> Strength to the sinew,
> Skin strong as stone,
> Oak strong as ash,
> Elm at the end,
> Earth over all.

Nonsense, really, but it did the trick with those half-romanised German officers, looking so civilised, but savages at heart, and all the time worrying about whether their sons will pass for Romans born, or whether they'll always show that touch of the tow-brush. The charm did it, that and the smell of the pig fat that all good Germans remember from their mothers' faces, and that they play too clean to bother with when they come within the Empire to make their fortunes. And the quick twist of my hand on the bone of the wrist, and Apollo helping me, whatever he did afterwards. It set the bone to rights, and both senior officers looked at me, and the Port Captain said:

'What do you want of us, Allfather?'

'Allfather? I know of no Allfather' — for this was the name that the Germans gave me when I was in the North, and it had brought me enough trouble all along the Amber Road, I wanted no more of it. 'I am only a simple traveller, and men within the Empire call me Photinus.'

47

After that, they treated me like someone important, even more important than a leading member of one of the richest trading families of the Empire, travelling incognito. I was someone they shared a secret with. The Port Captain pointed at Gwawl and asked:

'What do you want us to do with him? Shall we charge him formally, or would you prefer us to kill him — privately, that is?'

'No,' I told them. 'Why should I hurt a poor, helpless, demented fool? You see, he even believes his own lies.'

I ordered our clerk to give Gwawl a silver denarius, one of the new kind, one-horse and half copper, and that he had in turn to borrow from Cicva. It was one she had palmed from Gwawl's purse before she had let the sailors have it in exchange for the boat: and he knew it by his own toothmarks, and it made him swear more. But plainly there was nothing more that he could do there, and so he went away. I thought, though, that we hadn't seen the last of him, and no more we had.

Then I told the clerk we were more than ready to go and see the rooms he had for us in the inn, and if they weren't the best in Rutupiae, he would be in trouble. The Garrison Commander, however, put in a word, rather diffidently:

'Excuse me, All — that is, Simple Traveller — but there is no need for you to go to an inn. If you would be so gracious as to be our guest for the evening, in our mess — there are fifteen of us here tonight, all men of honour and breeding, and you shall have good food, real German food that you'll like, not that Mediterranean stuff, all soaked in oil.'

I accepted, graciously of course. I told the clerk to escort Cicva to an inn, and see that she had room fit for a princess, or there would be no knowing what would happen to him in the morning. I drew the girl aside and told her:

'As far as I'm concerned, you're free now, but you'll have to stay with me for a few more days till we can find a magistrate and make it legal. So don't get into any trouble tonight, because your legal position, and mine for that matter, might be a little ambiguous.'

Off they went in a rowing boat, and off I went with the two senior officers, but I called in at the Port Chancery before I reached the baths, and I borrowed the services of a couple of the official copyists. They would have to work all night to do what I wanted. It's a wonderful thing to have influence — or credit; influence comes cheaper in the end.

I must say, that handful of officers lived well, even if there were only fifteen of them in a house built to hold thirty at least, and still staffed on that scale with cooks and waiters. The bath had all the normal amenities, and I went in to dinner with my body oiled and scented, and my hair and beard combed Greek fashion, but in a toga, as befitted a Citizen born.

All the officers were Germans, born outside the Empire, and with twenty or so years of service apiece. So we had a real German dinner, only we reclined in the comfortable Roman way. I hadn't had a real German meal for years, nor did I again for years. We had hot and cold sausages of all kinds, and rye bread, and strong dark barley beer. Then, after we had sung all the traditional songs like 'Cole, the Bastard King of Britain', the guardship captain stood on the table and recited the latest border poem — 'Pictish Nell', it was called. Well, I mean, one party is just like another wherever it is.

But these were all elderly gentlemen, and so there were no games or fighting after the drinking. The place to see that is where there are old men and young men together, where the old men push the young men into it, to break their heads and spoil their clothes. Old men are too wise to try it, and the young men think of the expense, but can't say no to their seniors. Instead, here, the officers on early call went off to bed, and the duty officer went on his rounds, and only half a dozen of us were left to talk a lot and drink a little.

I said I was surprised to find so many men of their age and seniority living like this in a mess, not one of them married or even keeping women in the town — the law on marriage for the Army has got so complex in recent years that nobody is quite sure what is illegal any more. They all laughed.

'We're all married, more or less,' one of them said. 'We've all got families, legitimate or not, in Durovernum, and fine houses there too. We do five days here, and then three off there. It's a nice town, is Durovernum.'

It must be, I thought. It'll be worth spending a few days there before I move on if it's full of neglected wives. Then I remembered Phryne — it was getting harder and harder to remember Phryne — and I reminded myself that I was going to behave properly in Britain, even without hyena's hair. I asked what the Brits were like.

'Not too bad,' the Port Captain told me. 'If you don't mind the taste of butter and the smell of goose grease. The ones down here are not too bad, more like the Germans, but it's west of Londinium you meet the real Brits. We never saw much of them, in the Army. They look after themselves, with their own local assemblies and senates, and as long as they pay the wheat tax and do everything according to Roman laws, we don't interfere. The worst thing they can do is take their law suits to the Druids, like they used to before we came. That would really undermine our system, so the order is strict — kill a Druid at sight, we're supposed to. There hasn't been a Druid seen down in the South, not for twenty years.

'But they're not bad, the Brits, except the ginger ones. The red-haired men are killers, and as for the women — why, I wouldn't touch a red-haired woman, not for all the Gold in Ireland.'

'Much Gold in Ireland?' I asked, all innocence.

'Up among the Demetae you want to go for Gold. That's where the mines are. But it's no place to go if you want to keep alive. A lot of the Demetae still follow the old King, Pwyll, and we've never caught him. I did four months up at the mines there — no, don't laugh, it wasn't what you think. I had a turn as Guard Commander, and I didn't ask for another. Plenty of Gold up there, but what a place. I tell you, it rains four hundred days in the year. There's only one future for that country. They want to catch all the rain in buckets — they've got plenty of buckets, they worship a bucket. Then they can build an aqueduct across the channel, and across Gaul, and down into Africa, and they can pour all their rain into it and sell it down in Africa. And I tell you, if they thought it would show a profit, I think the Brits would do it. So mean they are up there, a man will walk five miles to have a look in your mirror to save wearing out his own.'

'But Ireland?' I pressed.

'Well, they talk about Irish Gold,' said another officer. 'But nobody's ever seen any. There may be copper, I've seen that come in. When I was supporting the Second Legion up there at Isca—'

'Supporting?' someone interrupted. 'Picking up, more likely!' It was lucky there was nobody from the Second in the room or there would have been some horseplay after all.

'When I was at Isca, I was telling you, we used to have Irish coming in in skin boats, selling dogs, mostly. I've never seen men as poor as the Irish.'

'Poor?' put in the unit accountant, who had been most helpful in getting the copyists to put everything aside to do my work. 'There are some Brits who are so poor, they can't afford charcoal or firewood to cook on. They burn the very stones out of the ground for fuel.'

'No!' I could believe a lot of things, I couldn't believe that.

'Yes, and the wheat won't ripen, they have to dry it in kilns. They won't eat wheat themselves, they only grow it to pay the taxes with. Themselves, they eat a kind of millet, oats they call it. But they make real beer, out of barley.'

'They're a cunning lot,' said someone else. 'Once when I was on outpost duty . . .'

And so they went on, telling tall stories of skirmishes on the hills north of the Wall, and weird tales of how other people, always other people, had been caught by magic. And so we talked our throats dry and our voices hoarse, and at last we all went to bed.

CHAPTER SIX

Next morning, I finished my business in the Imperial Chancery, and saw several packets off by the Imperial Mails, here and there. Then I had a boat take me across to the village and met Cicva and the clerk. The latter said that he had a boat ready to take us up river to Sturry, where we would be met by a litter, but Cicva said:

'No, it's a lovely day. I'd rather ride.'

'Ride what?' I asked her. 'We haven't got any horses.'

'You haven't,' she told me. 'I have. I've got four: and a groom, too.'

'You hadn't got them yesterday,' I objected.

'Well, there were some people last night in the tavern who thought they knew which cup the pea was under.'

I looked at the horses, which were fine beasts, and at the groom, who was healthy enough on the surface. But then I saw that there were six more horsemen, cavalry troopers, armed.

'What about these?' I asked as sternly as I could.

'The port duty officer came into the inn on rounds last night. I remembered Gwawl, and I thought the most useful thing I could win from him was the use of half a dozen men for a day.'

The girl had some sense, I admitted that. But it was annoying. I had visions of every woman in the island able to handle the pea and the cups, and where would the men be then? I told her, with as much feeling as I could put into my voice:

'Surely you know that this game is forbidden to women in the ordinary way? If it were not for my continuous intercession with the Gods Below, for all my fasting and prayer through the dark, you would have been struck dead in your sleep. Cicva, by the Gods Below and Above, I forbid you ever to play this game again.'

She glared at me. Then she laughed.

'As you order. But I tell you, Photinus, for this prohibition, you shall play Find-the-Lady across all the Isle of Britain.'

I swallowed that. I might have brought a witch back to the island, but at least she hadn't red hair. Two days later, after we had been to the magistrates, and Cicva had been properly freed and had a bundle of parchment to prove it, I helped her to sell three of the horses and the groom. She got up on the fourth to ride away, all alone, with her bundle of clothes strapped on the saddle in front of her. I asked her:

'And where are you going now?'

'Home.'

'And where's that?'

'And would I be telling you? But I might, though, if it meant any good at all. You're a hard man, and a clever one, Photinus, but I think that I could trust you if I had to.'

Well, well, I thought, as I watched her ride away toward Londinium. Trustworthy? I learn new things about myself every day.

Londinium

CHAPTER ONE

Durovernum was indeed a pleasant town, with its large houses set apart in their big gardens. I would have been pleased to have spent a few weeks there, because with so many wives mourning their husbands detained at Rutupiae it offered opportunities to any young man with a love of pleasure and a strong constitution. Alas, I stayed too short a time.

Our agent in Londinium, Leo Rufus, had a house in Durovernum, as had several other well-to-do merchants from Londinium. It was the convention to pretend that there was a hot season in Britain, as in a civilised land, and to have a country house to spend it in, as an escape from the great city. It was a real Roman house that Leo had, with atrium, triclinium and all the other rooms you find in the textbooks on architecture. The feature that worked hardest was the impluvium.

Leo Rufus was just like his house. Even his name was a sham: I knew enough about the Brits' language now to know that he had started life as Llew Gough. He was not, in fact, a Citizen of Rome, but it took some time before he let that slip, and then only because he wanted to know how much it cost to become one. But he talked as if he had spent most of his life in Rome (where he had never been), and he had nothing but contempt for the 'natives', as he called his own kinsmen. He spoke Latin to me all the time, so I saw no reason to let him suspect that I knew any Barbarian language.

The first evening he and I had a little quiet dinner by ourselves, reclining, of course. We ate roasted skylarks, which a true Brit would never do, and we drank real Falernian. Everything was like that, the real thing with no expense spared, but, of course, much more meat than any Roman would eat at one meal. Leo said he always entertained like this for the sake of the prestige of the family, but I made a note that we would have to adjust the rate of commission we were paying him. Of course, every time he had a guest he would have a good meal like this himself, at the expense of the firm, and the privations of this existence were dreadful. But it was I, as one of the family, who was paying for all this, and so I made no bones about making myself at home. Not quite at home. We were alone in the house. Leo apologised for the fact that his wife had returned to Londinium the very morning I had left Rutupiae. Leo himself was left to do the best he could with a mere two dozen slaves.

Over the dessert I showed him the Deed of Monopoly. He read it through. Then he observed, with the air of someone making a great discovery:

'This is a copy.'

'Oh, yes,' I told him. 'Do you think I would travel with such a valuable document as this on my person? I had the Chancery at Rutupiae make eight copies. The original went on by Imperial Mail to the Procurator's Office, and others in the same way to the commanders of the legions at Eboracum and Deva and Isca. This is the copy for your own records. You will notice that it is certified by the Port Captain and the Garrison Commander at Rutupiae: they advised me on how many copies to make and where to send them.'

I left him to worry over who had the other copies. He didn't like the idea of any of the business going out of his hands, but what could he do? I added:

'I have made it quite clear in my accompanying letter how confidential this business is. Faustinus would be furious if it were to fall through because of any careless talk. He is waiting for his commission too.'

That made him even more disturbed in his mind. But

I did not really expect what I said next to drive him so frantic.

'Go to Ireland yourself? You must be mad! It's quite impossible. No Greek could ever do it and return alive!'

'Why should it be impossible? I have been up the Amber Road: why should the Golden Road to Ireland be any different? I am used to long journeys in savage countries. I can rough it with anybody.'

'I am not thinking of your comfort.' It was a change for him to be so frank. 'Some Irish come here, a few, but all that nation knows what happened to Britain once the trade with the Empire developed. Therefore they have forbidden and prohibited and banned any Roman from setting foot in the island, and by Roman they mean any man from the mainland who talks any civilised language and wears boots and drinks wine. Wine, especially, they deny entry, for they believe that all the troubles of the Kings of Britain began with their thirst for wine, and indeed there is no denying that it happened so in Gaul, and in Gaul it all started with the Greeks of Massilia. So all the Kings of the Irish have agreed and compacted and decided that there shall be no trading nor bargaining nor intercourse of any kind between the people of the Island of the Blessed and us of the Island of the Mighty.'

Now these are the names that the Brits use in their language for the two islands of Ireland and of Britain, and I must say they sounded strange in Latin. Leo Rufus went on:

'And since this agreement, there have been horrible things and objects and relics that it is that have been returning. For I do not mean the stories and the rumours and the gossip, because there were always dreadful stories that came from the Island of the Blessed, and difficult to believe. But it is the actual bodies, and the heads, and the ships that we have been finding tied up to harbour walls in the dawn, with no living man aboard to say how they have come: but we all know why.'

'That is nothing to me,' I told him, scornfully. 'I once

came alive out of the hands of the Picts, and out of the very teeth of their King.'

'And it is thinking then that it is you are, that it would be making it any easier for you to go to Ireland and to return again?' It was when you had him worried that you could hear the touch of the woad in his voice, in the adenoidal sibillants and in the collapse of all grammar into a continuous passive voice and a flood of impersonal verbs. The British tongue is one that is best spoken slowly by an old man, as Latin is by a middle-aged one in a court, and as Greek is made for the slangy arguments of the markets of Alexandria and Tyre. 'The less that it is that it is that it is being said about it, that is the better it is that it will be.'

I thought that I had better appear to take some notice of his warning, though I knew quite well that it was the excuse of a lazy man for taking no action. It was quite clear to me now that any merchant with a grain of enterprise would have opened up trade with Ireland long ago. There is nothing a Barbarian king will not do for his own profit, and if all the kings had made an agreement, then certainly they would not have the slightest hesitation in betraying each other wholesale for the treasures of civilisation, for silk and bronze and glass and wine. Especially wine. It *had* been their greed for Roman wines that had split the great confederation of the Gauls, and brought down the walls of Alesia on Vercingetorix's head, and laid the whole province open to Caesar's armies. After he failed to conquer Britain as well, it was left open to the wine merchants to trade for two generations. Then when the Emperor Claudius came, the whole drunken country fell into His Sacred Majesty's hands like a ripe apple.

'I can hardly go back to my uncle Euthyphro — you know what he is like in a fury — and tell him that I had this monopoly in my hand and that even then I went no nearer to Ireland than Durovernum. I must go at least as far as the port for Ireland, even if I go no farther, for I must satisfy him as well as myself that there is no possibility of going any farther.'

Leo went out to his vomitorium, the pride of his house, which he showed to every visitor, and he went there not because he needed to but because he thought it was the proper and civilised and Roman thing to do, and he left me slightly fuddled and thinking of everything in threes and triples and thirds like a Brit. It gave Leo time to think, and when he came back and started on mussels in honey, he said:

'Even if you are to go as far as that only, and to learn something that will sound convincing in Rome, it will do you no good to go as a man in the counsels of the Consuls, in the confidence of the Caesars, in league with the Legates of the legions. I think that I know a man who, it may be, will be able to take you as far as the port for Ireland, and speak for you to the Kings of the Irish, if only you will go with him and live as he does and do as he says, and trust him with your life. First, I will have to send and dispatch and instruct a messenger to find him, and bring him to meet us in Londinium, and it's lucky that it is not long since I talked with him, and I know that he is not in the Summer Country, nor at sea, where he is for a great part of the summer. So if we go to Londinium in a few days, then this man will come and meet us, and it may be that he will help us if he feels it satisfies a whim of his.'

I had two days' rest in Durovernum, and then, the third day, Leo and I set out for Londinium, which is two days' journey by road, though a messenger in a hurry, such as Leo had sent off immediately after dinner on the first night, may do it in summer between dawn and sunset. We had a dozen Pannonian troopers, borrowed from the garrison, as escort, although I felt safe enough. Surely Gwawl, about whom I had said nothing to Leo Rufus, was now in pursuit of Cicva. But then I remembered how she had ridden off, in her red and white checked shawl, with its long tassels, and a bronze chain about her waist instead of the embroidered belt, and I wondered.

CHAPTER TWO

Leo Rufus had a house in Londinium which might have been a town house in Rome, six-storeyed and tiled-roofed. The ground floor was the warehouse. He had the entire first floor to live in, and he let out the upper floors for rent. Again he apologised, when we arrived, late in the evening, that his wife had taken it into her head to leave that morning for Durovernum. Perhaps I have a reputation.

That evening, on arriving in Londinium, I went to bed early. Leo promised that I should have at least one quiet empty day, and the following day again he would invite some of his trading colleagues to meet me, as probably the most influential and wealthy visitor to Londinium for some years. However, just as I woke, half-way between dawn and noon on that first day, Leo came into my bedroom and announced:

'You have a client.'

I thought he was being facetious, and I didn't like it. I am never at my best on waking. I snarled something like:

'If I'm a patrician, you're a Pharaoh,' but Leo stood back and the 'client' entered. This man did not really stand seven feet high. He only looked like it, in the undress uniform of his regiment, the Danube Rangers, Hadrian's Own. I leapt out of bed, and embraced Aristarchos, the son of Demons. Tall and lean, he was, and always walked like a horseman. His black hair, black as Gwawl's, and his cheerful black eyes, that charmed women everywhere, and his brown skin, telling of a sunnier home, were the best things I had seen for weeks.

'Why are you not still on the Danube?' I asked him. I

remembered the regiment he had, patrolling the river frontier, and on the other side of it, usually. Horse-thieves and cattle-stealers they were to a man, raised in Britain, and that is how he spoke the language like a native, though a rather disreputable native.

'All good things come to an end,' he replied. 'I'm having a period on the Procurator's staff. Oh Gods, I can't stand these cities in the summer.'

I agreed with him. He was, I thought, too clever for anyone to waste at a place like Rutupiae, however he might have liked it. I asked:

'What are you doing? I can't see you in an office, checking other people's claims for forage, though perhaps if you know all the dodges . . .'

'That's more or less the kind of thing. All this administrative stuff about trade and finance — you'd understand it, but I never will. Not that there aren't some interesting cases on the Marine side. It's funny how the rewards paid for rescues from pirates always go to the same people. But how about you? I heard a rumour, inside the service from someone in the Second, that you were on the way, but nobody seems to know why.'

I hesitated a moment. For an instant, I was tempted to tell him that I was merely broadening my commercial education and Leo's as well; I was going to do that in any case. But then I relented. With an island full of people like Gwawl and Leo Rufus, it was as well to have somebody I could trust. I told him a little of what had been going on. He whistled.

'Trade with Ireland? Now, if you could start that, it would be useful. The Eagles follow Trade you know, and the Second and the Sixth and the Twentieth are just waiting for the chance. You ought to come and talk with the Procurator.'

I shook my head.

'I have my own troubles. I'll start talking to officials when I have some taxes to pay and clearances to do. Faustinus' name on the Deed ought to ensure that I can work undisturbed.'

'As you like. Still, if you want anything done . . . or any entertainment, either . . . I can get you into half a dozen gambling clubs.'

'Will I meet any influential Brits there?'

'Not very likely. A sad lot, the Brits. Either they are trying as hard as they can to turn into Italians, in the hope of getting some kind of hereditary post in the administration, if they haven't got one already: or they've turned their backs on progress and are only interested in religion. And they are firmly convinced, most of them, that they are the favourites of the Gods, and that if they were conquered, then in itself it is a sign of the favour of the Gods. The reward of virtue is defeat. Odd, isn't it, what people will believe, if it makes them happy?'

'So all is quiet, except on the frontier?'

'Oh, there are a few who still don't believe the Empire is here to stay. They still pay taxes to the old kings. There's one, up in the rain hills, who is most troublesome.'

I remembered what the old men had said in the mess at Rutupiae.

'Pwyll?'

'Pwyll.' Aristarchos changed his tone, suddenly. 'But would you like to come out tonight?'

I shook my head.

'I have things to do. Later perhaps. Today, I have a little shopping.'

He laughed. 'You'll be soundly cheated, if you're not very careful. You ought to learn a few words of the language.'

'I'll try,' I assured him. He went out, off to the Office of the Procurator. I went in to the office of the family's agent.

It was a long and hard morning going through the books. In the middle of the afternoon I had a bite to eat, and then I unpacked my sword from my bag. I thought I could remember the name of the scabbard-maker I had been recommended in Bonnonia, and I even thought I could find my way, with directions from Leo. I refused his offer to come as a guide. I even refused to have a slave come with me. I wanted to see the town myself, with nobody to affect my judgements.

Londinium, of course, is just like any other provincial town, with the big buildings of marble in the official quarter contrasting with the low thatched houses where the natives live. Down there a civilised gentleman in his bare legs and his cloak is out of place among all the trousers and the jerkins and tunics of soft leather the Brits wear over their coloured shirts to keep out the rain. There are no people like the Brits for wearing bright colours. They move about like a bed of walking flowers, with their shirts and blouses and shawls in stripes and checks and patches. In my drab grey I felt most conspicuous. Still, a Citizen and a Greek ought to be able to carry off anything. I found the scabbard-maker in his little shop, and I told him who had sent me. He looked at the blade, and then he stroked the ivory of the hilt as if he could feel the lock of hair that Cicva had insisted on binding up within it, or as if he could hear the things, unintelligible to me, that she had crooned over it.

'I am trusting,' he told me in a soft voice, 'that it is no firm idea that you have for the pattern of the scabbard.'

'An artist,' I replied, 'must choose his subject.'

The old man smiled slyly at me. He asked, of course, when I was born and what stars had shone over me, and then:

'What is the name of the sword?'

'Name? Now, you may think it stupid, but in spite of paying so much for the blade, and taking so much trouble over the hilt and the sheath, I had quite forgotten the barbarian custom of giving a weapon a name. I thought a moment. All I could think of was the Brits' word for a blow. I said:

'*Burn* is all I will call it.'

'Then a hard blow it will be to you,' he answered. 'It will be ready in a week.'

I left him, and wandered through the mean streets till I came out on the river bank. I strolled for a little, watching the men fishing for salmon. The salmon they catch above the bridge at Londinium are the best in the world. Here and there clouds of seagulls fought about the places where men cleaned the fish. And then suddenly, on that summer evening, with the sun below my shoulder when I could see it in the broken cloud, out of a cloud of seagulls I heard a voice singing.

I tell you, it was the most beautiful voice I have ever heard in all my life. In it I heard the humming of the bees and the rustle of wind over the summer grass, the ripple of fresh water over shallows and the lap of salt water against the side of an anchored ship. It was a voice of cream and a voice of silk, a voice of honey and a voice of wine. It was a voice that brought the scent of roses, and of honeysuckle on a sultry night. It was a voice that brought the feel of air heavy and hot before the thunderstorm.

I walked towards the gulls, towards the voice. Out of the flutter of white the words came clear, some old song of the Brits, from days of old.

A handsome warrior rode down from Alesia;
A lovely young maiden he chanced for to see:
'Oh, sir, take me up in your chariot behind you
'To dance at a wedding till sunrise,' asked she.

I walked towards the voice. The birds rose in a great flock. She stood there, tall and slim and stately, wrapped from head to feet in a cloak that shimmered in white and gold. I stepped nearer. She slipped her shawl from her head to her shoulders, the tassels and fringes hung long and thick, to her knees. She showed her hair, red in the late red sun, shining like a helmet of copper, coiled in great braids and pinned over her ears. And as I approached her she floated away, gliding and smooth, but bobbing a little up and down as she went like a boat upon the water, light as a skin boat, and gleaming. And as she floated away, she still sang:

66

His mail it was gilded, his helm was of silver,
His shield was of bronze, enamelled in red.
Her blouse was of silk and her skirt was of linen,
Her rich golden hair was piled high on her head.

I remembered all that I had been told. The redheads are
the worst, they had said, everybody had said. I remembered all this, and yet I went forward. She bobbed away
from the river, down an alley. I followed. The thatched
roofs above us were covered with gulls. I pushed my way
between people and pigs, following the Lady in the Cloak.
I could still hear her voice.

They rode to the wedding, they danced at the
    wedding,
They danced to sweet music till daylight was near;
At cockcrow, the palace, the dancers, the pipers,
The maiden, all vanished: the warrior knew fear.

I knew no fear. I only knew that I must follow that voice
through the crowds and through narrow streets, across
courtyards and around corners. I wanted to find the Lady
in the Cloak, the lady of the seagulls, Phryne or no Phryne,
hyena hair or none.

His mail shirt was rusted, his helmet was tarnished,
His beard had grown long and his hair had turned
    grey.
The people around him wore strange-fashioned
    garments:
The walls of Alesia had crumbled away.

Now I was quite lost. I did not know the way back to
the river or back to the official quarter. It was nearly dark.
I did not know, I did not care, what would happen next
if only I could reach the Lady. I suddenly came out into
a kind of open square, surrounded with houses of a better
sort. A lantern hung outside a door. She stood under it,

the light on her hair. She had thrown open her cloak, and I could see the gleam of her belt of enamelled bronze. I walked slowly towards her. I heard her:

> So if you drive out on the road past Alesia
> Take no young maid up, whate'er she may say:
> For if you dance one night with the Princess of
>   Darkness
> It's all of your life you will dance clear away.

I was almost on her, I could smell the fragrance of her hair, I could feel her breath, I could hear the sound of her breathing in the silent, empty square. And as I almost touched her, the door opened behind her, she passed through, and it slammed in my face.

And then, as I stood a moment, dazed, it came. It is very clever to attack a one-eyed man. All you have to do is to come at him with his blind side. But it is advisable to be sure that you know which *is* his blind side, and this was a precaution that Gwawl had failed to take. He came rushing at me, and I stood still to the last instant, and then I leapt away, and he thudded with all his weight into the side of the house. He fell back on to the ground, winded, and his knife skidded away across the pavement like a flat stone across water, the water that the Lady had floated on, boatlike. Of course, if I had any sense, I ought to have run for my life; all I wanted to do was to stay and get into the house whose door had been closed against me, and I could not do that with Gwawl behind me. I flung myself on him, my knees into his black-and-white-striped stomach — or so I planned. But he was already recovering, and he rolled clear, and I nearly broke my kneecaps on the cobbles. He grabbed at my throat. I was worried about two things: I did not want him to get at another knife, least of all mine which was sticking in my belt, and I did not want to lose the other eye, so I gripped his wrists and hung on desperately trying to force them apart, the whiles we each tried to kick the other in the groin. As a result of this kicking, we rolled over and over in the dirt. At last I became conscious of a pair of feet close to my face. Next, I realised that the owner of the feet was waving a heavy stick, such as almost all the Brits carry, and he was obviously looking for an opportunity to strike. To strike whom? I had no friends in this country, and Gwawl had, I knew, at least two. And he had come prepared for this meeting, if he had not engineered it, and I braced myself for the blow. Of course, all this took scarcely enough time to repeat a line of Virgil. And then the blow came, and for all our mutual dodging it was Gwawl who was struck, and I rolled away and scrambled to my feet. I looked at my rescuer, idly swinging his cudgel and regarding the still figure of Gwawl with a satisfied air.

He was not a tall man or a heavily built one, rather spare and slender. He was about my own age. He wore shabby clothes of an indeterminate brown, but in the light of the lamp at the door I could see that he had round his neck a strip of coloured cloth, black streaked with yellow. As I looked at him and wondered what to say, the empty square suddenly filled with men, a score at least, and I realised that every one I could see near enough was wearing somewhere on his person a scrap of black and yellow. And it was then I began to wonder if those gay colours that Tacitus remarks on so idly had not some inner meaning. I had no chance to ask. One of the newcomers brought a bucket of water, and threw it over Gwawl, who began to stir. Another happened to be carrying a leather sack, and the first man took it, and when two others held Gwawl on his feet, the bag was pulled over his head and tied down to bind his arms. Then the men formed a circle and the leader pushed Gwawl across it, singing out:

> The badger's in the bag.
> The badger's in the bag.
> Heigh-o, heigh-o,
> The badger's in the bag.

And they pushed Gwawl across the circle, and every man he bumped into hit him — hands only, though, no sticks or knives. The more he staggered and cursed them from inside the bag, the more they, no, *we* all laughed, till at last he bumped into someone who was laughing so hard that he just fell over, and Gwawl escaped into an alley, running zigzag and bouncing from one wall to another till he finally bounced around a corner and so out of sight. We were all laughing after him.

Then I pulled myself together. There was no time to waste in laughing. I turned to the door. I raised the latch and pulled it open. I looked through the doorway to nothing. There was no house. It was merely a facade. Before me an empty waste stretched down to the river, strewn with all the rubbish of a city, broken pots and oyster shells and the half-gnawed carcasses of dead dogs and unwanted babies. No Lady. No one at all.

CHAPTER THREE

My second evening in Londinium, Leo Rufus gave a dinner in my honour for a few of his friends, all men deeply involved in trade with him, and by what I had seen of his books, once a man got involved with Leo it was not easy to disengage nor cheap to remain involved. Still, they seemed to bear him no malice. They were all romanised Brits like himself, and they lay there, eating roast goose in a daring manner and making sly little jokes I could not understand over the roast songbirds on a spit, just to show how civilised they were.

All the same, they talked in the most atrocious Latin, with the accents vile and the vocabulary pedantic, and the slang at least a hundred years out of date, and while they even corrected my quantities, and corrected them wrong, I learnt quite a lot. They talked of how trade had fallen off since the old freebooting times before the conquest, which none of them could remember, and how heavy the customs were, and how the Army was interested in nothing but the silver they cupellated out of the lead they mined near the hot springs at Sulis. When at last they went, Leo said:

'Come you down into the warehouse. I have someone you ought to meet.'

I followed. The warehouse was a big place, and at this time it should have been deserted, since Leo was a very humane man and insisted that all his slaves should get at least five hours' sleep a night. But now there were lights burning at the back, and as we picked our way between the bales, I saw a man sitting, eating a cheese, slowly, deliberately, with the point of a knife.

He was wearing an old brown jerkin with a hood, patched with leather at the cuffs and elbows, but showing at the neck a flash of colour, of black striped with yellow. And he had a belt — I was beginning to learn, now. No Brit will be seen without a belt, man or woman. The poorer people will wear belts of plain leather, and women girdles of the best cloth they can afford. But a noble by blood will wear a belt of Spanish leather with embroidery in gold and silver wire, and his wife a network of bronze chains. The more noble a man, the more expensive his belt. This man's belt was of plates of bronze, the size of my palm, enamelled in bright red with strange patterns of stags and bulls, garnet-eyed, and joined with links of Gold — Irish Gold.

He stood up, this man of my own height, whom I had last seen swinging a cudgel in an empty square. His light brown eyes looked into my one black. He pushed aside his thick brown curls, and took my hand.

'I had hoped,' said Leo, 'that the Master of the Western Sea might have come himself to meet you, but he cannot because he is at sea, or because he is old, or ill, or at a wedding, or for some other great and pressing reason he has failed to specify. But you may speak as you will to Pryderi, and not be deceived by his dress.'

'So it's you, is it?' Pryderi asked. 'Any enemy of Gwawl's is a friend of mine.'

'I am not so much concerned with Gwawl,' I answered, 'as with Bithig the Pict.'

I do not know what it was that made Leo look so concerned, the mention of Gwawl or of Bithig, or his discovery that I could converse in the language of the Brits, and might have heard anything in his house. And I had too, but that is another story. Pryderi continued:

'Well, Bithig is far away, and will stay there. I remember seeing you at the wedding. Missed you we did, especially at the May Feast. A real gap you would have filled.'

'I suppose that I would.' I felt that the whole subject was rather distasteful to me, anyway, however Pryderi might look at it. 'How is the . . . er . . . lady?'

'Well, you know, well. A bit regretful, in a hungry sort of way. But it will give me a little personal satisfaction to keep you two apart. Now, the Master of the Western Sea has given me a little discretion to consider any propositions you may have in the way of trade. Tell me, what is it exactly you are wanting?'

I explained the whole situation to Pryderi more fully than I had to Leo, who looked gloomier and gloomier as he saw the road to ruin opening before him. We ignored him, and he was reduced to a mere putter-out of the fires that Pryderi caused by oversetting lamps with his eloquent swinging arms. Northerners need more room to talk than do we unemotional southerners. But at the last, he just sat still and quiet, thinking hard for some moments. At last he observed, sadly and quietly:

'Mad. Mad you are, Photinus, and I always said as much. This is no easy thing you are proposing to do, like sailing across the Narrow Sea and selling a few pots of wine. If it were anyone else, I would walk out now and leave you. But seeing it is you, and seeing that your marrying Bithig makes you Royal, and seeing that all us Royals are brothers at bottom, then it is help you a little I will.

'Listen to the situation. There are four kings in Ireland, of the four parts of the island, but there is always one of them is High King. Now, if it is trading you want, it is the High King that you must persuade. But at the moment, it is quite the wrong man who is High King. However, I can find you an Irishman to speak to . . .'

'I'll talk to the High King. I have had enough of middle-men.'

'Politics is full of middlemen, Photinus. And this one — will it satisfy you to know that he is nephew to the King of the North, who is not High King?'

It did satisfy me a little. The King's nephew might well be the King's heir. I asked:

'When can I see him?'

'At the moment, he is the mate of a grain ship running between Lindum and Londinium, coasting and up the canals. Exiles, you know, have to do strange things. But he will be here on Friday night, and we can see him then.'

That would have to do. The interview was at an end. But not quite. As Pryderi stood up, I asked him:

'And the Lady? Who was she? Where can I find her now?'

'What Lady?'

'The one who sang: the one I was following when Gwawl attacked me. The one who went through the door with the lamp.'

'I didn't see any Lady. I just came round the corner by chance, and there you were, the two of you, having a lovely fight. Pity it was to stop you, and if it had been anyone else but Gwawl I'd never have stopped it. But I saw nobody else. Friday at dusk, then — here.'

He picked another cheese off the shelf and went off with it into the dark street.

CHAPTER FOUR

For three days, I led an exemplary life. Each morning I spent going over the accounts, till even Leo Rufus had to admit that I knew more about business than he did. Each evening, I stayed at home, and dined quietly, not even going with Aristarchos to one of the gaming parties he was so fond of: it would have been tame fare to me. Besides, I wanted to be so retiring that nobody would question my presence in Londinium, or notice when I left.

But in the late afternoons, till a little after dusk, I would dress inconspicuously, like a Greek sailor, and there were plenty of those about, and I would walk about the river banks and the quays looking for the Lady who sang. Everywhere I saw a cloud of seagulls I hurried, everywhere I heard any voice raised I loitered to listen. I went into every tavern, I inspected the girls in a hundred brothels, I haggled with every bawd and pimp in Londinium, and there are more there than in any port I have seen, because you have to do something to keep warm in their long cool winters and their long cold summers. But I could not find her, although I penetrated into every group in society where women might be expected to walk the streets alone. Yet, no one had see her, no one recognised her description. She had vanished, and the more I looked for her, the more I threaded the narrow alleys, the more I lost count of the corners I turned, the more eager I was to find her, the more her face swam before my inner gaze.

On Friday night, I was waiting in the warehouse when Pryderi came for me. He was dressed, even more shabbily than before, with a plain leather belt. I wore a heavy hooded grey cloak, and I had a long knife in my belt, and a heavy stick in my hand, as had Pryderi: most Brits carry a cudgel all the time, swearing of course in case of trouble that they need it to drive their cattle or to beat off dogs.

Pryderi led me through narrow streets that even I had not dared to penetrate in daylight, down into the sailors' quarter, at the east of the town along the river bank. It was as dirty and crowded a place as you will find in any town, and Astolat, as this quarter was called, was full of sailors' taverns. It stank of poverty and corruption.

'The only thing to do with this end of the town is to burn it,' I murmured to Pryderi, not too loudly, in case anyone might overhear me who was proud of the place.

'We've done it often enough, from one end of Londinium to the other, and the last was in my father's time,' Pryderi replied. 'The Lily is all right, though. That's where our man is waiting for us.'

It *was* fairly clean, by waterfront standards, and not too crowded. Pryderi called for cider — I had to pay, of course — but I wanted beer. I mean, there's good wine, and there's bad wine, and in a miserable place like Londinium it's nearly always bad wine. But beer — why, there's no bad beer, only better beer and worse beer. When I think of the time when I didn't drink beer — but I was back in practice now, and I drained the first pot at one gulp and called for another.

A little man alongside me dipped his finger in his pot and wrote on the counter:

```
R O T A S
O P E R A
T E N E T
A R E P O
S A T O R
```

It was clever enough, reading the same way up and down and back to front, but it didn't mean anything to me.

'And the same to you, Comrade,' I told him — I was

feeling in a friendly mood. 'Weren't you drawing fish in every tavern in Bonnonia the other night?'

He squinted at me in alarm, and then rushed out into the night, like a frightened hare. I turned to Pryderi who was complaining about the cider to the landlord.

'Muck, this, proper muck. All you can say for it is that it is wet. I suppose it *is* cider — it must be, because it isn't beer or mead, and it doesn't taste good enough for ditch-water. How they have the face to bring it into the country I can't think. Not your fault, I suppose: you have to sell what you can get. You ought' — this to me — 'to try some of my grandmother's elderberry. You will, too, as soon as we get down into the Summer Country.'

He said this last sentence very loudly and distinctly, and the landlord, who had been standing with his back to the counter and taking no particular notice of his customers, so that I had had some trouble in getting my second pot of beer, now turned sharply round and snapped:

'If you don't like this, then go you back to the Summer Country where you belong.'

And I suppose this must have been some kind of pass-word, because Pryderi immediately asked:

'And where is he now?'

'In bed with Elaine, the front-room barmaid. You can see him when — hey! You can't go up there now! a man's entitled to *some* privacy.'

'We're going up,' Pryderi told him, and went on muttering something about nobody spotting an old sweat from the Danube Rangers — Dredgers, the landlord told him, more likely — Hadrian's Own, that had seen more bloodshed than any man in the house. I slipped the patch off my eye and looked at the landlord with it. I had the garnet in, and somehow that carving always put people off, Hercules taking off the shirt of Nessus, delicate work, you could see the veins going into the kidneys and all the tubes of the lungs hanging out. And he saw the knife in my belt, and my stick, and Pryderi's, and so he stood back politely and let us go up the ladder to the top floor.

'Old sweat, indeed,' I said to Pryderi on the landing, 'and I know very well you've never been a soldier.'

'Indeed, and I was a regimental tailor for three months, and then they wanted to send the whole regiment back to the Danube, so I . . . left.'

'Deserted?'

'Well . . . not really. My cousin came back. I only took his place for experience while he went off to see a man who had seduced his cousin. Lovely head it was, too, when he took it, and dried a treat, very decorative. You see, for all the way old Aristarchos used to talk, one Briton looked just like another to him. Now, this ought to be the door. Do you think we ought to knock, or would it spoil the surprise? Let's go straight in and see how he's feeling.'

So in we went without any warning, but Pryderi was disappointed, because either the Irishman had just got out of bed with the barmaid or he had not yet got in. He was ordering his supper, and when he saw me with Pryderi he made no other comment than:

'Make it three times, Elaine, and the same for yourself.'

She was a big slattern, and I couldn't see any man of taste going after her. I suppose that I must have shown my thoughts in my face as she went, because the Irishman said:

'And is it thinking you can be of a better way of getting a room to yourself for a few hours? She only costs six coppers a time, for the house, but of course I always tip her and she gets a meal out of it.'

He did not bother about greetings. It was obvious he was expecting us. He and Pryderi showed for each other neither affection nor dislike, merely the attitude of two men who find it advantageous to work together, but who have otherwise nothing in common. I looked long at him, the first Irishman I had seen, I thought, though I was wrong about that.

He was a big man. He had long hair, down to his shoulders in the Irish fashion. The Brits wear it that way too, but while Germans cut their hair short, except Vandals, and wear long beards not cut or curled but combed, the Irish wear their beards long and neither washed nor combed but matted; the Brits are quite different, because they are unique among men in shaving off their beards and letting their moustaches grow, hanging down as long as possible on either side of their mouths. Pryderi's moustache was very fine, almost to his collarbones.

But the Irishman not only wore his hair long, he had combed it back and plaited it up on top into a ridge like the mane of a horse all ready for a show or parade. He had stiffened his hair with grease, and before this he had dyed it a bright yellow so that no one could tell what the original colour had been. It would have been most distinctive in Rome, but here in Britain men dress so fantastically that no one gives it a second thought.

The Irishman was dressed *as* an Irishman, in a way I had not seen before. I know that if your life has been passed in the centre of culture, then you will believe that all Barbarians wear trousers and that to let your legs go bare is the mark of civilisation. This is not true. The Irish go bare-legged, but no one could call them cultured. This man had taken a length of cloth, about fifteen yards long and two wide. This he wound two or three times around his waist, and then he drew the end up over his left shoulder at the back and across the front of his body down to his waist again at the right. The cloth was fastened with two big cloak pins of silver set with pebbles, of good workmanship but too flamboyant in design for my taste.

This Irishman had, however, made some concessions both to fashion and to decency, not to mention the climate, and he had on a fairly good linen shirt under the cloth. He had not changed it for some weeks, that was plain, but under the dirt I could make out that it had once been the colour of a Spanish orange, if you know the fruit, embroidered with a variety of flower motifs in bright green. The cloth itself was all of one colour, a dirty saffron, but I saw later that some of the Irish in the far north were beginning to weave their cloths in complex patterns of many colours like the Picts, from whom I suppose they learnt the art. Elaine came back with the supper, big plates of food of all kinds fried in butter. The Brits do not use oil, professing not to like the taste of it or the smell, though I think this is a way of hiding the fact that they are too mean to pay for it. They fry things in butter instead, which to us seems disgusting, since it is plain the Gods intended it for use only as a cosmetic.

'Can't eat this at sea,' said the Irishman, with his mouth full. 'It turns my stomach.'

I knew just what he meant, and said so, and finding that I knew what I was talking about in discussing ships he became more communicative. Then Pryderi asked:

'Anybody like my black pudding? I can't eat it.'

'You don't like it? We'll share it.'

'No, I like it, but it's a question of religion. All my family are descended from the great Black Pudding of Gabalva. I'll tell you some time. My house began in a fever of lust and greed, with a tradition right from the start of filial neglect, and I cannot think of a better way to power.'

'And you?' I asked the Irishman. 'What can't you eat?'

'What no one is likely to offer me.' He grinned. 'Dog, I can't eat, because when I was a child I killed a big dog, and so I got my name.' He paused, as if expecting me to say something. I kept silent. After a little he went on. 'And it is very considerate of you, and shows that even if you are a Greek, you are a noble born, and makes me ready to trust you, that you do not ask me my name. For if you did, I would not tell you, and if you asked me a second time, then I would kill you.'

He smiled again, very engagingly. I have known several men in my time who would kill for nothing at all but the whim and the enjoyment of it, Aristarchos, for instance, and they all smiled that same dreamy smile.

'Can you tell me your Clan?' I asked.

'Oh, yes. I am of the Sons of Mil, the noblest of all the houses of the Kings of Ireland. And I am of the nation of the Setantii, and I myself am the bravest and the strongest

80

and the cleverest of all the Setantii of Ireland and of Britain and of Gaul and of Galatia. So it is *the* Setanta that I am, and so you may call me till you hear my name called in victory on the holy soil of Ireland.'

Obviously, he could not risk anyone's using his real name while he was in the land of his enemies, because it would then be so easy to cast a spell on him. But he had said something interesting, and I went back to it.

'My mother is Galatian.'

'Why, useful that will be, indeed. For it is raising a fianna I must first be about. There is not a man will join me if it is thought I am in league with a Roman, and a Greek is not much better, though it is hating the Romans you must be as much as we are.' (I wondered where he had got that strange idea from.) 'But if it is a Galatian I am consorting with, then it might well be my own cousin within seventeen generations.'

I looked at the Setanta and dismissed that idea in horror.

'What is a fianna?' I asked him.

'Why, a band of brave fellows that will follow me to the overthrowing of the High King?'

'But why cannot you go back to Ireland and raise an army in Ulster?'

'For the same reason that I am in exile here in the Island of the Mighty. I could not bear to stay in an Ulster that the Connaught men had ravaged from end to end, and disarmed utterly so that there is neither sword nor shield nor horse trained to war in the whole Kingdom. No, it is here. I must raise a fianna, and arm them, and find weapons enough to fit out an army. I have been thinking over it for a year, and I know the very day that I must land in Ireland again. Now, you with all your connections can find weapons enough for an army. And if it is only a little matter you want in recompense, like all the Gold in Ireland, then it will be easy enough to let you have it, I promise you that. But, meanwhile, there are arrangements to be made, while I spend the winter in the rainy hills with Howell, and they will cost something in silver. But it will only be a trifle.'

'I can arrange that through Pryderi,' I told him.

'But then there is the question,' the Setanta went on, 'of getting the arms, when you have them, into Ireland, and for that you will need a ship.'

'Pryderi will see to that too,' I told him.

'I cannot,' Pryderi put in. 'There is a limit to my discretion, and I cannot here and now divert a valuable ship from the honest and peaceful trade it is now engaged in. Besides, I would not like to see it lured ashore and looted and burnt on the coast of Ireland, as has happened before.'

'But you promised—'

'To help. I will help all I can. You must come with me, Photinus, and ask the Master of the Western Sea yourself. I will help you all I can, but I cannot promise.'

'You give and then you take away again,' I said bitterly. 'If one of you does that, then the other—'

'I have my Gesa.' This was the Setanta in his pride.

'Your Gesa?'

'Every man of noble blood has his Gesa. It would not be just, or right, or morally praiseworthy, for a Son of Mil and a cousin of kings to exert his full strength against an ordinary man. It would be more honourable for me to contend with one hand tied behind my back. But that is undignified, and therefore I have taken on myself an obligation, that I must always obey, even if it be to my disadvantage. My Gesa is this, that I must never refuse to take what is offered to me, nor to give what is asked of me. And I have given what you asked for, all the Gold of Ireland. But if it is thinking you are that this is an easy burden to bear, then it is little you are knowing about it. And think, too, of the Gesa laid on my cousin and my enemy the King of Leinster. The Badger King may never refuse a wager, or a bargain, or a challenge once offered, however disadvantageous it may be.'

I hope, I thought, that one day I will meet this obliging monarch. But now I knew that the Irish were all mad, for no Greek would so bind himself. It was only necessary to find a man's Gesa, to see a way to destroy him. Pryderi snorted.

'Easy it is for them to take on a Gesa, and to think it so meritorious to accept odds. They are still a free people. If ever they are conquered, they will realise that victory is the only thing that matters. And then it will be too late. But come you down with me into the Summer Country, Photinus, and ask the Master yourself for a ship.'

I hesitated. Perhaps as far as that, but no farther. And quickly, so that I could get back to the Old City before the end of the summer, before the baby was born. And no farther. That was tempting. And I would not make myself any promises. I had told Uncle Euthyphro that I would see the trade started, and if it meant a month or two extra in Britain, then I would bear with it.

'Now, if it's there you're going,' warned the Setanta, 'it's not as a Roman you can go. You can be a Galatian if you wish, because you speak British with a strange accent.' This annoyed me: I was sure that no one could have guessed I was not born and bred in the island.

'With a new name,' Pryderi added.

'No, no,' corrected the Setanta. 'Clan first, name after.'

'All right, Clan then,' agreed Pryderi. 'Now, do you know your ancestry on your mother's side?'

'Not very far,' I warned them. 'Not more than twenty-one or twenty-three generations.' And I recited it, going back in the male line only but of course naming all my grandmothers as they came and inserting their fathers too. My two companions listened with care to my pronunciation of these outlandish names, now and again correcting me. And when I finished, the Setanta said:

'Plain, isn't it?'

'Obvious,' agreed Pryderi. 'Son of Lear, he is.'

'What does that mean?' I asked.

'Oh, a great house it was once,' Pryderi told me, 'and ruled all the island of Britain, but few are they and rarely met with.'

'But in the Isle of the Blessed,' added the Setanta, 'it is

an O'Leary you will be, and plenty of them there are and eager to welcome any kinsman from over the sea, especially if he is rich.'

'But what is it I can't eat?'

'Swan, of course.' They both answered together. I felt rather disappointed, because there is nothing I like better than a nice roasted swan. It is nearly big enough to serve as a dish for two, but if you are giving a party I advise you to cater on the basis of one swan per guest, since this avoids disappointment. Then Pryderi, in a doleful voice:

'This is all nonsense. There is no possibility, Son of Lear or not, of taking you down into the Summer Country as if you were one of us. It would be better, Photinus son of Lear, if you stayed here in Londinium and let me do all the work for you in the Summer Country.'

And let you have all the money to control, I thought. Not on any account. But I could hardly sound as distrustful, so I answered as ceremonially as I could:

'I come of a great and ancient House. Beside it your House of Lear is young and of little account. And I have sworn to all the heads of the House that I would go as far as the port for Ireland and bring back the Gold of Ireland. You talk of a Gesa which binds you. I also am bound. I can no more turn back from this journey than you, Son of Mil, could refuse me your cloak if I asked you for it.'

'Asked for it you have,' said the Setanta. 'And have it you shall.' He stood up. He was a head taller than Pryderi and me, and well built, though not gross or corpulent like Gwawl. He was, indeed, the kind of man I would have been pleased to have as Mate on any voyage. He went to the cupboard in the corner of the room, stepping gently over Elaine who had long since sunk into a drunken sleep. He turned to me again, his arms full of fur. 'Take my cloak, Photinus, that I cannot refuse you. And I will take what I think you have offered. You have offered me the head of the King of Connaught, to hang on the pole's end.'

I took the cloak, a splendid garment of blue-grey fur, strange to the touch and warm, lapping me from neck to heels, and hooded. This is what every sailor who can afford it wears in thunderstorms, for there is nothing that wards off lightning like seal fur. I turned to show Pryderi. He knew, as the Irishman knew, that I had no more suspected that such a cloak was in the room than I could fly. And that is why Pryderi looked at the cloak with open mouth.

'There is no further we need be looking for a name. Seal cloak asked unknowing shows that you are Mannanan.'

'But he is a god of the sea,' I objected.

'And is it not meeting him we all have been at some time or another?' asked the Irishman. 'And what is the loan of a name between kinsmen?'

For I had forgotten that it is the Brits alone among all the nations of the earth who are so bold as to take the names of their gods and goddesses to themselves, and you must always be careful in telling stories there to make it clear exactly who or what you are talking about. And I remembered too all my grandfather had always taught us about the essential nature of every name.

'Yes,' I agreed, 'I will be Mannanan the Son of Lear, on sea and on shore in this island and in the other.'

We talked on and on, and later when I lay in bed and remembered what we had said, I was horrified. I had agreed that somehow or other I would provide the means for a change of government in Ireland, which only could give us terms of trade. And what had I as working assets in this undertaking?

First, I had one man, and now, when I could no longer see him, and was no longer overborne by his personality and the air of power and menace in his stout arms and his massive fists, he did not seem such a great asset. I did not even know his real name.

And of Pryderi, my other asset, I knew nothing, except that he had found me the Setanta and that he only could help me to hire a ship that would face the winter on the Western Sea, for no Roman ship could float for long in the North except in the summer months, and then only in calm weather.

But, in the ship? We had talked of money, but in the end it was not money that the Setanta wanted, or at least not very much. But he did want what he could not buy, weapons. And it never struck him that I could not buy arms either. I had a permit for a sword, and one sword only.

I tossed in the darkness, and always in the night before me shone the Gold of Ireland, and I was frantic to think of it there, free for the taking, and not able to take it. And then, suddenly, I remembered something that Pryderi had said to the Setanta in one of the wrangles that had enlivened the evening. He had goaded the Irishman:

'Why, we in this island will have thrown off the Romans and will walk in freedom, when you in the Island of the Blessed still lie beneath their yoke.'

And it came to me then, that I had another asset. He did not stand seven feet tall, he only looked like it. And he had the ear of the Procurator.

CHAPTER FIVE

It took weeks of arranging, before Pryderi and I went off
into the West. There was a lot of work, at the Office of
the Procurator, because it was ruled that this was all a civil
matter, and a financial one, and that the military were only
there to obey. But whenever I could, at dusk, I would
wander about in the streets by the river, looking for a cloud
of seagulls and listening for a voice and yearning for a cloak
of yellow and white and for a head of red hair.

There was, however, one day I went back to the
scabbard-maker. I must say that he had done very well.
He had covered the beechwood sheath with thin plates of
bronze, patterned in scarlet enamel, and the bronze
between the enamel plated with Gold. Not a scabbard for
use, a scabbard for show, as I had asked. This was not
now a weapon I would ever carry into battle, even though
the blade was better than any you will find within the
Empire, a blade to cut down elephants. This now was a
sword to be borne before me, sheathed, point up, on that
great day when I would come before the High King of all
Ireland at Tara to tell him the terms on which my family
would deign to trade with him.

I received the scabbard from the maker, and I looked
at it. It was a real Brit pattern, all twisted lines and coils,
but meaningless. I peered at it way and way about, and
then I asked the maker:

'What is this pattern?'

'Why, bears. What else for you but bears?'

I looked again, and sure enough, if you knew, it was
bears all right. And I looked again at the X-shaped hilt,

and now it was less clear whether it was more like a man or more like a bear. But how should the scabbard-maker, or, more curious the blademaker, have known that bears were so sacred to my family?

Of course, when we left Londinium, I didn't wear that sword, on the belt of soft leather from Cordoba all embroidered with flowers in gold and silver wire that I found in a dark corner of Leo Rufus's warehouse. I didn't tell him about it, I just took it over. I wrapped the sword in my sealskin cloak, because there was no wearing that in the summertime, even though Britain is always as they say, two tunics colder than civilised countries. I didn't wear a tunic either, but I was dressed as a Brit, in blue shirt and trousers, good boots of soft Spanish leather dyed blue, and a jerkin of soft brown sheepskin to keep out the rain. It *was* raining, of course.

We left Londinium at dawn, as soon as the city gates were open. I had been up early, shaving off my beard, or most of it. I was very careful about how much of it I did take off, and by judicious clipping of the hair either side of my mouth I was able to give myself a real British moustache which reached down to my nipples and made Pryderi so jealous he did nothing but grumble for miles.

We each had a horse to ride on and another to carry our baggage, done up in bundles. I had quite a lot, because I saw no reason why I should not turn an honest penny on the journey. The horses were native ponies, and the less said about them the better. They were small, and very strong: if you don't mind your legs hanging down so far that your spurs hurt your mother the Earth and not the beast, then you can ride one of these ponies all day without a stop. But not two days running. I would have preferred one of the cavalry horses the Army use, with the Parthian blood, but it would have been so conspicuous, and Pryderi was dreadfully concerned with not being conspicuous.

Of course, I am disenchanted now with horses. I had one once on the Amber road, and he was a *horse*. He was a horse that would carry you a hundred miles in one day, and then again the next day, and then into battle on the third day, and in the pursuit on the fourth. He was a horse that understood the speech of man, and the very thought of man he would know unspoken, and obey. He was not got by any mortal stallion, I tell you that; he was by Divinity out of the Platonic essence of all horses. I rode him for three years, and at the end — I weep when I think of it. I killed him myself. I will not think of it.

But we had our packhorses, and they would cover, if they had to, thirty miles in a day on the hard roads. We went out by the road on the north side of the river, which cuts out a great bight of the Thamesis. It was a very busy road. After we left the walls of the City, we found that we could count on meeting at least half a dozen travellers going the other way in every hour. Some of them were ox wagons full of vegetables, beans and carrots going in to the markets of the city, and looking at the poor innocent plants shrivelling away on the carts I began to understand why the food in Londinium was so bad. But we did come across one group that was different. It was a military convoy, the only troops we ever saw on the road. There were only a dozen of them, just enough to stop the Brits from stealing the oxen for meat at night, and to wait on the very junior centurion who was in charge. I recognised him, I had bought him wine at that inn north of Lugdunum, but he did not know me, hardly gave me a second glance, just another Brit on the road.

Pryderi, though, nudged me to look at what was in the wagons. They were light, you could tell that from the way the cattle moved, and so the big baskets, the fisces, in them were empty. I knew those baskets, all right.

'Silver?' I asked Pryderi.

'Party from the Second Legion, at Isca, going up for the salt money for the troops,' he told me. 'There'll be enough silver going back, all in coin, next week, to keep a kingdom going for a year, and no more escort than you see now.'

'Easy pickings for someone,' I hinted.

'When the time comes,' agreed Pryderi. 'You see, they

know the south is quiet. There are no troops in the interior at all. Anybody who takes on a pay convoy risks having all the civil zone under military law again for years. It will have to be done at the right time and in the right place.'

I said nothing. Perhaps there were comments I ought not to make, things I ought not to know. We pushed on. The road crosses the river at a place called Pontes, and in the little town we stopped for the night. There was an inn where Pryderi was known well enough to be asked no questions. Nobody asked about me, either.

'It's the blue,' Pryderi assured me. 'Wearing that, you are known as a Bard, and whatever you do, however eccentric, like wearing a fancy eye, or a sword for that matter if you want to, people will pass over without a question, as being natural to the poetic mind. Respected you will be, and as a foreigner they will answer questions and tell stories that will astonish you, because they all know that the mind of the poet does thrive on marvels.'

I looked sideways at him. This is an island of deceit and duplicity and mists indeed, I thought, and if ever I hear the truth about anything, then it's lucky I'll be. It was easy already to fall into the Brits' manner of speech, and after speech comes thought, and after thought comes life, and love. If you talk in Latin and think in Latin, you must be dignified, and think in dignity, because there is no short or easy or comfortable way of saying anything in that language. But in Greek, as we speak it all along the coasts of Asia and into Alexandria, from Massilia to Trapezus in the Caucasus, everything is easy and full of slang and comfortable ways of thought. And yet, in this unconventional tongue, it is always possible to say what you mean, and to know that it will only have one meaning to anyone who listens. But while the Brit's tongue is also full of slang, it is vague and imprecise and soft at the edges, and behind the plain meaning of everything said you have to look for another hidden meaning. I decided to speak plain.

'If we are going to stay here all tomorrow,' I said, 'then I am not going to be idle, nor am I going to spend the day here at my own loss for the horses' comfort. Let us away to the hut that you have taken for us, and get to work.'

'Work?' Pryderi wondered as he followed me. 'Do not mention that word to me, that am a British gentleman. I do not mind a little usury, or profitable sharp practice, but not work.'

'And you a sailor?'

'Hauling at the rope, and straining at the oar, ten days together on the heaving sea, with not a drop of water nor a bite of bread to pass my lips, and often enough I have done it, why, that is not work. That is sport.'

'Indeed, then, it is not work that we will be employed in here, but sport, tomorrow, and art today.'

I unrolled one of the bundles that I had brought with me on the packhorse. Pryderi looked at it with interest.

'Leather?'

'Leather, soft leather. Guaranteed the best soft Spanish leather from fighting bulls of the plains.'

'Whose guarantee?' He fingered the sheets like a connoisseur. 'Not ten days ago this was baa-ing for its supper on the Rainy Mountains. You must realise, I have met Leo Rufus before.'

'And I have seen leather before,' I assured him. 'Now, as we came through this town, there was something that struck me, and it was this. I saw that there was a lack, and a scarcity, and a dearth, of one thing only, and that was — shoes. Boots I saw, of the kind you wear ploughing, and for fishing in the river, but no dainty shoes of quality on the feet of men or women. Come to that it did not seem to me that the feet were moving very quickly or that anyone was in a mood to dance through the streets.'

'And what did you expect?' Pryderi was a trifle impatient. 'Yesterday was the first of August, the day of the feast of Luggnasad, the end of shearing. There would have been a splendid time here, as indeed there was even in Londinium, if you knew where to go for it, and there is not a man, or a woman either in a country town like this who has not a headache.'

91

'Headache? I never have them, however much I drink.'

'Then lucky it is you are. But what you are going to do about this lack of shoes?'

'Why, we are going to make shoes.'

'Do we' — I was glad that Pryderi was counting himself in with me — 'do we know anything about that craft?'

'We can try.' I unrolled the leather. 'Hold out your foot. We'll do you a pair to measure first, and then some smaller and some bigger, as samples. Then tomorrow we'll sit in the market place and make them to order.'

I cut, and Pryderi sewed. He did it very well, and I remarked on this.

'Three months as regimental tailor to Aristarchos, and there is not much there is left to learn about clothing, or equipment, or how to make little economies which no one will notice till they have accepted the articles. Fit well enough, these do. Style is a bit odd, though?'

'That's the beauty of it. The women will all go for a new fashion.'

'A bit plain though, they are. They go a lot more for decoration, I tell you, around here.'

'I have thought about that.' I delved into another bag, in which I had brought a variety of oddments which I knew would be hard to get out in the West, like the gallstone of an ass, and an ounce of powdered unicorn horn, the ashes of a boar's pizzle, and the ground ankle-bones of a nanny-goat. Among all this were a few crystals of vitriol, which I dissolved in a cup of warm water. Then I added a few other trifles, and began to work with a piece of fairly clean rag. Soon the leather was a bright and striking blue.

'Will that do?'

'As long as it is fine tomorrow. But it is a foundation, and a ground, and a beginning. Allow me.'

Pryderi busied himself a moment with a few more of my little treasures. I was startled to see how much he knew. In a short while he had another cup full of a scarlet dye, thick, a paint rather. He took a hazel twig he had brought in from the hedgerow to clean his teeth with, and he dipped

92

the frayed end in the paint. Then, in one clean flowing line, he drew on the toe of each shoe a fish.

We made many more pairs that night, and painted them in blue and in scarlet, and in a variety of other colours. I made the shoes, and dyed the leather, and it was Pryderi's task to paint on the designs. I only painted one pair. I did that when Pryderi had made up several colours, so that I could spread myself, and then, on the toe of each shoe, I painted Aphrodite rising from the sea. And when I had finished I looked at the Goddess, and somehow I could not think where I had got that face from, because it did look familiar and not only because I had drawn it.

In the end, when our oil lamp had burnt too low to see, we had to go to bed. I had to abandon the ways of civilised men, and so I could not go to bed in my day tunic, but in the fashion of the Brits I stripped and put on a clean pair of trousers. Pryderi had so made fun of the style and the cut, to say nothing of the workmanship, of the pairs I had bought in Lutetia that I had relegated them to this use, except for a few pairs I had given to Pryderi, and I was half annoyed, half amused to see that he did, after all, consider them good enough for wear during the day. But as I took off my shirt, Pryderi whistled and pointed to the great scar that runs under my arm on my right side.

'That's a bad one.'

'I got that a long time ago, on the Amber Road. It was with my own spear he did it, too, you know the way things get mixed up in a mêlée. But I killed him, before the night was out.'

'That was a head worth taking.'

'No, I left it. There was nobody to play the head game against.'

'Head game?'

'Yes. You know, you throw the head up between two villages, and then wrestle for it, all in on both sides.'

'The Germans do that?'

'Yes.'

'And a godless lot they must be, indeed. A head is too

sacred a thing for that. Once you take a head, the thing is to carry it home, and vow it to the Goose God. And then if it is not an important head, or if it were easy enough to take, you may hang it up outside your house, but if it were the head of a great enemy or the result of a desperate deed, then it is to the Gods you give it, either hanging it up before a shrine, or casting it into some sacred place. When we get to the Summer Country, I shall show you some of mine. I have to keep a bit quiet about it here. The Romans don't like it.'

I began to feel that I was travelling with a different kind of human being from myself. This man would be a suitable companion for Aristarchos. And yet, I felt I could sleep easy in his company.

CHAPTER SIX

Next morning it was a fine day. You may take it as given, that unless I tell you otherwise, every day I spent in that Island the sky was overcast, even if it did not rain. But that day it was fine. Pryderi went off and slipped a denarius to the man who allotted positions in the market place, and we settled down on quite a good pitch.

'You'll have to work hard to sell anything here,' Pryderi warned me. I answered:

'I've been selling all my life. There are plenty of men who can boast that in Alexandria they sold the Pharos to visiting Arab chiefs. I sold it there once to an Alexandrian.'

I stood up. Pryderi sat below me with a pile of half-finished shoes. I began to speak:

'My friends, my cousins, my kinsmen! Here am I, Mannanan the Galatian. I have come across the Empire, out of my own kindness and goodness of heart, simply and solely to benefit you. And that I will do. Listen all to me.'

And early as it was, there were already a number who did stop to listen to me. I had several advantages, like a foreign accent which will always disarm suspicion, and my great fur cloak, which looked rich enough to dispel any idea that I could be wanting to make money, since I had so much already, and my one black eye and one sapphire.

'You and I are brothers. We alone of all the world speak the language of the gods, who saw the foundation and the construction and the erection of the universe. And once, we were famous among all civilised nations for the quality, and the excellence, and the beauty, of our shoes, and our boots and our sandals.' I bowed my head, and swept my hand in a great circle, pointing to their feet.

'Those days, my brothers, are gone. Look at yourselves. Should we be proud of what we now wear? Should we want the Romans to come and see us like this? How can you hold up your heads, unless it be not to see your feet?

'I have not come, my brothers, to tell you Galatian stories, though I have some that would make your flesh creep. No, I have come to benefit you. I have come on a mission of pure charity.

'Look at these shoes, ladies and gentlemen, especially you ladies, just look. Start off by inspecting the craftsmanship. Look at the cutting! Look at the stitching! Look at the patterns! Where ever did you see styles like these before? And no wonder. Here, my companion is one of the greatest Master Shoemakers of the Age.' Pryderi stood up, bowed silently and sat down again. 'Personal and private shoemaker he was to his late Sacred Majesty Himself. All the shoes of the Emperor's Household he made, for all the ladies of the Court, as well as for the Emperor Himself. Why, his late Sacred Majesty was cremated wearing a pair of my friend's slippers, and there in Olympus He walks today, wearing them, and it was His express wish. What better warrant of quality could you have but this? Who would like to wear the shoes of heaven?

'Now for shoes like these, what would you say was a fair price? What do I say? Twenty-five silver denarii a pair? would that not be fair? But am I asking twenty-five denarii for a pair? I, who only came here to benefit my kinsmen? I who only came here to make you remember, and remember kindly, your brethren in Galatia?

'Shall I ask you for twenty denarii a pair, then? Shall I even ask for ten denarii a pair? No!! I have come to invite you to share in my own good fortune, because I walk in such shoes every day of my life. Shall I ask for five denarii a pair, that would hardly cover the cost of the leather and the dye, and leave nothing over to reward us for our labour? No!!! All I need here is enough money in my hand to pay for the night's lodgings for myself and my friend, and for a handful of musty hay for our horses, who are religious and given to fasting. All I ask is two denarii, just two little horses, for a pair of the most durable, the most comfortable, the most distinctive shoes you will ever wear.'

They sold like water in a city under siege. Long before noon we had sold almost all our stock, and I was already beginning to reckon up my profit — I estimated that I had made three pairs for less than one denarius. All kinds of people had come to buy, first the market people them-selves, and then farmers and their wives, and our greatest sale had, as always, been among the local lads buying what they hoped would get their girls into the long grass with them. But then as I looked at my last pair, a different customer arrived. There was a sudden thinning out of the crowd in front of me, leaving a space, and as I looked it was covered with a swarm of sparrows, hopping about and quarrelling for the crumbs and the grains of oats they found in the horse-droppings. And as I looked down, there appeared among the birds the feet of a Lady. It was feet and shoes I was looking at that day, and by the shoes this was a great Lady, the litter trade if ever I saw it. They were fine and dainty feet, and that was real Spanish leather that covered them, and dyed it was in a dye that would stand up to all the weather of the world. Dressed she was like a woman of the country. Not like the women of Pontes, who wanted to show how sophisticated they were and walked Roman fashion in tunics with a pallium to throw over their shoulders if the weather required it, which it always does up there.

I saw beneath her skirt of wool, fine wool, all woven in a check of light blue and dark blue and grey, there were a dozen petticoats. Each one was of a different colour. I raised my eyes to her apron, of fine linen, white, and embroidered with the flowers of the flax. This linen I knew, it had come from Egypt. About her waist was her belt, and this if not the belt of a queen was the belt of a queen's daughter or of a queen to be, for it was of a dozen strands of chain, alternate links of Gold and silver, and at the front it was fastened by a buckle of silver, the size of both my palms, studded with garnets. I looked farther up, to the full bosom hidden, half hidden, by a blouse of silk, white silk, but embroidered in its turn with blue silk in a Pictish pattern of whorls and spirals. I looked up to her shawl, and this was of cotton, white again, and tasselled, and it was woven through and across with golden wire, and the wire ran out to stiffen the tassels. And under the shawl I saw hair of a light lively red, and it framed a face well known, well known indeed.

There she stood like a rich and splendid trireme, beating back from a voyage to the Seres, all laden with silk and Gold and pearls and diamonds. Rich enough she was to buy up all the ocean, strong enough to beat off all attack. She stood before me with her flags and banners flying, her birds sang about her like a cloud of sail full drawing. And she spoke, in a voice that I surely had heard singing:

'How much for shoes, Mannanan?'

At the sound of that voice, all my bones turned to water. Somewhere deep down inside me the merchant said, 'Go on, tell her the tale, how they are dyed by a secret recipe known only to the ancients of Galatia, and how they would be cheap at a hundred denarii, and how you will reduce them for her, special for her, to a mere twenty-five.' But I could not do it. I looked at that oval face, the straight nose and the firm lips, and I looked down to where it looked back at me from my own shoes, and all I could say was:

'For you, my Lady, there is no charge. They are a gift. Take them as an offering to your beauty from your brethren in Galatia.'

She stood still for a moment. Then she called over her shoulder:

'Pay him, Hueil.'

A man came forward from the crowd behind, and I saw that he was wearing trousers in the same blue and grey check as her skirt, and more, that he was one of a group, four or five. He came to me, and picked up the last pair of shoes, then shook his head and threw them back on the ground. Then he stooped to where I squatted cross-legged, and in one swift movement whipped the shoes off my feet, the shoes on which I had painted Aphrodite, and stuffed them into his bag. He tossed me, contemptuously, a coin, and followed his mistress into the crowd. I went livid, I felt it, and for a moment I almost threw the coin back after him, but the basic sanity that is the salvation of every merchant prevailed, and I bit it. It was Gold, all right, not lead. I looked at it more closely. This was not the head of any Emperor. Wafer thin, the coin was about the size of my thumbnail. On one side was a horse, with a human head. On the other was a name, in crude Greek lettering — the coiner, however well he could draw a horse on the face of the die, certainly could not read. With difficulty I read it: Niros of the Treveri. Here, on a quarter of an ounce of Gold, this long-dead King of the Gauls still lived. But the coin, minted how many years, how many hundreds of years ago, was still new, and unclipped, and unworn. The outlines and the letters were as crisp as on the day when they were stamped out. This gold piece had never been carried in a purse to jostle its fellows and wear itself into dust. It was almost as if it had been carefully put aside against a day — against today.

The sight of the gold, Hueil's action, paralysed me for as long as a man might take to count to twenty. Then I sprang up, seizing Pryderi by the arm. All through my conversation with the Lady he had sat there, his back to us, huddled up, as if trying not to be noticed.

'Come on!' I cried to him. 'Follow the Lady! Find her!'

He looked up at me.

'Mad you are, Mannanan, I always said you were mad. There's no following her, not for a sane man.'

'Why? Do you know her? Who is she?'

'Know her? Of course I do, and so does every Briton who sees her go by. My own first cousin she is, daughter of my mother's sister, and named after my mother. Rhiannon of the Brigantes, she is, and a great Princess, and a wealthy one, because it is the Brigantes that have made their peace with Rome, and they get all kind of favours. But I would not have you talk with her, for that very reason.'

'Making your peace with the Emperor seems to be profitable,' I observed, holding out the gold coin.

'Ach-y-fi!' he said, which is the Brits' expression of disgust. 'And would I be touching that, knowing where it has come from?'

I thought this was a trifle extreme a way of showing that he was not on good terms with his cousin. I said as firmly as I could:

'Well, whoever she is, I must find her.'

I stood and I was about to make off into the crowd, where I could still see Hueil pushing along, when there was an interruption. Pryderi was gathering up the knives and needles and last and the rest of the shoemaker's tools, when two fat and scarlet men came puffing up to us like a pair of roosters in the spring.

'Look here,' said the redder and fatter of the two. 'And what do you think you've been doing?'

'And who do you think you are, when you have stood still long enough for your manners to catch up with you, and running hard they must be because they are so far behind.' Pryderi could be insolent when he chose, and I decided that as it was his language the men were speaking, I would leave him to carry on the conversation, which promised to become a little acrimonious.

'This is a formal complaint. We are the co-equal Chairmen of the Shoemakers' Guild of Pontes. We have been told, and informed, and warned, that you have been making shoes within the boundaries of the unincorporated Municipality of Pontes, contrary to the Charter agreed between the Guilds of the Town, and amended by, in particular, the by-law of the Fourth Year of Domitian, Chap Six, Clause Four, Para Two.'

'We were not making shoes. It was slippers we were making.'

'It is the same thing.'

'It is not at all the same thing.' By the light in Pryderi's eyes, it was clear that there was nothing he would like more than an argument at the end of his long silent day sitting at my feet in the market, his mouth full of waxed thread and needles, and if necessary, I could see, he would keep an argument of the type of 'You did' — 'I didn't' going for hours. The two men could see it too. The spokesman avoided the trap. He merely said:

'The terms "shoes" is general, and subsumes under it all slippers, boots and other footwear.'

'It does not,' Pryderi snapped back. 'Slippers are most clearly defined and distinguished and differentiated from shoes by a Law of Lud Son of Heli that was King of Londinium in the years before the Conquest. And it is known to every thinking man that it is precisely these laws treating of the definition of terms that are by the laws of the Empire and by the grace of the Caesars deemed to be the basis and the foundation and the substratum of all local municipalities and corporations, especially of unincorporated federations of Guilds.'

'Careful, you. It is our town you are in, unincorporated or not, and you will do what we say.'

'Force is it now? You can always tell if a man has a bad case that he would not argue in a court of law, when he begins to talk in terms of numbers and of possessions.'

'Another word, and you will be in front of the Magistrate, and there is little chance you will have in front of him, being as he is my brother-in-law, and treasurer of the Potters' Guild as well. Hand it over, we want every penny you have made by cheating this afternoon.'

'And there is not a single denarius we have made by cheating. That is defamatory, and it is before the Magistrate we will be arguing that, I tell you. I rely on the help of my friend here, who is familiar with the law and the Rescripts of the Empire covering this very point, and has the more important of them by heart, seeing he is a Citizen — of Rome, I mean, not of any little hamlet like Londinium or Pontes.'

There was a short pause. There is an advantage in having the kind of influence being a Citizen gives you out in the more distant provinces of the Empire, where Citizens born are rare outside the Army. The second of the co-equal Chairmen, seeing his chance, muttered something about 'never sue a Citizen, they've always got some pull somewhere,' which is true enough. The two officials of the Guild muttered more furiously after that, but so quietly they could only be heard by each other, and when Pryderi tried to put his head in between theirs they cursed him so roundly that even he stood back. At last the first Chairman said:

'All right, then. Keep what you've got, but clear out of town now. I mean now, straight away, this instant.'

Pryderi began to look fierce, but just in time the second co-equal Chairman said himself:

'No, not this afternoon, but tomorrow morning. We want to send a man ahead to warn all the other Shoemakers' Guilds ahead as far as Glevum.'

We didn't object to that. I was tired of making shoes. But the interlude had done the damage. The Lady had vanished, and try as I would, walking about the town, I could not find her again. I was able to do a little shopping, against the next town, investing the proceeds of the morning's work, the silver, that is. Not the Gold: I kept that.

It was dusk when I got back to the inn. Pryderi was in the main room, drinking cider with a rather motley set of companions. I joined them.

'I think there's a story here you would like to hear,' was Pryderi's greeting. 'It's about Gold. You buy old Blino a mug of cider, and you shall hear it.'

I obeyed. It was a very old man who sat there, very old indeed. As soon as he was satisfied that I really was going to buy him cider, he drew me into the darkest corner of the taproom.

'Not everybody I would show this to, you understand,' he whispered, suffocating me with the foul wind from his decaying teeth. 'But since you are a friend of him, then I will.'

He fumbled in his pouch and brought out a twist of black and yellow cloth. He untwisted it, and showed a ring, a Golden ring. It was made of Gold wire, fine as a hair, twined into a sixteen-fold strand like rope, big enough to go on his now shrunken little finger.

'That's Irish Gold,' he told me.

'How do you know?'

'Why, that's where I got it.'

'From Ireland?'

'No! nobody alive goes to Ireland. I got it out of a grave. Dug it out with an iron spade, I did, so I was safe enough. They won't never come back from Ireland to find me that way.'

'Who won't?'

'The dead, of course. That's where the dead go, to Ireland. I'm keeping this, like they did, to pay my passage, where every labouring man is paid in Gold, where there is neither hunger nor thirst nor pain, nor cold nor the bitter sadness of defeat, where age rusts not away the spring of youth, where men and women are for ever young, far in the Golden Island of the Blessed.'

His voice died away. I wondered how the rest of the poem had gone. He was past asking now. Cider and age had done their sleepy work. I raised my eyes from the Gold in his hand, and I looked over his shoulder into the face of a man with a squint. He made the Sign of the Four, as the Druids do, on face and chest, and was gone in the flickering light. I put the ring back in the pouch, and the pouch firmly into the old man's hand. If he had nothing now, why should he not have his youth again?

CHAPTER SEVEN

Next morning we took the road again. Pryderi looked suspiciously at the big packages I loaded on my horses and on his, big and awkward, but light as a feather. However, he said nothing, probably thinking that anything I told him would only spoil his peace of mind, if he had any left.

The road from Pontes to Calleva soon leaves the river valley, and goes up on to higher ground, a long belt of barren sandy soil, sour and good for nothing but growing timber for charcoal. Where the country was more open it was covered with gorse and heather. Sometimes the sun shone, and then I felt at home. It was good adder country if ever I saw it.

Calleva we reached at sunset. It is quite a pleasant town, in a provincial way. The only trouble with it is that there is no reason at all why it should exist. Usually a city has some reason for being where it is. Either there is a bridge, or a ford, or two roads cross, or there is a good site to build a fort. But there Calleva stands in the middle of an oak forest, on the edge of that adder country, with not so much as a little stream close by to give it an excuse for being.

Why was it there? Well, there had been the day, back in old Claudius's time, when the Legion had first pounded along into the wilderness, laying down the road as it went. Now it so happened that in that month the King of the Atrebates was spending the time eating up his rents in that particular dirty shabby little village, as he had spent the month before in another shabby little village, and as he would move on to a third when the country around Calleva was eaten bare. If you have no roads, and your wealth is in food and cloth, then it is much easier to go where your wealth is to consume it than to have it brought to you. So with the great decisiveness an Empire expects from its commanders, the legate of the legion decided that this must be the capital of the Atrebates, and that the country of the Atrebates must be governed from a great city here on this spot.

The kingdom, therefore, became the country, and the King became the hereditary chairman of a local senate, and his nobles became hereditary senators. Nothing else was changed at first, only the names. But the country had to pay a corn tax, and in wheat, too, which up to now they only grew to make a kind of beer out of.

Then there came the development. Under the pressure of the Procurator and his staff, the local notables marked out wide boundaries for the new capital they hadn't realised they wanted. They built walls, of earth first, with a stake fence on top, and they put a gate in each of the four walls, just like a legionary camp. Then they laid out two straight roads across the town, from gate to gate, just as in a camp, and where the Praetorium of a camp should be they built a basilica to serve as a senate chamber and as a court. It was a mud-and-wattle hall at first, but when I came to Calleva they had just rebuilt it in stone, and they were very proud of their marble barn.

Now, if the nobles were going to sit in the local senate they would have to live in their capital for some months of the year, and so each one built himself a house in the town. Of course, each one thought he would not settle there, but he would still live most of the time in his own farm-house in the country, which gave him his income. But the nobles reckoned without their ladies. You know how women are when they get together. They soon find out the pleasures of gossiping, and they object when their husbands begin to suggest that it is now time to return to the country. That is an end to the free and lonely life. So now the nobles live in the town all the year round, and their stewards bring them in their rents by the fine new road. Nowadays the nobles never see their farms at all, and their people who would once have followed them into battle even against the legions forgot what they looked like or even who they were. Only in a few wild regions, where the kings had refused to submit to Rome, or to live in towns, did the people still follow their ancient lords. But kingdoms were one thing. Clans were another, and even if a man forgot who was his king, he would remember who were his ancestors, and accept his relations, even to seventeen generations. And that, I thought, was why Pryderi was so careful about choosing his inns, and why he was so calm about leaving our property unguarded.

Very few people, however, would come and live in a town like Calleva, because there was nothing for them to do there, except to satisfy the demands of the nobles and their families, and of the lawyers who would come when the courts were sitting. There were a few craftsmen, protected by the nobles' insistence that there should be no market in the county except in Calleva itself, where they could easily collect the market dues and share them out equally. It was in the market place that we got into trouble. But that was on the third day there.

On the evening of the first day, we only put up our horses and carried our packs into the room we had been given. Then we went into the public room of the Inn, in the hope of supper. There were a number of people there, including the two middleaged men with the boy that I could remember from Pontes. They were sitting together in a corner playing Fichel. The rest of the clientele were discussing a particularly juicy rape case that was coming up the next day at the court. They went into a lot of circumstantial detail none of which had anything to do with the question of guilt or innocence, till I decided that the only possible verdict was an acquittal on the grounds of public entertainment. At last the landlady, who had been looking more and more uncomfortable as the discussion developed, said:

'I *do* wish you'd stop talking about it. You're all going

106

on and on like so many querns, and it's a dreadful headache I've got with it.'

'Headache? I'll tell you what to do.' I must have been feeling a little drunk and very conceited, in my character of the wise and experienced traveller. 'You ought to take three walnuts and crush them together in a pestle, but you must begin by cracking them so carefully that the meat comes out unbroken in one piece. Now, you must use a pestle of oak and a mortar of elm to mash the meat of the nuts into a paste, and the paste you must then spread on a platter of wood and divide into five exactly equal parts with a sea-shell — an oyster shell will do. Now one of these parts you must offer to the Sun, and one to the Moon, and one to the Wind, because there you have the three greatest causes of headaches, namely walking too long in the Sun, sleeping where the Moon can shine on your face, and facing into the cold Wind. Of the remaining fifths, the fourth you must put on your head, and fasten it there with a bandage of linen, spun from flax sown at the waning, and not at the waxing, of the Moon. The last fifth you shall eat. And then you will find that the headache is gone.'

And this is in my experience an infallible cure, because by the time you have done all this most headaches will have worked themselves out, and the cares of making the spell will make you forget the sickness if any remains. Now that I had my audience, I thought I would impress them some more with my Galatian wisdom, especially the man in the corner with a squint, who merely sat there saying, 'That is all magic and nonsense and an invention of evil spirits.' I thought it would be worth my while silencing him, to show the difference between real medicine, which is founded on logic, and magic. I explained:

'This is a most efficacious remedy which had never been known to fail. And why is it so effective, I hear you ask? I will explain it to you, I who am a philosopher who am used to examining the causes of things and the reasons behind the motion of the world, and in making things clear to even the meanest intellects, as I see here tonight. You are all aware that the ague springs from the marshy places, and is given off as a mist and as an effluvium from the stagnant waters. Now, I am sure that you all know that the surest way to cure the ague is to chew the bark of the willow that grows in marshy places. For every disease carries in itself the sign of its own cure, and every cure carries the signs of the disease proper to it, as if it were written thereon.' I am afraid that I allowed my language to become pompous, because the Brits are most impressed with this. 'If you ask me, doctors spend too much time examining the diseases they know, and then seeking cures to fit them. They would be better advised to find the cures first, and then to seek out the diseases against which they are effective.'

I drank some more wheat beer.

'Now, for any disease of the outside of the head, for the skull, for complaints of the scalp or for falling out of the hair, the best cures are made from the flesh of the Indian nut, which perhaps you have seen.' I was quite sure that nobody there would have seen one, for at that time I myself had only rarely set eyes on it. 'This nut is the size of a man's head, and it has hair that grows on it. Beneath the hair, you will find on the skin of the nut three marks that signify two eyes and a mouth, so that the nut is in every way the sign and symbol of the head of a man.

'But this nut is only good for ailments of the outside of the head, for if you open it, you will find inside a hollow filled with a little sickly juice, though I am sure that there are heads in this very room' (and I looked straight at the man with the squint) 'which are like the Indian nut in all respects.

'But for pains of the inside of the head, you must always use a cure made from the walnut. And why is this? If you crack a walnut as I have told you, so that the flesh comes out in one piece, then, as I would show you if the nut were in season and there were any walnuts here to be had, you would see that the surface of the unbroken nut within the shell is an exact copy, and simulacrum, and model, of the brain of a man when you have carefully removed the skull.

Now, it is no wonder that you should not know that, because I doubt whether there is anyone here who has ever looked on the surface of the uninjured brain—'

And a man at a table in the corner murmured, not loud, but very clear:

'I have.'

I looked at him. I peered into the shadows where he sat, and I began to have my suspicions. I went over to him, and I raised a lamp and I looked close at him, in his shabby clothes, all spattered with the muck of the roads and the straw of the stables where he had been sleeping till the russet of the cloth hardly showed. He was a good deal taller than either me or Pryderi, but he was very slender, emaciated almost, as if he had been fasting a long time. He was clean shaven all over his face, and that in itself was strange in a land where all men wear moustaches. His hair was red. I knew him all right. I looked at his plate, grilled kidneys and boiled beans, and at his mug of cider, and I said:

'Come, come, Taliesin. Last time I met you, you would eat no meat and drink no strong drink' — in public, I meant, and he knew it — 'and I wonder to myself, how it is, since it is a paying trade, you have given up being a Druid.'

And at once everyone in the room, Pryderi and the land-lady and the middle-aged men and the youth and everyone else except the man with the squint said 'Sshh! Ssshhh!!'

The landlord, who had up to now left the running of the place to his wife, came over and pulled me down on to the bench between Taliesin and himself. He said to me:

'Fine times it must be you are having in Galatia, and a liberty far beyond what we enjoy. But here we must be careful. Do you not know that the Romans killed all the Druids they could find when they first came here? It is unlawful for any Druid to do his holy work of judgement and sacrifice and prayer, or even to be seen within the confines of the Empire, or to walk abroad in the sight of men in this unhappy part of the Island of the Mighty. And plenty there are who claim to be Britons born who yet would betray this sacred patronage to torture and to death for the sake of money and for the favour of the oil-soaked wolves that are now so powerful. Some of our young men do still go over the seas to learn the Holy Law from the Druids of Ireland, but I do not need to tell you that of these brave lads there are none that do return. So, if we do hear, and suspect, and surmise, that there is a Druid travelling about the roads, in whatsoever disguise he may present himself, then there is nothing we do say about it to anybody no, not even to the Holy Man himself. And we understand, and it is essential for you to understand, that it may be necessary for such a Holy One to defile himself in the sight of the ignorant so that he may live to carry out the will of the Great that are invisible.'

'Aye,' confirmed Taliesin. 'It is for the sake of the fulfilment of my most holy vows that I must undergo all kinds of pollution.' He stuffed his mouth again with kidney. The landlord filled the resulting gap in the conversation.

'A virtue it is, and rewarded in this life, and in the time of transmigration, to give charity to a Druid. Therefore, it is incumbent on us all to assist this Holy Man on his pilgrimage to the Summer Country.'

The landlord was so pointed about this that I hastened to order another pot of cider for Taliesin, and one for Pryderi who joined us, as well as wheat beer for myself. I ordered our three dinners — for Taliesin agreed that his first dish of kidneys, being interrupted, had been a false start — to be brought to us in the corner. The landlord took this for an index of my desire to attain virtue, because when I went to pay our bill some days later I found he had not only charged us all double, but had made me pay for Taliesin as well. When I protested, the rogue said it showed how virtuous he was himself, in allowing me to assume a burden of charity which would certainly assure me future bliss.

I looked again at Taliesin's dinner, his second. I remembered what we all hear, that the Druids of Britain, like those of Gaul, are Pythagoreans, believing in the transmigration of souls, and living on vegetables alone without the taste of meat. I therefore had great pleasure in telling him something it had been obvious he had not known at our previous meeting.

'I've found out something about the Pythagoreans,' I told him with relish. 'I got drunk with a lapsed one in Byblos the year before last, and he tells me that the Bean is not a sacred thing to them, but unclean, and therefore they never eat it, while you, as I remember, used to live on them. And those kidneys you are eating, besides being made of meat, good solid meat, are bean-shaped and therefore instead of reducing the sin, as you imagine, they are adding to it.'

'And whoever said I was a Pythagorean?' asked Taliesin innocently. 'Indeed the vile slander has been spread by the Romans, who know no more of either doctrine than does my grandmother's cat. But we have little in common with the Pythagoreans except one element in our doctrines, and that little I shall reveal to you as the night goes on, or at some other convenient time.'

'As the night goes on?' I asked him. 'And where do you think you are going to sleep tonight?'

'Why, with you two. And it is not possible that you should be worse company than the horses.'

I could do little about it. I had to let him sleep in our room. I wanted to make him lie on the floor, but Pryderi, full of a reverence that did him little credit, gave up his own pallet to the Druid.

'I don't know why I allow it,' I grumbled. 'The last time I saw you two together, you were both ready to eat me. Going to quarrel over the marrow bones, I shouldn't wonder.'

'Appetising he looks, doesn't he, standing there without any trousers?' said Taliesin dreamily. Pryderi agreed.

'The right thigh, the champion's portion. Promised it I was.'

'But even so,' went on the Druid, 'I was not expecting such a welcome, seeing I came out of my way to travel with you.'

111

'Travel with us? Certainly not! It's too dangerous. Citizen or not, I'll be in real trouble if the Government find out I've been concealing a Druid.'

'And who is there to tell them but yourself?' asked Pryderi, logically. 'You will be safer by far travelling with him than if you were in the midst of a legion, in the country.'

I changed the subject.

'In any case, I don't believe you were trying to travel with us. How would you have known we were on the road together?'

Pryderi, not Taliesin, answered me, too readily for my liking:

'Shoemakers' talk. Of course, you can't understand half what they say, their mouths being full of nails all the time, but still — it gets around.'

'True,' agreed Taliesin — you might as well try to shout down a waterfall as to get a word in edgeways into a conversation with the two of them together. 'If it is hearing you are about one Pryderi the Ingenious, and a young man from far away with only one eye who sells slippers to shoemakers' wives when they don't want slippers, then there is easy it is to come to a conclusion. By the way, when it was knowing you I was, there were two eyes you were having. Caw told me you'd lost one. What's that you've got there? Amethyst?'

'Yes. There's a little man in Corinth who does them for me. I'll give you his name if ever you need it. Do you like the carving?' I slipped it out and put it on the palm of his hand.

'Oh, indeed, and lovely it is, too. Hercules cleaning the Augean Stables, isn't it? Oh, the detail in that heap of manure . . . poetry in stone, I call it. An original design, mind you, seeing what it is for.'

'Perhaps. I have several others, but I like to suit my eyes to the occasion. I put this one in today in case we met Rhiannon again.'

That meant something to Taliesin, and nothing that he liked. He sat straight up in bed.

112

'Not Rhiannon of the Brigantes? Is she on this road?'

'He sold her some slippers,' said Pryderi: he seemed to think it funny. 'Hueil the son of Caw told me that she was going south to Dubris to spend the winter in Gaul. But there, you know what his Gesa is? He may never receive a gift, nor give one, nor speak the truth except in jest.'

'Why,' I asked, 'do you know this Hueil?'

'My second cousin on my father's side,' said Pryderi contriving by his tone to imply that I had asked a stupid question, carrying in itself its own answer. I wondered. Caw was a common enough name . . . But Taliesin was worried.

'Well, let's hope that he was jesting when he said it. Principal Chief Bard I have been to Casnar the Painted Pict King, and Bithig the Bitch. Trouble and tribulation and trial, shortage and scarcity and starvation I saw there, but ruddy Rhiannon is worse. I will say no more. It is not a subject I wish to pursue before I dream.'

Perhaps Taliesin dreamed. I did not. I lay awake for hours listening to the most tremendous snores. Kidneys were not his ideal supper.

In the morning Pryderi went down and brought us a breakfast of beer and oat bread. While he was about that I unpacked my bundles.

'Shield frames?' he asked. 'Where did you get those?'

'In the market at Pontes,' I replied. 'And finished shields they were selling, too, there, so plain it is that they will sell here. But what I did not understand was this, why men in a disarmed country, and women too I saw, should want to buy shields.'

'For decoration,' Pryderi told me. It didn't matter to me, of course, why people bought them as long as they would sell. 'It is hanging them up people are, inside their houses and outside them too. It is their family badges they are painting on them, to proclaim to all that pass their ancestry and their nobility, and the less noble they are, and the more obscure their ancestors, the more shields and the bigger and the gayer they will hang up, and the more they will

113

pay. So I understand the thinking there has been behind your purchase, but it is, indeed, the policy I am questioning. It would be more politic for us to travel with as little fuss as possible, and the fewer men that see us, and see us to know us, the better it will be.'

'Indeed, and that is nonsense,' I told him. 'There is nothing more suspicious than the traveller who has no reason for travelling. But who will notice or remember or think the worse of the travelling craftsman? No, the more things we make and sell, the fewer men will remember us.'

Pryderi grudgingly agreed to join in. I looked at the shield frames. They were great flat baskets, oval in shape, that would cover a man from shoulder to knee. How anyone would use such a thing in battle I could not think. I found out, later. But of course these shields were not meant for war, and so, instead of planks of lime and sheets of gilded bronze, they would just be covered with leather.

'Do we know anything about shield-making?' Pryderi asked me.

'We can try,' I told him.

'Well, the best thing we can do is to cover the frames with leather, dyed in a variety of colours. Then if we paint a sample pattern on one, we can paint the rest to order in the customers' own patterns.'

We set Taliesin to dyeing the leather, while Pryderi and I cut it out with our shoemakers' knives and stretched it on the frames and stitched it. By noon, all the frames were covered and the leather was drying. We ate a light midday meal of a sucking pig between us, and then I told the others that I would work on a sample. I took a blue shield, the same beautiful heavenly blue as the shoes, and I made up dyes and colours from the variety of substances I carried in my bag.

It was a beautiful picture, I must say. I chose as a subject the marriage of Thetis and Peleus. There they stood, their divine beauty scarcely veiled by their flimsy garments, but Thetis further hidden by the shimmering of her form as she changed from one shape to another. The muscles stood

114

out on Peleus's arms as, still at this late moment, he clung to the wrist of his unwilling bride, while Chiron prompted him over his shoulder. In the background were all the gods and goddesses, with their emblems, and with only one exception. And She, too, was present in Her own way, for the Apples of Discord fell among the throng. It was, though I say it myself, a masterpiece of art, and it is a great pity that it has not survived to be handed down to all posterity as a supreme example of what the mind of one man can conceive in colour and form and balance and symmetry. And for sheer workmanship, too — there was not the space the size of a finger nail over the whole surface of that man-high shield that was not covered with some part of the story or other: here you might see the arms of Peleus, the gift of Zeus, there Thetis' Golden urn, and in one place, the size of a man's hand, I had drawn the city of Troy, and Golden Achilles in his chariot. And yet, as I looked at it, it seemed there were things that were not quite right, though I could not imagine what, in Peleus's moustaches, in Thetis' heart-shaped face and the swell of her lovely breasts. I looked and I looked, but I could not think what it was that should disturb me so.

This painting took me the latter half of the day, and when I finished, it was nearly dark. But there, in the twilight, Pryderi took another shield, and a tiny disc of scarlet paint, and a chewed hazel twig. He dipped the end of the twig in the paint, and on the azure surface of the shield he drew one line. It was a long sinuous line, and he drew it all in one movement, never lifting the brush from the leather. There we saw, when he finished, a great Pictish bull, head down, tail up, pawing the ground, ready to charge. I expected him now to fill in this outline with lights and shades and patches of colour, and to make the background rich with trees and grass and rocks. But no, instead he took the same brush and the same colour, and in the bottom half of the shield he drew a second bull, but this one facing the opposite way. Hideously bare and stark the whole shield looked, when he laid down his brush, just the two bulls in outline. Ah, I thought, tomorrow we shall see I will have to fill in that picture for you, when all the other shield blanks are sold and we want to get one off our hands. You will be coming to me, Pryderi, and asking for lessons in how civilised men paint pictures.

So in the morning he and I went into the market place. Taliesin excused himself, on the plea of business elsewhere. We two found a comfortable place at the base of a pillar, and a couple of denarii to the market warden made sure that the lack of early booking would be overlooked. And I stood there, with my great picture shield covering my body from neck to ankle, as we see painted on old vases, and I began to talk.

'Comrades and brothers, listen to what I say.' Of course they always listen, it doesn't cost anything, but once they listen they may, may perhaps, buy.

'Proud am I of my ancestry. Proud am I of those who came before me. Proud am I that I can recite the names of my progenitors, to the fortieth generation. And so should you be proud, that can do as much. But do you show your pride in your houses? Do you hang on the walls the signs of your noble birth and the deeds of the great kings from whom you are sprung? I know you do. I know that it is only the cost, and the dearth of men who are skilled in handling the brush that holds you back from honouring each several one of your immortal ancestors. But now all your problems are solved. Here we are before you, shield- and sign-painters by appointment to His late Sacred Majesty. Out of pure piety, and love for our kinsmen, and desire to improve the palaces of our native land, we have come to offer to you shields painted and decorated in any pattern your ancestral piety requires, and that merely for less than the cost of the materials. And such a small sum we only charge because it is well known that no one values a free gift. But do not delay, because we wish to be equal benefactors to all the nations of the Isle of Britain, as much to the Silures and to the Coritani as to the Cantii and to the Atrebates. Come now while there

116

is still time, and while we have any shield blanks left to paint on.'

And they came — oh, Zeus, how they came. They pressed on us to buy. But to my chagrin, there was not a man who wanted to buy my shield of Peleus and Thetis, even though we swore that it showed Dylan the Son of the Waves, nor did anyone want anything in that style. In fact, they said bitterly that it was rubbish like that which was all one could buy nowadays, and that good honest old-fashioned art like Pryderi's bulls could not be bought for love or money. And indeed, when I thought of it, it *was* in pictures like his that the Brits embroidered their linen and painted the outsides of their houses, in bright lines on the whitewash. So I talked and sold and haggled, while Pryderi sat with bowed head and painted bulls and sea horses and chariots and the geese flying high.

So, with great profit, we came to the end of the morning, and Pryderi was painting the last shield blank with a wild boar, and I was even wondering whether it would not be good trading to wipe out my Thetis and let him spread his swine over it, if only it showed a profit, when I realised that the crowd that had thronged about me all the morning had fallen back, and that in front of me instead of people were a flock of pigeons, all cooing and coocoorooing and sweeping the ground with their amorous breasts. And even as I divined what it was, I heard a voice say:

'That's a pleasant daub. I would have preferred Eurydice, of course, but there's no choice.'

There was never a voice like Rhiannon's, singing or speaking. Smooth and clear it was, like cream pouring out of a jug, whatever language she used, whether Greek or Latin or the tongue of the Brits. Sweeter by far it was than the murmuring of the doves, that still swarmed about her feet like bees upon a lime branch. A voice it was to make your hair stand on end with love and lust and desire for beauty in the dark as well as in the light. I looked up to where she stood, Hueil and four other men behind her.

Oh, have you ever seen the Imperial pleasure galleys on

the Lake of Trasimene? Splendid they are in scented cedar-wood, with figureheads of ivory and rams of bronze. Each mast is a single fir tree from the groves about Olympus, and the yards from strange and secret woods, from the sources of the Nile. Of cloth of Gold are their single sails, the shrouds and stays of copper wire, the dead eyes are carved from ebony and the blocks from the wood of life. The handles of the oars are lapped in the hide of the gentle unicorn, and the rowers' benches cushioned with velvet stuffed with down. The tacks and sheets and braces they twist from the hair by virgins, vowed to the Great God Neptune in Colchis by the sea.

So I saw Rhiannon stand there in the market. The infrequent sun was shining on her Gold and copper hair. About her shoulders she had thrown, to hide her splendid bosom, and veil from the eye of covetous man her silk and cotton blouses, a cloak of strange and shining cloth, of the fine, close silk from Samos, the warp of white and shining thread, and all the wool of yellow. Thus in that fine and shimmering Gold and white, fastened by a morse as big as a man's two hands, of bronze inlaid with Gold and emeralds, Rhiannon bargained with me for my painting. So I began to talk, and I took my tune from some brown pedlers I once met, men from, I think, India. I told her:

'Aye, this is a masterpiece, Great Lady, a painting fit for the Gods. It is on work like this that I rely to keep my children from starving through all their long lives, without their doing any work themselves, because all they have to do is to say that it was their father that painted this shield, and in any civilised place a grateful Government will feed them at the common table and clothe them out of the public purse, out of sheer joy that a man could exist who could bring such beauty to birth.'

'That is as may be,' she interrupted, and at the sound of her words I would have given her anything. 'How much?'

But the inborn skill of a hundred generations of merchants was too strong in me at first. I answered, without thinking:

'How much? You ask how much, Great Princess, for the

118

work of all my life, for all my stored-up skill, for all the knowledge that went into compounding the colours and priming the ground? How much is the wisdom of all mankind worth? Think of the great emotional experience that went into it, that was necessary before I could conceive of such a scene' — and looking at it dispassionately, I had to admit that I had given to Peleus a look of sheer lust that I would have given a great deal to have achieved: I mean, at my age it would have taken something pretty ripe to have aroused a response like that. I went on:

'But let us be looking, Great Lady, at the hypotheses of the matter. Supposing that such a painting were for sale, where should we start the bidding? At two hundred denarii of silver? At—'

She looked at me coldly and said:

'Three.'

'Glory be to all the Gods. At last, Lady, for the first time in all my life, I have found someone who would truly admire and value great Art, who would start the bidding at a price higher than even I would deem proper, at a price which would almost cover the cost of the materials and the hire of the splendid studio where I did the work. Hear, all of you who stand round' — though it was painfully obvious that the only people within earshot were Rhiannon's bodyguard, their cloaks much streaked with birdlime, for everyone else had retired to a safe distance, though whether to be safe from the men or the pigeons I did not inquire — 'hear, all the men of Britain, this Great Queen values my work at three hundred denarii!'

'Not three hundred, you fool. Three denarii. New ones.'

'Oy-oy-oy!! Do not mock a poor artist, Great Lady, do not make game of a humble man who labours with his hands day and night to bring beauty into the world, and has nothing in his purse but what will bring him a crust of bread tonight, and a dip at the common fountain, and leave to lie in the corner of a stable seeking the filth of the horses for warmth! Look, Lady, look at these nymphs' — and I traced the outlines of their bottoms lovingly, taking care, however, not to touch the surface in case the paint was still wet — 'see the warmth of affection I put into them, the delicacy of the brush strokes, the vibrating movement of their draperies . . .' The draperies seemed to vibrate because while I was painting Thetis' attendants, Pryderi was telling dirty stories, and I laughed so much at the one about the Old Woman of the Bog and the Pedlar's Mule that I couldn't have drawn a straight line to save my life. 'How could you think of such a paltry sum in the same moment as seeing these little darlings? Let us say fifty. Great Lady, a mere fifty, to anybody else it would be a hundred, but special to you, Lady, special to you, I will charge only fifty.'

'I might pay twenty,' she said cuttingly, '*if* I were buying it in the dark, and there was no other picture in the market, and I were anxious to cover up a bad spot on the wall in a room never seen except by candlelight.'

'At twenty denarii you value it, my Lady? Then I will not ask you to pay twenty denarii for the great crowning glory of my life. I will not ask you ten, or even five. Lady, I grant it to you freely as a gift. I will take nothing for it. I say, I give it to you. Take it away quickly before I repent and take it back again. I am already in tears at the very thought of losing it.' And I pulled the hood of my cloak down over my face, but not so far that I could not see, and I wept bitter tears, most convincingly, loud and wet.

Rhiannon picked up the shield. She put her arm through the strappings. It looked, in spite of the painting, very martial — I still wondered why the Brits liked shields of that size and shape. She called over her shoulder:

'Hueil! Pay him!'

Hueil came over. He looked me straight in the eye a moment. Then he flung a coin down into the dust. I felt outraged at this insult to my dignity, but I picked it up, all the same. I mean, Gold is Gold, and it can all be spent. Hueil walked away, brushing feathers from his cloak and all the pigeons flew off after Rhiannon in a swarm. I tied the coin in a corner of my shirt, and I looked around for

Pryderi. He emerged from behind the pillar. I was about to start to discuss with him the disposition of the profits when a large and important-looking man came up to us.

'Are you the two who've been selling shields here?' he asked.

'And lovely shields they were too,' answered Pryderi, though I was pinching his arm as hard as I could, because this man had petty official written all over him. 'Now, if you want one like that, then just tell me your name, and your clan, and your nation, and the name of your father, and I will have one designed and painted and executed that will tell all the passers-by unmistakably and clearly and plainly how rich and great and powerful is your descent.'

'That is all I wanted to know,' the minor official replied. 'An obvious admission. I am the treasurer of the Guild of Shieldmakers and Armourers of the County of the Atrebates, and though it is disarmed we are, and have been for many years, and there is no making of weapons allowed, so that the main concern of our members is with the welfare of the poor and sick among us, yet still we have the monopoly of the making of shields in this Country, under the provisions of the municipal by-law "Whatsoever person" of the seventh year of the Emperor Hadrian. And this Country, which extends from the southern edge of the Oak Forest to the banks of the Thames, has for its centre and chief place this town of Calleva. And I have not seen any record that you have paid a contribution into our common fund, as is good and right and proper.'

Now the last thing that I was willing to do was to pay for what by now amounted to a burial club of well-to-do tradesmen to eat an extra dish at their annual feast if there was any way out of it, but for the moment even I could see no way out. But Pryderi caught on something.

'The making of shields.' He rolled the words around his tongue. 'There is a fine phrase for you. There is a fine legal phrase. It insinuates the activity of a trained man, who has passed through all the stages of his apprenticeship, and who can cut the wattles and plait them into a basket, who

121

can plane the seasoned lime planks, who can tan leather and dye it, who can beat out sheets of the red bronze and emboss it and enamel it. All this is comprehended in the phrase "the making of shields". No, there is no ambiguity there. "The making of shields". A splendid craft.' Pryderi looked sideways at the official, like a cat at a mouse it wants to make a move to escape. Then he struck, fast and accurate as a shark. 'But we have not been *making* shields. We have been supplying them, and we have been assembling them from materials made for us by other trained and skilled shieldmakers in other towns: and it has been for citizens and councillors and senators and noblemen of your town and of all the County of the Atrebates that we have been doing it, and I can recite to you all their names, and their attributes that I painted on the shields which we *assembled*. So it will be all these gentlemen as well as us you will be having to prosecute if this comes to anything, if it is that there was an offence which it is not saying that there was I am there was.'

The official spent a little time disentangling Pryderi's meaning from his syntax, which had grown a little wild, and that not by chance. Then he said:

'Deceived it was they were, all these respectable people. They could not know that you were not members of our Guild nor of any Guild affiliated thereto nor licensed to act as if you were being members of our Guild, and they will so testify.'

There was a point there that Pryderi could have kept the pot a-boiling on for hours if he had felt so inclined, but he was tired, and hungry, and, especially, thirsty, as he confessed later, and so he returned to an earlier point of attack.

'It is showing, you will have to be, that your by-laws have been infringed by our making and supplying shields. Now in the first place, it is showing you will have to be that either of us both made and supplied shields, and that is difficult, because although you may be able to prove that one of us sold shields, you will not be able to show that he made or painted shields, or that the other, though it may be he painted shields, ever supplied or sold or even presented any shields. And it is then showing you will have to be that the painting of shields, which is all you will have any evidence for, is covered by that clause, and sentence, and phrase of your by-laws that concerns the making of shields, and it is tolerably certain I am that it is not, and that if you appeal to the by-laws of other towns on this point, then there is no parallel you will find. Now my friend here is of that opinion, and he has had experience of all manner of courts throughout the Empire, though it was always Not Guilty it was they were finding him, the Gods be glorified, and it is easy enough we will find it to hire lawyers, better than any that usually find it worth their while to practise in a hole like this. Now, is it willing you are, and only the hired treasurer and all, to commit the members of your guild to an expensive lawsuit when it is plain that it is not the by-laws of your own Guild you are knowing yourself?'

Well, the official, poor man, hummed and hawed to make a brave face of it, but of course in the end he agreed not to begin a prosecution, as long as we promised him not to do it again, and that we could easily do as we had used all the shield frames, though not all the leather and the dyes. And on top of that, Pryderi terrorised and browbeat him, by threatening to blacken his name to the Guild members, into giving us a silver denarius to pay for our dinner at the inn, to which we merrily returned, but not till I had myself made a few purchases in the market.

At the inn, we found Taliesin already waiting at a table for us. We called for our supper — the argument with the treasurer and my bargaining had taken more time than you might imagine. The inn was unusually luxurious for Britain. There was a real choice of dishes for the meal. I could have sheep's head, breast of lamb, shoulder of mutton, or a sheep's stomach stuffed with mutton offal minced, and then boiled. I began to realise that by leaving Londinium I had entered into the land of the Sheep. It is

123

mutton that the Brits mostly live on. Cattle they keep, but only for milk, and to boast about how rich they are. Their real life is based on sheep, which clothe them and feed them, although they will deign to eat pork when it seems appropriate. I remembered bitterly that at Pontes I had a choice of leg of lamb or stewed beef, and I had chosen the lamb as being more of a rarity in my life. Alas, alas, what we miss through ignorance.

However, I chose a dish of sheep's brains, and beer with it, and we chatted on this and that, till suddenly, apropos of nothing at all, Taliesin said:

'And if it is Ireland you are thinking of, then I am thinking it would not be a wise place for any man of this island or from farther east to be going to. For the Irish to come here is one thing. But for a human being to go there is another, because it is doubtful it is, I am telling you, whether the Irish are human in the sense in which we use the word.'

'What do you mean?' I asked him.

For answer, he turned towards the door, where looking timidly into the room were two people, an old blind man with a kind of lyre which is popular in those parts of the world, and an older woman. He beckoned them over.

'Now, Tannwen, my daughter,' he said with all the assurance of Priesthood and thirty years (or less — I was never quite sure), 'sing us your old song about the Western Ferrymen.'

The blind man struck a few chords on the lyre — it was soon obvious that he knew nothing about music, but merely beat a rhythm and was there simply out of charity on Tannwen's part — and the old woman sang, in a kind of monotonous repetitive melody:

The people down in Menevia that live by the edge of the waves,
The fish and the weed are their portion, for they are the Dead Gods' slaves.
They shut themselves in their houses on the night of the Samain Feast;

They sit with their eyes to the water, they sleep with
their backs to the east.

There comes a knock on the lintel, and the Fisherman
walks to the sand.
He sets his boat on the wave tops, and he paddles away
from the land.
The boat sits low in the water, the Fisherman hard
strains he,
For heavy it is as if packed with men, though no man
does he see.

When they come to the Isle of the Blessed, where the
Green runs down to the Grey
The boat grows light and the dead go ashore, before
the beginning of day.
But the Fisherman waits till he is paid, as he waited in
days of old;
For every Blessed Soul he bears leaves him a scrap of
Gold.

Oh, that is the Gold of Ireland, treasure that floats on
the waves,
Collars and bracelets and cloak-pins, that the dead bring
from their graves,
Though live men may go to Ireland, no living souls
come again.
From the Isle of the Dead and the Blessed, the island
beyond the rain.

Nonsense, I thought, just nonsense, as sensible as the
doggerel metre it was sung in. But I wouldn't be going to
Ireland, not till the land was safe and settled and merely
another good place for the family to have an agent. Then
I might, *might*, go across and choose the agent. That
could wait.

CHAPTER EIGHT

The next day we rode from Calleva to Spinae. There is, at least, some reason for Spinae's being where it is. It is the place where the road to Corinium and Glevum leaves the road to Sulis and the Lead Hills, on the high ground above the crossing of the Kennet. But there is no real town there, although it would have made a much better place for one than Calleva. There are two inns, and a few small houses, and, where the roads part there is a kind of permanent market, where the peasants sit and sell off odds and ends of country produce to people who pass by. There is quite a good clientele, as a number of the travellers to Sulis are wealthy.

We clattered down into the village, Taliesin on his rather horrible horse, which kicked and bit everything and everybody in sight, and all of us loaded with the light bulky packages I had had so much trouble in picking up in Calleva, but which were, Pryderi noted with relief, the wrong shape for shield frames. We had an argument about which inn to stay at, and my two companions insisted for reasons of their own on our stopping at the dirtier and smaller of the two, even though I was paying. We unloaded the horses into a hut where we could all sleep on straw pallets on the floor. I stroked my parcels lovingly before I opened them.

'These ought to sell well at the Forks,' I said. 'All we need is a few hours' dry weather to sit out.'

'What are you going to sell this time?' Pryderi's voice betrayed a certain loss of patience and confidence.

'Saddles. We're going to make some saddles tonight.'

'Do we know anything about making saddles?'

'We can try.' I unwrapped a package. 'I've got some saddle frames here, best second-quality beech, warranted well seasoned, at least three weeks since they were cut. Never mind, this leather will cover it all. It's a good thing I brought so much of it — I wonder why Leo Rufus couldn't sell it. Now, if we can make up some of the blue dye, we can have a fair stock by the end of the evening.'

'But you can't sit on leather and beechwood,' Pryderi objected. 'What about the horsehair for stuffing?'

'Horsehair? No need for that. Why do you think I cut all those rushes when we crossed the Kennet? Now, we can all start by cutting out, and then stuff later.'

'No,' said Pryderi. 'Taliesin can do all the stuffing. I can cut and sew, but he can't handle iron.'

I hadn't noticed it before, but now I came to think about it, Taliesin always ate with a bronze knife and he always shaved with a sliver of flint, and otherwise he never did touch iron. But while he worked on the saddles by lamplight I asked:

'Are we likely to have any more trouble with the local guilds?'

'Am I going to have trouble, you mean. The answer is, no. Spinae isn't any kind of municipality, incorporated or unincorporated.'

'If it comes to that,' I went on, 'could we really have argued our way through a court on those charges? Were the charters as specific as you said they were?'

'How should I know, boy?' Pryderi laughed all over his fat face. 'I can't read.'

Luckily there was no one in the inn that night who could read or tell a story. I should have slept peacefully, but instead I dreamed. I had not dreamed in Calleva, and that is why I know that nothing will ever happen there, but in Londinium I had dreamed of fire, and here on the road to Sulis I dreamed of battle. I remember a little. All through a day, I dreamed, we had stood against an army that came at us from the East, and towards evening they had fallen

127

back, exhausted, and left us holding the field. And yet at that moment, a new army came at us from the West, along the road, and though they were as many as we were, yet we laughed, because they were too late. And I woke from that jumble of weary men and dead horses to find the dawn breaking bright and clear on a fine day for sitting by the roadside and selling whatever we wanted.

Pryderi and I sat there at the Forks, and the first four saddles we had made, and that Pryderi had painted, went very quickly and easily. But the last saddle stuck, and nothing I could say would persuade anyone to buy it. Of course, it was the old story you find all over Britain. Nobody will try anything new. This saddle was entirely my own work. I had painted it in the latest civilised style as I had the shield, with splendid details and gorgeous colours of the battle between the Lapiths and the Centaurs. This was much superior to the simple line patterns Pryderi used, and I'm quite sure that it wasn't the art that people didn't like. No, I know what it was. I had fitted the saddle out with an innovation just coming in then from Scythia. I had put two straps hanging down from the saddle, one on each side, and a loop on the end of each to put your big toe in. It was supposed to hold you on the saddle and let you use your hands more and give your knees and thighs a rest. Myself, I think it is a mistake in technology. I have tried it myself, and I didn't like it at all. It took twice as much effort to stay on, and you couldn't get off in a hurry if the horse fell or anything. Besides, there was all the trouble of riding barefoot.

Anyway, whatever the reason, nobody wanted to buy it. I began to think that I would never get rid of the thing, and that perhaps we would have to carry it on, or even use it ourselves. Besides, it was getting late, and I began to see us spending another night in Spinae. Then I noticed a scattering of birds among the sheep droppings. Even Calleva was a decently clean and cultured town, and they kept the streets quite tidy in a civilised way with pigs, who foraged everywhere and got rid of all the garbage people threw out of doors, just as they do in Londinium

128

and Rome. But in Spinae, and in all the other little hamlets we came to after this, it was sheep they used, and the horrid things would come up and take the bread out of their mouths if people weren't careful. I began to see why the Brits ate so much mutton — it was a way of getting their own back. But when there was a chattering of starlings among the droppings, I didn't have to look up, nor listen for the chink of money bags. I began, automatically:

'Great Lady, Great Lady, look here at this saddle. A masterpiece it is, a marvel of the saddler's art, brand new and incorporating all the latest improvements and innovations brought straight from Rome. This is the way to be in the fashion, Great Lady, to be the envy of all your peers. Buy a Scythian saddle, made for the men who ride the great plains of grass not only all day but all the year. On their horses they eat, and they sleep and do all that they wish to do, and that without fatigue, and it is all due to these straps which they use to stay on their steeds while their hands do other things . . .'

'Let's see a two-seat saddle, then,' said Hueil with a snigger. 'For otherwise one generation of Scyths will have to last the life of all the world.'

I ignored him.

'Now, Lady, just look at this decoration, at this painting,' and I looked at it myself and the more I looked at it the more I realised that the side of the saddle I had facing me showed the rape of a mare-centaur by a one-eyed lapith, and the centaur's anguished face, turned back over her shoulder as she tried to unseat the unwelcome Greek who tried to mount her, was that of Rhiannon. I could not remember consciously trying to do this, and yet, how our actions betray our thoughts. I could not for the life of me remember what was on the other side, so great was my confusion now as on every occasion I had seen Rhiannon, but I hoped that it was nothing to give offence, as Hueil was bigger and nastier-looking than I was, and there were the four other men, and Pryderi and Taliesin had run away. I went on:

'Here we have the peak of the painter's art, born of a skill built up over years of practice and hard study. Twelve hours a day this painter worked, Great Lady, all the days of his life, for forty years and more, till he was able to produce such a scene as you can see here. And look at the leather, Lady, look at the leather, feel the quality, genuine Cordoban, double-tanned for durability, double-stitched for strength, double-stuffed for comfort, the ground just the right colour to match your shoes. Most Mighty Princess, how could you ever forgive yourself if ever you missed an opportunity like this, a chance to buy his gem, and at such a price, too. And what is the price? What am I asking for it? Do I ask—'

She cut me short.

'Why do you talk so much, Mannanan? You know that you could sell me anything, even yourself.'

I looked up at her, for the first time at the Forks. Have you seen the fishing-boats come in to sunny Naxos, the low sun glinting on the white and purple sails, loaded down with tunny, octopus and cuttlefish, oysters and mussels and sponges from the deep? As you see the skipper, leaning on the steering oar, smiling in joy for wealth and hope to live another day, so I saw Rhiannon, smiling as she bent above me, as a spear-fisher smiles looking down upon his prey. There was a necklace about her neck, of mussel pearls on golden wires, and her head piled with its copper hair was bound in a coral wreath. Her white and yellow silken cloak parted to show her linen blouse, embroidered with sea anemones and the weeds of the shore. She was a sight to drive any man mad. But I remembered, I was a Greek, I know logic and how to think and all the rules of Nature, and I drew myself up and I told her:

'I am a Citizen of Rome, and of another city older than Rome, and I am no man's slave. I am not bought or sold.' I shifted back the folds of my sealskin cloak, which I was wearing that day to look more the great and rich merchant which I told the passers-by I was, and which indeed I am, greater and richer than any in Britain, and I showed the jewelled hilt and the bronze scabbard of the sword Burn, so that Hueil could see it. 'I give myself where I please, and for no price that anyone can pay. I do not give myself to anyone who asks for me. But I will give you, Rhiannon of the Brigantes, this saddle.'

And that was the first time I spoke her name. Hearing it in my voice changed her temper. She turned and spoke sharply:

'Hueil!'

He bent and picked up the saddle, and threw a gold piece in the dust before me. I picked it up, and bit it, ostentatiously. Then I told them:

'Beware, Lady. A gift thrice refused brings bad luck.'

She had the last word, of course. She called:

'Tell me that again, in the Summer Country.'

And off she walked, her cloak billowing out in the wind like a sail, but her shoulders beneath it were shaking with — what? Rage? Shame? Laughter?

I went back to the inn, where I found Pryderi and Taliesin already saddling up the horses. I tossed the gold piece in the air before them.

'A fair rate of profit,' I told them.

'Count your money with care,' Taliesin advised me. I looked at the coins. The first was struck by that old King in Gaul. The second — on the reverse was a tangle, dots and squiggles, not intelligible to any human being, not even to a Brit: it was just the pattern they always put on coins. But on the obverse was a head, crude, but recognisable: it was an attempt to draw a real man, someone who once walked the earth, and the artist had seen him, had known him. And above his head, some letters. With difficulty I read them: *Tascio Ricon*.

'Tasciovanus, you would have called him,' said Taliesin. 'My ancestor, and Rhiannon's, and even Pryderi's. It was he, the great King, who defeated Caesar, and drove him back into the sea, never again to see Britain. That was in the days of glory.'

Like the first, it was new, crisp, unworn, unclipped, a

marvel in a coin twenty years old, let alone nearly two hundred. But that the third coin, that I had received that day, should be in such a state was even a greater marvel. For a stater it was, a gold stater of Alexander, the Greek who conquered the world, and had he lived there would have been no need to call myself so often a Citizen of Rome as well as of my own city. And Alexander, remember, was not a Greek of those outworn cities of Attica, but a Macedonian, as far from the line of Themistocles or Solon as we of the old towns of Asia. But this stater — I looked at it. I knew the die well. This had been struck in the Old City, in my home, in my very house, by my own ancestor. These coins showed common ground between Rhiannon and myself. They were not choosen foolishly. I would not spend them easily.

CHAPTER NINE

We rode out of Spinae immediately, keeping our faces hidden as we went past the other inn, the one with a fine modern bath, for there, it was clear, Rhiannon would be staying. Beyond the Forks, we soon entered the Forest, and I began to wonder where we would sleep, because it was getting towards dark. But an hour's ride west, Pryderi suddenly turned his horse off the road, and we followed him along a half-hidden path till we came to a hut, built, I suppose, long ago by some charcoal-burner. While I unsaddled the horses and hobbled them, and Taliesin fetched bundles of green bracken for our beds, Pryderi went into the hut. He came out again with, to my surprise, a hunting bow and a boar spear.

'I feel like a taste of decent meat,' he grunted and slipped into the woods. By the time I had lit a fire he was back, calling me, and I brought a packhorse and followed him to where he had killed a great stag. We got it back to the hut fairly easily, slung across the horse's back, and there we did all the real butchering, burying the offal and hanging up the joints and the hide. We ate well on venison steaks broiled on sticks over the fire, and mushrooms Taliesin collected, of several different kinds which I had not seen before, but which he swore were harmless, and so they were, except that it was them, I suppose, that made me sleep so sound in the open air till Pryderi woke me to stand the last watch by the fire against wolves. Or perhaps it was the cider. Up till now I had drunk beer among the Brits, but my two companions had brought with them no beer but only a jar of cider, and then I began to realise what real ecstasy was. I will not hear a word said against beer, if that is what all around you are drinking. But if you have the choice, then cider is a drink for kings. I tell you this, once the Germans begin to taste cider, they will soon forsake beer utterly and plant apple orchards where once they grew barley.

But it was cider and venison again for breakfast, and then we travelled on to a village a little way from Cunetio. We stopped eventually outside an inn, and this at last was a real Brits' stopping place. The other inns where we had slept had all been possible, just possible stopping places for civilised men who weren't too particular, but this was no place for anyone who was not native born. We had stopped in the middle of the day for a bite of cold roast venison and an oatcake we bought from a girl at a farmhouse by the way. All alone she was, and baking like a mad thing, for every other soul was in the fields at the last of the wheat harvest.

I remarked that I had already tasted enough of that stag to see me through a lifetime. Pryderi laughed.

'And it's more of him you'll be having for your supper, but it's depending I am on him to pay for our beds too.'

Sure enough, he was able to persuade the innkeeper that it would be just to take the carcase of the deer, and the hide and horns, to pay our bill.

Now, this was the first British house I had stayed in, that is to say, the first built in the British way. For all the nations of the earth build their houses with straight walls, and it is only the houses of their gods and their graves that they make round. But your Brit likes to build himself a round house, and simple it is to do. First of all you mark out a circle on the ground, and around this circle you dig holes two or three paces apart. In each hole you set an upright post, twice the height of a man. Then you join the timbers together with light rafters, and this you can thatch, leaving a hole in the middle of the roof for the smoke of the fire. Perhaps the house is not big enough for you. All right, then you draw another circle outside the first, and set there another ring of uprights, and thatch the roof between the inner and outer rings, and if you feel so inclined there is always room for another circle, because you have all the island to cover if you have a mind to. The walls you then fill in with basketwork well caulked with mud, or even with a few courses of stone. If for any reason you are not satisfied with one open hall to live in, then you can join uprights together to make booths, and so this inn consisted of a great round house, with an open hall at the door, and a ring of booths at the farther circumference.

We exchanged our deer, then, for the use of a booth for a night, and glad we were to get into it, because the luck that had brought us dry, if not fine weather now deserted us. The cloud got lower as the morning wore on. The girl who sold us the oatcake was looking anxiously at the first few drops showing on the flagstone at her door, and awaiting the rush home from the fields. By the time we reached the inn, three hours after noon, the rain was falling steadily in a monotonous drizzle, not heavily, but thoroughly. I was tolerably dry myself, because I put on my sealskin cloak, and that shed the water like — well, have you ever seen a seal? The other two had their soft leather jerkins, but all the same we were all glad to get indoors.

The innkeeper seemed almost to expect us, or perhaps it was my fancy, and he gave Taliesin the same exaggerated respect as had the man in Calleva. Of course, beside the inn he had a farm, and his stacks of oat and wheat stood behind the house. He was ready enough to talk about the weather and the prospects of the harvest while his wife and servants bustled about, as if they were expecting a busy evening. Other travellers came in. There were the two middle-aged men and the youth I had seen in Pontes, and then a little man with a squint leaned over me, too close for my liking, and said:

'There is one flock, and one shepherd: one vineyard and one true husbandman.'

What that meant I had no idea, and so I only said back: 'And a pretty small farm that must be, brother.'

It seemed to satisfy him; at least, he didn't speak to me again that evening.

The dinner was good, nine-year-old mutton since the venison hadn't hung long enough for the landlord's taste, stewed, with onions and leeks and turnips and oat bread, and oat dumplings in the stew. We ate as only men can who have ridden all day in the summer rain. It was a warm evening, in spite of the rain, and as the inn filled with people, men and women, all in their dripping cloaks and sweating under them, the room turned into a good imitation of a steam bath, except for the smell, which was of bodies and not predominantly of scented oil.

All the people present were Brits. Any Greek or Roman on the road would have taken one look and preferred the open road, which would in any case have taken him to a civilised tavern at Cunetio, where they would use oil to cook with. There were all sorts in the inn, and all free men and women, no slaves. If you go outside the Empire, or to these hardly settled places, whether among Brits or Germans, you find that there are very few slaves. A rich man may have a few women captured in battle or kidnapped by pirates, who are used for grinding corn and other heavy work in the house, but apart from that a free man, or woman for that, does everything for himself. That, of course, is just why these areas are so backward. A civilised man, if he is to live a full life, has to be backed by power not only to grind corn, but to cut and carry fuel and mine metals and smelt them. But the Brits, if they will not use slaves outside the household, are doomed to barbarism for ever.

The room, as I said, became very full, but you can drown any discomfort in cider. We were busy denying any virtue to lifesavers, and singing a song popular in the neighbourhood called 'Bran, the Bastard King of Mona' — I noticed that Pryderi was not showing a single trace of black-and-yellow — when in at the leather door, out of the rain, there came six people, dripping wet, sodden, half-drowned, squeezing, water out of their hair, out of their shoes, out of their cloaks, weeping with relief to be inside, the tears running out of their wet eyes over their red chapped cheeks. Rhiannon it was standing there, like a wrecked barge, swamped, mast and spar sagging forward in a tangle of rope and splinters, and floating she was in her own private lake of fresh water that she had brought in with her.

Her five followers, Hueil first, wetter even than she was, pressed behind her to help her off with her leather cloak and the leather overskirt in which she had ridden. She flung the garments behind her without looking, and scattered the flock of ducks which had waddled in after the Lady.

The landlord went towards her, his eyes on her belt of hexagonal plates of gilded bronze, but whether he wanted to assure her most humbly that this was no place for such a great Princess as she, or whether he wanted to tell the five of them to go and hang themselves on lines till they had drained enough to mix with decent folk, I never knew. Rhiannon pushed him aside, and looked around the room.

Her eyes fell on my face. She walked towards me as I sat in that booth behind the table. She walked like — have you ever seen a bireme of the Imperial Navy bear down on you all cleared for action? Cruel glitters the ram of iron as it cuts the swell, cruel beat the oars in time, cruel fly the flags. The sail is furled, that it shall neither take fire nor press the rowers. The gilding and the carving is stripped away, and black she is painted and not a man who is to be seen but has hidden his face behind a mask of brass. So Rhiannon came to me, her face a mask of anger, terrifying and awful. I looked about me in terror. On my right sat Pryderi, still as a corpse, his stern face held steady by an effort of his will. But on my left — Taliesin was no longer there.

Before I could ask Pryderi, or even ask myself, where the Druid had gone, or where we could go, Rhiannon stood in front of us. I could have sworn that her red hair was

137

itself on fire, sending as it was great clouds of steam to the roof. She bent down and wrenched off her shoes. She flung them down on the table in front of me with a bang. Shoes? You have never seen shoes in such a state. The blue colour had run and the Gold leaf had floated off. The threads that stitched the uppers to the soles had broken in some places, and in other places had torn through the leather to run three or four awl holes into one. The soles themselves were worn into holes the size of oyster shells.

'Shoes,' she said, spat, rather. She beckoned to Hueil. 'Shield!'

He held it up. It had been a good shield, once. The limewood panel had warped. The leather cover had split in some places and was peeling away from the curling wood, and in others it had blown up into great hollow blisters. And where, oh where, were my Thetis and my Peleus, my nymphs and gods and goddesses? All had run into one horrid brown-purple splodge, which even as I watched dripped dye onto the clean floor straw. It is a dreadful thing to see the work of a man's hands spoiled by a woman's stupidity in riding in the rain.

Then 'Saddle!' she said.

Hueil threw it at Pryderi, who was too terrified, or too dignified, to duck, and it bounced off his face and fell back on to the table in front of me. It was the worst of all. I could now remember what I had painted on the side which faced me. I had shown the lapith leading the she-centaur away captive, a rope around her neck. But it now existed only in my mind, and in Rhiannon's. The wet, and the stress between horse and rider, had twisted the frame. And then with the heat between saddle and horse's back, or between saddle and that lovely bottom, even through nine layers of skirts, the ripe seed heads of the rushes had germinated, and sprouted, and thrust through to cover all the surface of the leather with a dense green fuzz.

Everybody in the room crowded round to see. I could hardly hear my own teeth chattering, as they did in face of Rhiannon's fury, for the 'Oohs' and 'Aahs' of horror and disgust. Pryderi's nose was bleeding, and though his dignity forbade him to move his hands he kept on trying to wipe his face on my shoulder, so I told him what I thought of that and it hardly helped to calm me. Rhiannon, having thus gained an advantage, proceeded to use it, and addressed the crowd in that lovely creamy voice of hers, and indeed it was the first time I had heard it properly without the twittering of birds, and now there was no other noise at all, because all the people were silent clustered in a semi-circle behind her and glaring with her at us.

'Men of Britain!' she said, and that miserable raggle-taggle of batteners on travellers and sellers of watered beer and tough mutton and of shelter under leaky thatch all straightened up as if the words meant something.

'Men of the Isle of the Mighty! How long, I ask you, how long? How long will we allow foreigners to cheat us? How long will we be carried away by a curious accent, by charming infelicities of phrase? How long will we be put off our never-ending search for quality and true value and honest dealing by strange tales of the impossible and by the enchantments of Syrians and Greek pedlars? Are we always to be dupes? I call on you all to be witness.

'These men have sold me at different times shoes, and a shield, and a saddle. The price was high, but the price they asked was higher. What profit they have twisted out of our brothers and sisters down the road I can only guess, but believe you me, their saddle-bags are heavy with Gold. Aye, I know what the law is now, "Let the buyer beware," but I call on you to witness that there is an older law than that, a law of the Gods and not of the Romans. Even a merchant must speak truth, and the meanest and poorest buyer must know what to believe. Remember the great motto of the Blessed Ones who are now gone from us, driven from us. "The truth against the world," is what they said. I call on you all at the last to stand for truth.'

This was a new approach to business morality. How on earth can you proceed in the way of trade except on the assumption that the man you are dealing with is a liar, and that he is stating a case that appears to give you the maximum benefit while in reality it is himself that it profits the most? To suggest that a trader should ever speak the truth betrays ignorance of the whole basis of a merchant's thought. In any case, it is obvious that the innkeeper, and indeed everybody else who tried to sell me anything in the whole Isle of Britain, would disagree violently with Rhiannon in practice whatever they might say aloud in her presence. But I was unable to break into the flow of her speech to put my point of view, because she never drew breath.

'A saddle, and a shield, and shoes, they sold me. Warranted to last till the day of the transmigration of the whole earth they were. The colours were warranted fast and the workmanship good, and now look how much their word is worth. See what has happened to this costly merchandise after one shower of rain! See what they think to foist on us here in this land where rain is our daily portion!

'My brethren!' Her voice rose, and even I felt a surge of indignation against all dishonest traders, so persuasive was her speech, in manner if not entirely in content. 'My brethren! What shall we do with these men who cheat us? What did we do by the old law?'

Some of the people shouted, 'Hang them,' and others shouted, 'Burn them living,' and these last included Pryderi who prudently supported the larger party till I reminded him that it was likely to be himself who would be the first sufferer. They would, I was sure, keep the best bit to the last. He urged me:

'Say who you are. Are you not a Citizen of Rome? Appeal to Caesar. Demand to be tried by a Roman magistrate. Such an appeal they will not resist, even in their anger. And once in front of a civilised court, as you call it, you are safe, for who would think of preferring the word of a pack of us miserable Brits.'

And I ought to have done it, I should have done it, but there was something held me back. I said:

'No. I have come into this country dressed as a Briton,

140

and as a true Briton I will endure what must be. I will depend on my own unequalled skill and power.'

'Then it is a Gesa you have taken on yourself,' replied Pryderi. 'A vow it is you have made on the presence of death that it is not on legerdemain nor on trickery nor on fine words that you will rely while you are in our country, but that what you have undertaken to do, that you will do yourself.'

It was, I agreed, one way of looking at it. After all, I do trace my ancestry back through sixty noble warlike generations. And as we spoke, Rhiannon went on:

'Thieves! Liars! Cheats! Men of the island of Britain, men of the Isle of the Mighty! Rise up, great nation in your wisdom. Judge these men for yourselves, judge them for me, judge them and execute judgement.'

For a moment I would have thrown myself on the floor at Rhiannon's feet, begging for mercy, but then I glimpsed Pryderi sitting there, arms folded, bleeding, and I caught my courage together and I stood up and I said:

'Let no man be judged unheard, men of the Isle of the Mighty, descendants of Brennus. Here I stand, a Son of Lear, and I demand to know two things. By what law am I judged, and what is the penalty?'

The landlord stepped forward as spokesman.

'As for the penalty, that is simple. If a man sell short measure or worthless goods, then he is the property of the buyer, for the buyer to sell or to keep, to let live or to die, as it pleases him — or her. In olden days it was thought most fitting for the buyer to give such a man to be burnt as a pleasing offering to the Gods. But as for the law, why, we will go by the law of the country as it always was, and as it always will be when the Romans are gone. It is the nobles and the princes and the kings who administer it, and it is the most noble person in the room who shall pronounce judgement. And there is no denying who is the most noble person here, for who is more noble than a princess of the Brigantes, and even here among the Belgi we acknowledge that. As indeed we would acknowledge any prince or king,

141

aye, even a king of Demetae. There is no judge greater than a king of the old line, except it be a Druid.'

'Yes,' said a clear tenor voice from the doorway. 'Except a Druid.'

Taliesin stood in the entrance. But not the Taliesin who had come with us, the ragged man in dirty brown, with muddy face and matted hair. Now he was wrapped in a robe of fine white linen that hid him from shoulder to foot, and I will swear that he had grown a head taller. His hair, red as Rhiannon's, was clean and combed and sleeked down with water. Upon his head he wore a wreath of oak leaves. The leaves were fresh, and the broken ends of the twigs were oozing sap, but the acorns, now in early August, were already hard and dry and brown-shelled and ripe. In his left hand, thrust from beneath his linen shirt, he held an apple, and in his right hand he held a sickle of the rich Gold of Ireland. And on his breast, held by a Golden pin, were a pair of bright green leaves and between them on the stem two fresh white berries. Whenever did you see the berries of the mistletoe ripe and smooth and plump in August?

It was late in the evening of a summer's day. It was still light enough to ride, but in the inn the servants had long lit the torches. The rain had stopped, but we could not see the setting sun for the low grey cloud. The air was misty. The whole land smelt of the warm steam. The birds were silent. Outside even the rooks and the pigeons of the woods had ceased to call.

In all that stillness, Taliesin the Druid walked through the filthy inn room. The floor was covered with straw littered with the bones and refuse of years of feasting. And I swear that I saw the straw move itself aside that his feet might touch only the sacred earth. The oak tables were stained with the spilt drink and gravy and littered with the fragments of the evening's dinners, and I saw the table legs bend back as the wood shrank least Taliesin be defiled by the touch.

The old men in the room knelt before Taliesin, and the

142

young men held their hands before their eyes that they might not be blinded by the radiance of his brow and the glory of his face, for they had not seen a Druid before in all their lives. He came to Rhiannon, and she went down on one knee before him, her skirts spread about her feet. She drew her shawl over her glorious hair, for respect, and the fringes of her shawl before her face, for modesty.

There stood Taliesin, walking as a Druid in a land where no Druid might walk abroad in freedom. He faced the rack and the cross and the fire, the lash and the salt mine and the beasts, and that for the sake — no, not for the sake of my life, nor of Pryderi's, nor for that of friendship in the abstract. He came for the sake of truth. Courage is a kind of holiness. I knelt before Taliesin.

He looked at Hueil. Hueil scurried around the room, and found the biggest chair in the place, one that stood in a corner, with arms and a high back. He lifted it on to a table, the highest in the room, and stood back. Taliesin still looked at him. Hueil looked puzzled, and then he began to burrow into one of Rhiannon's saddle-bags. Out of it he brought my Lady's cloak, that enormous garment of silk, shot yellow and white, shimmering Samite of Gold and silver. This cloak he spread over the chair, which thus became a glittering throne.

In an instant, without seeming to move, and certainly not making any jump or violent movement, Taliesin was seated on his throne, his arms crossed on his breast, the apple at one shoulder, the sickle at the other, so that he looked like some ancient Egyptian King, carved in the red rocks of the Nile. And then in the silence of that crowded room — for the alley that had opened to let him through had closed up again and it was plain that every Briton for twenty miles had come to hear him and see the Druid — Taliesin spoke:

'The truth,' he said. 'The truth against the world.'

Rhiannon rose and stepped forward. I too moved and stood beside her. I was her equal in this trial, as I had not been before. I never doubted an instant that I should

143

subject myself to Taliesin's judgement, nor did I remember that he was my companion on the road. I never hoped for an instant that he would bend his rule to favour me. I only saw a Druid, and I bowed before my Judge. Rhiannon spoke first, as the plaintiff.

'Master of Light,' she said. 'It is for truth I call, for truth and justice. From this man I have bought three things.' And I accepted this new state of affairs, that the case was brought against me alone and not against Pryderi. 'My Master, I bought of him a shield, and a saddle, and shoes. Not for a shower of rain did any of these last. I ask you for justice by our ancient laws. This man has said in my presence that he is not bought or sold. He says that he belongs to no one. Let him then, my Master, be given to me. Let him neither be bought nor sold, but confiscated and devoted to compensation.'

She stopped. Taliesin did not look at her. Neither did he look at me, but I knew it was my turn to speak. I said:

'My Master, I have sold this woman nothing. Thrice I offered her gifts, and thrice she refused my gifts. But the goods she took, and Gold she flung in my face. I have not spent it, the coins I have here still. I give them back.'

I took the three old pieces of Gold from the fold of my shirt where I had twisted them. I tossed them gently across the room, one by one, and all present saw them shine in the air, saw Rhiannon catch them. And she opened her hand, and we all saw there, not three pieces of Gold, but three cockleshells. Easy enough to do, you will say, if you know how: but who did it?

Taliesin looked down at us from his throne. He had called on truth, and the truth was come upon him. I knew the signs. The God had come upon him, the Muse, the Awen the Britons call it, though whether the Awen is to them a separate God, to be worshipped, or merely the abstract epiphany of divinity in its essence I never found out.

When the Awen comes on a Bard you cannot mistake it. The Bard does not go into a trance. He is conscious all the time of what he is saying, and indeed it seems to him that he sees suddenly of his own unaided intellect the reason and above all the truth behind all things, and he realises at once how he can express what he knows so that all can understand. So now we heard, as Taliesin's voice deepened in pitch and changed in tone, not the even measured speech of the impartial judge, but a strange chant, the song of truth.

'In all the world is like and unlike, like married to unlike, equal and opposite, completing and complementing. East there is and West, dawning there is and sunset. North is there, and South, heat is there and cold. Being is there and extinction, life and death, seeing and unseeing, seen and unseen. Those who are vowed to the truth must walk in the midst of lies, and the Sacred One of the Sun must call on the Gods Below.

'So Rhiannon and Mannanan, equal and equal, opposite and opposite, hear you me. To you Mannanan of the House of Lear, who may no longer call on the Unconquered Sun because so long ago you did the will of the Unconquered Sun, to you I give Rhiannon, Queen of Those Below, to keep to the ages of ages, to serve you and to serve, through life to death and beyond death.

'Rhiannon, Princess of the North, Lady of those that are gone, I give you Mannanan, Photinus the Greek, man of many names and many lives, last Lord of the Amber Road. He who is no man's slave shall be your slave for ever.'

He stood up, and out of his oak-leaf wreath there rose a wren, ticking loudly. Three times it flew around the room and then fluttered out into the open air. It was the only bird I ever saw that took no notice of Rhiannon. It flew away. I did not know it then, but it was at sunset on that very day that my son was born and Phryne died.

Ours was the first case of the evening, but to my surprise it was not the last, and indeed it was the only summary hearing, the only dispute that belonged to a court of first instance. There came up to stand before Taliesin a long series of pairs of men, each with a dispute to settle, one already judged by a village gathering, and appealed from

145

there to a nobleman or a prince, and now referred at the last to a Druid for final solution. It was clear, too, that Taliesin had been warned of each case long before and was ready with his judgement, with all its references to times of old and the decisions of kings long gone. And it was intriguing to hear how each pair of adversaries, especially where the case concerned land, made their arrangements to have the case heard in a Roman court, so that the decision could be ratified and made safe against any desire of the Government to overthrow it, and so presented that only one Roman verdict would be possible and that the same as Taliesin's. Indeed, I wondered, who rules this land?

Fifteen of these cases there were. Fifteen times the Druid fulfilled his function, which is nothing to do, I found with sacrifices and rites as Caesar imagined, but is a business of preserving the laws, which in a society where no man can write or read is a more difficult matter than you may imagine.

And then at the end, after the fifteenth case, and I can guess how it happened, since I have done the same myself, there was suddenly a red glow from the brazier in the centre of the inn, and the whole room was filled with a cloud of choking smoke. When it cleared, of course, there was no Druid but a dirty-faced man in ragged brown clothes was sitting at my side.

And then the feasting began. All the local people were trying to nerve themselves to go out and home in the dark, and that of course uses up a great deal of cider. And Rhiannon came and sat down opposite me, as if nothing had happened at all — her retainers found themselves somewhere else to sit and drink — and everything was quite ordinary, except that a crowd of Britons in a corner were singing a cauldron song, the first time I had heard such a thing:

Oh, the cauldron on the fire is a pot that some adore,
But the cauldron that we worship is the little one on
the floor.
Yes, the little one—

and they all thumped their drinking cups on the tables, bang-bang-bang-bang:

> Oh, the little one on the floor.

I leaned across and I said to Rhiannon who sat opposite me, as Taliesin had now moved to be next to her and opposite to Pryderi:

'Now, I am your master, and you must leave your journey to Sulis or wherever else it has struck your fancy to go, and come with me wherever *I* wish.'

'Indeed,' she answered, not angrily, but half laughing, and there is little I like less than being laughed at. 'It is you that must go wherever your mistress tells you, and follow *me* you must if it is your mistress I am.'

Taliesin, now recovered from his Awen and as stupid as the rest of us, opened his mouth to speak, but I felt Pryderi kick him under the table as he said:

'A cock there is to every hen, and a bull to every cow, and a dog to every cat. Fight they will and must till one has the dominion, and evenly matched this pair are for cleverness and wit and for mischief and for stubbornness, and it is patiently I am waiting to see which it is will take the other along.'

'And there is true it is what you are saying,' Taliesin agreed, now all innocence of face and voice. 'But interesting and informative and inspiring it would be to hear where she *is* going.'

The crowd in the corner were still singing:

> Pots of bronze and pots of iron on the charcoal flames
> are stood:
> But who would light a fire 'neath a cauldron made of
> wood?
> 'Neath a little one (*bang-bang-bang*) 'neath a little one
> made of wood?

Some kind of riddle, I thought. In the middle of this

147

nonsense I felt a little more intelligent approach to the problem would be helpful, so:

'And to where might you be going, Lady, if I may be so bold to ask?'

'Boldness is it now?' and her blue eyes flashed, and her cheeks glowed with pure enjoyment of a quarrel, because she was one of those people, and there are men as well as women, who enjoy nothing more in life than a dispute with an opponent fairly matched, and I am not saying that I am not one of them. 'And how far is it you are meaning your boldness to go? There are limits, and I hope you know them, to your impudence in the face of your mistress.'

'My boldness will go as far as I like with my own,' I replied, 'but your boldness itself goes too far. Wherever you may be going, or think you may be going, it is leaving it you will be and coming down with me into the Summer Country.'

'And where else is it thinking you are that I am going? I am bound to the Summer Country for the winter, and it is there I will go whether you come with me or not.'

And for some reason Taliesin leaned back on his stool with a look of relief on his face, and nearly overbalanced, and we very nearly deafened with the singing behind us and the banging of pots and fists and even of feet on the tables.

> Let the Romans sip Falernian, and the Germans swill
>   their beer,
> While we Brits taste life immortal from the cauldron in
>   the Mere.
> From the little one (*bang-bang-bang*) from the little one
>   in the Mere.

'*Yes*,' she hammered bang-bang-bang back at me. 'I will go there if I please.'

If she pleased, indeed. I glared at her. The party was nearly over, there was no one left in the inn room except the few who would be staying for the night. I felt I had

148

drunk too much, and I decided, while the others arranged who was going to sleep in which booth, I would go out and dispose of some of the cider. It was so hot inside that I pulled my sealskin cloak around me, and in doing that of course my sword fell out of the pack, and I was slightly drunk so that it seemed less trouble to pick it up and take it out with me. I felt better out in the open air, and I tried to recover myself and understand precisely what was happening, and though it had all seemed quite clear and, indeed, welcome in the fury of the opening of the trial, when the mob were gathered round me and behind Rhiannon, with axes and cudgels and all kinds of intricate agricultural implements like gelding shears and branding irons, I failed to see now how the situation had changed in any way, for though I had found the Lady — my thoughts rambled on and on. I breathed deeply and groped my way round the inn and into the rickyard.

Everything had now grown quiet. I wondered if the other three had noticed that I had gone. I leaned against the stack of oats, and considered improving the taste of their bread for them. When I had finished, I stood still again. I listened. I could hear someone moving. Now, that was strange. There were men moving about, a lot of them. And they were taking care to be quiet. That was the strange thing. If they had been about normal business, as might just possibly happen around a farm or an inn, then they would be moderately careful to be quiet, but only so far as to escape things thrown at them by sleepers awoken out of turn. But these men were trying to be quiet as the grave, hoping to wake no one. I clutched the sword hilt under my cloak.

Well, there's a thing, I thought. If I shout I don't know what will happen, and it's up to no good they are. So I pulled up my hood about my face and stood closer to the stack and listened to the feet squelching in the mud.

Then all of a sudden, people started shouting, lots of people, men and women, and I began to feel glad I had something behind me, and of the way I was standing in the angle between two stacks, to shield my blind eye too. While all the shouting went on round the inn I heard someone coming, very quietly, around the side of the stack. I sensed him rather, just smelt him and heard the half-breathing, and when he came round the corner, backwards as if he were watching something I caught him across the side of the head with my sword, still in its scabbard — I didn't want to do any damage we couldn't repair just in case it was a friend. Down, of course, he went, and I knew that he wouldn't move for a little time, at least. But after that there was a sound of shouting and running my way, so I pulled a mass of oat sheaves down over the pair of us. I'd had time to look at his face in the glow from something that had been set afire, a stable or something, and I knew him now all right. It was the lad I had seen in the successive inns, the one who was travelling with the two middle-aged men.

I lay there where I was safe and listened to the rumpus. I could hear Rhiannon screaming, but it was anger in that voice, not pain or even fear — she could look after herself and certainly nobody was doing anything drastic there. Pryderi was holding forth in a fine flow of language, and then his voice died away in an unmistakable grunting as someone gagged him. And then, quite near, there was a voice I knew.

'What? Do you mean to say you haven't found him?'

'No. He isn't in the inn, or in any of the huts.'

'Flaming Greek! You never can rely on them,' said Gwawl. I would have recognised that voice even through a gag, and that was how I wanted to hear it. The other voice, too — it was one of the middle-aged men who had been with the lad. Gwawl went on:

'Have you seen Lhygod?'

'No, not since you came. Must have gone ahead. Shall we look for Mannanan? If we set the place afire we'll smoke him out.'

'No. It will attract too much attention, and it won't be any good if he's gone off into the woods already. But if

150

we take these three away he's bound to come looking for them. We can leave a few men in the inn till dawn, though, in case he comes back. Right. Off we go.'

I lay still till I heard the sound of horses. The lad was beginning to stir. I felt that, as Gwawl said, the woods would be safer for me. I took some of the straw ropes from the oat sheaves and bound Lhygod's arms, and with a shorter length I gagged him. Then I woke him up by rubbing his face in a puddle and pulled him after me, leading him by the neck like a horse. We plunged into the darkness of the forest.

CHAPTER TEN

We walked through the dripping woods in the dark. I heard
the shambling rush of the frightened badger, and the hoot
of the owl. Once there was a heavier noise, and I knew
the bear was near. The wolves, at this time, might come
by ones or twos, but, I remarked loudly, I would be all
right because I could leave them Lhygod to eat. I was
satisfied to hear him add a muffled terrified grunting to
the slight noises of the night.

Where was I going? I had not the slightest idea. I was
making, roughly west. I knew that it would do me no good
to ask help from the local farmers, who were all Belgi.
Pryderi's people lay farther west, I knew that much, how
far I had never asked, but not far, to judge from odd
remarks he had passed about the ability of Taliesin's brown
horse to stand up to the journey. It might be only a day
or two.

The grey dawn came on us slowly, through the rain-
clouds, and it was at about the moment when one can tell
a white thread from a black one at arm's length that we
came into a clearing. In it was a hut, like the one where
Pryderi had found the bow — had earlier hidden the bow,
he or someone like him. I wondered if there might be
something useful here. I quickly tied my prisoner to a tree
and went forward. I peered cautiously round the leather
curtain that closed the door of the hut. There was the sound
of snoring. I drew my sword, and with one swift slash cut
away the door. Then I shouted:

'Come on out.'

There was a moment of confusion. Then there crawled

from the hut, blinking in the daylight, such as it was, three men. I looked them up and down as they stood in some kind of line. They looked miserable and half-starved, but that was nothing: on each of them, one on his belt, one around his neck, one peeping out of his sleeve, I saw the welcome sight of yellow and black.

'I am a friend of Pryderi,' I said, risking being mistaken in that light about the colours.

'Then let us have a good look at you,' said one of them. 'Because it is a rare and strange being you are in these parts.'

'And who are you, and what are you doing here?' I asked them.

'We are Duach—'

'And Nerthach—'

'And Grathach.'

'We are the Sons of the Hard Dawn.'

'We are the men who come from the confines of Hell.'

'And we are lost.'

I looked at them. Three big savage-looking men like that, and lost.

'Where then are you trying to go?' I asked.

'To say we are lost,' Grathach explained, 'is a figure of speech. We know where we are, but we do not know where we ought to be. For it is meeting Pryderi we should be today, but where he is now we do not know. So as we are his men and all our life revolves around him, it is lost we are till we find him.'

'In that case, I can help you a little. Gwawl has captured him.'

Grathach looked worried. 'There is bad, that is. Late he'll be for the wedding, too, I wouldn't wonder.'

'What wedding?'

'His wedding, of course. He's getting married on the thirtieth day after Luggnasad.'

'He didn't tell me.'

'I don't suppose anybody told him, either. It's only just been arranged. Enough trouble we had finding her, too.'

I felt that it would be too confusing to inquire further. I merely said:

'Well, if you want him to be any use at the nuptial feast, or after it, you had better help me. We want him back.'

'If we could wait a week,' volunteered Duach, 'I could ride back to the Summer Country and raise a party from old Caw. It's his niece Pryderi's marrying.'

'We might have to fight Romans as well,' pointed out Nerthach.

'There'll be no fighting.' I was firm about it. I went over and led Lhygod out. 'This is one of Gwawl's party. We've got capital.'

'Now, we can soon find out where Pryderi is,' said Grathach. 'There's always the old red-hot poker up the backside to make a man talk.' I was gratified to notice that Lhygod went a pale green colour and made choking noises. I insisted:

'No torture. Just a straight clean death. Now, is there anywhere around here that is fairly easy to see and good for a public hanging, because I think that will be the best.'

'Oh, yes. The mound of Arberth.'

'How long will it take us to walk there?'

'Why walk? We have horses.'

And so they had. We four rode, but Lhygod, hands and feet tied, we threw over the horse's back like a sack. We went west and north, till we met the road, and then we kept west over the flank of a chalk hill, past a line of barrows that marked the path of the Green Road, the Ridgway. And then, coming down from the Ridgway, down around the shoulder of the hill, we saw in front of us a great mound, an enormous barrow hundreds of feet high. It was more like one of the Pyramids of Egypt than anything else, and like them it had been built of great lumps of chalk, carefully cut and squared. But that had been long ago, and now the blocks had been weathered and rounded and the cracks between them filled in with dust and mud, and green moss and even grass now grew on what had once been white and shining walls. There was a path that led up to the top of the mound, but now one could only with difficulty see that it had once been a spiral staircase to a flat platform.

'Is it a burial mound?' I asked Grathach.

'Who knows?' he answered. 'It has many names, and most people call it the Hill of the Sun, or the Hill of Sul, who is our Goddess of the Sun. But what we used to use it for, and have done since time immemorial, was something quite ordinary. It used to be the Hill of Judgement of the kings of the Isle of the Mighty, and on top the High Kings of all the island, for we had High Kings once, would sit to give judgements in all manner of cases, their crowns on their heads and their Druids sitting at their feet to guide them in the law. But it is also called the Hill in Arberth, for Arberth is this land, and Arberth is the name of the village that lies to the north.'

'It will do me very nicely,' I told them, making my voice sound as off-handedly evil as I could for Lhygod's benefit. 'First we will take this wretch up to the top, and then I want you to go to the village and find me three beams, strong enough to bear the weight of a . . . lad, and a hammer, and nails.'

This they did, and Grathach, who only looked stupid, remembered the spade I had not mentioned, and also brought a chair for me to sit on.

'What shall we do?' he asked me in a loud voice, so that all the passers-by on the road, and all the people of the village of Arberth who had come out to watch, could hear. And I answered him in the same way:

'Build me a gallows. Build it high and build it strong, that it may stand here for a hundred years to show what happens to those who steal Mannanan's property. Dig holes into the hill, and set the uprights well into the soil. Nail the crossbar firmly so that it will not give, and throw the rope over. Then we will set the noose about this young rat's neck and pull . . . pull . . . pull . . . slowly and watch him kick. But do not work too fast, because it would be a pity if there might be anyone who would have too little time to see the justice of Mannanan.'

155

It was still only the middle of the morning. I looked about me as Nerthach and Duach took turns with the spade to sink the holes. To the east of us wound the Roman Road, and to the west of us, and in both directions it disappeared into the forest. To the north I could see the village of Arberth, and it was surrounded, I could see, by a circle of stones of the men of old, and another line of stones ran away to the east. But to the south, crossing me from left to right, I could see the line of the Green Road.

It was when the lads had finished sinking the holes and we were about to put up the first post that I heard scuffling on the path, and the grunting and blowing of a man out of condition, almost drowning Lhygod's sobs which grew louder as the holes were dug deeper. Then round the corner of the path the face of a man appeared and spiralled up to the top of the mound. He was a big, stocky man, very thick built indeed, with linen tunic and fine wool trousers, boots of Spanish leather, and a Gold chain around his neck. He looked the part of a merchant. He looked at the poles, and he looked at Lhygod, and he asked:

'Why sir, what are you doing here? Why are you putting up these timbers on this mound?'

'Simple enough it is,' I replied. 'Last night, I was walking hither and thither among my oatstacks, and necessary it was, because the mice have been at them lately. But of course when I came they all ran, and all I was able to catch was this one little mouse.' For that is the meaning of Lhygod, which I took to be some kind of a pet name. 'Therefore, I am going to hang this mouse by the neck till it be dead, for a warning to all the big rats of the Isle of the Mighty, and indeed of the Isle of the Blessed also, that I will have mercy on neither great nor small till what has been taken from me is returned.'

'Oh, but come now,' and his voice was smooth and silky as if he were trying to sell me something no sane man would take as a gift. 'Surely vengeance like this is beneath a great lord like yourself. The death of so little a mouse will not help you. I have always wanted a little mouse to

156

play with, as a pet. Come, sir, sell it to me for five pieces of Gold . . . or should I offer ten? It is only a whim of mine . . . Oh, yes, I can pay, I can pay, I am a trader of some repute in these parts.'

'I will ask you something.' Never, I thought, fight an enemy on his own ground. 'If I take five Gold pieces, new minted and not yet clipped, and I buy a hundred amphorae of Gaulish wine, and I sell them for two hundred two-horse denarii, and with that I buy one thousand cheeses and I sell those for forty thousand copper sesterces, then have I made a profit or a loss?'

'Now, if you will repeat that slowly,' he stammered, 'and let me send for my abacus and my tablets and let me inquire the price of cheese and how many sesterces there are in a sestertia—'

'Any merchant carries all these things at his fingers' ends, and would have answered me in a moment,' I said sternly. 'No merchant you.'

And Nerthach and Duach took him by the shoulders and the ankles and rolled him down the sides of the mound, and he scrambled up on to the road and ran as fast as he could towards the wood from which he had come.

Then the lads got the cross-beam up on to the gallows, and they made a great deal of fuss about it, banging away with the nails fit to wake the dead in the long grave mound I could see, and at every bang Lhygod sobbed the more. But when they had finished, a head appeared over the edge of the mound as a man strode up the spiral path as easily as if it were the level ground. He was dressed as an officer of an Auxiliary Regiment of Cavalry, in the German fashion, with his shirt tucked into his trousers and his trouser legs tapered to his boots. His breastplate was polished, and his helmet shone, with a yellow plume set crosswise. I wondered idly what regiment he thought he was in. Before I could ask him, he began to ask me, in a Latin thickened with an accent that might have been that of Friesia or Pannonia:

'Now, sir!! What are you doing here? Do you not know

that the administration of justice in this country is the task of Caesar's officers? Are you indeed preparing to carry out a hanging? Hand your prisoner over to me at once!'

I shifted my position in my chair so that the handle of my sword came before his eyes, and I answered him mildly enough:

'I am merely ridding my land of vermin. Last night I was taking the air in the rickyard, hoping to catch the mice that have been eating up all my grain. But they saw me coming and ran away, and I was only able to catch this little one. Therefore I am setting up this high gallows, and here I will hang this mouse, as a warning to all the big rats within the Empire and outside it that I will have mercy neither on great nor small till what they have stolen is returned to me.'

'A mouse, is it?' he mused, twirling his moustache between finger and thumb, and I felt pity for a man whose chin had been so recently scraped clean. 'Now, if, as I see, you have a large performing mouse, I would be glad to buy it as a regimental mascot. Expense is no object. I will reclaim it from the regimental funds. Will you take twenty Gold pieces . . . forty . . .?'

'All right, German cavalryman,' I answered him. 'Tell me this — is the World Tree an oak, or an ash, or an elm?'

He looked at me a moment in confusion.

'Why,' he stammered at last, 'the most sacred tree of all must be an oak tree.'

'You are no German Cavalryman,' I told him, and Grathach and Duach took him by the shoulders and the ankles, and rolled him down the slope, and pelted him with lumps of chalk as he ran back into the woods from which he had come.

It was now half-way through the afternoon. The men from the Confines of Hell threw the end of the rope over the cross-bar, and began to make a noose, trying it on Lhygod's neck for size and remaking it several times because it was too large, or too small, or not tidy enough. And while they were laughing over this, the head of a man appeared as he walked slowly up the spiral path. And this was not a merchant nor a soldier, but a Druid. His clean-shaven face peered out from his white headcloth, and his white tunic brushed the ground before his feet. On his breast was a shrivelled leaf, which might have been mistletoe, and on his head was a wreath of oak-leaves, the ends of the twigs fresh broken and oozing sap, and the acorns, since it was mid-August, still unripe and green-cased. He came to me and he said:

'What are you doing here, my son? If you wish to offer sacrifice, it is not for you to carry it out, and there is no law in this isle that allows you to hang an offering to the Gods. Let me have this man, so that at Beltain I may shut him in a basket and burn him alive.'

'Why, this is no man,' I told him, 'but a little mouse. I was taking my ease last night in the rickyard, where the mice have been troublesome, but when they heard me coming they fled, all except this one, which I caught. And I propose to hang it from this high gallows, so that all this vermin, of this world and the world that is to come and the world of the Dead, shall know that I will have mercy on neither great nor small till all that I have lost is returned to me.'

'Then if it is a mouse, my son,' said the Druid, and I was full of admiration for a man who could talk thus so soon after his moustaches had been scraped from his upper lip, 'I would indeed like to possess it, because it is foretold that when I die I shall be transmigrated into a mouse, and so it would be unworthy of me to allow anyone to kill what may, in time, become my own wife. Therefore, let me buy it from you as an act of piety, and though I have no money of my own, yet I am entrusted with certain funds to be disbursed in charity, and therefore I could offer you for this mouse sixty pieces of silver . . . of Gold . . . eighty pieces of Gold . . .'

'Druid!' I spoke to him without reverence. 'Tell me this. What is white and black, of the sky and not of the sky, of the earth and not of the earth?'

He looked puzzled. Then he said, 'I must have some time to consult my sacred books.'

'You are no Druid,' I told him, and Nerthach and Duach were ready to roll him down the slope again, but I merely said to them:

'*Pull!*'

With relish they began to take in the slack of the rope, but as the rope tightened Gwawl shouted in his proper voice:

'Stop it! Stop!'

We looked at him., He had thrown off the Druid's robe, which was only a bed sheet he had stolen from the inn the night before, and he stood there in his black and white shirt, but clean-shaven now.

'What is there I can give you for this mouse? Name anything you want, even to the half of my Kingdom.'

'First,' I said, 'tell me who is this mouse.'

'This is my wife,' said Gwawl, 'new married, and this was the only way I thought she could travel safely from her own Iceni across a land full of desperate men like yourself, and at the same time have my two men keep an eye on you. And treat her carefully, I beg of you, because she has just found out that she is pregnant.'

'Then if you want her back,' I told him, 'you will have to pay for her, and sorry I would be to have to hang her, for I like her as well as any woman I ever met who did not speak a word to me.'

'Yes, yes,' gasped Gwawl, sweating with worry. 'I will exchange her for Rhiannon.'

'And besides Rhiannon?'

'Yes, then — you may have Taliesin too.'

'And besides Taliesin?'

'No, no: you cannot ask me to give up my real prize, my ancient enemy.'

Grathach gave a playful tug at the rope, and the mouse stood on tiptoe, gurgling.

'All right, then. I will send back Pryderi also.'

'And besides Pryderi?'

'What? Will you give me no profit at all from this night?'

'None at all. Let us have back also Hueil and his four men, or their weight in Gold if they are dead, and our horses and all our baggage unrobbed and untouched.'

'All that I will do, only let me have my little mousey back.'

'And bring them before the sun is set, to the road below this mound. And then let us see you go, vowing not to molest us again on this journey, as we will not molest you.'

And so we agreed.

The Mere

CHAPTER ONE

How far from the Mound of Arberth to the Summer Country? Far enough, with five men wounded. Hueil had an arm broken, and his four comrades were hurt each in a different measure — this one had his jaw broken and most of his teeth knocked out, that one had been struck in the face with a burning log, and so on. Pryderi had merely been kicked many times in the ribs, so that he found it painful to ride far in a day. Taliesin had been tied up, no one daring to offer any more violence to a Druid, and indeed that violence had been enough.

'For the first time in my life,' he told us, 'I regretted that the laws of my holy order forbid me to curse any man. But I did as well in my own way.'

'How?' we asked.

'Why, I drew in the dust with my foot, and I told each man his fate, and how he would die. And there is not a man there who will not die a dreadful death, violent and horrible beyond belief.'

Now whether he truly divined this or not I do not know, but I have no doubt that his prophecies will all come true, because there is no surer way to drive a man to court disaster than to foretell it for him. What we believe, happens.

Rhiannon they had kept apart, and she told us that Gwawl had made sure that she was treated like a perfect lady. It would, of course, have been easy to trace her, had I let Duach go to fetch a band of men, by the hawk that hovered above her all the day.

We moved along the old Green Roads, crossing the new

stone roads of the Romans, but not using them. This was for ease, not for necessity: no troops march along the new roads any more, except once a year the Pioneers, replacing cobbles and clearing out the ditches, in case it should be ever necessary to hurry the legions down into the West again.

We stayed in farms at night. The people knew that we were coming. These were big farms, set well apart, because the Britons live thus and not in villages. Often the farms would belong to nobles, who now lived all the year round in the County Town, like Calleva or Sulis. Of course, a noble would never now go near his farm, but he liked at least to think that he had a house in the country where he could, if he ever wanted to, entertain his important friends if he ever made any. And it was at least a good thing, 'my house' and 'my estate' and 'my tenants', to talk and exaggerate about.

A number of these houses were quite comfortable, by provincial standards. Usually they had changed from a cluster of round huts into a series of straight-walled rooms, like the rest of mankind build, and the farmyard had changed into a paved courtyard. Sometimes the owners had gone as far as building the walls of stone, or even brick, and in a few cases they had put on a layer of plaster in the slim hope that some day they would find someone to come and paint them with some civilised scene. And in one case, the floor had been made ready in the dining-room in case the owner could ever afford to have a ready-made mosaic put down.

Heating, of course, was still primitive, charcoal braziers set wherever it was convenient. Still, they were somewhere to stay, since the stewards or bailiffs or what you like to call them were always eager to take us in, and as far as I could see never charged a denarius, or complained about the bird droppings in the room where Rhiannon slept.

We went west, and then south, and after that west again, to skirt the Lead Hills. You could, on clear days, make out the haze of smoke from the smelting furnaces at the mines. There were the nearest Roman soldiers, and not many of them: they would be little interested in the surrounding country, but would only be wondering how long it might be before they were relieved. And these men, and their lead, came and went by the new road, north of the Hills, that went through Sulis to Londinium.

All the hills were quiet now. The Army had gone from village to village and from house to house a hundred times, in the few years after the conquest, and seized every sword and helmet and mail coat. The chariots, too, belonged to the nobles, and they had also been brought in. You never saw so much as a real shield now, not the stout lime-wood panels, three-layered, bronze-faced and iron-rimmed: only the flimsy painted leather screens that Rhiannon's escort still carried. This was an old-fashioned area, but, even so, you never saw a Roman here either. Only, once every seven years or so, the surveyor came through, re-assessing for the wheat tax. Now *he* needed an escort. Otherwise, the peasants obeyed their lords as they had done before the conquest, or rather they obeyed their lords' stewards, because their lords never came any more.

Still, there was no need to go inviting trouble, in such a big party of ours, and that was why we travelled by the old Green Road, and spread out into small groups between farms, coming together for the night. We met few other travellers, and most of them were rather curious. We so often overtook or met single men with packhorses, two horses to a man, and each horse with two baskets, not big so they must have been heavy, or so I thought. What was striking was that always horse and man were black from head to foot: not black by nature which would have been understandable, but black with some dirt or other, grimed into white skin and brown hair beyond any hope of washing. The baskets were black, too. I took them for charcoal-burners, and I said so to Pryderi, one day. At this, he laughed, and the next time we met one of these men, he stopped and called him over.

He was a short man, and close to you could see the sweat

167

running channels in the dirt, and the hands and arms covered with the scars of labour filled with the black and looking blue underneath the skin. The man came to us, and we got down to talk, as is only polite, while he sat down, balancing himself delicately on the heels of his feet, and doubling the backs of his thighs against his calves, so that only his feet and not his back side touched the ground. It was the art of a man who works hard, and does not spend his strength unnecessarily on standing up.

'Go on, ask him what it is he carries,' said Pryderi. Hueil and Nerthach, riding ahead, reined back and waited for us. The Dirty Man looked at my blue clothes, and nodded to them, not to me, politely, but respectfully, as though granting through good will and not through obligation, some slight deference to a social superior. I asked him:

'Is this charcoal?'

'Charcoal? Wood coal? Would I be selling you the worn-out ashes of other men's second-hand fires? No, this is earth coal, the best.'

'Earth coal?'

'Easy it is to be hearing, and understanding, and knowing, from your question, though it is very well you are speaking the language of the Gods, and only making a few mistakes in the grammar, and in the order of the tenses and in the mutations, and sometimes being indistinct in your appreciation of the fine gradations of meaning, that it is from far away and from foreign parts and from a distant land that you have come, and travelled, and ridden.' He spoke in a thick accent that I could hardly follow, but he had that easy flow of language and wide vocabulary and subtle sense of rhythm which are common to all Britons. 'No, it is not charcoal, it is the earth coal.'

'Let me see it.'

'Aye, I will let you,' he began, and it was obvious that he was about to launch out again into one of his interminable sentences, the only saving quality of which was that like all the Britons he was careful to begin each one with the main verb, but Pryderi passed him a leather-bound flagon of mead. The Dirty Man took a long, long swig. When he lowered the bottle from his mouth, he began to undo the basket with his free hand, saying as he did so:

'Aye, sweet it is, the mead of the bees, sweeter than water, sweeter than death. But not so good it is as water to quench thirst. There is nothing like pure water from the spring to wash out the dust of the tunnels and the grit of the caves. In return for this, I will even let you have a piece of the earth coal. For it would not be right, nor fitting, nor lawful to give you a piece without payment and without price and without exchange. Into the very guts of the earth we go to gain it, and we cut it out from the roots of the hills. Into the heart of the rock and into the liver of the world we make our tunnels to find it, and there we hear the friendly spirits of the earth our mother. They warn us, when it is time to close our tunnels, and when they wish to bring down the roof so that the earth may rest fallow. And it is only the foolish man who stays when the spirits warn.' He took another long draft at the mead. 'Aye, here is a lovely piece for you, and worth the buying.'

Now, what he said about it being wrong to give the stuff away I could well understand, having once been a doctor myself. When you have some skill or access to some commodity, and this has cost you a great deal of work in the past, then it is an act of impiety to the God who gave it to you not to show how much you value it by asking for it the highest price you can get. And if a man will not pay the price you demand, then he must go without. If he cannot pay for a fire or for food or for a doctor's knowledge, then let him die of cold or hunger or disease. It is blasphemy for him to ask for food or firing or treatment free, and it is blasphemy for anyone to have pity on him and help him for nothing. This is the basic law of all religion, and the foundation of the science of medicine: no man is entitled to life unless he can pay for it.

Anyway, this man looked into his pannier, and brought out a lump of something, I couldn't see what at first, it was only a small piece and he hid it in his closed hands.

169

With a look of complicity in some dark deed he put it into my hand. It was, to all appearances, a piece of stone, black, and sharp in contour, newly broken or quarried. It was soft, though, as stone goes. I could break it into little splintery pieces with my thumb-nail, pushing along straight cracks to split it into layers. It stained my fingers with black. When I split it along the cracks, the fresh surfaces caught the light. I was puzzled.

'What is it?' I asked.

'If it is not knowing that you are,' the Dirty Man replied, 'then it is guessing you will have to be.'

I turned it over and over.

'It is too friable to be building stone. Likewise it would never serve for paving, even as occasional black pieces in a mosaic. It might, however, do for the black in a wall mosaic. Instead of using it as it is, perhaps you grind it down and use it to colour plaster black for wall designs. Or is it a dye?' I spat on it. 'Probably not, since it doesn't dissolve in moisture. It might, though in oil, though I haven't any and I can't try it. I know it isn't jet, since it is much too brittle to turn on a wheel. So, I suppose it must be an ore of some kind. What kind? Not iron, or lead, it is not heavy enough. But . . . tin is light. That's it, I have it. It's tin ore.'

It was rather humiliating, I must say, to show a fine example of the methods of the sophists as I did then, and to be laughed at, but all the same Pryderi and the Dirty Man did laugh at me. Pryderi said, when he could.

'Not to worry, you weren't to know. I'll show you tonight, you won't believe me otherwise.'

At that moment, the next section of our party came round the bend in the road behind us. The Dirty Man looked at them, moving on with the clusters of birds singing in the bushes at either side, and he asked sharply:

'Who's that?'

'Well, boy,' Pryderi seemed to be ready to settle down for one of those irritating riddling chats the Britons are so fond of, and he was using his peasant voice to do it in, 'that one in front, well, Taliesin that is, Taliesin of Mediometon.'

'Oh, aye,' said the Dirty Man, unimpressed. 'The Druid. I seen him before, I did, and not much to look at now, is he? But her — who's she?'

'Her? Oh, well now, that is . . '. Pryderi paused, savouring it. 'Her, well she's . . .' and then it came in a rush — 'Rhiannon of the Brigantes, Rhiannon herself, that is.'

'Rhiannon herself? Herself? Here? Already here?'

The Dirty Man was of a sudden out of breath. Rhiannon clearly was a different kind of being from us, or from Taliesin. He stared as she came nearer. As she approached, the wood on either side of the path was full of the scurrying of wood-pigeons, and jays, and tree creepers, and the songs of the thrushes and the warblers. The Dirty Man had pulled his old horse to the side of the road, and now he stood beside it, his hands raised level with his face, spread out, palms forward, his head bowed, the universal attitude of prayer. Rhiannon came level with us and reined in her horse. The birds fell silent.

'What is it, my son?' She gazed down at the Dirty Man, who did not dare to look her in the face. Rhiannon at this time was, perhaps, twenty-two or twenty-three, in the grand flush of her beauty. The Dirty Man was at least forty, nearing the end of a hard life. His drooping moustache was flecked with grey.

'Bless me, my Mother, Mother of Those Below,' he asked her. 'Give me good fortune. Let me find the seams below, fat thick seams, rich and good, that will kindle and burn and give warmth to make men live and cook good food. Keep the choking mist from my lungs a few more years, and let me not be burnt in the great floods of flame, nor drowned in the blaze of waters. Let me not be caught behind the falls, and let your messengers tell me when the roof comes down. Only for a few years, my Mother, only for a few years, till the boy is old enough to come into the seam and feed himself, and his mother if need be.'

'Be content my son,' answered Rhiannon, speaking

slowly and with ceremony. 'Those who toil below are not forgotten by those who dwell below. You shall not come to your end till the boy can dig for himself. And this you have not asked aloud, but only in your heart and I will grant it you. You shall not die like the common run, standing or lying and in the light of sun and moon. You shall die like a man, crouching amid the falling stones and in the dark. When it is your time, I shall take you to myself in the bursting roof, quickly in noise and fury and in the blackness. This I grant you, my son.'

Pryderi and I mounted. We all passed on. At the next bend in the road, I looked back. The Dirty Man still stood by the wayside, his hands still held before his face. His horse patiently cropped the grass behind him. The birds sang again about Rhiannon.

Soon after that day we came to the crest of a hill. The sun shone almost level from a little west of south. In line with it, out of a great stretch of open country, a hill stood up, a tall round hill the shape of an upturned bucket, an echo of the mound of Arberth, but taller, much taller. Pryderi pointed.

'See that? Once we're past that, we're in the Summer Country. That's the place to be, for the winter. Spending winter in the Summer Country, there's lucky you are.' He spoke like a peasant, laughing like a simple man at the play on words, 'Just let's get past the Glass Mountain and then we'll be right till the spring.'

I took little notice of his Glass Mountain or any other strange names. Far, far away, something shone. It might be, it might not be, but I was sure, too, that I could smell it, faintly, faintly . . . it gave me life. Somewhere within a day's ride was the sea.

A mile or two down the forward face of the hill we came to another farm, and we were greeted by rooms ready for us, and stabling for the horses, and food ready in the pot. But this time it was no Steward who stood to welcome us. Hueil dismounted, his arm still bandaged, and stood to receive us at his own door. It was a fine evening, almost warm by our standards, overpoweringly hot to the Britons, and we sat to eat in the courtyard, around a brazier set there for comfort and light and not for heat, and we sang, quietly and in harmony, out of joy at being surrounded now, not by mere friends, but, most of us, by our own kinsmen.

'Where's your keepsake?' Pryderi asked me of a sudden. At first I couldn't understand what he meant, but then I remembered, and out of my wallet I took my little piece of black stone. Pryderi took it, and fingered it for a while. Then he leaned forward and put it into the fire.

'Watch!' he told me. For a little while nothing happened, it just sat there black and dead. Then the stone began to glow at the edges, and little blue flames started from it. I remembered the officer at Rutupiae who had said, 'They're so poor, they burn the very stones of the earth for want of wood.' Pryderi explained:

'The people near here dig it out of the earth and peddle it about the country. It is good for fires. The Romans buy a lot of it for smelting the lead.'

'It is the gift of the Gods Below,' said Rhiannon. 'It will be the salvation of the Isle of the Mighty.'

Well, you know how women prattle. I saw a lot of it used later, and it does indeed burn very well, once you can get it to light, and that's the problem: you have to get a good wood fire going first to kindle the stone, and of course if you can do that, what's the use of looking for anything else. So who on earth would want it? It's so heavy to carry, and takes so much trouble to dig out, that it will never replace the charcoal. No, there's no future for earth coal.

CHAPTER TWO

It is a strange place, the Summer Country. It stretches between the Glass Mountain and the sea, from south to north. On the east, the boundary is the bluff edge of the Lead Hills. On the west is the ridge that marks the edge of the Deer Moor, a desolate bare country where only the wild beasts live in winter, and where the sheep graze in summer. Between them is a low ridge that men call the Apple Land. I will tell you why.

On either side of the Apple Land a river flows to the sea. And each river is ponded back by the tides into a marsh, so that swamps stretch from the edges of the Apple Land, east to the Lead Hills and west to the Deer Moor. That low land is covered in alders and willows, and little humps of land stand out of the swamp, which in winter are islands in the floods. And on a clear day you can stand below Hueil's farm, and look over the Summer Country, and count a hundred little smudges of smoke, and every one is a farm in the marshes.

We came down from Hueil's farm and we entered the marsh, the horses following a firm path. We skirted the base of the Glass Mountain. I suddenly realised, at the foot, that we were passing through where once a village had been. The ruined houses, deserted these fifty years, were overgrown with weeds. There were only two farms still occupied. One of them had a farmyard, fenced in on three sides, and on the fourth butting against a rock-face, and within that a barn against the rock. The people of the place looked incuriously at us as we passed. We said nothing. We did not talk to each other on the long road into the marsh.

The horses went well, carrying us down into the Mere. They stepped delicately along the track beaten out by the hooves of countless cattle. We passed into the meadows of long sweet grass, dotted with clumps of trees, and the ground about the track grew softer and wetter, and the grass longer and coarser, and the trees grew thicker and closer together. I realised that we were now riding along a made road, of logs laid crosswise in the way, covered with layers of gravel. It was a firm road, wide enough for two packhorses to walk abreast with a man between to lead them. It might well have supported even a wagon.

In some places about us the ground was firm and in the bright meadows, too wet for sheep, grazed the little black cows you find everywhere in Britain. In other places you could see the water gleaming around the roots of the grass. Soon there were open pools, and wider lagoons, between ridges and tussocks of stiff reeds and bulrushes. There was no riding here, or walking either, off the track, but there was not enough water for a boat. In some places the lagoons were shallow, mere low-lying fields filled by the summer rains; but some of the pools were deep and black, good places, I thought, for pike. Now instead of scattered clumps of big trees, there were willows and alders on the edges of the pools, and between patches of scrub, too dense for a man to push his way through quickly on horseback, or even to think of entering on foot. There was no choice but to follow the track.

Deeper and deeper we went into the marsh. The water looked like lead under the cloudy sky. There was now no sound but the scuffling of hooves, and the occasional twittering of birds following Rhiannon. Pryderi rode with me, and behind Taliesin went with Rhiannon. Nerthach and Duach brought up the rear. Both Rhiannon and Taliesin looked straight ahead, with faces emptied of fear or joy. Only, from time to time, Grathach far ahead broke the silence with a sad and shapeless song, too faint for me to hear the words. I did not know where we were going, or what we would find in the Summer Country. I tried not to guess.

We saw no people. There *were* people living in the marsh, sometimes so close to our road that we could smell their fires, but we never saw them. There were piles of willow withies cut and stacked by the side of the log road, and stacks of logs, too, sometimes, ready for the charcoal-burners. There were boats on the lagoons, crude things carved each out of a single log, blunt-ended, just enough to keep a man afloat while he fished. We still saw cows where the ground was firm enough: they must have belonged to somebody, I thought. There was nobody to talk to us, or to watch us, that we could see. But I was sure that we were seen, and watched.

Now we had been moving for half the day, with never a stop for food or rest. There was very little open land now, only the thicket and the marsh and the narrow road. It was now too narrow for two horses abreast, and I followed Pryderi. The willows hid the hills on either side. The Glass Mountain had long since vanished. There was nothing to be seen at all but the thicket, either within arm's reach on either side, or a spear's throw away across black stagnant water, covered sometimes with green slime. Beavers fled from before us into their lodges, and otters, water dogs, as the Britons call them, looked up from their fresh-captured fish on the far banks and watched us without fear. Herons stood in the reeds to see us pass. Moorhens and duck went about their business unheeding. This was no place for men.

I felt lost. I was lost. We were far from any human contact. There was an end now of houses and wine, of fires and the friendly talk of wise men. There was nothing but thornbush and grey cloud and water. There were no hills, no firm ground, nothing to which a man could cling, nothing real, nothing definite, only infinite marsh. All was lost. I knew that this was the end of the world, that all that lay before me was delusion and disaster.

I had vowed myself to the Gods Below, and now it was the Mother of the Gods Below who rode behind me, displacing the Priest of the Unconquered Sun, on whom

I might no more call for help. I knew now that I would never return to the real world, that there was no real world, that whatever I might see in future would not be the world. I had passed through the Gates of the Dead. I would never return. I was alone. I was dead.

The scrub grew denser. It closed in on both sides of the path. There was only a narrow gash in the green wall ahead. Grathach, in his cloak of striped black and yellow, moved his pony through the gap, and was gone. Pryderi checked his horse a little. I touched his shoulder:

'Forward?' I asked.

'Forward,' he replied. 'There is no other way.'

The path wound through the wood. The green waterfalls of the willows curtained me in on every side. I turned left and then right with the path, and left again, I moved here and there, twisting around the trees, turning in my horse's length. Pryderi was too far ahead to be seen. The twists of the path became more and more violent, more frequent. I became dizzy clinging with knees and heels and arms to the horse as he scrambled among the soggy tufts and the fallen branches, black with rot and speckled with red. I was lost and alone in this wilderness, it was death, it was Hell, this *was* Hell, to wander for ever with no hope of ever arriving, no hope of any rest or any end.

And then I came to, not an end, but a beginning, a choice. The path forked. One way went to the right, the other to the left. There was no telling which way to take. I sat still and listened. There was no sound, no sound of horses' hooves, no sound of feet. There was no voice to be heard, not even Grathach's song, nor the songs of the birds. There was no one in the marsh, no one on the path, no one before me or behind. I was alone. I had no help. I must decide. And yet, I was sure that I was not alone, that eyes watched me, alive or dead, that nothing I did but was known. And I understood that whatever I did now I must do alone, that there would be no help from any being.

Which way to go? I sat, and I listened to the silence,

177

and I sniffed at the air. There was no sound, nor the smell of fire, nor fresh tracks on the path, nor horse droppings nor broken twigs. But somewhere, along one path or another, I would find the Master of the Western Sea. And where would he be but by the sea?

I put my hand into my wallet. I took from it a shell, one of those rare Indian shells, glossy and striped in cream and brown, and speckled over with black. The mouth of this shell is a slit, all set along with teeth that never move or grind together, and if a man puts his ear to the mouth, then he can hear the sea, however far he may be from it. And that I tell you is true, for by such a means I have heard the sea in the middle of a desert, and on the top of a great mountain. And there in the marsh I put the shell to my ear, spitting first on the ground, because I had no other offering to make to the gods of the place, whoever they were. I turned to my right, and I listened, and I heard the patter of little waves on a beach, rattling the stones in the undertow, and so faint that it could hardly be heard. And then I turned to the left, and I heard the great waves of the ocean, driven by the west wind, tumbling and crashing in ruins of foam, seas to crush ships and drown whales and take up great stone jetties and cast them into the market-places of towns. If there were ever a sea worth the Mastery, then this was it. I turned to the left.

I followed the twists and turns of the path, and whenever it forked, as it did every hundred paces, I listened to the sound of the sea, and I went where the storm was loudest, though never a breath of wind touched my face, there in the prison of the Green Marsh. I forded little streams and splashed through shallow pools, and even my weary horse began to scent some hope ahead, and himself to sniff the air. And then, of a sudden, there was a wind, a wind in my face, and I sniffed it like the horse, and what meant nothing to him was the smell of nectar to me, the smell of the salt sea. And now I had no need of the shell, I faced always into the wind, and when it veered, as winds will, I veered with it, heading into it, so that the evil spirits of the place should not swamp me. And at last on the wind I smelt smoke, the smoke of a peat fire, and sometimes I thought I could hear the sound of voices. The thickets became sparser and the meadows more open, and the ground about the path was firmer. Instead of the otter's half-gnawed fish among the rushes, I saw the padmarks of the fox, and instead of the beaver's dam, my horse avoided the molehills among the buttercups. There were cows again, and it felt to me as if the path were slightly, very slightly, up hill. And then it was not a path but a road, the gravel beaten down into the spaces between the logs, and through the trees I could see hills ahead. The wind blew strongly, and the grey cloud thinned above me and cleared from before me, and by the height of the sun as I rode into it I saw that I was travelling to the West.

And then in a sudden I was clear. In a marsh I had once left all I loved. Now I had come out of the marsh again, and I was a new man. I reined in my horse, and I dismounted because where I had come I must go on my own feet. I threw back the borders of my sealskin cloak, and I laid my right hand on the jewelled hilt of my sword. I flaunted my boots of cordoban leather, and my trousers of blue wool of the first shearing of the virgin ewe. I let all men see my shirt of silk, blue silk from a world away, and the Gold chain about my neck from which hung an Amber globe, and the Gold morse that fastened my cloak, set with Amber, and my belt, plates of ivory engraved with strange scenes of the chase and sewn to elephant skin. Wealth I showed all who cared to see, the most precious things in the world, Gold and Silk, Amber and Ivory. And so I walked to meet the Master of the Western Seas.

I came across the open meadow towards him. We were under the bluff edge of the hills on the Western side of the Summer Country. The scarp sheltered houses scattered along the side of the marsh, above the flood level. Three hundred paces from the place where the path came from the woods stood a crowd of people, men, women and children, not in a shapeless mass, but ranked in order. And in the centre of the line Pryderi stood at the right hand of the Master of the Western Sea.

For who else could it be, seated there on a throne made out of the beak of a ship. The jutting forefoot was heaped with cushions, and the figurehead, a flying goose, spread its wings above him. He answered my belt of elephant Ivory with one of plates of the walrus's teeth. His boots were not of soft leather of the cow, but of the hide of the whale. The Gold chain about his neck suspended on his breast a pearl the like of which no man has ever seen, for it was as big as his fist. Instead of a sword, he held in his right hand a grapnel, three-pronged, of silver, the handle set with sheets of mother of pearl, and in his left hand he had the horn of a wild ox mounted in Gold. And his hair and moustaches were as white as the skin of the great white bear he wore for a cloak. But in all his splendour, I knew him, and he knew me. I walked steady and straight towards him, not looking round though I knew that a score of men had followed me in the marsh and were now behind me in the meadow. I halted three paces from him. He spoke first:

'Photinus-Votan-Mannanan, whoever you are. What is it you want of me?'

I knew I must stand up to him now, or never again.

'Caw!' I addressed him. 'Caw! Master of the Western Sea I know you. I stole your ship once, and I stole its cargo, and I even stole you. Now I have come again to you for a ship, and this time I am willing to pay.'

'And I tried to kill you myself,' he answered calmly. 'I spoilt your water and your food. These things happen at sea, where there is no law except that a man may live if he is strong, and must live if he is wise. But are you indeed the man I knew then?' He turned to Pryderi. 'What kind of man is he?'

Pryderi looked at me dispassionately.

'On land, I grant you, he is a man of skill and resource, a man who is not too proud to work with his hands, and to produce works of art according to his lights. And he is a keen bargainer in the market-place, and able to turn anything into money, even rotten rags and green rushes.'

'What else do you expect?' asked Caw. 'He is a merchant. Is he nothing more?'

'He is a man who will take a Gesa upon himself, and will keep it, even when he is in danger of his life.'

'Any man may keep his Gesa, for fear of the Gods, or even for fear of the vengeance of men,' said Caw.

'He is a man who will keep his word when there is no profit in it,' said another voice. I knew this voice. I turned to it. There was a wreath of coral in her hair, and about her waist was a belt of silver chains, the equal of Rhiannon's, linked as it was and buckled with Gold. But even today she wore above her nineteen petticoats, an apron I had bought her. 'He kept his promise and he set me free, though he did not know who I was or where I came from or what vengeance he was giving me. Hey, Photinus,' cried Cicva. 'Have you finished the hyena's hair?'

'But that was a little thing,' said Caw.

'There is more,' Pryderi told him. 'When he was tempted to follow the love of his life, he did not, but he still pressed to the West, wherever she might go.'

'And so might any man for money,' objected Caw again.

'But time was when he was offered all he has worked for, and that he refused, to redeem his love. And he did not redeem her only, but his friends too.'

What he meant by that I could not think, because I could not remember I had refused anything of importance. But Caw asked:

'Where is the man I used to know? He was one who would do nothing except for profit, and who would run after any woman in sight, aye, and catch her too. What has happened to you, Photinus? Is it only that you have grown old like me?'

I thought a little. Perhaps I had changed. I was not conscious of it. But perhaps in the old days I would not have left Pryderi to chase Rhiannon, I would have redeemed her alone and never thought of Taliesin, I would never have left Cicva, or Lhygod for that matter, unviolated. Was I becoming more temperate, less realistic in my prime? There was more than that. I answered:

'When I first went into the North, I went for no reason but to save my skin, and I had no one but myself to please and no one to answer to. That I gained great profit from it was an accident. Then I did not know it, but I followed the great plan of others, and I was a tool in the hands of the Gods. But now, I have come into the West to carry out my own great plan, and I will do only what I will. And I do not will that for my own sake, but I am doing it for the sake of my family, and to them I am responsible. I may not follow my own desires, no matter how attractive they are. I am not my own master, but I tell you this, I am master of my own grand design, and that I will carry out, though thrones fall and kings die, yes, even though I die.'

'And what is my place in this grand design, Photinus-Mannanan? What do you want of me?'

'I told you. I want a ship, and for it I can pay.'

'No, Mannanan. You want of me more than a ship, and for what you want, no man can pay enough. Sit here, and watch, stay with me a winter, and see what it is you are asking.'

Men brought a chair, with arms carved in the shape of swans, and placed it at Caw's left hand, and there I sat, and looked across the meadow to the edge of the wood. And from the wood I saw Taliesin come.

Now he was dressed again as a Druid, in white from head to foot. His oak-leaf crown was on his head, and the sickle and the apple were in his hands. In stout shoes he came across the grass, and I looked at the people expecting them to kneel before him, but they did not. They cheered, they waved their arms and shouted:

'Taliesin! Taliesin the Blessed, the Radiant Brow.' The women sighed and whispered and oohed and ahed and said:

'Oh, the Holy One, how beautiful he is, oh, there's lovely he is.'

The little children ran forward to touch the edge of his white garment, while their mothers warned them not to dirty it, and there was small danger of that, because their hands had been washed a dozen times that morning in readiness. And the men, oh, the men, they began to sing, intricately lacing together their Pythagorean patterns of sound, they sang the cauldron hymn I had heard before, and why it was appropriate to a Druid I could not think.

Some people praise a cauldron on a fire of flashing flame,
But a cauldron on a cold cold hearth brings the Brits immortal fame:
On cold ashes (*bang-bang-bang*) brings the Marsh undying fame.

That was the song they sang as I watched Taliesin come to us, and sit on the chair prepared for him on Caw's right hand, a great throne all carved with dragons and sea-horses, and painted and gilded. The voices rose to a fortissimo, and then stopped, suddenly, cut off. Out of the wood came Rhiannon.

Had you ever seen, even in your dreams, the ship of Theseus beating back to Athens from flaming Cnossus, you would know how she looked. For on that voyage, you will remember, the Athenians failed to change the black sails for silver. When Aegeus saw that black ship of mourning, he flung himself from the rocks for sorrow. And it would have been understandable for any man to have died for the love of Rhiannon as I saw her that day. She came to us, barefoot across the grass, wrapped in her splendid cloak of white and Gold; and in the midst of the space, as Theseus should have struck his black sails, so she threw down her cloak, and we saw her clad from head to foot in black; her blouse, long-sleeved, was of black linen, and her skirts sweeping the ground were of black wool. Her shawl about her shoulders was of black silk, and she lifted her arms and arranged it about her head to hide her glowing hair.

183

She came to us, and Caw stood to let her pass. Taliesin and I remained seated. She came to us, and as she came, all the men knelt. Caw knelt. Pryderi knelt, Grathach and Duach and Hueil knelt. I slipped from my chair and I knelt. And most wonderful of all, Taliesin knelt. The great Druid, the Most Holy One of all, he knelt. Here amid the men and boys of the Summer Country, the great priest of the Unconquered Sun knelt before the Mother of Those Below.

The men knelt. The women stood. They closed about Rhiannon as she went towards the house prepared for her.

CHAPTER THREE

Now you may think that I had had enough incident for one day, and that it was by now too near dark for anything else to happen, and so did I, but to my surprise, no sooner had Rhiannon vanished than someone brought me a fresh horse.

'What for?' I asked.

'Wedding, of course,' answered Grathach, laughing so evilly that I was afraid for a moment that it was to be mine, since the Britons as a whole, Picts or not, are wont to make such arrangements without consulting the main actors. However, it was Pryderi's wedding, to Cicva, and I was honoured by being allowed to take part in the chase. For the Britons maintain the fiction, and fiction I assure you it is, that every woman is averse to marriage, and will flee from it as from a wolf. Therefore, Cicva mounted a horse of her own, a white one to be the more easily visible, and rode three times around her own house, while Pryderi and a dozen of us rode after her, whooping and screaming, till at the end of the third circuit, Pryderi rode up alongside his bride and struck her on the shoulder with a twig at which she collapsed into his arms. I must say that running your wife to earth is a good deal less dignified than buying her.

At the ensuing banquet I sat on Caw's right, the happy couple, as I hoped that they would be, having the top table to themselves. Now one expects a wedding feast to be lavish, with imported delicacies, like chestnuts and olives, and enormous quantities of staple foods like mutton and oatbread, and enough drink, cider and beer and mead, to bath in. But there was more to the feast than that, held as it was in Caw's great roundhouse. And I don't mean Taliesin, who ate only boiled beans and drank only water, for now he was among friends and no concealment was necessary.

I lay back and belched towards the end of the meal, for it was the first food I had had since dawn, and I had had a long hard ride, and then a rousing gallop to give me an appetite. And I wiped the sweat off my face with my napkin, and then I looked at the napkin. Fine linen, it was, and there were enough of them matched to give every guest the same, not merely to use but to take away afterwards. Egyptian they were, but not fancy, nothing to look at till you did look at them. They were expensive, and I ought to know, because I had handled them myself, or a batch very like them, the year before, and I remembered thinking that I couldn't afford them for my house, and I am not a poor man. Caw's clothes, too, were very good, not only the furs but the linen and wool, and Cicva's; and the old lady who bustled round and waited on them was using the remains of a silk dress for a duster, and in most places I knew, if a silk dress had gone that far it would still have been worth while to unravel it, thread by thread and weave it up again into something else. It puzzled me.

I looked at the plates we ate from, and the cups we drank out of. They were not silver, they were only pottery, but when you looked again, what pottery! No Briton ever threw those pots. They were made in Gaul, or perhaps even in Italy — I was too polite to turn them over to see the potter's mark, but I could see they were expensive, and yet nobody was upset when a cup was broken. It costs a mint of money just to transport the stuff, mostly on the packaging. The hangings on the wall were in good heavy wool, thick enough for blankets, woven in the spiral patterns I was used to now, and I know well how much time it takes to set up a loom to weave it — dearer than embroidered. And the tables were painted too, and the chairs, in those patterns, and not amateur work.

186

And yet there was a lot missing. All the things that strike the careless eye as signs of wealth were absent. There was no silver on the table, and no bronze either except a few spoons and a wine strainer, which was merely an ornament as there was no wine, and no pile of broken empty amphorae outside either. There was none of the rich and splendid enamel work that I had been seeing so much of, except for personal pieces like the belts that more important people wore. No, the casual eye, for instance that of the ill-trained and well-bribed local tax-collector, would not have seen any indication that this was not the house of an ordinary marsh farmer.

I said nothing about this. I would have liked to know but the easiest way to find out was just to say nothing. So I said nothing. That is the only way with Barbarians, just don't ask. Ask them anything and they freeze up and don't say a thing, or else they take pleasure in telling you the biggest lies they can imagine. But, of course, they *do* want, really, to tell you about how wonderful they are, and how clever, and if you don't ask them anything they finally burst, and they are so put off by this display of non-curiosity that they will often tell you the plain and simple truth. So I asked nothing, and at last, when everyone else was singing dismal cauldron songs, Caw, that tough old man, broke, and began to tell me the tale of the people who lived in the Mere.

'You will be wondering, doubtless, as so many do, how it is we live out here on the edge of the world. Pleasant and happy is life, and decent is death, though far we are from our homes and the graves of our kin. In Gaul once we lived, our fathers were men of power, on the edge of the Ocean that nobody ruled but we. We sailed our ships up and down the rim of the world, from Spain to the Scillies, to Ireland and Anglesey, and up to the land of fire on the edge of the ice. Great were the ships we built, and stout were their sides, of oak beams dowelled together with pegs of elm. Never use iron in ships or your end will come soon. The oak and the iron are foes, that fight to the death,

187

and we who worship the oak would never dare to take an iron knife with us into the grove. See how the Holy Man, who is priest of the oak, never touches iron, though he may hold Gold or bronze.

'So our fathers were Lords of the Sea, and carried their cargoes of tin and of copper, of corn and wine and Gold, and all the nations knew that they were proud and rich. But then *he* came, the bald old man of the South, eager and grasping to steal the whole of the world. He did not know the meaning of decency, no not he, and he did not even dare to meet us fairly. He came at us in rowing boats, whatever the wind. His men tied sickles on their long poles, and then whenever they got close to one of our ships, they would cut the halliards and bring down the great leather sail and if they could cut the stays the mast would go too.

'Conquered were the proud Venetii, beaten was the hope of the world, bankrupt and ruined and broken the kings of our nation. Those who were willing could stay and pay homage to bald-headed Caesar, the stinking oil-eater. But some of us said we could not abide it, we would go out and find a new country. We sailed to the north and we came to the marshes, a desolate land that no nation governed, and we built a town beneath the Glass Mountain. When we thought that all was recovered, Claudius came to conquer the island. How could we live in a settled city, where tax-gatherers might come to count and to number us? We left our town, we left our temple, we moved a few miles to live in the marshes. Here are we safe to live out our days, in hunger and hardship and bitter poverty. We are too poor and too insignificant for noble or tribune or quaestor to see us.'

'Yes,' I agreed, spitting out the stone from a dried plum from Dalmatia. 'Poverty is a dreadful thing.' I remembered the talk I had heard in Londinium. It was not conquest that hurt the Venetii — it had harmed, say, the Atrebates little. No, it was the Roman fiscal policy which insisted that all trade with Britain should go through the Channel ports, where it could be taxed, and the dreadful penalties inflicted not only on any Britons who dealt with smugglers but also on any merchants who might try, in Gaul, to hire a ship in the West and trade any other way. The Venetii had seen their ships destroyed, and even if they had been able to rebuild there would have been no further employment for them. But some of those ships still remained — I knew, I had once stolen one from Caw himself, and there might be others. If there were no others, what was I doing here? Oak-planked they were indeed, and pegged with elm, but on to frames of ash, and elm-decked, and these two woods had no quarrel with iron: and they were not rowed, but driven by a great lugsail of leather, that would let them beat into the wind. Were there indeed any left? And if not, where did Caw's wealth come from?

I wondered about that all through the evening. We were all very merry. At the end of the evening, Grathach and Nerthach complained, as we made our way to the house where we were to sleep, that I was very drunk: I must have been — they dropped me twice.

CHAPTER FOUR

I must say that Caw stood up to the drinking very well for his age. We drank till two hours before dawn, and the sun was scarcely beginning to rise when he woke me and hurried me out into the thin rain, clutching my cloak and sword.

Silently he led me along past the sleeping houses, set far apart, because it is a characteristic of the Britons that they hate their kinsmen and each man's ambition is to live where he cannot see his neighbour's smoke. We did not walk far, only to an arm of the marsh where there was a small boat, hollowed out of a single log, hidden under the branches of a willow. We got in and paddled away from the houses, north-west. I had the choice of either wearing my cloak and being hot and wet, or of taking it off and being cold and wet, in the strong west wind and driving rain. I was dead weary from lack of sleep. I soon had corns over my bottom from sitting on quite different places from the ones you use to ride a horse, and all the rest of me was stiff — there were so many muscles I had not used since I sailed into Ostia. After hours, all I wanted to do was to lie on the bank and die, but Caw hurried me on.

When we cleared the north edge of the Apple Hills, we could see the edge of the Lead Hills east of us, like a long cliff, and the column of smoke from the Mines, but only when we came, as sometimes we did, out of the patches of willow and alder that stood up out of the waters. Well after noon I was ready to refuse to go any farther, and the only thing that gave me any hope was the strong smell of the salt sea.

Neither of us spoke much, except what was necessary to keep her head the right way, and among the willows it was more like choosing roads in a city than steering a boat. But at last, of a sudden, Caw barked:

'Up there, left, up that backwater!'

We came left, into a narrow channel, which widened out as such inlets often do, into a broad expanse of shining mud. And there, beached, was a ship. A real ship, I tell you, not a skin boat or a single log, but a ship. This was one of the Venetii, all right. High she stood out of the water, or would stand when she was afloat, with sides of oak planks, and decks of elm, and a high poop to help her ride a following sea. She had a single mast stepped a little forward of amidships, and the yard was down on the deck, but there was no mistaking it — she was rigged with lugsail.

There she lay among the leafy willows, with a couple of men scraping the barnacles off her timbers. We pulled ourselves up a rope on to her deck. A man sitting at his ease in a shelter under the poop got up to meet Caw, bowing to him. He had First Mate written all over him, mainly in his attitude of extreme indolence while his men worked. Caw said to him:

'Keeping well is it you are, Madoc? This is him.'

'Oh, you, is it?' said Madoc to me. 'Here, have something to eat.'

He held out a plate, full of gobbets of some anonymous meat. On the bank, someone had a charcoal brazier and was frying some more. I looked at the food cautiously. You never know what Barbarians may, or may not, give you. They might well have been trying me with Swan, just for the fun of it. I asked:

'What is it?'

'If it's wearing it you are, then it's eating it you can be,' Madoc told me. 'Seal this is. Fresh, too — only killed three weeks ago.'

So I ate it. I looked around. The hatches were off, and there were a couple of men in the hold, trimming cargo, for the ship was obviously ready for sea, though where

191

the water was that could float her was a mystery. On the bank, men were loading panniers on to packhorses. The strange thing was, that the cargo being trimmed in the hold and the cargo in the panniers was the same — dull grey bricks. Lead, I thought. I asked Caw:

'Where do you get it?'

He knew what I meant. He grinned.

'From up there.' He pointed to the smoke on the Lead Hills.

'Buy it?'

'Aye . . . in a way. You see, there are men we know who go in and out of the mines, and carry in the earth coal they use to smelt the ore. And there are other men there, in the mines and in the melting shops, who will do a great deal for very little, because it is very little they have, nothing at all, you might say, except their lives, and a twist of rag about their loins. So they will do, you understand, anything for a bite of decent food, or a jug, or even a sip, of cider. And there was once we even smuggled a woman in, and she stayed a week, and made her fortune, but she said she wouldn't do it again — too tiring.

'So men who carry earth coal in carry lead out, and lead in again. I suppose you know, there is more in lead than lead.'

'Silver,' I breathed. 'There is always silver in lead.'

'Aye, silver, and that is why the legions work the lead here and farther north, and if it were not for the silver they get out of it they would not stay in this island at all. So we take, let us say, perhaps one ingot of new smelted lead in five, and north we go to the Picts, and there it is arrangements I have with men, kings mostly, who will cupellate it for me. But we have to cover it over somehow, because book-keepers and centurions would come very expensive to bribe, as you may imagine, so it is pure lead we bring back, and send it in with the coal.'

'No wonder you live so well in the Mere,' I told Caw. 'A very pretty scheme. It does you credit.'

'As long as no one finds out. The tax-collectors don't

192

notice what you have if there isn't Gold or silver on the table. And why shouldn't we live well? It is our land, and our hills, and our silver, and our lead. Why should we not charge a little rent?'

Then he drifted off into conversation with Madoc, and I sat down a little against the bulwarks, and somehow or other I fell asleep. When I woke up, my head now thoughtfully pillowed on a cushion of swansdown, we were, where I most love to be in ordinary times, at sea!

I leapt up, reaching for my sword, and cursing at Madoc, who was at the steering oar, and at Caw, who was conning us between the mudbanks, and this was difficult because we were, in general, working in the opposite direction to the one where the wind came from.

'What are you doing with me?' I demanded. It was clear that they were still on speaking terms because they had left me my sword. Caw answered, in his careful way, between orders to Madoc:

'It was thinking, I was, that if it is proposing you are to trade on the Northern Seas, then it is the realities of the situation you should be knowing, before it is any obligations you are taking on yourself and on your family.'

'Whatever the realities,' I replied, 'I am in too deep now to draw back.'

'But I am not,' said Caw, flatly. 'I have not yet decided whether I will entrust a ship of mine to you, and it is more I am wanting to know about how you behave at sea. And so I thought a short voyage would be a fine experience for you.'

'A short voyage? And what good will a short voyage do?' For I thought he meant a day and a night aboard. But he answered:

'We will be back for Samain. Seven weeks let us say.'

'Seven weeks? Seven *weeks!* No! Take me back! I have traced Rhiannon all this way, and now I have found the Lady, then I will not lose her again for you.'

'Quiet, boy,' said Madoc. 'It is in the Mere that Rhiannon must stay now, till Samain and past Samain to midwinter.'

'And there is no going back now, Mannanan,' added Caw, 'either for you or for us, because we held the ship a week to wait for you, and if we stay another day the weather will be too bad for us to return.'

There was nothing for it. A-voyaging I went, and if I were to tell you the whole story of the voyage, you would hear only the usual travellers' tales. We went to the land of the Western Picts in lead, and from there in wool and tanned leather to the Land of Norroway, and brought back walrus ivory and the hides of the tame deer to the land of the Picts where we loaded again with lead and silver, now separate. And I found, and it is true, that in these parts of Ocean, the waves at the end of the summer are as high, and the winds as wild, as anywhere in the Mediterranean in the depths of winter, when we prudent captains will not leave harbour. And more, I found that it is a common thing for the ships there to go altogether out of sight of land, not merely for a day or half a day, as we often may to cut across between two capes with a perishable cargo and an expensive crew, but for four or five days together between one island and another. And at the end, beating home south into a south-west gale, it took even all my strength and skill to hold her steady.

And you would not believe even the most ordinary stories I could tell, how we married Madoc to a mermaid when he was drunk, and how Caw won the crown for telling the saltiest story at the Salmon Feast of the Picts, and how we moored at an island so that Coth the son of Caw could cook for us, and it sank beneath him and left him floating, spouting out a cloud — oh, I could tell you tales for seven weeks of what we did in those seven weeks, and of each of them you would say, 'Oh yes, but I heard that tale of so-and-so.' So I will not bother.

But in seven weeks' time, we returned to the Mere, and we beached the ship where no man would find her. Then, in a skin boat, Caw and Madoc and I paddled back to Caw's house. And it was two days before the Samain Feast.

CHAPTER FIVE

My bad luck came at the Samain feast. It had to come, because there is no good luck lasts for ever. Samain is the feast at the beginning of November, when the Britons bring in their sheep from the hills to fold them in close to the farmhouse, safe from wolf and bear. And just as the animals are folded in, so the family and the nation are folded in, and the house is full not only of the living but also of the dead and those who are yet unborn.

Most people believe that the dead go down to Hades. There they exist for ever in dirt and rottenness, envious of the living, and therefore most people fear the dead. But not the Britons. Why, they say, should a man be afraid of the mother who bore him, and the father who fondled him and taught him to live? Why should he fear the grandmother who nursed him to sleep as a toddler and wiped away his tears when he fell over his own feet and kept for him the best titbits of the kitchen and the sweetest apples? Why should a man fear the comrades who fell at his side in battle or slipped from his outstretched hands into the waves, or the loved ones who died in his arms of fever or dysentery?

No, the Britons know better. Their Samain Feast is a feast indeed, and the Happy Dead are welcome. And so are all wayfarers. That is why I sat at the feast next to Caw, who as befits the head of the house sat with blackened face upon a ploughshare. And next to me, coming out of the mists the day before, only a day after we had landed from the northern seas, was the Setanta.

Towards dawn, when we had drunk and eaten everything

in sight and were too full to go to the larder for more, the Irishman turned to business, as was his custom, always optimistic that other people would be more fuddled than he was and easier to do business against, and always wrong. He said:

'I am ready. I have a fianna in the Hills. I could move now, if you had the arms, but I would rather you waited till the spring.'

'I must wait till the spring,' I told him. 'The arms will not be ready till then.'

'But have you a ship?'

I looked at Caw. I waited to hear. It might all have been in vain. The Master of the Western Seas said:

'You have a ship. You have a ship for this trade, and for all trade you may wish to do across the Irish Sea.'

Far in the east, the dawn had begun, over the Lead Hills. In my impiety and joy and pride I forgot the Gods Below that all in Britain worship, and I forgot that Apollo had bade me worship him no more. I stood up on the bale of straw that had been my seat, and I lifted my hands to the advancing Chariot, and I called as I had done all my two-eyed life:

'All Hail and Blessing to the Unconquered Sun!'

And fate came on me, and I slipped from the edge of the bale. The hilt of my sword tore at my side, and I knew that the old wound was opened. I felt the blood run down, and I screamed, and I fainted with the pain.

CHAPTER SIX

That day after Samain, they took me to Caw's house, where he lived now alone, a widower. I lay on a bed, my shirt off, while everybody who had any pretensions to medical skill or knowledge — and the two do not always go together — fussed around me like so many broody hens.

Taliesin had the first try. He looked wisely at the nasty gash, oozing blood and yellow pus through the bandages.

'The sword is no use. I suppose the weapon that did the original wound—'

'Lost long ago, on the Amber Road,' I groaned. It hurt me to breathe deeply.

'Then I am sure you will not be having the gallstone of a male ass, which is a sure cure for such afflictions.'

'In my wallet.'

Taliesin looked a little disappointed. However, he picked it out, and examined it for a while. I said:

'Have you used it before?'

'I know all about it.'

'Perhaps you do, but have you used it?'

'Well, no, not in the . . . well, it isn't flesh, is it. Should we say in the lava? Rub with it, don't I?'

'And not too hard. It's got a surface like pumice stone. *Aaaaah!*' It hurt, too.

'I'd better put something soothing on it. I don't suppose you've got any lion fat . . .'

'The yellow pot.'

'Oh. Powdered ostrich egg-shell?'

'In that twist of parchment — the one with the green lines on it.'

'Ground mummies' testicles?'

'In the small phial. Be careful, it's hard to come by.'

'Do you think I don't know that? And Phoenix ash?'

'The vulture-skin bag.'

'At least, I've got a pestle and mortar. I think I know the right proportions.'

He beat together the ointment in fury, using some very appropriate incantations. He laid across the wound two hairs from the head of a blonde virgin, and that is something very hard to find in the Summer Country, smeared on the ointment with nine strokes of a swan's feather, being the proper instrument to my clan, and bound it up with a strip of the horseblanket last laid on the back of a white gelding. I must say that in their knowledge of medical science the Britons do not lag behind doctors in more civilised countries: they only suffer a great deal from shortage of quite elementary necessities, like bottled moondust and salamander skin. I made a mental note that the family might as well begin business in this field in the islands.

For about two days, the wound seemed to mend, and at last I was so bold as to get out of bed and walk about. Nothing went wrong for at least an hour, and then I coughed, and the whole scar opened again. It hurt dreadfully. Now Caw came to look at it, and he had a remedy which was beautiful in its simplicity. He merely clapped on to my side a hunk of whale's fat, blubber they call it, and tied it there with a length of whale skin, reasoning that the strength of the whale would pass into me and give me energy to resist all strains. The blubber was strong enough, all right. The fish had been dead for three months, and when at last I got up and went out of doors, people could smell me coming half a mile away, and all the dogs of the Summer Country came to the point of interest, and some even from farther away. And I did well enough, since the smell meant that I could endure to breathe only in the most gentle fashion, but at last, through sheer boredom, I yawned, and it was all to do again.

Then Cicva decided she would take a hand. First she washed off the whale blubber, much to Caw's annoyance, but she pooh-poohed him away.

'Men!' she said. 'They think that they know everything.'

'But instead, *you* know everything, my girl,' I teased her, but of course she didn't see it and answered:

'The only things I didn't know, you taught me.'

'Thank you. Now what are you going to use?'

'First of all, spider's web, because although it is so thin it holds the weight of the spider, which is a great beast in comparison.' So a whole web, taken with the dew on it, and lifted from the bush and brought in whole and unbroken — and how many webs the children of the place spoiled entirely I have no knowing, but there must have been mourning throughout the halls of Ariadne — she laid across the wound.

'And now some soothing ointment we use a great deal where I come from, up in the Silures. Most of it is goose grease, and that provides the softening. But there are other things my grandmother taught me to use, such as meadow saffron and foxglove, and they will stop the pain and the itching. Now, we have that on thick, and then I will tie it up in a strip of linen — here, one of Caw's napkins will do, if I tear it up like this . . .'

I said that there was no evidence of poverty in the houses in the Mere, and no expense would have been spared if there had been anything to spend on. However, it was plain that the Britons here were doing as well as any civilised doctor.

'Now, what I really would like to do, and what would do you good,' said Cicva, 'would be to tie up both your arms so that you can't scratch. It's scratching that opens it every time, whatever we do.'

'I don't scratch.'

'Indeed you do, you scratch like half a dog with two dog's fleas.'

'Well, and how do you expect me to behave with this itching like it does as long as I lie still? And as soon as

199

I move it tears, and then I can't feel it itching for pain and bleeding.'

'Then shall I tie your hands? There's not much you can do with them, lying here.'

'No, you may not tie my hands. I refuse to have anyone tie my hands.'

'All right,' she said crossly. 'There's no need to make such a fuss about it. It's not good for you — or for me, either.'

Well, I know that it is quite common for a doctor to prescribe restraint for a patient, but I wasn't an ordinary patient, I knew too much for that. Besides, I knew very well that no human means could heal the wound. I had offended the Sun Above and the Gods Below. Only those Gods together could heal me.

All the human attempts followed the same pattern. First the side felt better, the pain subsided, and then the itch. Next, there would be a firm clean scab over the wound. All would be going well. Then I would get up to walk. And in a moment, all would be undone, the wound would be open, and the blood run down.

'Nothing there is for it now,' said Pryderi, after two weeks of this, 'but seeing Rhiannon.'

'If it comes to that?' I asked angrily, 'why isn't she here? Either she belongs to me, or I belong to her, as Taliesin said, and in either case she ought to show a little interest.'

'And is it not for you to be showing a little interest in her!' countered Taliesin. 'It's carrying you we'll be doing.'

Hueil and his brother Coth the Cook took the ends of the bed on which I lay, and moved out of the house into the rain. Cicva threw my sealskin cloak over me. I could not remember now how long it had been raining; I could not remember when it had not been raining. The edge of the Mere was now nearer to the houses. My bearers' feet splashed through what had been firm meadows. We took a narrow path between the flooded fields, between clusters of willows that stood leafless out of the water. We came to the Deep Pool of the Mere.

Many are the gates to the World Below. Out on the green sea there are whirlpools, that engulf ships and men, and spin them down into the green dark, and these are the least known, and the greatest and the most powerful, because there is no return. But on land, there are the mouths of volcanoes, spouting fire and lava, and into these men had leapt to seek those who have gone before. There are caves both in the mountains and on the seashore, and it is in these that men have buried their dead, and it is into these that wise women have gone to speak with those who have left us and who now speak with the wise of all the ages. Out on the level plains there are marshes and bogs and places of Green Moss, and on the level shore there are sinking sands and into all these men have thrown their sacrifices to those who rule our deaths, believing, as some do, that no ordeal is as grim as death, and that those who rule our lives may hurt us as they wish, if so be they do not kill us. Life, say some, is worth the clinging to in spite of all indignities. I do not agree. I have lived long and I have travelled far, and I have seen men suffer things to which death is a feast. But whatever one's opinions on this, who can doubt the wisdom of making offerings by casting booty into a bog?

Of all the gates into the World Below, the surest and the deepest and the swiftest are the Black Pools in rivers and lakes and marshes. Bottomless beyond reach of plumbline, their surface smooth and unruffled by storm or rain, they lie beneath steep cliffs or smooth banks, and there for many generations wise men have come to make their offerings.

Such a pool there was in the Mere, where the river flowed against a bluff. In a backwater, the water gleamed no more than lead, the surface stirred no more than does a mirror. Only sometimes the great pike moved, hunting for what he could catch, and there was enough, for it was to the hungry Gods Below that the Britons of the Mere gave the scraps of food that even the dogs left. And here, on the bluff above the Deep Pool, Rhiannon sat.

She sat on a tripod, looking to the east, over the dark water. Above her head they had built a booth of alder boughs, thatched with the rushes of the Mere. Her food was the broth of nettles, and a fungus that grows on the trunks of trees, thrusting out in a fleshy shelf. I knew it as a boy: we called it Dead Men's Ears.

Rhiannon looked out across the flooded, sodden Mere. Little pools were become great lakes. Lagoons where in summer a man might wade a mile and never wet his knees would now float a trireme. The river, in the dry of the year a faint drift of leaves and twigs across the marsh, was now a strong current, sweeping whole trees to the sea, faster than a man might run. As a galley of pleasure is beached for the winter, her mast unstepped, her oars unshipped and stacked against the eaves of the boathouse, her sail of scarlet linen furled and carried under shelter, her cushions of velvet and of cloth of gold taken to grace my lady's boudoir, gilt flaking and paint peeling from her sides — so sat Rhiannon above the Mere. She was dressed in rough sacking, black, all black. She wore no jewels. Her hair had ceased to shine. Her hands, through hunger, were transparent, only the blue veins opaque. Above the waste, hardly sheltered from the rain, unwashed, uncombed, her nails uncut, she fasted for . . .? She waited for . . .?

Only the birds did not forsake her. The rooks cawed in the trees across the pool, the heron stood and watched. The kingfisher dived as if to seek out the sleeping swallows. Starlings hungrily combed the grass.

The sons of Caw put down the bed. They went away. I spoke:

'Help me, my Mother.'

Rhiannon did not answer. She sat and looked across the marshes. I asked her again:

'Help me, my Mother, for your birds' sake.'

Still, she did not reply. I waited a very long time, an hour or more. Then, I took courage.

'Rhiannon, my Rhiannon. By him that gave you to me, I challenge you. Speak to me. Who are your birds?'

Still, for a moment she said nothing. Then we heard the sound of wings in the east, and we both watched as the great birds went over us as an arrow. And after that, she sang: at last I heard that splendid voice again.

Spirits now wending
At full life's ending
As Wild Geese flying
Not regretting, sighing,
In trust advancing
Through low clouds dancing
Faint like stars glowing
To new lives going
Passing and fleeting
Sounds of wings beating
Living, not dying
As Wild Geese flying.

That was all she sang, and she sang it only once. Yet it was not an hour after dawn when we heard the wings, and when she finished singing it was the grey twilight of a December afternoon under the clouds of Britain. Then she spoke, not sang:

'Tell Pryderi: the goose has flown.'

'Have you no word for me? Can I not be healed?'

'Oh, Mannanan, my son, my father, my brother, my husband! Come to me at midwinter. Come when the Thorn flowers.'

Uncalled, Hueil the son of Caw and Coth the son of Caw came forward. They picked up my bed, and they carried me back to the house.

I spoke first to Pryderi.

'The goose has flown, Pryderi. Rhiannon said, the goose has flown.'

He bent down, and he took ashes from the fire and threw them on his head. He smashed a pot that stood by, and with the sharp edge of a broken fragment he slit open the front of his shirt. He said:

'I am going to the Demetae.'

Madoc, who stood by, spoke:

'You cannot face the winter seas alone.'

They went out. Cicva, silent, threw the end of her shawl over her face, and followed. Caw watched them go, then:

'It is no kin of mine. They will lay him in his house, new built, on his bed new made. Every man who comes will bring a stone, and they will fill the house about him with stones and earth, and they will build the house about outside with walls of cut stone and they will whiten it. And that is an end of him. And an end of much more, too.'

'An end of whom?' I asked. Caw did not answer. Suddenly, with the air of a man throwing off unpleasant thoughts, he asked:

'And Rhiannon — did she say nothing to you?'

'She sang one short song, that lasted a day. And she showed me the birds, and what they are.'

'But for yourself?'

'Caw — when do the thorn trees blossom in this country?'

'If Rhiannon told you — well, then, it is a secret thing above all the other secrets of the Mere, and there is not a Roman who knows of it. Listen to me.

'Below the Glass Mountain there is a tree, and to look at it, you would think it no different from any other thorn tree, growing where it do on the firm ground on the edge of the Mere. But every seventh year, something strange do happen, and every seventh seventh year, it is something wonderful that happens. Because, every seventh year, the thorn do bloom, and blossom, and come into flower, and that not in the spring, but at the middle of winter, and strange that is because there is no reason for any feast or worship of the Gods at midwinter which is a dreadful and bitter time. Now every seventh year, it is one branch or another only that flowers, and anyone may come and see the tree, and the tree alone. But every seventh seventh year, then it is the tree that blossoms, every branch, and it is then that the other holy things are shown, if the right people are there to show them.'

'And the right people are . . .?'

'Think, boy. They must all come by land, because the thorn came to us from the sea. And the people are a virgin princess of the days of long ago, and a priest of the days that are lately gone, and a pregnant queen of the times that are.'

'And this year is a . . .?'

'A seventh seventh year, and then the thorn is given great power over all those who come to it. And come to it you shall, Mannanan, though it was some pretext we were going to find to send you away for the midwinter. But if it is bidden you are, then bidden you are. Lie still, boy, lie still in my house till midwinter, because it is no more than twenty nights to go.'

The Britons, unlike all the rest of mankind, count their time not by days but by nights, and all their feasts are feasts of nights and not of days. And in the winter it is understandable, because the night is longer than the day. So I lived in Caw's house, and in the days, Hueil and Coth took me out, on my bed, to the lakeside, and I fished for pike, and never caught one. And in the evenings, Cicva would come from her empty home and sup with her grandfather and me, and she taught me to play the games of Fichel, that the Britons play in preference to all games of dice. And in truth I did not really enjoy Fichel, because there is no chance in it at all, or delightful uncertainty, but a game of Fichel is played on a board with men, and is entirely a matter of skill and wit. There are a hundred different kinds of Fichel, and Cicva taught me to play them all, in return, she said, for my teaching her to palm dice and lose the pea under the three cups. And again and again she said to me:

'Be careful, Mannanan: you think that you have found your Lady, but watch in case someone does not move the cups again.'

CHAPTER SEVEN

The solstice came and went, and the lengthening of the days became noticeable, just. Before the solstice, the rains stopped, and the wind came round slowly through north to north-east. This wind blew cold, and there were one or two clear nights, and in the mornings the frost was thick on the grass, and there was a thin film of ice on the little pools. And yet, the time of year being what it was, it was mild, compared with the winters we had up on the Amber Road. Then, on the solstice, the sky covered over with low grey clouds, and the wind dropped, and all was very still and quiet, and I wondered how Rhiannon could still live there in her house, open towards the east, above the Dark Pool.

Towards evening, the snow started to fall. It fell steadily, in great light flakes, like the feathers of the wild geese. It covered everything, and made the grey light of the morning look dimmer still. In Britain, you get used to living in a perpetual twilight: but the white snow makes it less bearable. It fell all through a night and a day and the night after, till it was, as Caw said, the depth of a chariot wheel, or as I saw, up to the top of a man's thigh, if he cared to step into it.

Then we had a day without snow, and the sky was blue and it was bitter cold again, so that although the sunshine melted the snow on the surface, at night the moisture froze to leave a layer of ice over it. We lay close around the fire that night, with all the blankets and furs and sheepskins we could find heaped over us, and yet we were all cold.

In the first light, Madoc wakened me. He had a lamp, and I looked round to see that I was in an empty house.

Madoc had been the last to try to treat my side, and he had merely made me lie still, and told me to wash it well each day with warm water. Then he had gone out into the winter sea, and I had not seen him nor heard that he had returned. But here he was, making me take my shirt off so that he could see the healthy scab forming.

'That will do,' he said. 'You will just be able to walk to the Glass Mountain.'

'I am not in any fit condition to walk,' I told him. 'You can say what you like, but do you know what it feels like when that place tears open? If I'm going that far, I'll have a horse, or there ought to be enough water now to float a boat almost up to it.'

'Everybody walks to the Glass Mountain at midwinter.' He was firm on that, and as it seemed to be matter of religion, I agreed to try.

'I'll come when I've had my breakfast,' I told him.

'Decent people go to this rite fasting,' and as he seemed as ready to insist on that, I pulled on all the clothes I could find, with my sealskin cloak over everything and my sword handy under it, and I began to walk. At least we didn't have to go barefoot, as some mysteries would have had us do.

We crunched across the icy surface of the snow, watching our breaths before our faces. Then, into the marsh. We pushed by willows, and the icy twigs cut across our faces like iron wires. The log road beneath our feet was covered in a layer of glass, and I feared to slip and tear my side again. The streams and pools were edged with ice, but never fully covered in, or strong enough to take a man's weight. Most of the paths we had used to come from the Glass Mountain were under running water, and we had to take awkward twisting ways, known only to the cattle and the deer, and the badger even, who made them. To push through a maze in twilight, with never a firm footing, with nothing dry, with the clouds threatening new snow, oh, there are better ways of spending a day in midwinter. Even when, at noon, the clouds cleared, it became no pleasanter, because it got even colder.

Sometimes, now, we could even see the Glass Mountain standing up in front of us beyond its screen of bare branches. A little column of smoke rose from before it, vertical in the still air, white against the blue sky. We walked in silence.

We were not the only people on the road. There was no one before us, but here and there, at forks in the way, we would find little bunches of men, and women and children, waiting to fall in behind us. They were all laden with bundles of wood, and with bags. They too went in silence, except that now and then, from behind us, we would hear voices raised in a melancholy hymn to the Cauldron:

> Cauldron our hope, in frost and snow,
> Bring warmth in plenty from below.
> O'er flowing panniers, laden carts,
> Flame out of blackness warm our hearts.

I could not have sung. My face was so stiff with the cold that I could not move my lips. I could feel that the end of my nose was dead. My moustaches froze to my cloak so that to turn my head hurt. My side was throbbing and hot: I waited for the tearing pain, the warm that I now knew so well. Let no one say that what I won on this journey I won without pain.

At last, at last, we came out of the Mere, we climbed the sides of the Glass Mountain. We came close to the farm built against the rock. Now, I noticed what I must have seen before, that the branches of a tree showed above the fence. Leafless they were and winter-barren, but, plainly, a thorn. There were people standing about outside the closed gates. Closest of all, I saw Pryderi sitting on the snow by a brazier in which a fire of earth coal was burning. Hueil was with him. I came to them and sat down. It was nearly evening, and I was hungry and tired, sweating from the walk and yet freezing with the cold.

More groups of people sat down around and behind us, each group with its brazier, or lighting a fire of wood on the bare ground, sweeping up the snow into windbreaks. They sat, quietly, waiting. Even the children were silent, and did not run about or play. When I was a little warmer, I stood up and looked the way we had come. All the side of the hill, all the firm ground around it, all the road by which we had come, was speckled with fires, mirroring in the cold clear air the stars above us. It was now quite dark. There was a constant murmur from the people. Not the angry shouting you hear from a mob in riot, not the cheerful turbulence you hear from the crowd waiting in an arena for the Games to start, not the hubbub you hear from a market crowd: it was the gentle hum of voices lowered in reverence, saying meaningless things simply because the burden of keeping silent was too much.

Neither could I keep silent. I asked Pryderi: 'Who guards the shrine? Is it Druids?'

He turned to me. It was the first time I had spoken to him since he had heard me tell him Rhiannon's message. Now, as his cloak opened, I saw he wore a new belt, a simple one, only a threefold chain of Gold. Only that, only Golden links that would have held a bull, only the price of half a province. He answered me seriously. Gone now was his usual air of bantering superiority:

'No, boy. The Holy Ones are gone. Do you think we would have made poor Taliesin trudge all the way down from the other side of the Wall if there had been a Druid anywhere nearer in the island?'

'And why Rhiannon?'

'Family tradition. And once this is over, she won't have to do it again, unless she's still alive and a virgin in another forty-nine years.'

'Do what?'

'Very little. You shall see soon enough.'

'And where did you find a queen?'

'It is the wife of the King of the Demetae, that is Queen among the Silures in her own right, if she had her rights.'

There were too many people there, and too many people missing, for me to understand. I sat down and watched the stars go round. Sometimes people sang. Others came past us, seeking their places to wait. One man, squint-eyed, recognised me, and bent down to whisper into my ear, in Greek:

'It began with a word.'

I was in no mood for riddles or mysteries, and I thought his accent vile, so I told him sharply enough, but again in a whisper:

'The only word for you, brother, is *off*!!'

He went on. It was close to midnight. I looked across the eastern sky, from the Bear to Orion. They had reached their summit, they hung poised for the descent into morning. Others looked too. Everywhere, men and women were getting up, and looking towards the farmyard. There was a smell in the air, a smell of anticipation, of excitement, as strong as woodsmoke, as distinctive as a mask. Pryderi stood, and I stood too. There was a sound of rattling at the gate. Everybody heard it. Now nobody was seated. We stood, Pryderi and I, in the very front of the crowd, and we saw the gate open.

Taliesin opened the gate. He shone there as he had shone in the temple in the Mere, but now he shone more splendidly. He wore his mistletoe, fastened by a brooch of Gold wire a span long. Above it he wore a collar, a Golden half-moon that covered all his breast. On his left arm he wore an archer's wristguard, as if to take the blow of the returning bowstring when he had loosed the arrows of the sun, and this too was of Gold, and it covered his arm from wrist to elbow. His Golden sickle hung from a belt of a sevenfold Golden chain. The buckles of his sandals were of Gold. And on his head the oak-leaves were beaten of Gold.

He flung wide the gate. We saw into a farmyard. The ground was frozen, ridged with the coming and going of cattle, but cleared of snow. There were piles of hay and straw. The barn, built at one side of the yard, against the rock, was wattle sided and roofed with thatch, like any other barn. But there was another gate, in the opposite fence, and this too was opened. As Taliesin guarded one gate, so did Caw guard the other, dressed in his whaleskin and white bear fur, ivory-belted and ivory-crowned. But he, too, wore a collar, a half-moon of Gold. For tonight, then, he was divine, for this night, once in forty-nine years, he was, surely, Dylan, the Son of the Wave, that ruled all the seas of Britain. But if so, then tonight who was Taliesin? I did not ask, but Pryderi breathed the answer:

'Mabon.'

I should have known. This was indeed the Glorious Youth.

In the middle of the yard was the tree, not a tall one, just an ordinary thorn. Somehow it all seemed full of a coming and going of people, though if you tried to look it was impossible actually to see anyone, only the general impression of movement. Then from Pryderi came the spark of light, struck from flint with an iron blade. He kindled a torch, and soon others were lighting torches, fresh, not from their fires. The space where we stood, and somehow the farmyard itself, was now as bright as day.

And then, there was movement. Not in the yard, but above it. There was a breath of the east wind. The branches swayed. And even as we watched, the whole tree burst into blossom. We saw the buds open before our very eyes. In the time it takes a man to count up to a hundred, we saw the branches covered with flowers, white they must have been, but in the glare of the red torchlight they looked pink.

The two people came from the barn and stood before the tree. Taliesin stood back from the gate. Pryderi took me by the arm and led me through into the farmyard. We bowed to Mabon, but he was not the one we had come to see, nor Dylan-Caw, leaning on his eight-foot steering oar. We passed towards the tree.

The women stood on either side of the tree. First, I saw Cicva. She was dressed as a Roman matron, richly and splendidly, if a trifle out of fashion, and even there I found space to wonder, irreverently, whether the clothes had been stored away for forty-nine years. Her tunic was of white silk, with a Gold-embroidered hem and girdle to match, shining in the torchlight. Her shawl was of Indian cotton, trailing to her heels. Her hair was piled on her head, built up on a pad, adding half a foot to her height, and capped with a gleaming diadem set with emeralds and Amber. Her hands were loaded with rings set with the rubies and diamonds of India. Three months pregnant, she stood proudly there, and in her hands she carried a spear, a great long iron spear on an ash shaft. For a moment I had hope, but then I saw this was no spear I had ever handled. Just an ordinary legionary pilum.

But beyond her stood Rhiannon, all in black. Her clothes were of wool, not the fine wool of the fat sheep the Romans brought to the island, but the coarsest of coarse wool from the little native sheep that you don't see any more except up in the wildest hills. Coarse as sacking it was, and not even dyed black, but shorn from black lambs, black as the earth coal. About her neck was a necklace of jet beads, strung on a thong of deer hide, and another of mussel shells. Her hair hung unbound, uncombed, on her shoulders. On her left wrist, where her gown, rough cut, unhemmed, sewn of one piece, left her arms bare, she wore an archer's wristguard, but this was of polished stone, of polished flint. And in her hands she held . . . what? A cauldron . . .? a dish . . .? a cup . . .?

Pryderi led me forward to the tree. I knew now, untold, what to do. I rolled up my shirt, tore off the bandage, hurt though it may, to show the bleeding, festering wound. Cicva reached forward the point of the spear and touched the wound. Rhiannon reached forward the cup, made, I saw, of turned olive-wood; I thought, a strange thing to find here, though common enough in Syria. She held it to my lips, and I drank the wine, sour as vinegar, bitter as defeat, sweet as death. I felt weak and faint. I wished to go out through the farther gate, but Pryderi guided me to lean against the wall behind the tree.

There I sat, for hours and watched the crowds go by.

212

I saw the colours of every kingdom in Britain, and outside it. I saw the shields and badges of every clan and every family. There were lead-miners and copper-miners and diggers of the earth coal, and smiths in iron and bronze and Gold. There were fishermen of salmon, and men who went out on to the wide ocean to catch whales and men who dived to take oysters for their pearls and men who dredged limpets and mussels for food. I saw the old women who dig for cockles, and glean in the fields, I saw men who earn their bread as shepherds, and those who spend their lives hunting bear and wolf and the tall deer. There were men who break horses, and men who drive cattle along the Green Roads to feed the cities. There were merchants and innkeepers and brothel-keepers from the towns, and men who had sold themselves to the Romans to collect taxes, and men who hid in the hills rather than pay them, weavers and dyers and fullers, money-lenders and bankers. And above all there were the peasants, men who grew oats for themselves and wheat for the Army, and wore themselves into the grave trying to satisfy tax-collector and rent-collector and wife and child.

They were of all ranks. I saw King Casnar the painted Pict go by, in his red and green, and I thought that there were Romans enough who would give a year's pay to take him alive inside the Wall. I saw Leo Rufus, who had been so proud of being almost a Roman, yes, he came. I saw Gwawl go by, in his black and white shirt, and he saw me, and did nothing. Each came past, and drank of the cup, and if he was ill or hurt or deformed or maimed, there he was touched with the spear. And all came in silence, and — this I have never seen in any temple or at any rite before — no man was asked to pay. You may believe that or not as you wish, because it is the greatest wonder I ever saw, but it is true.

Only one man broke the silence. He was a short man with a squint. He saw the cup and touched it — and then he did not drink, but shouted in his barbarous Greek:

'False! False and unclean! Be not yoked with unbelievers.'

213

And he ran out into the night, but as he went Cicva lunged at his eyes with her spear, and he never squinted after that.

At last, the sky in the east grew pink, beyond the hill. Still the column pressed on, hurrying now. Then, of a sudden, the cock crew. Taliesin stepped forward and bolted the gate in the face of the men next in line. From the crowd outside there came a low moan of disappointment: nothing more. The ceremony was over, that was all. Anyone else could now wait for forty-nine years more. The last of the crowd passed through the far gate. Caw shut it after them.

The cock crew again. The Epiphanies of the Gods passed into the barn. After a little, the cock crew a third time. The two woman came out into the farmyard again, and the birds burst into a song in the winter morning. Now the two were dressed as I had always seen them. Cicva was in a plain blouse and skirt, but now, she too wore a belt of three-fold Gold, Rhiannon hid her splendid clothes beneath her even more splendid cloak of white and yellow silk.

The women came to where I sat. Caw and Taliesin, themselves again, followed. They all sat down. We huddled together for warmth, pulling the sealskin cloak over us, shivering for weariness. We slept beneath the dying torches.

Suddenly, we all came awake together. The sun was not high, we could not have slept more than an hour at most. We all stood up, rubbing the sleep from our eyes and remembering how long it was since we had eaten, and shivering in the cold winter air and eyeing the grey cloud that was beginning to drift in again from the sea, for the wind was now from the north-west. The wind has changed, I thought, The world has changed. There is something strange and new about me.

I turned to look down at Rhiannon. She was on her knees. I reached down and drew her to me, to her feet. I made her lean on my left arm: she was frail as a bird from her long fast. Then I realised what was strange about my world. Half a day before I could have supported nobody. I held her a little way from me. With my other hand I rolled up my shirt. I looked at my side. The running sore was healed, and my side showed the old scar as it had been when I first came into the Mere.

I let Taliesin help Rhiannon. I drew my sword and cut off the hem of the long silk cloak. I sheathed the sword and went into the barn.

Inside, it was just like any other barn, bare-walled, with bales of hay and straw lying about. I looked up into the rafters, and there I could just see the shaft of the spear. The wooden cup stood on the floor in the corner. I went to the rock face. I looked for the signs, for the stains of libations of wine and fat. I pushed aside the hay, and found the sacred place, a crack in the rock, a deep dark hole. I greased the blade with goose grease and lions's fat from my wallet. I sheathed it again, and I wrapped the scabbard in the gleaming silk. I thrust the weapon, point down into the hole. It went well down, but when it grated on the bottom I could still touch the hilt. The crevice was narrower at the mouth than inside. I could curl my hand around the hilt, but I could not then draw the blade out. The sword would stay there till the Gods willed someone should take it. At least, *I* had left some offering for my cure.

I went out again into the open air. Caw opened the gate, and we left the farmyard. The hillside was still full of people, all the people who had been there the night before. Every group had lit fires. We joined Madoc and Hueil, who were cooking, with a group of people from the houses in the Mere. There must have been a hundred fires close by, and from each of them came the smell of cooking, and a smell that I never thought to meet in all the Isle of Britain. Everywhere I could smell roast goose!

I sat down beside Pryderi, who had a black pudding in his fist. Everyone was handed a platter of roast goose, everyone except me. They brought me something else, that looked like goose indeed, but when I tasted it, I knew it — I was eating swan.

Everyone was laughing and blaspheming as they ate the sacred foods of their clans. Caw was telling Rhiannon, without shame, the story that had won him the crown among the Western Picts. It was like Saturnalia, that I knew well all my friends in Rome would be keeping that day. After the rite comes the time of laughter; when the strain of piety and sacrifice and of touching holy things that may blast and obliterate the unclean, is past, then forbidden acts are lawful and the topsy-turvy feast begins. We in the south have forgotten the rite, and keep only the topsy-turvy time. I leaned across Rhiannon, who was eating roasted skylarks on a spit, and I asked Caw, when he had finished:

'What does the rite mean? To whom are the spear and the cup sacred?'

He replied, 'We haven't the least idea.'

'What, you don't know?' I looked incredulously at Taliesin. He belched — his platter had been full of all kinds of meat and he was now sucking the marrow bone of a sheep — and told me:

'No, not these in particular. All cups and bowls and cauldrons are all weapons, especially spears, are or may be sacred here. Many places had their sacred cauldrons before the Romans came. But until, oh, just ninety-eight years ago, there was no cauldron here on the Glass Mountain, and even if there were there would have been no such great ceremony made, because there were so many at other shrines, and this place is inconvenient to get to. But, of course, the Romans have destroyed the other shrines, and that is why we hide this last vessel and worship it only in secrecy, and we pay it the same respect as we would to any other cauldron of life. That is the meaning of this rite, of the Druid, and the pregnant queen and the virgin princess.'

He paused to suck his bone, and Caw took up the tale:

'But as to how this cup and the spear came here, it is a strange story. Soon after the Venetii my fathers came here, not long before the Roman conquest, there came here

216

by sea an old man, a Syrian, I think, who said he wanted to find a place where he could settle and fast and pray till he died. Now that is just the kind of thing a Druid will often do, and so they let him build a little house under the rock, where the barn is now. He brought with him three things: he had the spear, and he had the cup, and he had a sprig of the thorn. He said they were precious and holy, and there is no reason why we should not take his word for it. And he worshipped them till he died, and that was not very long, and now so do we. But he never told us why they were holy.'

So that was all, I thought. They were not even very old, or anything to do with the spot, or even with the ceremony. But I was certainly healed.

CHAPTER EIGHT

When we went back to the houses in the Mere, life was quiet for a few weeks more. Rhiannon lived in Cicva's house, because she had been much weakened by her long fast and the emotional ordeal of the midwinter night. I lived with Caw still, and I went to see Rhiannon frequently, and heard her tales of the great days of the kings of the Isle of Britain, such as how the Great King Lear had two good daughters who cherished him in his old age, and how he was set against them and tempted to his death by his youngest daughter, and how she came herself to a violent and well-deserved end. But while I listened and tried to put these tales in poetry in their own language, I wondered what I was to do with Rhiannon when she was well. I could hardly take her home to the Old City, even if she had been granted to me, and in return I had been granted to her, and I could not be hers, I was Phryne's and I had sworn to Phryne, jocularly, but validly enough, in parting, that I would sleep with no stranger till I saw her again.

But in less than a month after the Midwinter Feast, Pryderi came to me and said:

'Is it not seeing your other friends you ought to be?'

'There's no hurry,' I told him. 'It can wait until the spring comes.'

'It is necessary for me to go to that region,' he replied, 'and there may be no other chance, and true it is, and you know it, that unless I take you there is no finding the way.'

That was true. I looked at the black winter and I shuddered, but go I had to, saying goodbye to Rhiannon. First, Pryderi took a log boat, and we slipped down through the

218

Mere towards the sea. The snows had melted — Britain is not like Germany, where the snow comes and lies for months. The Mere now was full, all the lagoons were great lakes where a man might drown a dozen times before he reached the bottom. The currents ran strong, and tree trunks and branches and dead sheep and all the other rubbish bobbed around us. We paddled hard into the north-west wind all the short day till we came near the mouth of the river, and there we found an empty hut on the shore where we slept the night.

Pryderi knew where to look for a skin boat. At the dawn we set off again in this, and I now realised that he proposed to paddle it across the Severn Sea. A man well may think hard before he sets out to sea anywhere in February: to go out on to the Severn Sea, and to do it in such a frail vessel — well, I kept on thinking that we must be both mad. But Pryderi kept on telling me that the skin boat was the only craft that would stay afloat.

I could never understand why a skin boat did float at all. It is a companionable way to travel, as the Britons' boats are nearly round, and the two men sit side by side on the single thwart. But how do they float? Everyone knows that a ship floats because the weight of the timbers press down on the water and the heavier the ship the better she will float, which is why you must make the keel of a ship out of the biggest and thickest tree trunk that you can find. And skin boats really have no weight to press down on the water, being made out of wicker and leather only.

We went down towards the smell of the salt water, past the backwater where the ship was hidden, or had been hidden, and between the high banks of the river. Soon, perhaps we were at sea, because the water was brackish, but in a maze of channels among wide banks of mud. It was the tides, of course. There is no rational explanation for them. It is quite untrue that, as some say, they are governed by the moon, because in that case they would always happen a definite time after the rising of the moon, and they do not; they vary in time from place to place.

In some places, too, the sea goes away only a little between the high and low tides, but in the Severn Sea we must have been near to whatever is the source of the tides, because the sea receded about four and a half miles.

We paddled out cross wind, over the sullen waves, bobbing about like a sea bird. We were more than a mile past the last green growing thing and I thought the water was deep, when we met two men walking up to their ankles only in the water. They had come out across the mud, with boards tied to their feet to stop them sinking, and they were pulling a sled behind them: they had stakes set in the mud even further out, to stretch nets between, and they were taking the night's catch back to the land. We left them behind, and in the slackening wind we paddled out into mist. After a while, when the grey water all round melted into the grey sky, I begun to feel even more depressed than I had felt alone in the Mere. We were now well away from the mud. I was completely dependent on Pryderi.

The tide now set strongly and carried us to the northeast, so that we had to paddle very little to keep way on her, but only to hold her head the way Pryderi wanted it. *He* seemed happy. He sang to himself in a tuneless, wordless song. I just paddled.

I looked into the grey mist. It swirled round us in curtains, our clothes were soaked with it, there was nothing to see except each other. Pryderi insisted that it was northeast we *were* heading, taking his bearings, I thought, from the colour of the water and the smell of the fog. I was completely in his hands, more at his mercy than at any time before.

Suddenly I saw something in the mist.

'Look!' I called. 'Dead ahead — it's land.'

'Too far left,' Pryderi grunted. 'Bring her round a bit. There's still enough wind to throw us off.'

Oddly enough, it was a comfort to find that he did not know *exactly* where he was. We came round a little, to the north I supposed, and passed under an island. It was long and flat and very low-lying. We came further right, and suddenly we were under the savage cliffs of another island, towering steep out of the water. The cliffs were covered with sea-gulls, which rose screaming when I shouted. But even so, my shout sounded so feeble in the empty mist that I was frightened then in case I might have offended some sea god.

Then I gained my courage. I had not been afraid in the fog, with the Berts, who were more dangerous than Pryderi, and that other silent ship going by. I need not be afraid here. I need not even paddle.

'What way are we heading?' I asked.

'North today: north of east tomorrow,' Pryderi answered.

I knew a king of wizards once: he taught me to whistle; and I whistled. We must have been a long way from the cradle of the winds, but at last the mist began to thin, and the breeze was on our backs, even though the tide was now against us. The early night fell, but at least now we could see the stars, and head towards the Dog Star, and hold it till we were suddenly unable to see it for the great cliffs that towered over us.

We landed on a shingle beach, and carried the boat up beyond the line of seaweed which Pryderi told me marked the limit of the tide. I was rather uneasy, because there is no knowing that the sea will stop today where it stopped yesterday, but I could not overrule him without appearing discourteous. I groped along the water's edge in the star-light, and picked up enough scraps of wood to light a fire, and keep it going through the night. We took it in turns to watch the fire and to sleep under the upturned boat.

At dawn we ate our morsel of cold mutton and drank a little cider, and set off again, with the tide. I was in a better mood for whistling that morning, and we had a wind to help us too, moving east of north along a coastline where the cliffs abruptly stopped and we had on our left hand a low shore and flats of mud. We passed the mouths of one big river, big for that island, though anywhere else in the world it would have been a trickle, and a narrower creek, and a long way after that the mouth of another wide river.

We turned into this mouth, trusting to the tide — we had sat out an hour of the turn staked on the mudflats and then paddled against the ebb and through to the flow again — to carry us up between the high banks of mud, mud, always mud, north to where we could see a long line of flat topped hills.

But it was some time before dusk, and much nearer to the sea than to the hills, that we came under the walls of Isca Silurum. We could see the walls, and the sentries at the gates, all wrapped up in winter order, which is nothing like any uniform the legions wear farther south. We came in to the wood frames of the quay, and someone threw us a line and helped us to scramble on to the bank.

There were the usual crowd of idle hangers-on by the water's edge, and Pryderi stood there in his black-and-yellow-checked cloak and looked at them. The front of his cloak fell open a little to show his belt of Gold chain. The loiterers all stood up from where they were lounging on stones and walls and bales, and I realised that those of them who weren't showing somewhere a trace of black and yellow were wearing the red with a thin white stripe that Cicva was so proud of. Pryderi didn't say anything, he just motioned with his left hand, and there was a rush to carry our bags and lift the boat out and stow it dry.

There were a number of more or less clean-looking houses between the gates of the fort and the river — not a city or anything like it, just an unplanned village. Pryderi walked up the street, and stopped at the largest house. I followed him. One of the men from the river bank went inside, and in a moment a whole family, men and women, young and old, children of all ages and hens and the pig all came tumbling out into the street.

Pryderi led me inside. There was a rush of people to bring us hot water to wash after our long journey, and also soap which the Gauls and Britons make out of fat and wood ash. It is very good for cleaning yourself, and I have often thought it would sell very well in Rome if only scented oils didn't have such a hold on men's habits.

Someone gave me a razor — really gave, I kept it — and I sacrificed my fine moustache, consoling myself that I could grow it in a few months as long as ever. When we were clean, I changed. Pryderi handed over his belt to one of his new friends, which surprised me, and I threw on my sealskin cloak again.

Pryderi carried my bag after me up to the walls of the fort. The sentry seemed at first a little doubtful about letting me pass. I told him I was going to see the Legate — not wanted to, was *going* to. He called the Sergeant of the Guard, who turned out to be a Standard-bearer and so senior enough to take decisions. This man could read, not very well, but he knew the seal of the Office of the Procurator in Londinium and he let us through with a legionary to lead us.

The main street of the fortress was in the usual confusion of builder's rubble. I don't know what it is about soldiers. They spend years building a fortress and making it a safe and comfortable place to live and work in. Then as soon as it's finished, they think up some new regulation which will allow them to tear it down and live in squalor again. They now seemed doing nothing more drastic than turning the whole fort round to face the other way. At least, they had left the Headquarters in the usual place, and we picked our way towards it, Pryderi looking round him like a provincial in the Forum.

At the door of the Praetorium, I slipped off my cloak and let Pryderi carry it with my bag, and when the Tribunes of the Staff saw me in my toga, all gleaming white, as if I were in Rome itself nobody thought of challenging my right to be there or to see whom I wanted. At that time, Citizens were scarce enough in Britain outside the Army, and here in the far West they were completely unknown. So I went straight in past the sentry and turned along the corridor — all these Praetorium buildings are exactly alike inside — and I walked into the office of the Junior Tribune without knocking or any other warning. I tossed the Procurator's letter on his desk and said firmly:

'I am ready to see the Legate. Now. Announce me.'

And of course the young fop was too impressed to do anything else but usher me at once into the Legate's office, where the great man was having a nap and wishing it were late enough for him to leave decently and go home without setting a bad example to his junior officers.

The Legate, however, refused to be impressed. He refused very hard. He told me, quite curtly, that he had received orders from Rome itself to offer me every assistance, and he had heard from the Office of the Procurator what assistance I was likely to require. He did not think it at all proper for the Civil Department to presume to tell him how to dispose of the Army's property and resources, and he himself was in fundamental disagreement with the policy, but there was nothing now he could do. Therefore, would I go along to the Primus Pilus and get what I wanted. And he hoped that I would not make any special effort to come and bid him farewell if I were in a hurry to leave, as he knew that I must be.

I went along to the office of the Senior Centurion, the Primus Pilus. I was furious. You keep on meeting this kind of treatment from Latins. Just because they're born in Italy, and Patricians, they think they own the world, and they are a close little clique of the 'right people' who keep all these ornate and profitable offices among themselves. It's people like our family, Greeks and Syrians and Africans, who really have the money and control all the trade and the real business of the Empire. *They* control the details of government. So they take no notice of us. They treat us like dirt.

But their days are numbered. Who do they think they are? Who do they imagine really runs the Empire now? It's the long-service soldiers, the centurions, who know what the legions think, and what the legionary thinks about is who's going to be Emperor and how much he's going to pay for it. And who looks round and takes the opinion of the meeting? The centurions, not the legates and the tribunes. These Patricians, once they *were* rulers, and they can't forget it now. They have not yet woken up to the fact that we have an Empire, not their cosy old Republic, and they're only officials now and not very well-paid ones either.

After that treatment I was steaming with anger. I don't like being treated as if I were a slave, by a man I can buy up twenty times over and out of my own money too, without calling on the family's funds. I went into the Senior Centurion ready for a quarrel if he offered it. But, of course, he was quite different, a man from just outside Carthage named, or perhaps called is a more precise term, Caius Julius Africanus. He was much more inclined to treat a Citizen with respect, being a Citizen born himself, even though he was a provincial too. He did not trust Italians any more than I did. Oh, yes, Africanus knew all about my business, and all about me, which was more than the Legate did.

'Just look at this,' he said, as one harassed man to another. 'Here's the letter from the Procurator. The Legate just passed it over to me with "see to it" scrawled in the corner. That's what he always does.'

'At least it shows he trusts you,' I offered. The Senior Centurion looked at me. Then he described the Legate in detail, in a small vehement voice. I was impressed. I've heard many a sea captain do worse, and the delicate conjunction of epithets brought joy to my poet's heart. At the end I asked:

'But you *have* done it?'

'It's all ready when you want it. Tell me where you want it sent, and exactly when, and I'll do it. There'll be no questions asked about the ship. Don't tell me anything about it, either, I don't want to know.'

'There's another party supplying her.'

'I don't think we dare have you bring it up here. There are too many eyes to see. I tell you what, we have a signal station at the mouth of the next river, but there's a creek a couple of miles nearer here. We'll set off in a wagon train as if we were going to the signal station, and meet you in the creek.'

225

'No escort,' I warned him. 'Just hire wagon-drivers around here. You'll find a few ready and waiting.'

'Don't tempt me — I won't ask. But when?'

'I will set sail on the day the first shooting stars fall from the Lyre. It will take two days to get to the creek. Can you meet us then?'

'By the Calendar, that will be the end of April. I will watch for the stars.'

'I will expect you.'

'I will be there.' He looked at me. 'Where are you going to sleep tonight?'

'I think my man has found somewhere in the village.' Pryderi was, I supposed, sitting where I had left him, on the step of the Praetorium, looking around him curiously.

'Nonsense. Aristarchos said I was to look out for you, Photinus. You won't be safe in the village tonight, it's Imbolc. Would you like to come and dine tonight with the centurions? It's a regimental feast. You can sleep in my house.'

It was wonderful to be addressed by my own name again. I accepted.

'But your man will have to sleep in the village,' Africanus continued. 'We can't have any Brits in here tonight. It's not etiquette, not in the Second. I'll send an orderly to take you down to the baths. He can have your man take your bag down there for you, and he'll carry it back for you himself.'

That was what I did. I went to the baths, outside the fortress, and I went through the hot rooms and the cold rooms, and I lay and luxuriated while they scraped me down and oiled me well till I smelt like a civilised man again. Then I put on a clean tunic and it took nearly half an hour to get shaved, the barber was so good and careful. Then back into my toga, and into the fortress again.

The Primus Pilus has a house of his own, while the junior officers live in little apartments at the ends of the huts where their men sleep. Thus it is very seldom that all the centurions of a legion meet together except on the parade ground. This was one of the occasions, and the feast was held in the Regimental Burial Club House, which alone in the fortress had a room big enough to hold us all with a kitchen near by. The room was warm, with real under-the-floor heating. I remarked on this to Africanus, as I stood at his right hand, receiving his Centurions as they saluted him, and introducing me.

'Yes, that's what makes these big forts almost untenable here in the North. We can never get enough fuel. I have something like three hundred men permanently at work all the summer cutting wood and piling it for the winter, and it takes over a hundred wagons because we are cutting it so far away.'

'Why don't you use earth coal like they do at the mines?'

'Impossible. It's too heavy. It would cost too much to bring all the way, on packhorse.'

Africanus greeted his Centurions as they arrived, one by one. This one, he said, was from Byblos, this one from Lutetia, one from Carnuntum, one from Bordigala, this one from Bonnonia even — all Citizens born, from all over the Empire except Britain, and except Italy. I was glad to see that, no Italians. More than half of them, though, were from Gaul and not so different from the Britons. It would be legions down in Egypt that would have British officers. It was the usual kind of regimental dinner, but notable for the absence of the Tribunes and the Legate, and for the presence of every Centurion in the fortress. That did not, of course, mean every officer in the legion, because about twenty of them were away on duty, on detachment at smaller stations. Still, we made four tables when we lay down to eat.

First, of course, we burned incense to His Sacred Majesty. Then, still in silence, we were served with the traditional bowls of wheat porridge, and each of us took his ritual three spoonfuls and his three sips of ration red, that horrid bitter wine. And that one dish, in theory, *was* the meal. Then we were free to talk, and to eat a real civilised meal all cooked in oil, and drink good Grecian wine, with resin in it. After a few glasses, I asked Africanus:

'I know that every legion has its own feast. Why does the Second have a feast on the Kalends of February? Do you celebrate a victory?'

I asked that partly because I wanted to know, and partly because I knew that a stranger, if present, must ask such a question, otherwise one of those present must lay aside his military cloak and pretend to be a stranger asking. Prompt to his cue, the most junior Centurion stood and began to recite a lesson learned by heart.

'Think, brethren, why we are here. Tonight is the night of Imbolc. Tomorrow night, and for weeks to come, the Brits will watch every night beside their flocks as the lambs are born. Therefore they feast to cheer themselves for the long vigils ahead, waking in the cold lambing shed. Now on this last night of freedom from care they drink and sing in every village throughout the land. If ever we are to expect rebellion, it is on such a night, when men are drunk and tempers are hot. Therefore, it being a feast of the Brits, the Legion stands at its post, every centurion watching throughout the night, neither any soldier venturing out where he might cause offence and begin a riot. For from a riot may begin a war. On this night, brothers, let us watch, being armed, all through the night, knowing that our comrades of the Sixth and Twentieth watch also. Therefore we sit here together, ready to take our places on the parade ground, with the Standard-bearers and the trumpeters at the door.'

He sat down, sweating with the anxiety of remembering the whole thing. It was quite obvious that with what he had already drunk, it would not have been much use sending him on to the parade ground, nor any of the other officers either. I was glad the Standard-bearers were sober, being the senior under-officers. At that moment, the Night Duty Centurion appeared. He stamped up and saluted the Primus Pilus in a stilted tone:

'All quiet in the town — *sir!*'

'Take a glass of wine after your labours,' answered Africanus, this obviously being part of the ceremonial. The

Duty Centurion drained it at one ceremonial gulp, and then less formally held it out for more. I asked:

'Is it really all quiet in the town?' I thought I could hear something far away.

'Quiet at Imbolc? There's never been such a thing.' The Duty Centurion took a third glass. 'I need this. I've never heard so much uproar. Half the hills seem to have come down for the feast, and they've burnt a couple of houses. And do you know what they've been shouting? They're shouting for Pryderi!'

Some of the drunker centurions laughed, but the soberer ones sat up and asked for the words to be repeated. I asked, as innocently as I could:

'Who is Pryderi?'

'Pryderi?' said Africanus. 'Why, he's a thorn in our flesh and no mistake. Down in the far West, there's the Demetae, and they've never submitted to Rome, they haven't, though nobody would mind if only they kept quiet, as most of them do. But the King there is called Pwyll, and it's his son Pryderi who does a lot of damage, cutting up wagon-trains and burning small posts. Then the nation here are the Silures, and they submitted all right, and we built them a city a few miles east, at Venta. But now some of them have quarrelled with the ones who submitted, and they follow another branch of their Royal House, and there has been a rumour that Pryderi has married into that family. If that's so, then there'll be trouble around here next. He has done us a lot of harm already; I swear, if ever I have him inside this post, then Pryderi will take a long time to die.'

'Do you think it's true?' asked one of the younger officers, who was itching for promotion as was clear from the way he had been flattering Africanus — he thought Africanus couldn't see what was going on, but the Primus Pilus was an old hand. 'I could take a century down there and find out.'

'True or not, they're shouting so loud you can make out the words, "Pryderi, kindle the fire," ' said the Duty

Centurion, and one of the Gaulish Centurions opened his eyes wide and told us:

'Sounds like the old man is dead. It's the head of the family kindles the fire on Imbolc night.'

The ambitious young man still pressed:

'I could go down there at the run, and we'd have him in half an hour.'

'No, stay here,' said Africanus. 'If you did go out now, you'd want half a cohort at least, and all you'd do would be start a riot, if not a revolt. This is how it usually begins, and we're not here to start risings, we're here to prevent them. If that means staying in here and not giving offence even if the Brits call us cowards, then that's what we'll do. If it's fighting you want, there'll be enough of that by the summer's end.'

I thought it better to change the subject. I asked:

'Is it your custom not to ask the Legate to your feast?'

Everyone laughed. The Centurion from the borders of Armenia explained:

'We never ask tribunes, not since Carantorius insisted on billeting half a cohort in a village for Imbolc, about forty miles west of here, where the Via Julia meets the sea, and they were slaughtered in their beds. "Making them realise the Army are their friends," was what he used to say, but they weren't friends of the Army. We gave him a good tombstone, but there were two hundred and odd other good men dead as well. Forty years ago that was, but still . . . And we would normally ask the Legate, but this one . . .'

'Useless,' put in Africanus shortly. 'Perfectly useless. What does he, or any of the Tribunes either, know about this legion, or how to handle men? Look at old sourpuss up there. Fifteen years ago he did a year as tribune with . . . the Seventeenth, wasn't it, and everybody knows the Seventeenth. Since then he's been wearing out his toga in one office after another in Rome, counting the obols for cleaning the drains. Now, here he is, just because he's from a Senatorial family he finds himself a Legate, with a legion, and four regiments of cavalry, and the government of a quarter of the Province. That's all he's interested in, feathering his nest to pay his debts so that he can go back to Rome and have his year as Consul.'

'It's not as if he even *tries* to be a good general,' added the Duty Centurion. 'We've only had him out on an exercise once since he came to us. We took two cohorts on a long march up the valley. End of the first day, what happens? We halt, and I'm Senior Centurion, and I get on with my job, digging in, and you want to, up there, with Pryderi about. Then I look round. Where's his nibs, and the young Tribune he had with him, you know, little Peach-bottom? Are they placing pickets, noting routes of attack? Not a bit of it. They're finding a pretty place by the stream to pitch their mutual tent, where the rude dirty soldiery won't disturb their idyllic night out. Sets the troops a bad example, too. I hope he's not with us if ever we have to go into action.'

'If ever we go.' Africanus stood up. The rest of us who had been wandering about and chattering now the serious eating was over, resumed our places, and lay down properly. The Standard-bearers and their escort had returned to the chapel, and the slaves left the room. The most junior Centurion shut the doors. Africanus went on:

'My comrades, honoured guest, it is time for the toast. Remember, as you drink it, that our brothers of the Twentieth at Deva, a hundred miles away, are drinking it with us. A hundred years ago, we two legions came into this savage land. For forty years we fought against the savages, till at last we made peace and brought all this fertile quarter of the island into the Empire, and the great northern desert we left to the Picts. The Sixth at Eboracum can hold the Wall.

'All this time, we two legions have waited for the word to move forward to add the next province to the Empire. Here on the shore of the Ocean we have built our fortresses and amassed our stores, ready for the last great invasion to carry us to the edge of the Ocean. We have waited long for the word to march. It has always been our pride that whenever the word would come, we would be ready, if need be, to *march* into the very sea itself. If this winter we are cold, we must cheer ourselves that we need not march into the water, and we may warm ourselves by going into the saw mills to work and turn the wood that should have been our fuel into ships that will keep us dry. For I can tell you now, the word has come at last. Soon we *will* march. Gentlemen, I give you, in greater hope than formerly, the annual toast. I hope that I now give it for the last time, and with it I couple the name of our guest, Photinus the son of Protagoras. Gentlemen, I give you — Next Year in Tara!'

I felt a tear in my one eye as I looked around. There they were, thirty-five centurions, from rear rank to front, of all ages, of all levels, and all men of action, hard and ready to fight. The lamps flickered on the brackets on the walls, and showed off the splendour of the plate. The officers were in their dress uniforms, each man in a cuirass made not of iron and boiled leather, but of scarlet velvet, padded to look like armour and trimmed and faced with Gold thread. Because it was Imbolc, and they were ready, each man reclined on his scarlet military cloak, and on the floor behind him each had laid his dress sword, and his parade helmet, and these last were gorgeous things, with face masks like you see gladiators wearing in the parade before the Games, gilded all over and each waving its plume of scarlet horse-hair. Several of them wore Phalerae, those medals of silver and Gold given only for bravery in the field, fighting against savage Britons, or the more savage weather.

They all stood, and I sat. All these brave men, to whom honour and the eagles meant more than Gold or power, men who knew what it was to endure, they all stood, and they drank to me, to Photinus, who was granting to them the prize they had always sought. They lifted their wine cups and they shouted:

'Next Year in Tara! Long live Photinus!'

And then they cheered and called for a speech. When there was some kind of order, I stood and said:

'Gentlemen, I am making you a bridge across the Sea. I have made the way clear for you, and I have done that without going there. But I want to come to Ireland in the end. You have invited me to one feast, gentlemen. May I now invite myself to another? Next Imbolc, I will feast with you in Tara!'

'Never, with old Pig's Bladder in command,' hissed the Duty Centurion, who was rather coarse-mouthed, being an Illyrian.

I turned on him.

'When you go, you shall have a real general.'

I saw to that next morning. I went back to the Praetorium, and wrote a letter to Uncle Phaedo, sending it off with the military mail, partly for safety, partly for speed. It was short. I said: *Rejoice. Foreclose.*

I had sent him the contents of Gwawl's wallet. Already my uncle would have bought up all the Legate's debts. Within two weeks, now, the Legate would be broken.

While I was about that, Africanus suddenly came into the Registry saying:

'I'm very sorry, I quite forgot this. Aristarchos left this letter for you when he came through.'

'What was Aristarchos doing here?' I asked.

'What does Aristarchos ever do? He just passed by. It is my belief he was going native again. He's done it before. All I know is, he borrowed a Standard-bearer and five other good men — all Gauls, and, come to that, all from the same nation. All Setantii. After Pryderi, perhaps? With Aristarchos, you never know, and you don't ask. Here it is.'

I took the letter, and I went aside a little where no one could hear me read it. It was from my father. He had sent it to Uncle Euthyphro, and he to Leo Rufus, and he sent it on through Aristarchos, as he had no idea where I had gone, only a suspicion, and Aristarchos knew. It was quite short. I read it through twice. Then

I threw the end of my toga over my face and stood silent for a while.

Africanus watched me, also silent. When I uncovered my face again, he asked:

'Is there anything I can do?'

I stood there, mechanically cleaning the vellum with a piece of pumice, to use again. When I could speak, I answered him:

'I have a son. My wife died in August.'

CHAPTER NINE

I went from the fortress gate alone. As Africanus said, it was better that he should not know where I went or to whom. I walked out of sight of the sentries among the houses of the British village. True it was that some had been burnt the night before, but not the one where I had changed and left my British clothes.

Pryderi was waiting for me. We went in silence, as soon as I had changed, down to the riverside. There were a number of men to see us off. I had not met them before, but I could tell their rank. After a winter in the Mere I knew the subtle differences of dress, and I would no longer confuse a noble in his hunting clothes with a peasant in his market-day best. Not since I had seven kings at my marriage have I had such august helpers to steady me into a boat. Nor did they speak to us. Anything they had to say to Pryderi, any agreements, any plans and policies, they were the work of the night before. They were committed.

We paddled all that day in silence, and in silence we spent the night on a beach as before. We had no breath to spare, trying to make the most of tide and current as we crossed to the south side of the water. Besides, I mourned a wife: Pryderi had taken possession of . . . a patrimony? . . . a dowry? . . . both?

On the morning of the second day, however, we felt less numb. We paddled with the shore close on our left hand, and we were caught by the current of a great river, wider and stronger than any river of Italy or Spain, wide almost as Nile itself, and I was glad we had cider enough to pour a libation to Sabrina. And then, as we paddled, Pryderi began to sing, a sad and lovely melody, and the words were old, but there was little doubt that he had chosen them carefully:

We listened in the sedges to the song of the birds of
    Rhiannon,
The song of the thrush and the nightingale, and the ever-
    ascending lark:
Yet there is no living bird on the wing that sings like
    the birds of Rhiannon,
The songs of our loves who died long ago, who wait
    for us yet in the dark.

Blackbird and finch still sing to us on the banks of the
    Summer River,
But the song of the dead who loved us will never be
    heard again.
Love that is given for no return will return to the giver,
Love that demands love in return earns no return but
    pain.

We paddled ever south-west on the lead-dull waters. We heard the cries of the gulls and the slap of the water against the paddles and against the side of the boat, and we panted in our haste to drive the craft with the current and against the tide. I thought of Phryne, now dead, and I wept till fresh Sabrina merged into the sea. Perhaps she was no Helen, no Juno, but she was — I found it impossible to be coherent. Flung innocent into marriage with a man who knew worlds, who knew Hells she could not imagine, a man who at first had thought of nothing but his dead love in the North, she had been quiet and peaceful and forgiving and tolerant, and obedient, not as a slave, but as a partner. And she had always been there. There had never been a moment while I was in Britain when I had not known that Phryne would be still there waiting for me. I knew all the time that the moment I walked up the quay from the ship and came into my house she would be offering me her bread and oil. Nobody baked bread like Phryne, she always baked her own bread; she even ground the meal herself if it was for me. She said slave girls never would, no not could, would, grind the wheat flour fine enough for me. And it would be ready when I came home, however long I was away, a month, three months, two years . . . Now it would never be ready again.

And what of my children? My sister Xanthippe — my grandfather had won there — would take little Euphrosyne fiercely, proudly, to her own house, defying any claim by Phryne's parents: Xanthippe had five sons. But the baby — how could he survive? My grandmother would scour through the houses of all our friends and through the markets to find a newly delivered slave who could suckle him, even if her own child died: they would try to make him suck goat's milk on the end of a rag. But there was little hope. I am cursed in my children. I have two sons, and a daughter in the North whom I will never see again: and no son in my own home.

And no wife. There was no one now to wait for my return. I need never return. Only as long as the Gold came back, I might stay here for ever, or go where I pleased, might live or die. Now, I might please myself.

The grey waters, the grey sky, the colourless gulls that swooped and passed, all made my mood. I dug my paddle with fury into the swirling tide, keeping her steady in the wilderness of currents. I cursed the useless birds that jeered at us. Now I was at the deep point of the mood that had possessed me all through the grey and misty land of Britain, the land of twilight and soft shadows, the land of deception and melting form, the land where nothing is what it seems to be or claims to be. Now it had struck me down when I seemed to be most successful, most secure. The Army was at my disposal, I could dismiss a Legate who was more powerful than any Barbarian king, and I would soon bring down not one but four Barbarian kings. I had a ship that would live on that stormy sea even in the spring when no skin boat, no galley, could keep it, or carry an army. And my enemy, Gwawl, was defeated, dismissed, made harmless as he had been on the night of the thorn. All the Gold in Ireland was in my hands. There was nothing more I need do. I could rest here, or wherever I liked, and wait for the treasure to come to me, and I could do what I wished with what I had.

In the grey dark that succeeded the grey day we came to a landing place in the reeds, and climbed a gentle slope to a hut. It was not empty. Three men sat there, waiting for the hard dawn that should come, men that came from the confines of Hell. They had fire for us, and food. We ate and ate in silence. At last Grathach asked:

'Will they come, my Lord?'

'Some,' answered Pryderi. 'Not many. Enough.'

'Silurians?' I asked. I did not know how far I might go, I was overbold, I thought.

'They are beginning to see now,' Pryderi told me, 'how they have been cheated. They submitted, and that not after a hard fight, on a promise. The Romans said they would protect them from the Irish. And that they have not done. The Irish still raid. Last year they came under the walls of Venta itself. All along the coasts of the Severn Sea they come, except in the Mere. They do not come along the shores of the Irish Sea, either. We Dematae are not disarmed, and north of us, in the Rainy Hills, they dare not face Howell. But the other coasts — they raid as they please, and the Romans can't stop them. Now, Mannanan, see if you are more powerful than a legion. They are yours, now.'

'Who?'

'The Leinster men who raid, from the south-east of the island, they are the men you want. It is in their country, in Wicklow, that the Gold was found. They have the streams rich in metal. Turn them back to mining Gold, and they will be too busy to bother us.'

'And then, Pryderi, you will submit, and go to live in Venta, or build a city just like it far in the West, or in the Mere?'

'I will never submit to the Romans.'

'The future lies in the towns, Pryderi. It is the Guild of Shoemakers and the men who peddle earth coal who will rule this land in the end. Submit, Pryderi. There is no other way to power.'

'I will never submit. I am a king.'

'I know what it is. You are jealous of the Irishman, the King's nephew, the Setanta. You want to be like him, to lead a fianna, to ride into great battles, to topple monarchs and empty thrones. It is too late, Pryderi. Submit and be rich and happy and have power.'

'I might be richer than I am, and have more power, but I would not be happy.'

'Is it only the luxury of your pride, then, Pryderi, that keeps you in rebellion? Is it the mere pleasure of knowing that you are doing what you like?'

'Here my Gesa, Mannanan, to which I have been obedient since I was a child. It is this: it is never to forsake a friend, or forget a wrong, or forgive a Roman.'

He said no more: he rolled himself in his cloak and lay on his bed of dry bracken. There was no more to be said. I too slept.

They woke me a little before dawn. Grathach brought me hot mutton soup and bread, and as I scoured my bowl he said.

'Up the slope straight, and there is a path. Follow it to the end, not turning to the left nor to the right—'

'Will you now forsake me?' I asked.

'No, you cannot be forsaken here.' Pryderi on his bed was calm, not offended. 'Do you not know where you are? You are at the south end of the Apple Country. When you reach the north end of the ridge, turn to the west, and in the reeds by the huts at the end of the path, you will find boats moored. Then you can cross the marsh to Caw's house. As for us, we have no time to take you, and we trust you enough to let you go alone wherever you wish. We have other business that will not wait.'

I made west along the path, among the orchards of cider apples. And now I knew why the Apple ridge was sacred,

239

for though every tree was bare of leaf, yet each in the winter dark shone golden green and silver dotted. On every tree the mistletoe hung down.

I came in mid-afternoon to the edge of the ridge, where the Mere in winter flooded round on all sides. There I did find a boat, though I had to look for it, and in the end pick the smallest and lightest from a cluster cleverly hidden under a willow. The rain came down on me, and splashed in great circles into the marsh, as I pointed the bows up stream and paddled hard against the current in order only to make track straight across it. I waded to push the boat through shallows and lay flat to creep under low branches Where we had walked in the summer the flood would now drown a man. At last, I came to the edge of the main stream, rushing down from the hills inland with the force of a herd of frightened cattle, roaring and tossing. I struggled to hold her head, I saw lost all the way I had so painfully made north along the ridge. All the knowledge I had ever had of the sea, all the skills I had learnt in ships, all were useless against this sweet fresh water, whirling me back to the sea. I strained down to my heart, my back cracked, handsbreadth by handsbreadth I moved towards the opposite bank, taking first one mark to head for, and then losing it far up stream, and then another, and losing that too. And suddenly, as I thrust away a log that playfully butted me and almost turned me over, I was in calm water, and close under the opposite shore, under the west bank, on the surface of a calm black pool, a backwater where the water did not stir. I had lost my paddle in that last struggle with the ash tree. Now I splashed with my hands till I came near, and grounded on the mud beach. I did not think, I just pulled the boat up far from the water, as one always does. Once a sailor, you never forget. Then I climbed, foot by foot, ledge by ledge, up the bluff till I came where Rhiannon's hut had been, where she had sat for so long fasting and gazing out over the marsh. I sloshed soaking down the hill and by the last path to Caw's house.

Later, fed and warm and full of cider in the lamplight, I said to Caw:

'But would not cider pay you better than silver? There is no cider even in Britain like the cider of the Summer Country. You could sell it from here to Londinium, to Rome itself. I could arrange it all, act as your agent, and once it came into fashion at the Imperial Court, it is Gold you would be handling and not silver, and it would not take too much influence then to free you from the wheat tax. And it would be safer, too.'

'Attractive you make it sound, don't you?' He laughed. 'No wonder it is rich you do get by buying and selling. No, boy, it's the sea that is my real love.'

I changed my tack.

'How many of those great ships have you left now, Caw?'

'Well, there was another, but that one you stole from me. Now — to tell the truth, we only have the one.'

'After this one voyage for which you have promised her to me?'

'Back to the silver.'

'Why don't you build another?'

'It takes time to build a ship, time and space and skill. We could never do it, even in the Mere, with no one knowing. And what would we use another one for now? We cannot trade except as I do.'

'But if I were to trade with Ireland, then would you not think of building more? And then, you would not be a hunted pirate in the Mere, but you would have a style and a title and a place in the Empire, and under the Emperor it is you only would be the Master of the Western Sea.'

Caw sat silent, cracking walnuts with his teeth — fancy, a man at his age with his own teeth! Finally he said:

'I'll think about it.'

We went to bed. I was almost there, I thought, almost there. Soon I would be able to trade across the Irish Sea in all weathers and all the year, with an Ireland peaceful and settled and pouring Gold, rich Gold into my hands.

All I wanted in the Mere, almost all I wanted, was in

241

my hands. Now there was no thought of home, no obligation, no loyalty, no promise to keep me back. I was free to take what I wanted out of all the island, to take what was mine, what had been given me and what had been promised me.

I walked along the edge of the Mere in the grey morning. I came to Pryderi's house, where Cicva sat grinding at her door, grinding flour fine enough for Pryderi, and Rhiannon with her.

'Where is Taliesin?' I asked.

'Gone,' replied Cicva. 'He is walking back alone through the land as he came, from nation to nation, judging the people and telling them what is right and just to do, whether it please the oil-eaters or not. Why should you want him now?'

'I wanted a witness,' I told her. 'I have come to claim what is mine.'

'And what is yours?' asked Rhiannon. 'I too may claim what is mine, what I too have been given.'

'You are mine, Rhiannon. I will take you now. You can plead neither sanctity nor weakness nor strength. I will take you with me back, through Rome and through Ostia, past Brundisium and Athens, through Alexandria and Byblos to my own home in the Old City. Come, Rhiannon, I have children there who need a mother, and I have slaves who need a mistress. I have a great house in the town, Rhiannon, with a hundred rooms, tables of ivory and beds of ebony, laid with all the silks of India and scented with the strange woods the Arabs bring out of the Desert. There we eat well, Rhiannon, of bread and meat, and fruits and nuts you have never seen and have never heard of, and that not at feasts but every day. And wine, Rhiannon — we can drink a different wine every day for a year, and not exhaust my cellar. I have the wealth of ten kings in the Isle of the Mighty, Rhiannon, and in my own town I have the honour of a king. Roman Governors treat me as a man of importance, and merchants from all over the world bow low to me. And they will all bow low to you, Rhiannon, and bring

242

you presents, because you are mine. I have an empty house that waits for you, Rhiannon, and an empty bed that waits for you. I will take you now, Rhiannon, back out of this land of mists and shadows into the real world.'

'And would that honour me, that am a princess already?' she asked. 'Mannanan, you are mine, given to me. Now I will take what is mine. Come with me to the North, Mannanan, to my own people of the Brigantes. Come and live there with me, and all will honour you as a king, because I bring you. You will have mutton to eat all the days of your life, and oat bread, the fine fruits of the forest, blackberries and elderberries, cobnuts and blewits. You will have wool to wear and to sleep on, pure clean wool, through the hot summer days up on the heather hills, through the long winters in the dry cold air.'

'I have a farm also,' I told her, 'up in the hot dry hills. I too have my herds of sheep, and I wear wool of my own breeding, that my own husbandmen have sheared, that the women of my own household have combed and spun and woven and sewn into cloaks and tunics, and into blankets for the winter nights when we shall lie warm together and listen to the wolves outside. There we shall smell the wood smoke, and drink the resined wine that we ourselves have trodden out, and on the bread baked of our own wheat we shall sprinkle oil we have pressed from our own olives. If you wish, Rhiannon, you shall never see a town again.'

'If you spurn the throne of the Brigantes,' she told me, 'and will not be turned from trade, then stay here with me in the marsh. Here we will eat and drink in plenty, since it seems there is nothing you think of except eating and drinking. We shall have venison and hare, wild duck and moorhen, carp and salmon, oysters and mussels, snails and milk-caps and horns-of-plenty, And I will be kinder to you than you to me. I will let you go out and trade, wherever you will, up to the Picts and across to the Land of Norroway, anywhere.'

I looked narrowly at her.

'But not to Ireland?'

'And what cause is there for you to go to Ireland? You have no need of trading there.'

'I have no need to go to Ireland. All I want done is done by others. I have used the weapons that I know, money and persuasion and planning, to make a hundred men each work at what he thinks he wants the most, and none of them even knowing the others exist, and by all that to bring about my desire. My work is done. All will now come about whether I go or not. I will only be an encumbrance. I need not go. We can leave now, Rhiannon, we will be home by the end of the spring, by the hot blue sea, listening to the first cicadas among the flowers in the grass, listening to the shepherd boys piping. Come, Rhiannon, let me take my own.'

'You are not going to Ireland?'

'There is no reason why I should go to Ireland?'

'There is no reason why you should seek the Gold in Ireland. You have been telling me of all the wealth you have. What more can you add to that?'

'I must bring it back. I told my family that I would bring it. You will understand this, Rhiannon. This is my Gesa, that what I have said I will do, that I will do, and neither the love of women nor the fear of men will deflect me; no, not for all the Gold in Ireland will I break my word.'

And then Cicva spoke:

'And it would have been well if there were Brigantes who had taken that Gesa, for it was the Brigantes who said they would not submit, and then they submitted and the great castle of Stanwyck they surrendered without a blow struck.'

She spoke with venom. I had not realised that Cicva hated Rhiannon so much, that she envied, from here in the Mere, hiding from Roman eyes, this princess of a surrendered house. Rhiannon at least could ride across all the island unchallenged. But Rhiannon did not hear her. Staring at me, she shouted:

'Then take their Gold back to them,' and at my feet she threw three coins, three coins I knew well. I stopped to pick them up as she went by me, and then I followed her out.

She ran across the grass, round Cicva's house, towards the fence of the paddock. Hueil was there, acting as guardian of the Mere in Pryderi's absence, and he was preparing to go boar-hunting in the thickets of the Deer Moors. He had two horses saddled there, and Rhiannon ran past him and swung up on to the one saddled for her. I could not think where she was going. Half I remembered the ritual chase when we had caught Cicva four months before: half I hazarded that in fact she had nowhere to go, she just wanted to run away, to escape, to flee from me anywhere.

I rushed to the fence and swung up on to the other horse. Hueil, who had only just fastened the girths, looked at me in surprise. Then he grunted:

'You never know,' and before he slapped the horse on the rump he handed me up the boar spear.

The horse twisted to bite me, and I recognised him. It was Taliesin's evil-tempered brown again, a horse I hated. But it was the only one ready, and I belaboured his flanks with the butt of the boar spear and prepared to see if he would go.

Go? Oh, yes, that brown horse would go. You can forgive anything to a horse that *will* go, that will run his heart out the day, the one and only day, when he must. There was only one horse I ever had that went better, and he was dead, long dead. Rhiannon looked back and saw me following.

At first she thought she could play the old game, and keep just out of reach till my horse tired, while hers was still fresh but it was hardly a furlong before she saw that if once she hesitated, if once her horse pecked or stumbled, then I had her. She set her horse at the paddock fence and cleared it. Jumping is not something you do lightly if you have only one eye, but by now I was in such a state of suppressed anger and excitement and general rage with the whole world that I just pointed the brown at the fence and let him go, shutting my eye in case I lost courage. Every fence and hedge we came to the black jumped, but the

245

brown, stupid blundering, marvellous brute, went through as often as over, and where the black cleared a stream, the brown went in and I was soaked. And this did not soothe me.

We left the edge of the Mere, and climbed the hill up on to the open moor, where there were no sheep at this time of year, but only deer and wolf, and the chance of bear or boar in the woods. It was into the woods Rhiannon went, seeking a twisting path. The brown did not care for paths. He went into the scrub all right, but he galloped straight as an arrow. Very soon my clothes were torn to pieces by the thorns, and I was glad that I had flung my sealskin cloak to Hueil as I mounted. It was a wonder that the horse did not run head first into a tree, or that I was not brained on a low branch, but by cutting corners we stayed with Rhiannon as she went, went north-west towards the sea, away from the Mere. Did she choose the way on purpose, or by the accident of its giving us a firm path? I did not know. I followed. We were in sight of the sea now, a paler grey line under the line of the grey clouds. There was a thicket ahead of us, and Rhiannon made for it. I saw a disturbance there, and I thought 'boar' and then I saw men and I still thought 'hunting party'. Rhiannon vanished into the thicket, and the nearest man was close to me, running towards me with a spear. I had scarcely time to think, 'Funny kind of spear to go after boar with,' when I was close to him, and I knew him. It was one of Gwawl's friends, the older of the two middle-aged men who had escorted the Mouse from inn to inn. He came at me with his spear, and as he lunged, I pulled the brown horse round and down we came, knocking the middle-aged man flying. I fell clear: I wouldn't have done that if I had been using one of my own saddles with a strap for the toes.

I rolled away from the threshing horse, still holding the boar spear, and got up just in time to receive the charge. I sidestepped the spear point, and the shafts crossed as we pushed against each other, sweating and straining for the advantage. Suddenly, we both gave together and each went

246

staggering back. He was quicker on his feet, for all his age, and came back at me with the spear levelled. There was only the one thing to do, and if it did not succeed I would never know it. I poised the boar spear, regretted briefly that it was not very well balanced for the job, and that I had no chance to find another, and threw it, with all my might, when he was barely two yards away.

His run carried him past me. He fell on his side. The point of the spear stood out two fingers from his back. That, I thought, is the end of you, and who knows . . .? I bent to take his spear from his hands, and someone jumped on to my back from behind. There were a number of them, filthy men, smelling of dirt and fat, but of salt and the sea beside. They held my arms and turned me round to face the thicket.

Gwawl stood before me. He wore still his black and white shirt, and a pair of trousers he had bought in Lutetia and Cicva had won from him and given to me, cheating the Berts, and I had given Pryderi and Gwawl had stolen back. He stood there and laughed in my face.

'That was fair,' he said, jerking his head to the body on the ground. 'When a man armed meets a man armed, then there is neither blame on either for seeking blood, nor on the victor for drawing it. There is no call for vengeance here.'

'Where is Rhiannon?' I asked him.

He ignored the question. He went on:

'By every law of my people, I ought to kill you now, and save all the trouble that will come. But there was an oath I swore, and a bargain, and I must keep them. I may not kill you, Mannanan, in this land I may not kill you. So I must leave you.'

Someone had unsaddled the sweaty brown horse, which had remained standing cropping the grass and watching the fight unconcerned. After all, what concern was it of his? They flung the filthy saddlecloth over my head, and wrapped me in it, and tied my arms to my sides under it. Then they spun me around, and someone, Gwawl I think,

247

struck me half a dozen blows across the face, not hard, but sharp, contemptuous.

I staggered about, trying to wrestle my arms free, trying not to breathe the sweat on the blanket, hoping that I would not step badly and break my ankle. I wrestled and struggled as if it were Gwawl himself I was fighting, and in a way it was. I wrestled as if it were Hercules I was faced with. Then suddenly, dimly through the blanket, I heard more hooves and shouting, familiar British voices, and in a few moments, someone was cutting through the rope and letting me breathe again.

Madoc asked:

'Who were they?'

I rinsed out my mouth with the cider someone gave me. I said:

'I don't know, except that it was Gwawl.'

Hueil was kneeling over the body.

'Irish,' he called. 'Wicklow man here, I think. Nothing of value, though, except his knife.'

They brought me the brown horse again, and handed me my bloody boar spear. Someone asked:

'What, doesn't he want the head?' but I ignored that. We set off again, through the thicket, where we found Rhiannon's cloak, of thick yellow wool, on the ground, and then down a steep narrow valley onto the coastal flats. The way was clear, with the marks of hooves and broken branches. The beach here, I knew, was shingle, with a bank above the sea. We could see a group of something on the bank and made for it. When we came closer, it was a group of horses. We reached them and went up the bank into sight of the water.

Far out across the bobbing waves we could see the skin boats, a dozen of them, big ones, already setting the lug sails that they too used, all paddling hard.

'Too late,' said Hueil.

'Wicklow men,' said Madoc. 'If you wish, we can be at sea in six hours. I will find a crew here, and we will pick up warriors in Pryderi's country. Or we could wait for Pryderi, but I do not know how long he will be. Then we can raid the coasts of Wicklow till we find her.'

I looked into the setting sun. Somewhere out there, on the leaden water, being carried across the February sea in a basket covered with a little leather, was Rhiannon, the glorious Rhiannon, that was worth the greatest ship that ever was just to carry her across a little stream.

'No,' I said. 'No, I will see to it myself. I *will* go to Ireland and find her, at the proper time.'

CHAPTER TEN

Two mornings later, I stood on the bluff above the Dark Pool, where Rhiannon's hut lay in ruins. I stood looking into the waters. To whoever dwelt there, to Those Below, I vowed, in bitterness, the whole of the Island of the Blessed. And as an earnest, to Those Below I gave, first, Gold. Three Gold coins, ancient but unmarked, I threw into the water, one by one, in order of age. And then I plucked the eye from my head and cast that in too. Not my real eye, you must understand, but my most expensive one, of diamond, carved with a scene of the judgement of Paris.

And then, quietly, Pryderi too came to the waterside. I had never seen him like this before. He was armed. He had on a short mail coat, to the waist, and an old-fashioned helmet, plain and unornamented, round and setting close to the head. The long sword, too, at his side, so long that he almost tripped over it, was plain-hilted and in a plain leather scabbard. A man who goes into battle wears no Gold or jewels. And Pryderi had been in battle. His forearm was caked with clotted blood.

He carried a big leather bag. He put it on the grass. From it he took a cloak of scarlet wool. Next, he took out handfuls of silver, dozens, hundreds of silver denarii, and piled them on the cloak. Plainly, though, there was more, much more, in the bag. Last, he brought out a head. His fingers sank deep into the close cropped black hair. The face was that of a man in his late twenties. He had had neither beard nor moustache: I thought it was a Thracian face if ever I saw one, but it was, I was glad to see, no one I knew. The look on the face was of surprise, nothing more, just surprise.

Pryderi laid the head on the cloak among the silver coins. He turned up the ends of the scarlet cloth to form a bag, and tied the mouth with a leather strap. Then he swung the bag backwards and forwards once . . . twice . . . and the third time, he let it go and it sailed out and fell into the deepest centre of the pool. Weighted with silver, the head went straight down to Those Below. And I have no doubt it pleased them more than Gold or diamonds.

Ireland

CHAPTER ONE

When the time came, Caw and Pryderi saw me into
Madoc's ship at the river mouth.

'Don't lose the ship, whatever you do,' Caw warned me.
'We won't ever be able to build another without a pattern.'
So that was settled in his mind, I thought. He had never
said anything about it before. But all Pryderi told me was:

'If Cicva has a boy, I'll name him after you.'

Which name of the many, I thought, as we swept her
out through the channel and into the shallow Severn Sea.
We came between the islands and made the mouth of the
creek at dawn on the second day.

There was someone on the wharf waving a red cloak.
We tied up and Madoc's crew put down a gangplank. I
went ashore and greeted Africanus. He had come himself,
he said, to be sure that there was no treachery. Talking
of that, I asked after the Legate. Africanus laughed:

'He's gone. There's a rumour he went bankrupt soon after
you were here. True or not, he went back to Rome in a
hurry last week, and he took young Peach-bottom with
him. I'm glad of that, too — sets a bad example to the Brits.
We haven't had a replacement yet, and with luck we'll be
without one for the rest of the year. Of course, old ox-
head would have commanded both legions when we go,
but now it'll be the Legate of the Twentieth. He'll be all
right. You can put too much store on regimental loyalties.'

I agreed. The thought of two legions going ashore in
Ireland under a general that none of the senior officers
trusted was chilling. But if the troops trusted the commander, then the battle, if there were so much as a battle,

255

was won already. Africanus and I stood there in complete accord and watched the wagons unloaded into the ship.

'I'm depending on you, coming down with all this material and only twenty men,' Africanus went on. 'We lost the half-yearly pay convoy a few weeks ago. Nobody's attacked that for twenty years — we just didn't expect it. There were only fifteen men, and a very junior Centurion. Pryderi ambushed them on the steep hill east of Glevum, and took the lot. Half a year's pay for nine thousand men, all in silver. All the escort killed. As for the Centurion, Pryderi cut his head off and took it away. Horrible thing. Not been anything like that as far east as this for . . . no, not for fifty years.'

'You are sure that it was Pryderi?'

'He told the carters before he let them go. He boasted about it. "I'm Pryderi, King of the Demetae and of the Silures," he said. "Tell Caesar to think again what he rules." Now we can't move anything along these roads without an escort. Pryderi! When I catch him . . .' He changed the subject. 'Are you keeping a count of this?'

'No. I assume that you're giving me all you've got.'

All he'd got? I'd never seen anything like the arms we were loading. For a hundred years, the Second Legion had been disarming the country. Swords and shields by the hundred they had confiscated and stored in the Fortress of Isca. They had stored them, and kept fifty men busy looking after them and greasing them and counting them every year, while the quartermaster grumbled about the work and how long it was taking Rome to make up its mind about them. Now Rome *had* made up its mind, and I had them.

You see, you cannot teach Barbarians to use Roman weapons, and on the other hand, you cannot ask Roman troops to use Barbarian weapons. These were Barbarian swords, not even German which the cavalry could use, but British. They were very long, three and a half or four feet from hilt to point, double-edged, and a palm's width at the hilt. Why were they so long? You shall learn, in good time.

There were shields, too, of two kinds. Some of them were like the ones Pryderi and I had made. Roman shields are oblong and convex. German shields are round. These were big, almost as long as the swords, and oval. They were flat and very light, a thin wood frame with a layer of boiled leather over, often covered again in the thinnest of bronze sheets. They had been, once, enamelled and set with jewels, like the scabbards and the hilts of the swords. But now all you could see were the holes where the Roman soldiers had wrenched out the gems. Who on earth would carry these into action I could not think: they were far too big to run with, and too light to stop a sword cut.

There were, however, a lot of smaller shields, round and a foot or a foot and a half across, just the thing for a swordsman. There was armour, too, mail shirts of iron rings sewn on leather, and other shirts of boiled leather which are almost as good as mail unless you are unlucky and get the full force of a cut with a really sharp blade. There were throwing spears, and a few pikes and axes. Besides this, we had helmets, almost laughably old-fashioned. Some of them were tall and pointed, others round like kettles, and many of them with horns or ridge crests of thin bronze.

And last of all came the things that made sense of the long swords and the big shields and the throwing spears. The wheels were about waist-high to a man, iron tyred, and light. There were great tangles of leather harness, and poles, and basketwork. All this we took aboard and stowed in the hold.

When we were loaded, the ebb tide was ready to take the ship out. I embraced Africanus.

'Why!' he said in surprise. 'I thought you were coming ashore with me. I have a room ready for you.'

'I've changed my mind,' I told him. 'Someone has to do the thinking.' I did not mention Rhiannon: how could I have explained?

'Well, then,' he warned me, 'don't get pricked with any of that sharp stuff. I want to see you there waiting for me on the beach on the first of August. And keep a few Irish wenches waiting for me.'

He stood on the wharf, waving his vinewood staff at us as we dropped out into the Channel. He was a good reliable man, was Africanus, and I wish I could have taken him with me on that voyage. But, of course, a Negro would have been *too* conspicuous on that expedition.

CHAPTER TWO

We beat down the Channel, against the wind that blew from the south-west. First we had a low marshy coast on our right hand, then high cliffs, and then sand dunes with great mountains close inland, their heads high in the clouds. The Alps are fifty miles high, we know that because Pliny has measured them, and I think that these mountains west of Isca must have been at least ten miles to the tops.

I took watch and watch with Madoc, heaving on the steering oar and bellowing at the men who handled the leather sail, a great lug fifteen feet square. Oh, there's nothing like being in a ship of your own, handling the winds as if they too were your subjects. You have to woo a ship when you first have her, finding out her little ways and fads, discovering what will make her yield, what will best satisfy you. And at last she lies open to your every desire, your slightest whim is her command, you no longer have to show what you want her to do, she anticipates your demands before you make them. And the weariness that comes after a long trick at the helm, the fatigue that lets you sleep on the hard deck, although the spray drenches you and a battle rages over the bulwarks — the lion too, they say, the lion too.

But there is no joy in a whore you hire or a slave girl you buy for your bed. If you spend no effort, do not venture your pride, then what pleasure is there? Likewise, there is no satisfaction in steering another man's course or carrying someone else's merchandise, what you do not know. But as on that day in the Channel, steering a ship you have hired for yourself, carrying your own goods to make your own fortune, oh, that is joy, that is happiness indeed.

At noon on the second day we had the sun at our backs, when we saw it, and on our right hands we still had savage cliffs, that soon gave way to a land of high mountains. And on the third day, the mountains were highest of all, higher than the Alps, though we never saw the tops, being wreathed in cloud.

We were near the estuary of a river, with wide sandbanks at low tide. We worked our way in to the southeast side, where a great rock rose sheer out of the water, the waves breaking at its foot. We would come in close, though, near enough to see people on the top of the rock and hear them shouting to us.

'The Rock of Harlech,' Madoc told me. We watched a crowd of skin boats put out from the shore, full of men. They reached us and swarmed aboard, shouting. I felt glad that I had taken the pick of the arms from the cargo for myself, a light mail coat and a helm, a small shield and an axe. No more swords for me. The men who came aboard were all Irish by their dress. I would have let Madoc push them back into the sea again if I had not recognised the patchy hair of the first Irishman, the Setanta, in the last boat to leave the shore.

As soon as they were all aboard, we made sail for the west. Madoc took her, tacking among the shoals. I stood on the poop and watched the Setanta as he handed out the first of our arms to his men. There was one man there the others called Heilyn, who took a tall spiked helmet with a ring on top, through which he threaded some red rags. He was not really seven feet high when he wore it, he only looked like it. I tried to hear what the Setanta was saying to him and then what the others were talking about. I listened hard. I received my worst shock of the whole voyage. I couldn't understand a word they were saying.

For a moment, wild thoughts raced through my head. Were they drunk? Were they perhaps not Irish after all? They sat about in the waist, delousing each other and relieving themselves in the scuppers and chattering away, and I couldn't make out a word of it. I turned to Madoc.

'What language are they talking?'

'Language?' he asked in turn. 'What language do you think? Irish of course.'

'Irish? Have they got a different language?'

'Of course they have!'

'Not like yours?'

'Not a bit. Quite different. I can't manage a word of it.'

Different? Different! All these months wasted! I was going to land in Ireland, in a hostile Ireland, not speaking a word of their language. I might as well be deaf and dumb. I nearly wept. Cheated! Why had nobody told me? This was just the thing those accursed Brits would think was a huge joke. All those weary weeks learning British just so that I could talk with the Kings of the Irish, and now to find that they could not understand me! There was nothing to do but to whelm my sorrows in food. I ate myself to sleep.

Before dawn, Madoc woke me — I was sleeping curled up under a skin boat on the deck.

'Wake up, boy. It is happy enough you ought to be, seeing it is a Holy Day that it is. Let's make it a bright one and a happy one, for it's standing away by noon that I would like to be.'

It was a Holy Day indeed. This was the first day of May, on which the British and the Gauls, and I supposed the Irish too, drive out from the farms the beasts that they have kept folded in close all the winter, out to the summer pastures on the hills. And this, being the end-of-winter feast, is the fire feast for them, when they build their bonfires on the hills and jump through them and wish. Beltain they call it.

Now, it was with a fire feast that I had come into the North before, and I had gained wealth from it, and ever after I had counted such a feast as a lucky day for myself. I stood there in the cold wind of early dawn, and I looked at the sky, the first time since the year before that I had

261

looked up at all the stars, all of them shining through clear air with never a wisp of mist nor any haze to hide them. There was a clarity here I had not known in Britain. All the winter I had groped in the mists of double meaning, till I had myself begun to think not in logic but in riddles. But here, now, I knew, I would be myself again. Here I would think and reason as a man, coldly and economically, and *know*, not guess, what I was about. Here at last, I would not be at the mercy of others. I would be my own master — no, I would be master of all around, I would be master of all Ireland before I finished.

In the shelter of a tongue of land, we dropped anchor, still on salt water, though near a river mouth. The Irish, and there were twenty-seven of them altogether, all armed, launched their skin boats and got down into them gingerly, weighted down as they were with mail. Armour does not float very well, in my experience. The Setanta tapped me on the arm.

'Is it the courage to come with us you are having, or is it staying where you are safe that you will be?' Of course he spoke to me in British, and as we had both had to learn the language deliberately, we understood each other perfectly.

'Naturally,' I told him, 'I must be at hand to protect my investment.' I was full of the confidence of the first flush of day. I went down into a skin boat with the Setanta and Heilyn and another smelly ruffian, a very hairy man called, it seemed, Callum, and we paddled towards the shore. At least they paddled. I lay back with an air of civilised polish. I had finished with manual work, I told myself. From now on it would be the Barbarians who did all the work.

Some way off the shore, the other boats stopped; that is they stayed in the same place while their occupants paddled like mad to save themselves from being carried out by the tide. We, however, went closer in till there was hardly room for a skin boat even to float.

As we paddled in, we could see three figures on the beach, and as we drew near to the shore, so they walked down to the line of seaweed and driftwood that marked the water's limit. As we came in so that we would have been better advised to get out into the water and wade, I saw that they were three old women, tall and gaunt, hooded and cloaked in dusty grey. They threw back their hoods, and while the wind dropped to nothing, their hair streamed back horizontal from their heads, streamed grey and dusty as their cloaks. We bobbed up and down, not ten feet from them, and we looked at them and they looked at us.

Their faces were lined and old and lifeless. They might well have walked out from the houses of the Dead. They pointed their fingers at us, their left forefingers, bony and fleshless, and they began to sing. In a high wailing voice they sang, a mournful wailing tune, a tune full of sadness and foreboding and warning. I have heard sounds in my time that few men have heard and lived. I have heard the scream of the wounded mermaid, and the cough of the crocodile in the night. I have heard the women wail for Osiris in the Sanctuary, and I have heard the rustle of the poison spider on my pillow. And nothing have I ever heard that chilled my flesh and raised my hair as did the sound of those three women, tiny, singing on the empty beach of Ireland. We sat there on the sea on the edge of the world, and in that song I heard all the gulf at the end of the Ocean open to swallow us.

I looked at the Irishmen. The Setanta was quite unconcerned. He explained to me: 'It is the Morrigan.'

I knew a little about this, as much as any Greek does, and that was not much. The Morrigan is what the Irish call the Mother, but there in that wild land on the edge of Ocean, the Mother is still a conquered goddess, wild and unforgiving and hostile to all living men. The Morrigan is the wild spirit of all the women of the land, and the farther you go from the warm countries where kindly men rule, the more clear it is that men and women are two different kinds of being, as different from each other as dog from cat or horse from cow, and the fact that they can breed together, and that they both feel an unsuperable need for each other and a bitter hatred and rivalry, is as accidental and irrational as the tide. It was in answer to this impossible bond that I was coming myself to the land of Ireland, and here stood the Morrigan, the spirit of woman, to bar my way.

The Morrigan may come upon any woman at any time, or on more women than one. Here she had come on three women, which is right, because anyone who has an upbringing like mine knows that three is the number for women, and seven for men, whatever the Pythagoreans may say.

'What are they singing?' I asked. It was clear enough, really, but after all the shadows and double meanings of the magical Isle of Britain, I was not ready to accept anything as simple and plain in its meaning.

'They are forbidding us to land,' he answered. He spoke to the other men, and they began to paddle us away from the shore. I had to take a paddle too, because it is very difficult to make way against the tide and the breaking waves. I looked a question at the Setanta, because I had no breath to speak.

'We cannot land where the Morrigan has forbidden it. We must go back out to sea.'

'Are you going to abandon your invasion because they tell you to?' I was incredulous. Religion is one thing, but money is another, and I had invested a lot in this expedition. It was worth a curse, I thought. There is no curse that cannot be lifted for some appropriate payment. If Gold will not do it then blood will.

'I will not abandon this,' the Setanta answered, short of breath.

'Go somewhere else?' I panted.

'No, we must land here.'

'When?'

'When we have made a new voyage.'

I liked that idea even less. We had now reached the cluster of skin boats, half-way between Madoc's ship and the shore. We looked back to the beach.

'Now,' said the Setanta. 'You may count the waves. We are out beyond the ninth wave.'

I counted. 'So we are. If we return, it will be a new voyage?'

'It will that.'

'But if we make a new voyage, will not the Morrigan forbid us again?'

'Now it is the witches of the Queen of the West that they are, and it is paying them well she had been to forbid us to land. It is earning their money they have been. Now it is earning their other money they will be, and it is not seeing us that they will be intent on. Witches are very expensive. The Queen cannot afford to hire them for more than one cursing in the day, and we can only hire them for the one abstention, but praise be to the Gods, abstention is a longer act than cursing, and it is good value we will be getting for our money.'

'My money, you mean.'

'If it is pedantic you are meaning to be — yes.'

'So it is all a paid performance, and not the Morrigan at all?'

'No. It is here they are coming to curse because they are paid, but it *is* the Morrigan that is on them, and she is my fierce enemy.'

I did not ask further after the habits of the Morrigan. I was too busy digging in my paddle and heaving the boat shorewards against the tide and the wind. The other boats came with us, holding back a little out of politeness, so that we should be the first to land. Above us, the cloud began to break. The sun shone on us, clear and bright. At last I saw the colours of Ireland, and I saw them true and clear. In Britain I had lived half a year and more in twilight and in mist. There you will see no clear colours. Even the bright yellow of Rhiannon's cloak, the scarlet of a centurion's plume, everything in the Island of the Mighty, was seen as through a mist, the hues degraded, unsaturated, the outlines blurred, all hard edges softened. But now, as we came to the Island of the Blessed, everything was flooded in a clear hard light that took me home. The saffron cloaks and the green trees beyond the strand glowed bright and definite. I shook myself. I began to throw off the languors and the uncertainties of the Island of Britain, where nothing is as it seems, where every meaning is both doubtful and double, and I prepared to return to a life of logic and certainty and simplicity.

We beached the boat. The Setanta sprang first ashore, drawing his sword. I followed, waxing my axe, and the other men from the ship, as soon as they had carried the boats up above the tidemark of seaweed, also brandished their weapons and shouted dreadful oaths in their own language, describing perfectly intelligibly what they would do to anyone who tried to bar their path. The Three Witches of the Queen of the West drew their hoods over their faces, and ostentatiously did not see us, only grunting a little when Heilyn went over and pressed purses into their hands.

We walked up the beach in a long line. The Setanta was in the centre with Callum on his left and myself on his right, and Heilyn came on my other side, and I was glad of someone to keep my back, being the first emissary of the Empire to set foot in the country, even if no one knew about it. We were ready to form a shield wall, but we were not attacked as I, at least, half expected. Instead, as we breasted the dunes at the edge of the beach, with the low sun at our backs, there was a great noise and a crowd of unarmed men came running to us out of the scrub ahead.

There must have been two hundred of them. This was why the Setanta had been so positive that we must land here, and now. They thronged around us, shouting and cheering, the weaponless men of the disarmed kingdom of the North. They offered us hunks of steaming meat, and barley bread and jugs of beer, but we followed the Setanta in refusing them with flamboyant ritual gestures of abstention. And of course, we had had a hearty breakfast of cold mutton and oat cakes and mead in the ship. Still, we came ashore fasting till the time should be ripe for us to eat.

The Setanta stopped in the middle of an open space, and someone brought him a bundle of dry sticks and a bow. He tore off the edge of his garment for tinder, and twisting a stick in the bowstring, he made fire just as we do in the Temple at home on great occasions. In Ireland, if not in Britain, the meaning of every rite was plain to see. When the tinder smoked, nine naked men brought him each nine sticks from nine different trees — oak and elm and ash, willow and alder and yew, hazel and apple and rowan. They piled the sticks in a cone, and with a good deal of blowing by the Setanta they were able to start a real fire. Then all the men rushed to pile on the wood, so that they all had a hand in the blaze. When there was a good roaring pyre, the Setanta added a handful of straw, and immediately the Northern men piled on damp straw and green leaves, until a pillar of white smoke rose high in the air, to tell all Ireland that there was a new champion come to challenge the High King at Tara, and that he had kindled his own Beltian Fire.

Then, and only then, did the Setanta accept food and we ate too. Madoc, seeing the smoke, brought the ship in and beached her, and his crew rigged tackle to swing out the bundles of weapons. Then the Northern men came around and received their arms from the Setanta himself, to each man a sword, and to the more favoured a helmet or a mail coat or a shield, and to the luckiest all three.

But while this was going on, other things were being hoisted out, wheels and chariot bodies and poles. For this was the ruler of the battlefield in the Island of the Blessed, and if the King of the North had none of these, then he could not hope to face any other king in battle. Heilyn called round him the smiths and the carpenters among the Northern men, and set them to work assembling the chariots. I watched. The wheels were as high as a man's waist, not the high frail wheels you see on the chariots in the Games. And while we fix tyres on our wheels in sections, nailed on to the rim, the tyres of these wheels were made in one piece of iron, jointless, and shrunk in some

267

magical fashion which nobody would explain to me, so that they hold hard to the rim without nail or rivet or any other fastening.

They fixed a pair of wheels on to the first axle to hand, and drove the lynch pins into the felloes. Then they lowered a body on to the axle and joined body and axle with leather straps. The pole, likewise, was hooked on to the front of the body, so that the whole vehicle was most alarmingly flexible. I asked Heilyn, who spoke the British tongue, but with a vile accent, as did a number of the other men with him, who appeared to be Gauls, of the nation of the Sentantii:

'How many have we?'

He answered, without looking up from his task of fixing a pole into the first body:

'Well, there's nearly a hundred wheels, but mostly not in pairs, and forty-two bodies, and some in a dreadful state, and only twenty-six poles, but poles are easy to make, and I haven't counted the harness — I should say we will be lucky to have more than thirty when we finish. And the work in putting them together — you know, they were all made originally by a group of double-jointed Scythian dwarves that old King Brutus bought specially for the job, and unless we can find some more of the same breed, and it's expensive they come too, in any slave market, then it's not much of a success we will be making of this.'

I left him, and returned to the Setanta, who had paused in his rearmament programme.

'What will we do for horses? I can't see any.'

'Indeed, and isn't it getting them we will be now? Wasn't it in skin boats that those fine boys were coming down from the North, and how would you be carrying a horse in one of them?'

It was true enough, and now that everyone was armed, and it left great heaps of weapons and armour over, little groups of the Northern men were drifting off in all directions. Heilyn went on assembling his chariots, and all the day long more parties of unarmed men came straggling in asking for swords. Before noon, we could see other columns of smoke to answer ours, for we were on the seaward edge of a great plain.

By evening, the men were returning in their little groups, not just men, now, but warriors, for their new swords were blooded and some of them were wounded. One or two were left behind dead and many more dead drunk, and these also were dead in truth before the dawn.

They brought us back the horses, all right, plenty of them, because we had landed on the horse pastures of the High King, and we were able to take the pick of his herds where they grazed. Not that the pick was very wonderful. None of them was big enough to carry a man. This is why the Irish have to use them in chariots, because any beast, however puny, will pull a cart. There is something in the air of Ireland which prevents any horse from growing to its full size. They will never be able to breed a horse in all Ireland that will carry a man on its back.

They didn't only bring the horses. They had cattle, dozens of them, to be roasted at the fire that the Setanta had kindled, and others we had lit from it. We must have cut down half the woods of the province before we moved on. And they had mead, too, by the gallon, because they had robbed the village where the High King's horse-herders lived, and burnt it, and thus lit the whole land in a Beltain fire such as no one had expected.

Yes, that was a Beltain night to be remembered. The Setanta had returned after . . . how many years of exile? One year, said some of the Barbarians, and three years, said others. Before I left Ireland I heard songs that put it at seven years. However long it had been, the Northerners were glad to see him again, and made it clear that he was even more welcome than their brothers and cousins who had gone to join him overseas and were now returned with him. Now I could see that about half the Fianna were real Irishmen, out of Ulster, but the rest were strangers, Gauls it seemed. They, and I, received dark and suspicious looks from the newly arrived Irish, straggling in by threes and fours to demand their weapons.

This is what Pryderi would like, I thought. Instead of creeping from a little boat in the very shadow of his conquerors, to land from a great ship on a beach, and be surrounded by stalwart, obedient, faithful warriors, so that he could give each one his arms with a lordly gesture. No wonder Pryderi was jealous of the Setanta. This, to him, was the true place of a king, and his true work, raising an army for a great battle.

All through the night, the Northerners came streaming in, drawn by the light of the fires and by the smell of the meat as much as by the glint of the iron and the skirl of the whetstones, and by the screams of the women dragged from the horse-herders' village as they were mauled and raped and passed from man to man. Other women came in, too, of their own accord, as they always do when an army camps for the night. The Setanta, always a gentleman, had four of the younger ones passed in to the ship as a gesture of appreciation.

All in all, I thought at sunset, it was not a bad day's work. Five or six hundred men, all armed, and thirteen chariots ready to use, and horses for them, and food for us all for a month if anyone would take the trouble to store it and issue it, not bad, I thought, not bad at all, for one day. For one day, the day that the Setanta began his war of conquest of the Queen of the West and of the High King of all Ireland, that would set all Ireland in a blaze of quarrels and disunity. Not bad, even if no one in the island knew it yet, for the first day of the Roman Conquest of Ireland. Two months now to set the pot a-boiling, and then the seas would be calm enough for the clumsy galleys the legions built, calm enough even for those to bring the Army across the wide salt sea, first the Second, and then the Twentieth in support, and four regiments of cavalry, big men sitting on big horses, that would settle the business of any chariots that survived the coming battles of Irish against Irish. But this would be later. Let the war come first.

When it was dawn, I saw we had the beginnings of a real army, two thousand men or more. The supply of swords and shields had long given out: the latest comers were given spear heads and told to go away and cut their own shafts. When the tide rose and the ship floated, I waved Madoc out to sea. Now, I was alone in Ireland, as far as anyone to talk to was concerned, alone amid these howling savages. In Londinium, the Setanta had merely looked a bit wild. Here, in the middle of a great crowd of men dressed exactly like him, and he now as dirty, with a winter in the hills, as the worst of them, he looked at once both horrifying and commonplace. Looking around, I could believe all the tales I had heard in Britain of the Irish cooking their enemies in cauldrons to suck their valour from their marrow bones, and carrying the heads around their necks for years, till they rotted on the string.

Of course, the lack of communication could soon be remedied. I went to the Setanta.

'I want a woman. Next girl you catch, a young one, I want her.'

'Have one of these,' he said, magnanimously. 'Why didn't you join in last night?'

I looked at the huddle of weeping, bleeding, naked bodies. This, I thought, is what Pryderi would want, this is what the other island was like before the conquest, when every king was as good as any other king, and any man as good as his master if only he were strong enough. But the legions would settle that; as brutal perhaps in the first months, but in five years there would be roads all across the land, and inns by them, and even Rhiannon could ride unguarded and unharmed wherever she liked. And, I swore it, if Rhiannon had been treated one-tenth as badly as these women, then there was not a man in the south that I would leave alive, I would not grant one his life, no, not for all the Gold in Ireland. But now I replied to the Setanta, as casually as I could:

'No, thank *you*. They've been well used, too well used, overused I should say. Anybody may have been tramping about there. I want something . . . how shall I put it? I want something a bit cleaner and fresher.'

271

The Setanta called over our boat companion, Callum, who seemed to have a great following of his own, and translated to him, and I dangled a few links of Gold chain before his eyes. He was going off to forage anyway, and even if he had farther to go than the day before he was back not long after noon with horses and cattle, and half a dozen likely wenches to choose from. I picked the cleanest, to the accompaniment of a good deal of cheering and jeering from the warriors, and after a few days' hard work — and it went as hard for me as for her — I could make out a great deal of what they were talking about, though I never got as far as being able to make poetry in Irish, as I had almost done in the British tongue. The two languages were not all that different, after all. The grammar was almost the same, only most of the words were strange. When I could understand what the warriors were jeering and could jeer back, I was satisfied, and I let her go off to some of the best jeerers, and she could assure them that at least some of what they said was true, and the rest false.

After we had been there a week I began to get impatient. I had nothing to do, except sit still and learn Irish and watch them put together more chariots — we had nearly forty in the end. I also watched them training the horses. They had to be taught to run when they were told, and stop when they were told, and stand still whatever happened around them. One advantage of where we had landed was that some of the horses had been trained already. But there weren't many of the men who had been in a chariot before, and so we had to find a number of the lightest who could learn to drive. This was a thankless task, because you had one driver and one warrior in the chariot. The driver had to control the horses and satisfy his master, and if anything went wrong it was the driver's fault, and if there was success it was due to the warrior. And the driver had no way of defending himself. I thought that killing the driver was the easiest way of stopping a chariot, but the Irishmen assured me that wasn't the way to go to war at all. Noblemen fought noblemen, and left the drivers out of it.

We had to train a dozen horses, at least, for each chariot, since no horse could charge more than once in a day. And a number of the younger men were as unskilled as the horses, and had to learn how to hold a sword or a spear or an axe or whatever else they had been lucky enough to get. But apart from this, we did, effectively, nothing, except to eat up the country. After a week I went to the Setanta and asked him:

'What are we waiting for?'

'We are waiting for the High King. What else would we be waiting for?'

'Waiting for the High King to do what?'

'To come to Tara, of course.'

'What? Isn't he at Tara?'

'And why should he be now at Tara, seeing that it is neither the Feast of Tara, that they hold every seventh year at Samain, and it will be held again this winter. Nor is it the feast of his consecration as High King, for that was years ago, and it is ourselves will hold it, I am telling you.'

'How far are we from Tara?'

'Perhaps twenty Roman miles.'

'Then — if the High King is not at Tara, why do we not just march there?'

'What? Without a battle?'

I looked at him. I could not help saying what I did. It was in my interest to see a battle, to see as many battles as possible in the coming two months, and yet — something in me made me speak, made me want to show him how wrong his actions were, how absurd his manner of thinking, how — I could not contain myself.

'Battle? Why do you Barbarians always want to fight battles? Battle is the last resort of politics, to use when all other ways are barred. Battle is waste: waste is effort, waste of health, waste of blood. Why fight at all if you can get what you want by any other means? Speed is all we have. We could make a quick rush to Tara now, could have done any time the last week, and make you High King, or your uncle, or anyone you choose. As for the present High King, we can send one or two of your Northerners to assassinate him under pretence of making their surrender, or better still, we could bribe his bodyguard to murder him privately. So all the waste could be saved.'

The Setanta looked at me as if I were a child.

'Oh, you merchants. Why is it always only the end you look at, and never the means? It is how a thing is done that is important, not only what is done. Whoever is to be High King, he must show it, not by walking into Tara in the dark, but by killing his rival before the eyes of all the Island. If we shed no blood, no one will believe we rule.'

This is the way of the Barbarians. I knew he would never rule, not with all the four armies of Ireland broken against each other, and the legions wading ashore and the Eagles flying over Tara. That he did not know. He went on:

'But if it is any comfort to you, tomorrow the High King will indeed be at Tara, and we will be going that way too, and the day after that we will fight him, and the armies of the West and of the South.'

You'll fight him, I thought, not me. I'm not going into any mêlée with only one eye. Nevertheless, while the others sharpened their swords, I honed the edge of my axe. You never know.

CHAPTER THREE

Next day the Army marched. Our troops had come down from the North in skin boats, or by foot along paths that clung close to the sound of the breaking wave, to steal the well-broken horses and come at the High King from a direction he did not expect. Now, therefore, we marched north of west, to Tara.

We must have been five thousand strong, all told, and we covered a great square of country. For besides the men, we had the cattle we had stolen in the country round about, and the horses, and droves of swine, and all the women we had stolen as well, and who now wouldn't be left behind, after the way of women in a land at war, and their children came, and children who didn't belong to anyone who would own them now, but who had to come with the Army because there was no other way for them to beg a few scraps to eat.

We trampled over the grass of May and left it a great scar of mud, because it rained the day we marched, as one might expect, after weeks of dry weather. We strewed the countryside with half-gnawed bones and worn-out shoes, piles of ordure and dead babies and all the other litter an army leaves behind. This, I thought, is what Pryderi would like to see again in the Island of the Mighty: I wish he were here to see it now.

The chariots had been painted in gaudy colours, and hung about with bronze and silver bells, and charms of all kinds, in place of what they usually hung on them. For the journey, the colours were covered against the dust with sheets of coarse cloth. And men pulled them, because it was important that the precious horses should not be tired out or cast shoes or break legs before the battle.

We covered about fifteen miles in the day, and when we halted we were, they told me, in sight of Tara, but there was never a city I could see where they pointed, only a few scattered huts between me and the distant hills where the sun was setting. But what I could see only too well, and see better in the dark, was the long line of fires that answered our own. From our farthest right to our farthest left the fires shone hard and bright in the clear dry air, for the hard east wind now blew the rain away. I could see clear and harsh the figures of men who passed between us and the flames. So we lit our own fires, and we made our force look bigger, as I was sure the High King had done, by lighting two fires for every man and a fire for every woman.

We cut down a forest to feed our fires, and we slaughtered all our cattle, so that every man could have the hero's portion, the thigh, to eat, and the rest we threw away as not juicy enough. The women stuffed themselves on what was left and then the straggling children, and the dogs quarrelled over the bones, and the mangy wolves crept out of the thickets and scavenged at the edges of the camp, and wished it were the next evening, because they knew, they knew.

There was mead enough for every man to get drunk, and stay drunk till Doomsday, as indeed a man will if he thinks Doomsday is tomorrow. So get drunk they did, all of them, before midnight. I went to the Setanta, who was still sober enough to speak, and I suggested that he should get a line of pickets out, in case the High King tried to rush us in the dark. He laughed at me. The Irish never do such things, he told me. They have no sense of prudence at all. Now you or I, if we had an enemy, would have used some intelligence when he left himself vulnerable, would ambush him with a knife in the dark, or put an arrow in his back in a narrow way, or burn his house over his head — or safer, when he was out of it. But the Irish believe in meeting their foes face to face. No, said the Setanta, there was no need to be afraid of anything.

I did not agree. I looked for Heilyn, or Callum, or any

of the men who had come with us in the ship, but they were not to be found. Drunk, somewhere, I thought. Will there be no sentry in the night over all this army of the North? No, none but I.

I remembered how our army lay. Before us there was a wide level plain. It is only on such ground that you can fight in chariots. About midway along our front was a mound, a burial mound of the men of old. On our right, there was a thicket, and between the mound and the thicket was an area of scrub willow, knee high or higher. Our left flank was quite open.

I moved through the host, my sealskin cloak open to show my mail coat, one eye black and one glowing red, ruby red. Nobody was sober enough to ask what I was doing, or to deny me anything. From one group I took a jug of bull's blood, hot and steaming from the heart, and from another I had a jar of mead. In a bowl I put the fat from around a bull's kidneys, and the thigh of a porker. These I balanced on my shield, a round bronze shield, enamelled, once set with garnets. I balanced the shield on one hand, and in the other I had a black cock.

I turned my back on the host of Ulster, and I walked towards the host of the High King. I went over the open ground in the dark, and there was not the least sliver of moon nor any star to be seen; yet I did not step into a mole-hill, nor trip over a drunken sleeper nor an amorous one.

I came to the top of the mound, a low mound raised perhaps five or six feet above the level of the plain. I set down the tray. I took from my bag a knife, a bronze knife, broad of blade, and I began to dig. I knew where. It was an old grave and much honoured, the grave of one of the long dead kings of the country, and full, if only I had had the courage to open it, of Gold and jewels. But I found the funnel between the stones that led down to the mouth of the King. First into the funnel I poured the bull's blood, hot and still steaming, full of life and strength, and after that the mead, full of the warmth of the sun and the busy stirring of the bees. Then I offered the fat and the meat, and I put them into the hole, that the waking Dead might eat and be filled, and not hunger after me. Last of all I took the morse that fastened my cloak, a Golden pin, Indian Gold, not Irish, and I threw it into the hole. Phryne gave it to me. Phryne was dead. I gave it back to the dead. I did not fill in the hole.

I stood on the mound that led to the land of the dead, the grave mound that all the British and all the Irish believe is a gate to the Land Below, where we who live may meet those who are dead and those who yet may live. I had paid my private debt to Those Below. That would have whetted their appetites. Now I would show them how to feast, now I would draw out life for them. Now they would have a feast indeed.

I stood on the mound in the blackness, and I looked toward the host of the High King, where the fires died uncovered and the filth of men was poured out on the earth, and I saw that they were ready. And I took the High King and all his host, and I devoted them to the Gods Below, I sacrificed them to the dead who sought their lives. I sang in the ancient tongue the rite of the Gods Below, that our ancestors first brought over the mountains out of the plain, when Greek and Trojan, Persian and Egyptian were one nation. I asked the questions, and I answered them too, for want of anyone to answer them to me.

'And you came to the crossing of the river, and what found you there?' I asked myself, and I answered in the dark:

'Waters swift to the knee, waters cold to the belly, waters bitter over the head.'

The fires opposite me guttered and died as if the waters indeed rose over them. The host of the High King lay down drunk to sleep, and they dreamed: oh, yes, they dreamed. Their dreams did them no good.

'And you came to the crest of the mountain, and what found you there?' I chanted, as I have chanted it before in the Temple of the Old city. And I sang the response, as I have sung it to my Father, and as my nephews have, and my son will sing to me:

'I found the heart out of the chest, and the liver out of the trunk.'

The darkness was thick enough to touch, thick enough to feel. This was a darkness that I called upon myself, a darkness that felt and thought and knew. With this darkness I cursed the host of the High King. The black cock lay still at my feet looking at the Holy Line. I asked:

'And you came to the gate of the pass, and what found you there?'

And who was it, then, that answered:

'I found the flesh of a thigh, and the marrow of a bone.'

For Those Below now stood beside me on the mound. First came those who had gone below and returned, before they died for ever. Ulysses and Aeneas, who spoke with the dead across the stream, my kinsmen both — the same blood ran in our veins and one flesh, living and dead, we stood upon the mound.

Next, but farther off, stood Orpheus who went below to seek his love, and lost her again, through love, and Gilgamesh, who was before him, and Persephone who stands half of every year before the throne below, and Pwyll the Old, Pryderi's forefather, who ruled a year in Hell in Arawn's place. They all came, and stood beside me on the mound. They held up my arms, and with me cursed the host of the High King.

To bring the friendly dead was one thing. To bring the just Gods was another, those who favour no man, who cannot be persuaded. Thoth and Adeimantus. But all the night I stood upon the mound in the cold dark, the worst May frost in a man's life, and the sweat upon my skin froze within my clothes. I sang the words I may not here repeat in the language none may know I speak, and at last the great Judges of the Dead stood beside me to judge the High King and all the host and condemn them for all the evil they had done. But they judged the host of the North, also, and they judged me. But that I did not know.

Last I sang up the named and the nameless Gods Below, the gods who do not care for justice or for right or for any man, and it is these gods above all who rule the world from their place below, rule the Sun and the Earth and all the other gods. They hate all things living, and they seek only to draw us down to themselves and suck out our life. These are the gods that no man worships, but the gods do: that men and gods fear, and will never tell their fear. They feed on souls. I promised them food in plenty.

And at last, they too came to me on the mound, and the ice crackled in my eyebrows as they came past. It was the last frost of a mild winter, and it blasted all the fruit blossom throughout Ireland, so that there was no cider pressed that year. And who ever before knew of frost out of a starless sky?

There came a gleam of light over my right shoulder, and I heard a rustling and a scraping before me. The light became stronger, and the cloud faded from the sky, and at last the sun shone full over the horizon behind me, and all the cocks of Ireland crew, as they had done under the Glass Mountain on Mid-winter's eve. Before the cock at my feet could crow, I bit off his head with my teeth, and I tossed the struggling body into the hole in the mound. And then those in front of me saw and heard the head in my hands crow louder than ever a whole bird sang. And then the head too I threw into the hole, and I pushed the earth back over it with my feet.

Behind me, I knew, there lay the host of the North in a drunken sleep. They would not stir for all the ghosts of the world. But in front of me, men came gently forward over the frost-white grass. The High King was a wise man, wise as I, and a worthy enemy, for he knew what war was about. He had thought, as I thought, that a determined rush by a few determined men would settle the matter for good and all, and so it would have done. If the Setanta were to die, who would stand here?

There were about two hundred of them, young men and strong, the High King's household troops. They came steadily and stealthily on, looking up at me as I stood before them on the mound, my arms stretched in prayer, so that they knew well enough what I was about. I sang my hymns to the Gods Below as loudly as I had done throughout the night, and yet they took no notice of me, they did not so much as throw a spear. They would see to me later.

But when they were well within a spear's cast from me, when their line stretched out to lap round the mound on both sides — then I stopped singing, and I dropped my arms. Their whole line stopped as if they saw another line rise up from the ground to meet them. And so they did. Had I not worked all night for it?

Each man of the household looked at the line that rose before him, and each man cowered behind his painted shield. Each man looked into the face of the man who stood against him, a sword's reach before him, shield to shield. And each man saw himself not as he was, as he might see his image in a pool, or even in a mirror if any man could cast and polish a sheet of bronze large enough to reflect a whole man. No, each man saw himself as he would end. This man saw his own ribs thrust up and out from a spear stabbing from the ground, and that one saw his own gut pour out on the earth from a slashing sword. Men saw their own skulls smashed by axe blows, their eyeballs hanging down on their cheeks, and their brains grey in their hair. They saw their faces shorn away, they saw severed arms held in good arms, they saw themselves try to hop on one leg and the stump of a thigh.

Now many a man, and a brave man too, is sickened by the sight and smell of his own blood steaming on his arm, or at seeing a limb of his, or even a finger, warm on the ground. But hot blood is one thing. Stale blood is another. The High King's household did not see themselves as they would be that night, fresh dead. They saw themselves as they would be in a week ahead. The clay of the grave clotted on their rusted mail, those that had not been rudely stripped. Their rings were torn from their fingers and their ears. Their clothing hung in stinking rags. Maggots teemed in their gaping wounds. Worms writhed in their empty eye-sockets, those that still had their heads. Their bellies swelled, and their navels showed the green spot of corruption. The stench of the grave hung like a curtain before them. And worst of all, it was not only the edge of the iron that had emptied those eye-sockets or laid bare the teeth within the cheek, or cracked the marrowbones. The wolves howled in the woods, and the crows hung in great cawing crowds above us and filled the trees. The household of the High King looked at themselves, and they knew themselves by their painted shields, and by their garments, what was left, and by the scars on their bodies. They looked at themselves, and they did not stay to look twice.

If I then had had a hundred men ready to follow, there would have been no battle that day. The household rushed back through the ranks of their own army, and spread the tale of terror, and not a man of them struck a blow in the battle that day, though all of them died before the sun set.

Then the crows rose from the grass and circled above us, and from the South and the East there came in the kite and the buzzard, the souls of those who have done evil and are condemned now to live on carrion. And there was only one who could have sent the birds, and it was for her that I did battle. I would not have raised Those Below on the mound for all the Gold in Ireland: I did it because only thus could I conquer all the land and find the mistress of the birds, the Lady of Those Below. And with Rhiannon's birds, my own wolves came howling on the flanks. All the birds and beasts were working their way towards the rear of the High King's army, so as to have a shorter way to go for their dinner. And the host of the West saw this, and it did not make them more eager to fight.

The noise and clatter of all this, the cawing of the birds, the shouts of terrified men, a dawn chorus of a kind we seldom hear, woke all our army as nothing else could have done. There was a great shouting and blowing of horns, and in less time that it would take a stammering man who was not very sure of his arithmetic to count to a couple of thousand or so, they had formed a line of sorts, but

282

well behind me, leaving me alone on the mound. And there I stayed.

Our warriors did not look very well, most of them. That is one reason why Barbarians fight so savagely. Usually they have been drunk the night before, and there is nothing like a raging headache to put venom into your sword strokes. Or so they tell me. I don't have headaches. Going into a fight drunk is quite another thing. I'll fight a drunken man any day, but a man who is sobering up — never!

The line of foot soldiers was not very straight or very steady, I looked for the men who had come in the ship, especially for Heilyn and the Gauls, but they were nowhere to be seen. I decided that they had deserted, as Barbarians often do, and mercenaries usually do, before a battle. But, if our army had formed a line, so had the High King's, and what a line. It overlapped ours at both ends, not because there were many more men in it than ours, but because their men were spreading out so as to have room to run away, while ours, having nowhere to run to, were clinging together for warmth. But that was the enemy's first line, and there were three more of the same strength behind that.

Later they made songs about that day which claimed that we were outnumbered by twenty or thirty to one. It always feels like that, even if they're only three to two, because all the spare men go loose and you never know where they're going to come from next. At my best count, they were four to one at most, and fifty chariots to our forty, and we were better off for chariots because we had all the trained horses. Men were running about, pulling off the covers to show the painted sides, and harnessing the horses and fitting the scythe blades to the sides — not to the wheels, of course — which discourage anyone from getting close enough in to hamstring the horses. Of course, someone always tries it and ends up in seventeen pieces.

The few chariots we had ready were already out in front of the foot, and to my surprise they were singing the old song we so often hear at the Circus before a race, when the charioteers are trying to get their spirits up. The words were a reasonable translation of what we are used to:

> Throw an obol on the grass,
> Save a Charioteer's ass:
> Yarahoo-oo . . .! Yarahoo!!
> Throw an obol on the grass and be saved.

These were nothing like the racing chariots you bet on, though. They had two men, one small and light to drive, and the other big and strong to do the fighting. It was he who needed the big shield, to cover him from shoulder to calf — his shins were behind the low wicker sides. He had a long-edged sword for slashing at anyone who got near enough, though the scythe blades made sure that nobody did, so he had for his main weapon a bundle of javelins. If you have ever tried throwing a spear from a moving chariot, you will realise that the vehicle's main effect is on morale. The charioteers were thinking of their own morale; they sang:

> Riding by the Liffey,
> Hear the warrior wail,
> Save me, Chieftain, save me,
> All Connaught's on my tail.
> Throw an obol to the sky.
> Why should charioteers die?
> Yarahoo . . .! Yarahoo!!
> Throw an obol in the sky and be saved.

And all our line of foot screamed, 'Yarahoo!!' to keep up their spirits, and they needed it, with the High King's chariots riding out in front of his line, and getting their dressing straight, no fuss, no sweat, very careful, as if they were riding in a triumph, not going into action.

A fine sight it is, a line of chariots, and lucky you are that you will never see it the way I saw it, coming on at you at the trot, very earnest and deadly and full of all the

284

confidence in the world. There I stood on the mound, and I could see the line of them rolling on, the hooves very quiet in the ground soft still after the previous day's rain. They were spreading out on my right and my left and obviously going to lap around me on either side.

The High King's chariots covered the half-mile between the two hosts quite slowly, when you consider they were all eager to fight, but they were saving their horses for that last dash, when you can let them strain as they will against the rope loops about their necks and it does not matter if they half-strangle themselves now. Our little group, twenty ready now against their fifty, came forward in a bunch on our left. They hoped there at least to stop the enemy curling round to come against our foot from the flank. They were very steady, waiting to be loosed at the last moment in a spoiling death ride in the hope of slowing the enemy down before they crashed into our infantry. Some of the latter were already drifting away: the others were none too steady.

Then suddenly, out of the willow scrub on my right, a group of men stood up, shouting and screaming some kind of challenge, mother naked most of them, except for their swords and helmets. Oh, yes, I knew who these were. I did not only recognise Heilyn and Callum, my fellow rowers, and all the other men from the ship: these, I knew, were the Gesatae that Caesar and Tacitus tell us about, warriors vowed to death and so fighting with no protection, to ensure it comes. But an opponent who is not defending himself, but intent on killing you, is very hard to deal with, and if you can kill one of them, then it is clear that you are a hero yourself. So it was no wonder that the chariot line carried out a manoeuvre which does not sound impressive till you try it, remembering now it was being done at the canter, and the whole squadron moving faster and faster, with each warrior wanting to be the first to draw blood and every driver wanting to satisfy him. The whole line of fifty chariots changed front half-left and swept towards the right of the mound, leaving our chariots facing nothing and all our infantry on the right exposed to the full fury of the charge which twenty Gesatae would do nothing to halt, however hard they died.

And then, as the first chariots, because the line was ragged now and had lost its dressing, entered the scrub of dwarf willow, one of them tipped over on a broken wheel, and the horse of another fell, and a third swerved hard left and crashed into a fourth. And into the jumble of smashed chariots the rest hurtled, and in the twinkling of an eye the scrub was full of broken wheels and snapped poles, of kicking horses rolling on their backs tangled in their harnesses, and men trying to get free and throwing down their swords and shields as they dodged the flailing hooves. And the Gesatae were among them at once, and a hundred or more of the foot from our line. In that moment, whatever happened later, the battle was won, and it was Heilyn who had done it, Heilyn and the Gauls from the ship, and Callum the Hairy, the only Irishman among them. They had stretched ropes among the scrub, to trip the horses, and thrown down spikes to hurt their feet, and dug deep holes to break their legs, and scattered big stones to break the chariot wheels. Like all battles, it was won the night before by men who thought: I was not the only sober man that night, nor the only sleepless one.

The few chariots that survived went west like the wind, the drivers urging on the horses in terror. Into the ranks of the High King's army they swept, unstoppable, and before they could be slowed down they had caused as much damage as if they had been enemies, not friends in distress. They punched a wide hole in the line, and now it was the Westerners who were beginning to slip away. The crows cawed impatiently. The Gods Below had begun to taste their feast. They would not rest, now, till they had had their fill of lives. There were few men on that field who saw Beltain again. Few men on either side.

I waited for our own chariots, and now there were thirty of them, to charge in their turn, but they hesitated. Out from the turmoil of the High King's line came a single chariot. I looked at it with the keen sight of the one-eyed man. It was the High King himself, there was no doubt of it. Tall in his chariot, with his long black hair trailing behind him in the wind from beneath his shining helm, Gold gleaming on his neck and wrists, his mail flashing where it caught the sun, his great bronze shield shining red, he came charging alone towards us, and our chariots hung waiting there. Out from our line to meet him rode the Setanta, the Champion of the North.

It was like something out of Homer, and I saw it all from where I stood on the mound. The two chariots rolled on towards each other. The men in the lines were shouting and screaming. I had half a mind to try and get back to start some betting going, but then I reflected, if the North lost who would there be to pay me?

Round and round the mound the chariots raced, in opposite directions, the Setanta with the sun, the High King widdershins. Each driver kept the other on his left as they passed twice on each circuit. Twice on each circuit they passed and each time they passed the warriors threw their spears. Five times the spears were cast, and five times both missed.

Then, on the sixth pass, each man threw his last spear. I was watching the Setanta, and as the horses nearly collided and then swerved violently apart, I saw him stagger as a spear bit deep into his shoulder. I followed him on, but when I looked back to the High King, I saw that his driver was spitted, and he fell forward over the front of the chariot among the horses' feet. The beasts kicked and stumbled, and the chariot overturned, and the High King of all Ireland rolled in the dust.

In the time it takes to tell, the Setanta's chariot was all the way around the mound again, and when he saw the wreck, the Setanta clapped his driver on the back, and the little man pulled up the horses in their own length, and that takes strength. The Setanta leapt down, pulling out the spear and throwing it away, any way; it nearly skewered *me*.

The Setanta was white with passion, and his hair, stiffened and streaked with dye and grease and whitewash, stuck out behind him like a horse's mane. The veins were big on his forehead, his eyes almost started out of his head, his mouth was distorted into that square shape you see on the statues of the Furies, and his limbs were flailing like an octopus's: you'd have sworn there was never a bone in his body. Blood was running down his arm, but if he was in pain, the High King was worse. *He* was half stunned still from his fall, but he groped for his sword and shield on the ground, and then he came to his feet. But as soon as he put his weight on his left ankle, it gave under him, for he must have twisted it hitting the ground all in a bundle as he had. He staggered again, trying to hop on his right leg, and the Setanta was on him at once smashing his shield into the King's face, and hacking and chopping at him as he went down.

The King squirmed on the soft grass, all cut up with hooves and already splashed with the Setanta's blood. The Setanta danced over him, screaming like a wild thing, and hacking and stabbing at him aimlessly, tearing through leather and mail, almost for the mere sake of hurting the man. But this man could not be hurt any more. The body turned into a bloody mess as the Setanta hit it again and again, with edge and with point, in full view of both armies, who all stood still and silent as the grave. Even the crows had ceased to caw.

At last, the Setanta bent down and cut once, carefully. He stood up, holding the High King's head, all gashed and bleeding, and took it to his chariot and tied it by the long black hair to the pole. Why else does a warrior wear his hair so long? While this had been going on, the driver had taken no notice but had calmly changed the horses. The Setanta stepped again into his chariot. And then all his army shouted, and for the first time I heard his name. He was safe now, no witchcraft could hurt him, I could hear it and remember it, as they all bellowed:

'Cuchullain! Hero of the North, Cuchullain!'

The charioteers were now all in line, all forty of them. They began to sing:

> Throw a neckplate or a pin,
> Save a charioteer's skin.
> Yarahoo . . .! Yarahoo!!
> Throw the Gods Below a pin, and be saved

The chariot line began to move forward, Cuchullain the Champion of Ulster in the centre, slowly at first. The whole area where they had waited sparkled as if covered with dew. Every man had indeed thrown down some jewel of Gold or silver, a cloak-pin or a kilt-pin, a necklace or an armlet, jewelled and shining, as an earnest for his safe return.

CHAPTER FOUR

There wasn't much of a battle, if you are thinking of a civilised battle, where two armies clash in a long line of fighting men, pushing and striking at each other, till one line goes back and back, dwindling and shrinking and the last of them die where they are because they have nowhere that their honour will allow them to go back to any more. In Barbarians' wars, the real business of a battle is over beforehand. By some means or other, a duel between witches or between leaders, one side is convinced by the other that it has lost, before ever a blow is struck by the rank and file. Then the losing side runs away, and very sensibly too. Their enemies run after them and kill all they can catch, and that is not many. Most men who die in battle are struck in the back. Any man who is willing to turn and fight when he has to will be let alone.

Before our chariots were within spear throw of the army of the West, their front line broke and ran, and so did the support lines when they saw there was no protection in front of them. The chariots ran into the shapeless mob and right through them. The scythe blades caught a few men, and the warriors in the chariots stabbed as far as their spears would reach and occasionally threw them at a tempting target if it stood still, but not often because they were afraid of running out of spears. Our foot followed them, almost as much of a mob as the defeated enemy, but going more slowly as soon as they reached where the front line had been, because they kept on bending down to pick up weapons thrown away, and to rob the few bodies. As this undisciplined mass came level with the mound, they drew me with them, waving my axe. Such is the power of a crowd.

I found myself running shoulder to shoulder with Heilyn, who had, sensibly, not stayed naked any longer than it had taken to tempt the chariots against him. I looked at him through the tangle of hair and whiskers and the grease of a winter in the hills. After a few paces, I said to him in Greek:

'Are we running all the way? This mail is heavy.'

'Slow down, then,' replied Aristarchos. We did, and watched both armies disappearing into the distance. We paused to look at the body of the High King. He still had all his jewels: Cuchullain would return to strip him later. His sword lay near him. I looked at that. The weapons we had brought from Britain in the ship had been old-fashioned, native work a century old. This sword was far older in design, whoever had made it, and whenever. It was long and two-edged, pointless or hardly pointed, the sides running parallel almost down to the tip. The hilt was topped by a pommel of Gold, a Golden ball through which the iron tang protruded, to be turned over and hammered down again. The iron, though, was poor, not even as good as Roman, let alone as good as the fine metal the Germans use. Any good iron in the islands, I had been told, was kept for chariot tyres. The High King had fallen at the last on his sword: the blade bent under his weight.

I might have taken a few souvenirs, for Cuchullian owed them to me, but old women were already coming out to crouch around the body, old women in dusty black, their white hair streaming down their blacks, with the lice moving in it like a ceaseless wave. They sang the death song, in a high reedy tune, the tune that the witches had sung to us on the sea shore. I watched them a little: then I thought, 'Even Rhiannon will come to this'. And it was a death song I too had sung all night on the mound. I left the women to the dead I had made.

Other corpses were scattered over the plain. This was no Cannae, but it was enough. All had been struck in the back. Most had been robbed of their weapons already, and some of their heads. Those men of the North who had not been armed out of the ship had gone into battle armed only with their thick cudgels pulled out of the hedge and with their knives. Now everyone had a sword, and there were shields and to spare, and even a few mail shirts cast off by those who felt that the time taken to strip was worth exchanging against the extra speed after it.

The crows were already busy on the dead. These souls of evil men found no famine for their wicked beaks. They could afford now to take the eyes alone, and be filled. The rest would be eaten soon enough. The wolves were slinking out of the woods on the edge of the rout, tearing at the men who lay, living or dead where the armies had passed. When night fell the mangy starving beasts would come further. I looked at my companion. We had both seen battlefields before. We had no need to rob: we had no wish to stay. I asked:

'Which way is Tara?'

'The way nobody is going,' Aristarchos answered, pointing a little north of west. 'I've never captured a city by myself.'

'No more have I,' I agreed. 'Do you think we could sack it? You might even get a mural crown.'

We turned half right and made for the cluster of huts a mile or so away. There was nobody to stop us. I stuck my axe through my belt. Aristarchos sheathed his sword. We slung our shields on our backs. He asked me, casually:

'How was Africanus when last seen?'

'Thriving. The ships should be nearly all ready by now. The Second will embark by the end of June, and the Twentieth will be here in August, weather permitting.'

'Splendid. Now we have scattered the armies of the West and South. By midsummer I shall have the army of the North spread over half the island, with concentration impossible. Before the end of the year, the whole island will be part of the Empire.'

'Yes,' I nodded. 'It will be this year in Tara for the Second, at last.'

We swaggered into Tara. Not alone. A dozen or so of the winded, or windier, footmen had fallen in behind us.

Entry into Tara at the head even of this bedraggled little vanguard of a victorious army would have been impressive if only there had been a city for us to enter. When we came close the cluster of huts became a scattering of houses, spread over a mile of country, all mixed up with barrows and mounds and earthworks of doubtful purpose, middens and manure heaps and furnaces, smithies and fields of barley and vegetable plots, and animals grazing, pigs and cows, and dogs and children running everywhere.

There were a lot of people around, men and women too, most of them busy at one thing or another, weaving or beating iron or bronze, or chipping away at wood, and one or two bards, sitting with what looked a little like lyres but weren't, obviously practising their spontaneous improvisations for a feast to come. Our miserable little army killed the first two lads they came to, minding pigs, but all the other people around looked so shocked that they stopped killing at once and clung together in a little group and looked embarrassed.

Aristarchos and I went up to a large and comfortable woman who was boiling soup over an open fire.

'And a fine day it is indeed,' Aristarchos said to her, in a conversational manner.

'It is that: but it was raining it was yesterday, to be sure.' She straightened up and looked at us. 'And who was it that won, then?'

'Us, of course. The North.'

'Indeed. I was thinking, I was, that that was how it would be.' I wondered whether she had had a bet on it, but I remembered that the Irish are very little given to gambling, which was why the King of Leinster's Gesa must weigh so hard on him. She asked:

'And what was it became of the High King?'

'Cuchullain cut his head off.'

'Indeed, and improve him vastly I'm sure it would, for it was a face like a bladder of lard he had on him. And if he lost the battle and lived, then it would be dreadful bad luck for him for the rest of his life, and he might have lived for many years.'

293

The logic confused me. Still, there seemed method in it. I asked:

'Does this happen often?'

'Constantly. Isn't it the three High Kings we've had in the one year, and never a grain of sense among the three of them? And none of them properly consecrated, although when I think of it although the rite is so well known there is never a king that has followed it so exactly that there is arguing he can ever be that he is High King with no shadow of doubt. And when it does happen, it is a terrible time we have finding the horses, and it is white mares they have to be, pure white, every time.'

'You have to find the horses every time?' I didn't find it possible to believe what they told me about the way the High King wedded his kingdom, I still preferred to think of the bridal chase I had seen among the Britons.

'And who else would there to be doing it? Why, do we not live here rent free for that very purpose, to be finding the horses for the High King, and to be making the Feast of Tara for him, and to be forging his sword, and to be making his coffin if indeed there is enough of him left to need a coffin. Mind you, whenever there is a battle, there are usually one or two of us that do get killed, but it is by accident only and not through malice, and it is worth a little risk, you will agree, thinking of all the other advantages of living here.'

'Oh, yes, there must be great advantages in living here,' I agreed. These were quite a familiar people, slaves of the God, living around the Temple, and serving the Priest King, whoever happened to be Priest King for the time being. I asked:

'And where is it that the High King is living?'

'Why, 'tis in his own kingdom that he lives, and it is to Tara that he only comes on the Feast of Tara, and to the Hall of Tara that he and his warriors will go after the battle for the feast. And sure, it is there you will be wanting to go now, is it not?'

'And if it was wanting to go there we were, then which way is it we would be needing to go, now?' The rhythm

294

of their language, even of their way of — no, not thought, a Barbarian cannot think, let us say of their pondering and puzzling — it was infectious. Besides, obviously nothing of any value was to be gained by staying here.

'Why, it is past the mound that the hall is. And if after the feast tonight there is nowhere to sleep that you are finding, then it is in my house that you are welcome to sleep the night.

'Oh, good!' Aristarchos and I both exclaimed together, and then we glared at each other because there is something about the air of the island that is very relaxing to both physique and morals, though it is a fine and keen edge it puts on wit and logic and understanding. But she went on:

'And it is my husband that will be very glad to meet you. That is Cullain over there at the smithy. The one bending horseshoes out of billets of cold iron.'

'It must be very strong teeth he is having,' I was moved to remark.

'Indeed, and it was a strong man he was in his prime,' was her answer. We bade her good day and walked on towards the mound, and round it to the hall. We both spoke together. I said:

'There ought to be some pickings of Gold and silver here, if no one has been here before.'

Simultaneously, Aristarchos remarked:

'I wonder if there will be anything to eat.'

We both laughed. Aristarchos said:

'There is the difference between the soldier and the merchant; you want something to sell, and I want food. But there is nothing to buy, and no one to sell to, and we neither of us had any breakfast.'

We soon caught up with our little band who had gone on in front while we had been talking to the woman. They were straggling forward in an irresolute way, looking about them like worshippers at Delphi, impressed by everything they see, from statues to horse droppings. We two took care only to speak Greek when they could not hear us. We led them round the mound and came to the Hall of Tara.

295

This hall was the biggest of its kind I had ever seen. It was of the usual British type, round but very big. The roof was held on circles of posts. There were seventeen posts in each circle, and there were nine circles one outside the other. We went in. The hall was empty. No Gold, no silver. Not even good wool cloth hung on the walls. Only the bare oak pillars and the mud-and-wattle walls and the rough thatch. Later we heard talk of pulling it down and rebuilding it in the new Roman style some of the Irish had seen overseas, with straight walls, but there was no thought of making the hall as it stood at all good to look at or comfortable.

Inside, there was a big fire in the centre, venting its smoke through a hole in the ceiling, and bales of hay and baulks of wood strewn around haphazard for people to sit on, around the fire and in the alcoves. Otherwise there was nothing. It was bare as a barn. There is something in the Irish character which forbids them to make their places of worship at all ornate or richly decorated.

Outside the hall, though, were big open fires, and men were roasting huge bloody carcases whole on spits. Others were baking bread of a kind, flat barley cakes on flat stones. Aristarchos went over and picked up a loaf and tore it in half. We stood and wolfed it, hot and fresh. Someone handed us a pot of barley beer, and we shared that too, swig and swig about. One of the cooks looked up and asked:

'And is it waiting for the feast you are, then?'

'And for what else would we be waiting?' Aristarchos answered. 'Would you not be wanting to know who it is that won, and who it is that will be feasting here?'

'And why should I worry my head about that? There's little difference to us, one king wins or the other king wins. And indeed, it is always the new king that it is that is winning.'

It was now a little after noon. Aristarchos and I took our bread and beer, and we lay on our backs on the side of the Mound of Tara, a great grave mound of the men of old that is the centre and the heart of Tara. We lay and we looked up into the dark blue clear sky, all flecked with the burning white clouds of May, with never a fleck of grey on them. The air was so clear, with never a trace of mist, it might have been at home.

And so I and Aristarchos were like two small boys again, let out from lessons, and with nothing to do but to lie and watch the clouds. We teased each other as boys do, in our childhood dialects, though we had never known each other as boys; he in clumsy Thracian, I in the purer Greek of the Old City, the best form of the Koine that every civilised man speaks. We pelted each other with the heads of the grasses, and we blew the first seeds of the dandelions in each other's faces, and we played guessing games with the petals of the daisies. And after a while even this intellectual exercise was too exhausting. We lay still and listened to the birds singing, and watched the sparrows come for the crumbs of the barley loaf. I remembered all the birds I had ever seen, and these birds that swarmed about on the Mound of Tara, they were bolder and they were more numerous than any other flock, and they were of all kinds, and it was as if Rhiannon again stood with us. But for no reason, there were two things I was certain of. First, that Rhiannon would not come to me now, however many birds came winging to me from the countries of the dead, each singing, singing, to try to send some message of love and sorrow to those the soul had left behind, and frantic that no man could understand. And yet, a second thing came into my thought, and I was as certain too of this: that it was Rhiannon indeed who had sent these flocks about me in Tara, as a sign that neither in life nor in death would I ever be free of her to whom I was given, of her who was given to me.

And drowsier we grew, and even those thoughts melted in sleep. The afternoon lasted a thousand years, a thousand happy, happy years. This was the high peak of all our lives, for Aristarchos and myself. It was the high peak of all our time in Ireland, and never again would such achievements crown our dreams. This day we had fought a great battle and seen it won. We had taken the enemy's capital. The whole Island of the Blessed was at our feet. Blessed indeed were we in that day.

CHAPTER FIVE

Suddenly I was awake. The birds rose in a cloud above
us, their singing that had charmed us to sleep, that singing
sweeter than the song of women, changed to a frantic
scolding of terrified creatures, souls that now remembered
that it was true, that all was finished, that never again
would they talk as humans, that henceforward they had
no words to speak, only the twitter twitter of ghosts. The
sun was westering and lower. I nudged Aristarchos awake.
He followed me to kneel before the Druid who stood over
us on the summit of the mound. He was old, an old, old
man. His scanty hair was white and thin on his scalp. His
skin was soft with the tenderness of age. The mistletoe on
his breast was berryless. I thought back to things Taliesin
had said, and I knew from that who it was who wore the
leaf without the berry, and I trembled before him. I knew
who this must be. I knew the name.

'Cathbad,' I said. 'You must be Cathbad.'

'Mannanan, who are not Mannanan' — the Awen was
on him, on the greatest Druid of the Island of the Blessed.
I could tell it from the light in his eyes, from the rhythmic
chant in which he declaimed, not poetry, but prose — 'Son
of Lear who are not Son of Lear, Dark Son of the Bright
Sun, Bright Star that light the stars below, I know who
you have been, I know who you will be, and that you do
not. Sorrow and trouble you will bring on the Island of
the Blessed, but the whole blame is not at your door.

'Listen to me, then, Mannanan. Stay within the plain
of Tara! Do not cross the river in the south, or the river
in the north, or the great bog that lies to the west. Here

298

in the plain of Tara I can keep your head for you by day, and by night it is the Gods Below who will see you safe in the dark, because it is the darkness that you serve now, who once served the Sun. But once you leave this place, then neither man nor gods can save you, and your doom, and the blame for it, will lie on your own head.'

The Druid passed on. What he said had meaning and truth enough, but I laughed at his warning as I led Aristarchos into the hall. Once the legions came, how could the gods of the Irish harm me? If in this island I once burned incense before the bust of His Sacred Majesty, what could the spirits of the bogs and the rivers do?

I forgot it all as we entered the Hall of Tara. A horde of men sat about on the bales of straw and the tree trunks. Cuchullain the Setanta sat in the place of honour, looking south across the fire out of the door of the hall. The warriors from the chariots sat on his left hand and on his right in a circle around the fire facing it, and their drivers sat next to the fire, singeing themselves and keeping the heat off their masters. It is a thankless task to drive a chariot, and no work for a gentleman. But there was no place in the circle for Aristarchos or me, or for the hairy Callum or the other men who came ashore from the ship.

The villagers of Tara had stacked piles of wooden platters near the door, and we took one each and squeezed as near to Cuchullain as we could, and that was not very near. We only got into an alcove behind him. Nobody took very much notice of us or of the others of the Fianna, which annoyed me, and I began to think as little of Cuchullain as I had of the Legate of the Second Legion. And then I remembered what had happened to *him*, and I was happier.

The food was, let us say . . . different. The Britons eat what they grow, mutton almost entirely, with oat bread and beer brewed from wheat. They don't let principle interfere with their appetites except where goose is concerned. But the Irish have a fine idea of what is fitting for a noble to eat. The peasant may eat beef if he likes (while the Briton may drink milk, but when he kills a bull it is for the tallow, not the meat) and he may eat barley bread, and so does the noble most of the time, when he is at home and only being a herder himself with his clansmen. But when he is, so to speak, being an active noble, and going to war, or celebrating it, then he wants to eat in a manner fitting for a gentleman, as he thinks his father ate before they began to be bothered with all this business of the tiresome care of cattle and crops. Then he eats, not what he has killed himself, since this would take up too much energy and time that would otherwise be better expended on eating, but on what he thinks would not be beneath his dignity to chase and kill himself.

The carcases they had been roasting outside on the spits, so big they were that they were not fully cooked yet, were deer. Not red deer, or fallow, but the great elks of the deep forests, almost all gone now in Britain but still roaming in plenty in the dark woods of Ireland, as they do in Germany. This is the beast that the great dogs, which are the only export of Ireland, are trained to bring down. So, at the feast, we ate venison, because tradition said that it was a dish that a noble might eat. Great lumps of the half-raw meat were dumped on our platters, and we sank our teeth into it and stuffed our mouths, and cut it off close to our lips, and chewed for dear life till we could breathe again. We washed it down with beer and all kinds of unnameable native drinks.

Somebody dropped on my platter what looked a bit like a boiled baby. Aristarchos tore off a leg and tried it.

'Badger,' he pronounced. He knew the taste all right, he said; a man who had seen active service like he had knew the taste of many strange dishes. This was the only special treatment I had that day: only I had a boiled badger given me, and Callum, and no one else. I did not know then why.

I stripped the badger carcase; not bad, but not good — two at a meal would be too much, you may like to know, if you are planning a party. And we finished a hare apiece, and I had a hedgehog baked in clay, so that his prickles came off, and a spit of roasted larks, hoping that Rhiannon would not hear about it, down there wherever she was in the South-East. And we had a bowl of stewed mushrooms between us, Aristarchos and I, and he looked a bit doubtful, but, I assured him, I knew my fungi, and besides, how could there be any harm in mushrooms in the Island of the Blessed, where there is neither harmful serpent nor any other dangerous thing, except wolves and bears, and they are so near to man that they do not count. How else do you think that the land got its name?

Then the serious drinking started, after the food was half gone, and the singing. All the songs were melancholy and sad, enough to make a warrior weep, and that is what they did. Then a Bard called Amairgen stood up and sang an interminable song about all the earlier invasions of the Island of the Blessed, and how our invasion was the most glorious of all, and I was very hurt that he made it sound as if Cuchullain had brought over the sea all the men who fought with him, and he named none but the champion, as one would expect in an epic. But I was even more vexed that nobody asked me to sing. At last, it seemed that even if I were to sing, there was no one sober enough to hear me, and so I pulled Aristarchos to his feet, for he was as drunk as anyone, and I was terrified in case he began to talk in Greek, and back we went to the hut where the smith and his wife were, indeed, waiting for us. But it was not as luxurious as you might think because we had the room left in the hut after the smith and his wife, and their nine children and his five apprentices and seven other warriors, and the pigs had all got in before us. Mind you, next day we sent four of the warriors packing, and we killed one of the little pigs: all black the piglets were too, which some people might not like, but which suited me.

Next day, late next day, when at least some of my companions were in a fit state to talk, I tried to have a word with Cuchullain. There was the question of the Gold to discuss, and that would be a question of the conquest of the South-East, and that was where Rhiannon was. There would be no need to hurry yet; no harm would come to her among the Irish, I knew, not to a princess of an ancient house of Britain, not to the Mother of Those Below. But once the

301

legions landed, there was no knowing what the Irish might not do to keep her out of harm's way — her very presence in the island, they would think, would be a lodestone to draw Roman vengeance on them. They had no real idea what the Empire was about, or what the army was for. They saw it not as a great union of peace and trade, held together by an army of engineers and builders and messengers and administrators: they thought of it as a despotism in other interests than their own, symbolised by the fierce shield wall of the legion. The Irish knew well the rule of their own custom: but the rule of law that we live under in the Empire was beyond their comprehension.

However, there was no talking to Cuchullain, now the battle was over. He was surrounded all the time by his fine friends from the North, who came in to Tara all the day, more and more of them. Clan chiefs and pirates they were who raided the coasts of Britain and Gaul, and each other, but who were too cautious to risk the battle, because that was only for desperate men who had nothing to lose: they were ready enough now to share the pickings and rule all Ireland. The only man of importance who had been in the Fianna was Callum the Hairy, and he was the chief of the poorest and most desperate nation of all the North.

But the chiefs who came down brought their own warbands, and though many of those were only armed with cudgels or with knives tied on to the ends of poles, there were enough swords and spears dug out of hiding, now it was safe, to have filled our ship twice over. And there were slingers too, and if only they had come earlier, we would not have had those moments of terror when the chariots came at us, because I am sure that a squadron of slingers and another of men with long pikes would break up any charge.

But even the Northerners who came with their cudgels tucked under their arms were enough to frighten me away from Cuchullain. And not only me. The two dozen who had hidden out with him in the hills all winter, even Callum, who came at last in the ship and fought well in the battle, won it for him really, they could not get near to speak to him either. And this went on for day after day, and the longer it went on the worse it got, more and more important princes coming down from the North, and Cuchullain always too busy to talk, and we men from the ship now even shut out of the nightly feasts in the hall, where there was no room for any of us, even for Callum, and getting our food where we could, and not many of the smith's little black pigs left. And why wait, I asked, like this, why wait?

'We're waiting to collect the army for one thing,' said Aristarchos, who as Heilyn was getting his orders from someone who got them from someone who got them from some northern prince who occasionally saw Cuchullain. 'He won't sweep into the West with a little band like we beat their king with. Cuchullain wants to raise an army big enough to pour across the plain and crush all three of the other Kingdoms, and any army they can raise now. The Ulstermen want to do to the South what the South did to them. The Queen of Connaught has a new husband already, they say, and she claims that he is the High King now by right of marriage. But Conchobar says that he is High King because he was married to her first, and because they finished half the enthroning ceremony on him before the Westerners came sweeping into Tara to spoil it and Maeve went off with the King of Connaught. So now, the King of Ulster is on his way here to finish his consecration, and when he has done that, when he is married again to Ireland, then he can go back home safe to the North again, while we do the work.'

'We do the work, as usual.'

'We do, that. Have you noticed that they don't use any money here in Ireland?'

'No more they do,' I agreed. 'I suppose they do any trade they can by barter.'

'Oh, no. They have a currency, of sorts. The smaller unit is a cow.'

'And what is the larger? A dead elk?'

'No. Four cows, one slave woman they say. I have a feeling that the Ulstermen intend a certain amount of inflation. And a debasement of the higher unit. By the time they

303

finish, they hope to have a woman for two cows, and a horn of ale for two women.'

There, I thought, you have the whole lack of system in Barbarian life exposed. To a Barbarian, a slave is something to use for pleasure. We in the Empire know that nothing a slave does is equal in quality to what a free man does, whether you are thinking of a mason or a miner or a sailor or a ploughman or a prostitute. Therefore they use slaves in ones or twos, in bed or kitchen. But we use slaves only in large groups, and only in tasks which no free man will do, which no freed man will continue in. And if there were anything better than the fickle, mischievous, unhealthy slave to give us the power we want to break stone or pull ploughs or build, then we would use it. But there is, and can be, nothing else in nature that will ever serve.

It was the end of May when the King of the North arrived. He had taken his time, but now he came galloping into Tara in his chariot as if he were in a dreadful hurry to be enthroned as High King, or to finish his enthronement. And this, the people of Tara said, was wrong. By rights he ought to wait to the Feast of Tara at Samain to be enthroned, and to argue that his enthronement had begun at a Samain and been interrupted was surely better cause for waiting for Samain and starting again rather than finishing it out of season. And sure, had not the last three High Kings who had been enthroned out of season died a violent death? But, I reminded them, had the last forty-three kings not died a violent death, however and whenever enthroned? But, no, the people of Tara said, that was pure coincidence.

And sure, they told me, was it not necessary for the High King to receive the sovereignty at the hands of a woman, and that the right woman, and was not the right woman missing and had she not shown clearly that there was no High Kingship she would be giving to Conchobar now, and was it not only his word alone that we had that she had ever given it to him? So there were some that agreed with the King of Ulster, that it was only necessary for him to carry out those ceremonies that had been omitted, and others said that there was nothing for it but to begin again from the beginning, and with this last party it was said that Cathbad held. As for Cathbad, some said that he thought thus because the Queen of the West had paid him, and others said it was because the part of the ceremony that would be taken as done was the bull sacrifice, and he wanted his fill of the beef, which otherwise he would be unable to taste.

But the King of Ulster had his way, and the day after he arrived he was enthroned under the same blue sky, because there had been no rain since the day that we had marched to the battle across the mud of the horse pastures. I woke early and I climbed up with some other warriors on the top of the great mound, because I realised now that there would be no special treatment for me, whatever I was owed, unless I demanded it in some spectacular way, and I was not doing that while Cuchullain could in any way plead that he was bound by his overlord. The mound was a trifle far off to see everything in detail, but at least I got there. I saw the new High King ride up in his chariot, driving it himself, and showing his skill by passing so close to a standing stone that the felloe of the wheel scraped it and threw out sparks and yet the chariot did not overturn. But he did not do the other feat that was expected, driving his chariot between two other standing stones, because, some said, he had already done it once before, or because others said, he was afraid that the stones would catch him and crush him between them as they were supposed to do if anyone who was not by rights High King rode between them.

The King dismounted then and went to the flat stone on which he was to be enthroned, and they brought the white mare that the smith's wife had spoken of. I will not tell what happened then, because there are things a man may stomach to do in darkness in the rites of a mystery, but to do it in broad day in sight of ten thousand people as the High King must do — I will not speak of it. I will only say that I was sorry for the horse.

After it was over, the King killed the mare with the slash of an iron knife across her throat. Then he went from his stone to the cooking fire outside the Wall of Tara, and from that he went twenty paces to the west. There he piled brush-wood for a new fire, and returning to the standing stone he had ridden by he struck fire from it with his sword — and not really his own sword, but the sword with which by proxy he had won the High Kingdom, and with which his champion had cut off the old High King's head — he struck more sparks to kindle timber, and that he carried back to light a new fire.

They put three stones about the new fire, and on this a massive iron cauldron, and by the working of it I could see that this had been made in Britain and brought across the sea, though whether by trade or by theft I do not know: I think by theft. They had this full of boiling water already, or we might have waited all day for the next part of the cere-mony. The King began to joint the mare, and of course other men helped after the first cut of the royal knife. They hacked her into gobbets which they dropped into the cauldron, and they boiled the meat for some little time. Then when the King and some of his more favoured warriors and nobles, like Cuchullain, had eaten a little, His Majesty threw the rest into the crowd, lump by lump, and the men fought for them.

I did not join in this struggle, but Aristarchos did, and he came to me a little after licking his bloody fingers, because the flesh had not had time to be thoroughly cooked or even more than blanched on the surface. The riot merged with no further ceremonial into the feast in the Hall, to which neither he nor I nor any of the Gauls who came in the ship had been invited, and so we all went back to the smith's house, and there we found a cauldron of our own, and in it we put one of the little pigs and a couple of hares and a calf that we happened to come on by accident when nobody was looking our way because they were so engrossed in a fight between two of the Gauls who made more than enough noise to cover us and get up an appetite of their own. The cauldron we boiled on the smithy fire, and at last had it well cooked. There was not enough to drink, though, till one of the Gauls went off and reconnoitred the kitchen, and came back laden with mead jars, good stuff intended for the High King's own cup.

We sat there outside the smithy, which was only a booth open at two sides, and ate and drank, and talked about the good times one could have in Britain, and about how kings who wanted to keep their thrones paid their debts, and how at least that was a lesson Caesar had learnt, and how profitable it must be to serve in the Praetorian Guard at the death of an Emperor, all that was what we were saying, when the people of the village of Tara began to join us, and we had to talk more carefully, though they all agreed with us. We were all beautifully, ecstatically depressed, a fine contrast to the chieftains in the hall, who were, by the sound of it, in the grip of a different kind of ecstasy. Suddenly there was a movement in the circle, and the songs died. Cathbad the Druid had sat down with us.

I had never seen the Druid in all his splendour sit so near a smithy, or come so near meat cooked in a pot of iron. But this was no ordinary night, and this no ordinary place. He sat there in silence, and we all looked at him and waited to hear what he would say.

We waited for Cathbad to say something, or to recite some poem that would give us, even in a Delphic form, his real thoughts, because there are limits to the things a Priest can say to an all-powerful King. But he just sat and watched us, and listened to the small talk that sprang up again, how this man had killed three great chieftains in the battle, and how that one might have done better if only a cursed useless chariot had not got in his way, and men compared the armlets and collars they had taken from the enemies they had killed, and indeed this was what we had talked about every night for weeks now. Then all of a sudden Cathbad spoke, and spoke to me.

'Mannanan, whether you stay within the plain of Tara and keep your life, or whether you go out of the plain, and risk it, is all one to me. But it will all end in tears, and it is your doing, but there is no blame at your door: it is fated.'

And then, in the way Druids have, he was gone, and we did not see him again, that night or after.

307

CHAPTER SIX

There was a whole week of feasting, and even on the day after the last feast there was still no one but myself who was both ready and eager to march into the South and West. You can fight a battle with a headache, but you cannot march a mile. But the day after that, the new High King rode north to safety in Ulster, and the Champion of Ulster led the army of Ulster out of Tara, to conquer the island for the High King, and to bring back for him cattle and women without number, and most important of all, among them the Queen of Connaught for his bed and her cattle for his table or for his stud.

Cuchullain, then, led his army down to the river that was the southern boundary of the plain of Tara, and even in that country of no roads there were at least fords here and there, and the army had to come down to one ford and to one ford only. The chariots were at the head of the host, my chariots, all gilded and painted and set with gems, my chariots that I had brought in my ship, that I had bargained for and paid for, that I had broken a legate for, my chariots. And in the first chariot, with the head of the High King that was hanging by its hair from the pole, and other heads with it now, stood Cuchullain.

The Champion did indeed make a fine sight. He wore his particolour hair long down his back, as a challenge to whoever should want to take his head. So, I remembered, did Pryderi wear his. This, I thought, is how Pryderi would like to ride, at the head of an army, sweeping a country bare of women and food and beasts, and it is only for preventing this that he has this hatred for Rome. Oh, yes, war is a fine thing for nobles and leaders, even in defeat; but for the defeated, or the weak on either side, there is little to be said for it, and if you can think what that little is, then tell me, because I cannot think what it is.

Cuchullain now spurned the civilised luxury of a shirt. He wore only the long strip of saffron-coloured cloth wound round his body, held together by fine brooches of Gold and silver. This dress set off the muscles of his arm and back, rippling under the armlets and chains that he wore, of precious metals only; nothing so poor as bronze for him. The sword that had killed the High King he had given to Conchobar, and now he wore an old sword, brought down from the North, hidden away from the army of Connaught when it had tried to disarm the North as the Romans had disarmed all Britain. This was the oldest sword I had ever seen, a long chariot sword, double-edged for slashing, but this one pointed too. There was no ball to the pommel. Instead there spread out from the top of the hilt two wide horns of Gold, curling up like a new moon in the sky, and the tips of the horns studded with tiny chips of gems so that they glittered as the light came on them from all directions. And the bottom of the scabbard was likewise ornamented with horns, this time of gilded bronze for the harder wear as the chape bumped on the ground or the sides of the chariot, though it would be seldom that the sword would be worn except in the chariot. It was slung from a sword belt that went over his right shoulder, and was anchored to the garment he wore, but round his waist he wore a noble's belt in the British fashion, a chain of bronze gilt that went round his body four or five times before it was caught by a clasp.

Behind him came his army. You have seen a civilised army on the march, or at least you have seen soldiers, small detachments marching to join their station or stepping out proudly in a review. Are you thinking of those straight lines, dressed from the right, taking their step from the standard-bearer? You will conjure up those scarlet cloaks, all of a length, the line of shields held, however it breaks

309

a man's arm, all level topped. You will imagine the helmets, shining like so many suns, the legionaries' topped with spike or knob according to regiment, the centurions proudly tossing their scarlet plumes of horsehair. The breastplates shine, scoured smooth with brick dust, and the faces are shaved close as if they too were scoured, and every neck cropped, and crown too, so that no hair shows outside the helmet. Those are the two things that you will remember, every man is alike, and every man is clean.

That will not do for your picture of a Barbarian army, Irish or German. Every man is dressed differently, as he pleases, only that a fashion may run for a little through some clan or nation and give them at least a skim of likeness. The helmets they wear are of a hundred different kinds, knobbed or spiked or crested, round or pointed, with cheek-pieces or not, sometimes beaten out of one piece, sometimes built up of plates of metal on a cap of boiled leather, and whether it is of bronze or of iron is a matter of choice. Then some men will wear mail, and some do not, according to whether they have been lucky in war or in inheritance or in theft, and for cloaks they wear what length and colour they can catch. But you must not imagine this equipment as shining, because how can bronze shine when it is green with verdigris, or iron sparkle when it is pitted with rust? The cloaks hide their colours under dirt and grease, and every man wears his beard long for want of will to cut it, and his hair long as a challenge. And this army will not march in ranks, or in any order, but will push along in a great heaving crowd, every man only taking care that he is always near to his lord to recognise him.

So Cuchullain rode at the head of this crowd of warriors, by the way I knew that he would come, and there at the ford I waited for him. And when he stopped there, all his men came up and crowded close to hear what I said, as I knew they would.

Where the track came down to the ford, I had dug a hole. There was no need to seek out a standing stone of a burial mound: here was the boundary between the Plain of Tara and the rest of the Island of the Blessed, and every boundary is a place of mystery. Beside the road to the ford I had dug a hole, dug it with a stick sharpened in the fire. I dug the hole knee-deep before I was satisfied, and I heaped the earth on the south side, the unlucky side. I stood on the west side of the hole, and I barred the way to Cuchullain and his advancing army. He rode up to me in his chariot, and saw me there. The hood of my sealskin cloak was drawn over my face, but he knew me, and he knew too, and all his soldiers knew, why I held in my left hand a screaming black piglet, the runt of the litter, and in my right a knife roughly chipped of flint. Cuchullain saw the kicking squealing pig, and he stopped.

'How then, Mannanan!' he cried. 'Have you not had enough blood?' He gestured around. This was the way that the army of the West had fled, and the ground was covered with corpses. Some the wolves and the buzzards had torn: most had been stripped. Now the ribs showed through the rotting flesh, three weeks dead. The bellies had burst: there was a stench over everything. There was nobody whose duty it was to bury them. So they were not buried.

'I do not drink blood,' I replied loudly, so that all the host could hear me. 'But I know those who do. Those Below, the thirsty ones, shall they be filled tonight?' and I drew the blunt back of the stone knife across the piglet's throat. Cuchullain looked long at me. He saw my hair plastered down with fat, and it might well have been corpse fat for all he knew, and stuck with the feathers of the black cock. One half of my face was blackened with the ash from the fire, and one painted scarlet with a dye I had with me. From my red cheek glared my one black eye, and from the black cheek shone the red of a ruby. And Cuchullain saw, and all his army saw, that the blood of the black pig would flow into the pit, and I would curse all his army and himself and deliver them to the Gods Below as I had delivered the High King. Cuchullain changed his tune, and asked what I wanted.

'Pay your debts, Setanta, pay your debts!' For he was

still arrogant, with his army behind him. Now the battle was won there was no need for him to think that he could escape paying those that had won it for him. 'Before you came here, before I armed you, before I gave you your triumph and your kingdom, you promised me my pay. All the Gold in Ireland, all the Gold of all the mines, you promised me. You promised, Setanta, and you have not paid it yet. What have you promised the men behind you, and will you ever pay it? Pay me my Gold, Setanta, and then pay them!'

He did not dare refuse me, or try to put it off, there in front of all his army who had heard it. There is nothing will make an army melt away as fast as the rumour that the pay chests are empty. If that happened, then indeed he would feast with the Gods Below. Every man watched him and watched me with my hand on my knife. Cuchullain turned to his host and called:

'Who will go with this man into Leinster?'

A big man came forward, and beneath the hair it was possible to recognise Callum that had pulled the skin boat with me. Now his face was painted and his hair stuck with feathers so that he would have drawn attention anywhere in Britain, where he had before been merely an unusually hairy and dirty man. Now, though, he could dress for what he was, the prince of a little kingdom somewhere far away, and with him he brought his own kinsmen, perhaps five hundred of them, and almost every man of them had joined us on that first day. There was little enough attention he had had from the High King, though, for all that, or from the Champion till now.

'Callum the Hairy,' Cuchullain addressed him. 'Ravage Wicklow, and take Mannanan to the Rivers of Gold.'

I stood beside Callum, and we watched the host of Ulster pass, great crowds of ragged hungry men, ill armed and ill tempered, even now, and looking not for excitement or for glory but for loot, only for loot. Only in the middle of them marched a dozen proud and fierce men, well armed, Heilyn and his Gauls. Close behind the leading chariot they strode, ready to keep each others' back, or their leader's back. And as they went, so I saw pass for the last time the Champion of Ulster.

Nor did Conchobar ever see his nephew again.

I trudged south with Callum the Hairy, passing the river last of all, and while the host turned west up river, we turned east towards the sea. There were, as I said, about five hundred of us, and not a man whose name or whose face I knew except Callum. I had my axe in my hand, and my cloak on my back, and a little bag at my waist with my belongings, like a few spare eyes in case we were invited to a feast. I asked Callum where he came from.

'From far up there,' he said, pointing to our left. 'It is on the coasts opposite the Picts that we are living and it is across the sea that it is we would rather be raiding, because it is a fine land that the Picts have, and easy it would be to take it from them, but it is silver in plenty they have that lets them keep men always under arms in case we come, and the bread that those men ought to be growing they can buy for them.'

They were a crafty people, these men of Callum's, part of a nation of the Irish who called themselves Scots. They did not worship any living being, but their sacred thing, they said, was a ship, a stout wooden ship that had once cast itself up on their shores and had given them much silver, and been the foundation of such prosperity as they had. Besides, they said, it was more convenient to worship a ship, since there was no chance of sinning by eating it.

When we crossed the river, we passed into the land where Cathbad could no longer, as he said, protect me, but I remembered how little power he had seemed to have even in the land of Tara, and I laughed at him. There was nothing he could do to protect me that I could not do myself.

We marched on, our men singing the rousing chorus of 'Erch, the Bastard King of Leinster'. When we could smell the sea, we came to a village, a collection of huts by the water. We turned out the whole place in a twinkling, women and pigs and cattle. Beyond the village was a strong place, a rath as they call it, an earthwork around a circular farmyard, and a fence on top of the bank, and a gate in the fence that we easily broke in. The men in the rath we killed very easily, but there was nothing inside worth taking. The prince of the place was already dead across the river, and his women had fled to the west. Some of his own peasants had taken the rest of his belongings, mead mostly, and shut themselves inside the rath to enjoy them. Some of our men were for burning the place down, but Callum would not allow them.

'For indeed,' he told them, 'it is bringing our families down here we will be, and I will be king of this place, and I will reign from this rath myself.'

There we spent the first night, and when we went south we left a band of young men to hold it, and there we sent all the cattle that we stole, and there we agreed to meet if we were scattered. The young men had the women of the place to comfort them, and the pigs to eat. But we turned south into the narrow plain between the mountains and the sea, and all I could think of was Gold. I hardly remembered at all that down there in the South, by the sea, somewhere, was Rhiannon, and that is what Cathbad could not protect me from once I was out of the plain of Tara. For in the Plain, I thought of glory and honour and the rule of law and of love: but once I was across the river, there was nothing I remembered but Gold.

There was no one in that plain that expected our coming. I wondered why. Callum listened to me wondering as one listens to the prattling of a child, and then in pity teaches it to wipe its nose.

'Indeed, it is the country of the Eastern King that we are coming into, the country of Leinster. It was not to the taste of the king of this and to go to fight at Tara, for he has not been in this island for a year or two, but he has been wandering across the seas, and some say inside the Empire. But now he has come back, and he has brought him back a wife too, from among the Iceni, and a hard time of it he must have been having in making his rule felt again. For it is a proud people the Brigantes are, and impatient of any king.'

'But — the Brigantes!' I protested. 'They live in Britain.'

'So do some of them, and some of them live in Gaul, and the finest and oldest branch of the nation live here, although it is arguing and quarrelling they are always over which *is* the oldest and finest branch.'

Now I began to realise why Caw had been so unperturbed when we told him that Rhiannon had been stolen away by the Irish. And now, too, I first began to wonder whether she had, in her own mind, been stolen or rescued. From now on, when I thought of her, as I did infrequently, I only wondered when I should reach her in her palace in the capital of the Brigantes, when we should at last fall, as I thought we would, into each other's arms.

We went south, like a thunderstorm. We slept each night in the villages we sacked, with the widows and daughters of the men we killed, if we could catch any to kill, which was not often, or if not, then with the wives and daughters they kindly left us. And we ate their cows and pigs, but not many of them, because our real interest was in collecting a great herd together on the banks of the river beneath the fence of Callum's new rath. We spread out too, and covered all the country between the mountains and the salt sea, and we were no longer an army of five hundred men, but a scatter of companies of fifty or so, each just enough to settle a village. In these villages there were few men, I noted, however many women we might find. But almost every day, almost every hour, I would ask Callum:

'When do we come to the rivers of Gold?'

And he would answer in that ingratiating way that Barbarians have, when they know that the answer will be unwelcome and they do not want to hurt your feelings by telling you the truth:

'Soon, soon. Tomorrow, the next day, the day after.'

I realised, but slowly, that he had no more idea of where the Gold was than I had. Till at last we forded a little stream running east from the sea, as we did a dozen times a day, and I scraped my toes into the sandy bottom. I stopped dead there, with the mountain water icy cold half way up my calves, and I shouted in joy. Oh, yes, I'd seen sand like that before, the sands of the Maeander are like that, where Midas gathered his Gold, and gathered it all up, so that there is no Gold there any more. But this was Gold sand all right. I stopped where I was, I did that, and I bent down and I plunged my arms to the elbow in the bitter stream and I brought up a fistful of sand. I held it in my cupped hands, and then I swilled it round in my palm, watching for the glint of mica and I saw it, and then I knew that I had come to the Rivers of Gold.

'Callum!' I called to him. 'Callum! Is this the first of the rivers of Gold?'

'Rivers of Gold? Why, all the rivers of the Eastern Kingdom are rivers of Gold, that's what they call them. Why do you think that this is the first?'

'But look at the sand!'

'Sand? Why, it's just sand, like any sand. All sand is the same. What has that got to do with Gold? Come on, we'll hurry on to the next river and you can play in the sand there.'

I had no choice but to follow him. That afternoon we reached the next river, where it ran low among the rocks in the summer, cold from the mountain tops that we could see, and there was a big village. There were a few men there, whom we killed, because they didn't run fast enough, and a lot of women. But while the rest of the party rearranged the politics, not to speak of the morals of the place, I took a flat platter with a high rim out of a house, and I knelt by the river bank, where there was a little backwater with a beach of clean sand. And there I washed for Gold. I knelt there and I put handfuls of sand into the platter and whirled it round till the sand and the water climbed the side and swished over, and I looked in the bottom of the dish for the heavier metal that should be left there. I knelt there in the gravel and I panned and panned, while the sun went behind the hills, and even on a June evening the air grew chilly. And at last, when some of Callum's men came, to call me for supper they said, but they had never done such a thing before, and it was only out of curiosity that they walked so far out of the village, I was able to show them at last a tiny glimmer of Gold, a patch of Gold grains on my palm, enough to gild a third of the nail of my little finger.

It was Gold, real Gold, and all Callum's men, and their leader, crowded to see it, Irish Gold that they had never known, only heard of and not believed in. They made a celebration of it, or tried to, though in reality they did not think as much of the Gold as they did of the cattle they found, since the cattle they were getting for nothing, and the Gold was taking work, that they could see, and the metal I had got in all those hours of kneeling was not enough to buy the hind teat of a barren cow. But because I was jubilant, they rejoiced with me, and we drank late into the night, and looked out over the plain between us and the sea that was dotted with our own fires, and the hills that were bare of the fires of our enemies.

Next morning I went to Callum, because none of our men were in a condition to march, and it was not only the drink that did it, but sheer fatigue, overwork both on the road by day and in bed by night. I said:

'I want some women.'

'And wasn't it enough women we were having last night? There was that fat black-haired bitch with the green eyes — 'twas a dreadful game she was having with me, a dreadful game. Oh, Mannanan, it is an awful thing for a man to have to say, but it's too old I think that I am getting for this life. And anyway, what is it you would be doing with a woman in the daytime?'

'No, it's nothing like that, Callum. I want a lot of women, and I want them to work. You can have them all back for the night. Old ones will do. I'll be staying here for a little, and I want them to work.'

'And it's staying here I think we will all be, for a little while too, the way I'm feeling.' And stay we did, and the men were happy enough, for they had food and drink in plenty and women to wait on them hand and foot. But they let me have about thirty of them, assorted ages, to work during the day.

That first morning of work, I had all the women out by the stream. I made sure that each of them had a trencher or a platter with a rim or a shallow bowl or something like that to work with, not always the best things for panning, but they had to do with what they had, and they soon learned not to bring what would only make hard work. I showed them what to do, whisking the pan around and around. They all looked at me blankly for a bit. Then one of them said, in a bright but witless way:

'Oh, yes, like in the Gold dance.'

'The Gold dance?' I asked. 'What's that?'

'Oh, like this,' they all said together, and straight away they began to dance, and to sing a wailing song. It was a very complex dance, with many figures and a great deal of repetition, and in between each figure, or when they were not dancing principal parts, as some of them did, they were all the time panning, panning with their hands, though none of them picked up the pans they had, or seemed to know that they should. The first few figures I did not see, because I was too busy scattering salt and chewing garlic, and crossing knives and generally making myself secure against any spells they might be weaving. It would, of course, have been foolhardy to have tried to stop the dance in the middle, or all the stored-up power from the first measures would have been split out on me, and there is no knowing what I might not have turned into. But it was tempting, because the dance lasted a full hour of a summer's day.

Some of the figures were quite intelligible. They panned, and they worked bellows, and they poured out of crucibles, and they beat leaf thin with hammers, oh yes, you could have been a goldsmith as good as any in the world to have done all they danced. Then half of the women became traders from over the sea, and brought things to trade for the gold. They had cloth, in long strips, and jars of wine to drink, and cattle to milk, and most welcome, it seemed, of all, they brought the cauldrons, of bronze and of iron, to boil the food in. For you cannot boil a dinner in a cauldron of Gold, any more than in a cup of wood. And all the time, they made this continual panning motion, while they made their sacrifices and poured out their oblations, and charmed the rain down on to the hills to fill their streams.

When they had finished, I said:

'Right, now! You know what to do. Get on with it!'

They all looked at me, blank again.

'What, in the river? Put our feet in cold water?' They were horrified. 'We'd catch our slow deaths if we did, and die coughing and groaning and spitting blood. If cold water touches your skin, then it is death, slow death, and if it is hot water, then it is a quick death.'

Looking at them I could see how firmly they believed this. It was no time to try to convince them by argument. I had borrowed a whip of bull's hide from Callum, and I cracked it in the air above my head.

'I don't care what you think, or how you die. Into the river you go.' What I would have done if they hadn't gone, I don't know, I hadn't the heart to flog them, they were too stupid, but first one and then another waded gingerly into the stream.

'And what is it we are to do now we are here?' one asked. Heaven preserve me from ever again having to make women work.

'You know all about it. Get down there on your knees and wash for Gold.'

'Oh, he's mad,' one woman said, and another, a pert lass and very good in bed, I found, but no use at all in a practical situation, giggled and told me, in a confidential way:

'You don't get Gold out of streams, dear. You get Gold from over the sea. You have to find a city, and then you can dig it up out of the rocks between the houses. And they say the Romans will give Gold for dogs. I wouldn't mind seeing a few Romans around here, I wouldn't, be a change from you Northerners.'

'Oh, no you wouldn't,' another girl corrected her. 'Those Romans all smell of olive oil, they drink it instead of beer, they do, whatever it is.'

'Then if you can't get Gold out of the river,' I argued

319

and that was a sad mistake, to argue with them, 'where do you think the river got its name? Why do you call it the Gold River?'

'Oh, that's just its name,' they all chorused. 'There's a Red River and a Black River, and so there's a Gold River, or so the Bards tell us. Names don't mean anything.'

'But your dance — why do you call it the Gold dance?'

'Why not? Every dance has to have a name, or you wouldn't know which dance you were doing, would you?'

The more they talked, the more I became convinced that it was true, that they had forgotten what the dance was about. It was all one with the fundamentally irreligious approach they had to dancing. They had really forgotten that the rivers were full of Gold. But they had danced the Gold dance so often, I thought, that it was a miracle that there was any room left for the waters to flow between the mounds of precious metal. They had danced it forty or fifty times a year, every year. The words didn't matter, they told me, they made them up as they went along, about village scandals, and they would soon have some words sufficiently disrespectful to fit my case.

I drove them down into the water, cracking my whip, and I split them up into small groups, choosing the most likely places. I went from group to group all the day, watching to make sure that they were all panning in the right way, and ducking those who weren't. I was sure that they were doing it right. But there was not the glimmer of Gold in the pans, not a sparkle of bright metal, nothing but sand, sand, sand. I couldn't understand it all. It was *just* possible that they had been filching it away and hiding the dust, but it didn't seem possible after I had had the most likely thieves working naked for a few hours, so that they had nowhere to put the stuff. There was no Gold. Thirty women to pan a stream for a whole day and no profit — it was incredible.

We washed that stream for four days, working from the sea back into the hills up to the source. Nothing, not a speck. Mica we found, and plenty of that, but no Gold. The sand was right. The rocks were right. The water was right. Perhaps the earth had stopped breeding it, I thought, but that doesn't happen without the intervention of some God, and there would have been some memory, however garbled in the telling, of that.

There might be Gold in other rivers, I thought, and the women might know of it. They said they didn't. I threatened to have them tied and flogged, but by now our men were so demoralised that all they and the women did at this was roar with laughter. That was one of the troubles in Ireland, nobody took war seriously, and they had even less respect for trade. Irreligious, as I said.

So we moved south, to the other rivers of Gold, and we panned a fresh river every day, with fresh women. Every village had the Gold dance, and we had them dance it till their feet nearly wore off. Perhaps the words of the song, I thought, were more important than the women said they were, but it was past trying now to find out what it was. And they didn't know what the sacrifice was. I tried a number of things, pigs, dog, hen, child, and even once a sickly foal that would have died anyway but even so it was expensive. And yet there was never the smallest little nugget. I didn't try snake, because there are none in Ireland, but if ever you are going that way you might take a snake with you and try. There's not much hope, but at least it would be conclusive.

And then it came to the sixth morning, and we were on the edge of the sixth river, and I had all the women of the village out on the bank, and we had danced the dance, and I was telling them what to do, and here were a couple of cracks of the whip to be going on with — and I was interrupted. Someone was laughing at me. I glared at the crowd, and they all edged away, in the way frightened people have, from the offender. And the worst of it was that they were afraid of her, not of me, that was plain. She was an old woman, very old, with not a tooth in her head, and not much hair on it, shrivelled and bent, and the very look of her frightened me as much as it did the women. For this was someone as old as the women who

321

had cursed us as we landed, and much more evil, and it would not need any queen to bribe her to curse a man — she would do it out of spite and amusement. I snarled at her — my temper was wearing thin now — and I asked:

'And what do you think there is to laugh at? Just you keep quiet, or I'll be storing the Gold dust in skin bags — your skin.'

But she kept on cackling and screeching, till at last she had had her laugh out, and then she pointed at me and cried hoarsely:

'The Gold, the Gold, the Gold is gone, there's none for you to find. The Gold, the Gold, the Gold is gone, all washed away to the salt salt sea, swirled away to the cod and the conger, sunk to the weed and shells at the bottom. It's gone, it's gone, it's washed away!'

Up to now, I had refused to believe it. And it was flung in my face, and all at once I knew it was true. Perhaps, men had washed and washed these streams till all the Gold was taken, all smelted down into the collars and bracelets that were now all buried in the graves of the Isle of Britain. It was possible. But no, I could not believe that. I looked at the women, and I knew better. Out of their greed, they had danced the streams dry. In impious laughter they had danced the Gold dance for its own sake, and not for the Gold, and they had, through a myriad repetitions, danced all the Gold out of the hills and down the streams, out into the deep deep sea. In one instant, there alone with all those women on the river bank, I understood all the story of the Gold of Ireland, and in that instant I realised that there was that in Ireland which I would have done better to have prized and sought before all the Gold in Ireland, and she was still here somewhere to the south of me. And I looked across the stream to the land of the Brigantes of Ireland and I prepared to march forward towards Rhiannon and my life, when all at once there was a tumult.

Tumult is a nice and glorified and poetic word for it, and too dignified for that noise. There was the bellowing of a thousand rather anxious cattle, the screaming of five hundred rather frightened women, and the deep panting of as many terrified warriors running north for all they could go. The whole mob came sweeping past us where we stood, a little above the ford where they had to cross, and we watched them come over the river. And bringing up the rear, blowing aside his whiskers to urge his people on, looking like Death, Death received and Death bestowed, was Callum. He gestured to the ridge behind, where the tips of spears caught the sun.

'Run, run!' he cried. 'The Brigantes are on us!'

CHAPTER SEVEN

So began that dreadful flight that lasted, as far as I was concerned, for two whole days and two whole nights. For others it lasted longer, for they crossed the river into the Plain of Tara, and for others it ended sooner in a spear thrust or slashing swing of a sword.

At first we formed a great square of movement, men and cattle, pushing north as fast as we could trot. An easy pace, you think? Oh, yes, easy enough for an unarmed man for an hour or so, with nothing at the end of it but a crown of laurel or a horn of ale. But to keep it up for days, with a coat of mail and a helmet, and a sword or an axe or a spear, and with your own life as the prize, why, that's another thing.

Behind us as we went we left our trail, a great belt of land where the grass was eaten and trampled, and the houses burnt, the fences about the paddocks and the folds pushed over, the fruit trees cut down, the wells fouled and the fords muddied. Soon we were leaving other things, bags of food and water bottles, spare shoes and bronze bowls and cloaks, and mine among them. And then, more sinister, mail coats, and helmets, and at last shields and spears and swords thrown down by men who only wanted to run. We left men as well as women gasping by the wayside, with knees or ankles twisted in the mud, or their soles worn into raw blisters, or snorting or spewing blood. I could never understand what came over the women, for they ran as fast as the men even when no one guarded them. They urged the cattle on, they rushed forward to captivity as if it were the goal and object of their lives. Caught up, they were, I suppose, by the general frenzy around them.

I know that I was. I belted along for the first few miles as hard as I could go without falling over the cows in front of me. After a while, though, I remembered Socrates at Delium, and I went faster till I could catch up with Callum.

'We wouldn't have to run so fast,' I shouted to him, 'if we could discourage the Brigantes.'

Callum considered this for a few hundred paces. He was a realist. He didn't slow down till the next ford. Then he stopped at the water's edge and looked at the men who were passing. We were by now well in the front of the retreat, being by nature more determined than our followers. Callum caught one man by the arm, and then another. He was not indiscriminate. He let most of the fugitives go by. He collected about thirty men. None of them were in their first youth, but they were strong men, heavy-handed and savage. Every man of them still had his weapons, and held them as if he knew what these things were for.

We waited in the bushes above the ford, on the south bank of the river, till most of the rout were over and the first pursuers appeared. Young men they were, running lightly and easily, scarcely out of breath, delighted at outrunning their elders, which experience had taught me is never a thing to do in war if you want to live. Their spears were already bloodied and they slung heads at their belts, taken from men too tired and broken to resist. We were different. Youngsters, I said. They had no chance. We charged down on them, and though they tried hard to remember how they had been taught to fight, we killed eleven of them before you could shout a warcry. We only had two wounded. We took the heads, of course, because it was the thing to do, not because we could afford to carry trophies, and indeed we dropped them down the next well we came to. You see, the sight of his friends' bodies, headless laid out in a neat row across his path is enough to make any man wonder whether precedence is so important.

We pushed on. It had begun to rain, breaking the long dry spell that had begun with the Battle before Tara. I could only hope that the rain had the same effect on our pursuers' spirits as it had on ours. I fought seven times in those two days and two nights. Five times we laid ambushes, and twice we were ourselves attacked, for the Leinstermen soon called back all the lads from the forefront of their army, and those who came on after us were old warriors like ourselves. And what I could not understand was that some of them bore wounds already, sword cuts a few weeks old, and yet the army of Leinster had not come against us before Tara, and I wondered what had been happening in the Eastern Kingdom. I was glad that I had once been taught the finer points of using an axe by a Lombard, not named Bert, and I soon had heads enough to hang all round my belt by their long hair, if I had wanted them.

When we held the field, we took the heads of the enemy and also we picked up the bodies of our own dead. And their heads we took too, and carried them with us till we could scrape a little hole in the earth and bury them out of sight. Because you cannot leave your comrade's head for his enemies to hack off roughly and insult, and at the last stick up on a stake for the crows to peck out the eyes.

But we ran most of the time, and there was nothing that I had to eat but a piece of dried beef that I picked out of the mud, and a quarter of a barley loaf and two raw carrots I took from some women who were fools enough to let me see they had food. We were no longer now a solid square of movement. The men in front were hastening to get their beasts out of the Eastern Kingdom and across the plain of Tara and home into the North, and each made the best speed he could and took the easiest path, while Callum the Hairy played the prince's part and held back the pursuit, and gave them time. We were but the wreck of an army now, and the warbands of Leinster roamed among us at will and cut off first this herd and then that.

Sometime in the darkness of the second night, I fought for the eighth time. There were only six left with Callum then. Some had been killed, and some had fallen with weariness, and some were just lost in the dark or in the press of cattle. Men rushed at us out of the darkness, and split us, so that every one of us was fighting alone, and I the most alone, twisting and turning always the same way to guard my blind side and striking at shadows with my two-foot axe. I spun and dodged, and ran to escape, because there comes a time always when there is no more to do than run, and you must give up and acknowledge that there is no more that you can do. I blundered westward, or so I thought, up hill and over bog and through copses, till at last I tripped over a root and I fell flat on my face into a hollow in the ground, and I lay there winded and sobbing with shame and terror and fatigue, and there at last I slept.

When it was well light I awoke. We had been on the left flank of the retreat. I had wandered far out, into the shoulders of the hills. I got cautiously to my hands and knees and looked down the slope. Far away was the great scar that the herds had cut across the pastures, and the ruin of dead beasts and dying men and wailing women, and the crows and buzzards and the wolves gaining all the profit of the night. But otherwise there was no army to be seen. The pursuit had swept on. There was nobody now to be afraid or to cast cowardice in my teeth. The host of Callum the Hairy had gone and so had the army of the King of Leinster, gone on north towards the river which I could see in the far distance. Across the river lay the Plain of Tara. There I might be safe. Cathbad would protect me there.

CHAPTER EIGHT

I began to make my way to the north, moving carefully from one clump of trees to another, trying to keep out of sight. I shivered for want of my cloak as much as from fear, and I turned my head this way and that lest anyone, or anything, should come up on my blind side unseen. I kept moving. I was not only afraid of men. There were wolves around.

But I did not look round enough for all my care. I came at last to a place where I could lie in a hollow and see through the parted grass the mound and the rath which Callum had marked to be his own, above the river. The rath looked empty enough. There was no movement above the fence. There was some smoke, but a fire need not mean living men: I had seen enough burning houses in my time, and families dead around their own dinner a-cooking. The pursuit had turned inland along the banks of the rivers hours ago.

I lay and watched for a time. When I was beginning to think it might be safe enough to go forward and see if there was anything to eat inside the rath, there was a noise behind me, of someone clearing his throat. I whirled round and on to my feet, my axe at the ready, blade vertical before my face, my hacked and battered shield on my arm. A man stood in front of me, ten yards away, his sword at his side, his arms folded. He was not really seven feet high, he only looked it, in his pointed helmet, centuries old, with a bunch of red ribbons threaded through the ring on top. Heilyn Aristarchos had given me warning of his coming lest I killed him. Lest *I* killed *him* — I laughed bitterly at the thought.

'Well?' he asked me in a dull toneless voice. 'Where is all the Gold?'

'There is no Gold,' I replied. 'Have you anything to eat?'

He brought a lump of roast venison, dried and dusty, out of the fold of his cloak. We divided it equally, every scrap. I told him my tale. His was the same. But at least all Callum's men were of one mind, and they tried to drive together one huge herd to drive back to Ulster. But the men who went with Cuchullain into the West did not even do that. As each man found he had enough cows or women to suit him, he would leave the army and go home with them. And as the host went west, so they spread out and the whole army dwindled away, not to nothing, because Cuchullain still kept together his chariots, and the Gauls who had come with Aristarchos held with him, and another band of the Setantii, Irishmen. And these were all that were left to face the wrath of Queen Maeve as she came in a second cloud of chariots against them out of the West. And then Cuchullain had done as Callum did, and fought skirmish after skirmish to hold the Connaught men off the wreck of his army. But as he retreated so his army grew, because like a snowball it swallowed up the stragglers who had no cattle, and soon the skirmishes were more like battles, but the retreat went on for all that.

'Then, two nights ago,' he told me, 'I took a small band off to the right of the road, to try to draw the Queen south after us. We fought with their right flank near dusk, and we were cut to pieces. We scattered in the dark, and here I am at my rendezvous, for it was at this rath that I promised to meet my Gauls. If any are alive: I am almost certain none are.'

'Who were they?' I was bold to ask.

'Oh, Setantii, all right,' he assured me, 'all related to Cuchullain. But how was he to know that every one was a soldier, sworn to Caesar, three of them of the rank of standard-bearer, and every one anxious to hang on his breastplate such Phalerae as would make every legion and every regiment of horse in the Army salute us as we passed. And there is still hope we may have it yet. This rath —

where better for the legions to build Praetorium, and govern all Ireland?'

'Soon it will be done,' I assured him. 'Just think, now all the roads of Britain are scarlet with the marching troops, coming down to the boats on the edge of the Irish Sea. All we need do now is to reach the landing beaches before Tara, and wait till the ships appear. When the Liffey itself is full of galleys, then we can come out and collect our praises and our crowns for settling all Ireland in such a turmoil they will never notice what is happening till they are conquered.'

'I hope my Gauls will see it. But they know the ways of this kind of war as well as I do. Make for the rendezvous, and then carry on, and never wait for the men who may never come. But they may be in the rath.'

We trudged down, miserable, through the fine rain that never stopped, and we climbed the path to the gate in the long fence. The gate itself still lay on the ground where it had fallen when Callum himself, under a rain of stones instead of water, had cut through the leather hinges with his sword. The village between the rath and the river had been burnt, but inside the courtyard the houses still stood. There might be food there. We looked at each other. Then Aristarchos nodded.

'There may be food. We'll go in.'

We moved forward, through the open gate into the court. We could see nobody about. And then, there was a shout, and we turned to see a dozen men in the open gate, warriors, splashed with the mud and blood of a three days' pursuit. And in front of them he stood. He was big and grossly fat. His black-and-white-striped shirt was stained with moss. His hair, now grown long down his back, was streaked with whitewash. Picking a chicken carcase he held in both his hands, his royal state made obvious by the massive Gold collar around his neck, stood Gwawl, the Badger King of Leinster.

There he stood, triumphant in the gateway. He spat chicken bones at our feet, and he laughed. He said, in Latin, to taunt me the more:

'Well, Mannanan-Photinus! Who is it now that controls the Gold of Ireland? You have the Monopoly Deed: but I have the monopoly of you. This is my day of victory at last. You cheated me between Bonnonia and Rutupiae. You hid in the mists in the Channel, and my ships missed you. You rolled me like dung in the streets of Londinium. Now it is my turn to do what I like.'

'Do what you will,' I told him. 'Your days are numbered.'

'But at what a number,' he insisted. 'Soon your days will be gone. Do you wonder why I do not kill you now, myself? I promised my cousin, Rhiannon, when I saved her from you, that I would not kill you, nor harm a hair of your head, and no more I will. But I have also promised my other cousin, Maeve, that I will send you to her, bound, and that I will do. And she has her own ideas of sport, and it is not quickly that you will die, nor easily.'

And there was no doubt that he would do it, and there was no knowing how long it would take the legions to bring the Queen to heel. And by then we would be dead. I still held my axe, and Aristarchos his sword, but there were a hundred men in the rath now, with poles and nets, to take us alive like wild beasts. My own skill with axe and shield had brought me alive out of the first stage of the retreat from the rivers of Gold. There was no cheating in Ireland. Now I must bring us both alive out of the Island of the Blessed with my own unaided brain. There was only one thing left now to fight Gwawl with. I called on the man's Gesa. I said:

'Gwawl, or whatever name the Irish call you, I call on you to play against me. Play me three games of Fichel. At each game I wager my head if I lose, but if I win, then you must give me what I ask, or play another game.'

Gwawl looked at me hard, and then he called in a tone of anger to his men:

'Find me a Fichel board.'

And they routed about among the ruins of the stronghold, and they came to us with a Fichel board, the board of the Fichel of the Nine Men.

Now this Fichel is played on a board that is nine squares

to the side, as other Fichel games are played on boards that are of seven or eleven squares each way, or on oblong boards of different sizes. And it is played without dice or the least interposition of chance or of divine favour. In this game, one player has the king, who at the start stands in the middle, and the other has the eight men who stand in the four corners in pairs. And the king must move one square at every turn, and the men one square only at a move. The task of the men is so to hem in the king that he cannot move, but the king, if he can, may kill the men if he catches them alone. Now the object of the game is not the same for the two sides. The men can win only if they kill the king. But if the king is still alive by the end of whatever number of moves the players have agreed, then the king has won.

So it was that I sat at the Fichel board to play against Gwawl. And it was I that took the king for each game, since, I pointed out, I had come alone into the rath as the king into the Fichel board, outnumbered and shut in.

Now, the first game we played was a Fichel of seventeen moves, the Game of the Warrior, and a speedy game was it with a sure end. Because Gwawl was not used to my style, in twelve moves, six to him and six to me, I had killed four of his eight men, and there was no hope that the others could hem me in. Still, he would not surrender, being a king himself, and he played out the last sterile moves while his men watched by the flickering light of the fire, because the dusk had now fallen.

When all the seventeen moves were played, Gwawl glared at me. He asked:

'What then is it that you are wanting of me?'

'That instead of giving me to Queen Maeve, you send me and my man here' — because it was easier to pretend that Aristarchos was someone of no importance — 'back alive to Cuchullain.'

'That I will do,' said Gwawl, because he was bound by his Gesa to respect his wager and to pay it, whatever other promise he must break. But there spoke a voice from the darkness beyond the fire:

'That you cannot do.'

We stood, and we all looked into the shadows, and it was Cathbad the Druid who stood there, and we knew him by the white of his robe and by his voice and not by his face, which was swollen with weeping for all the dead of Ireland that had fallen because I had come to seek Gold. He stood there, and he began to intone a poem, in the terse evocative style that was even now old-fashioned and dying out in favour of the complex rhythmical metres that imitated hexameters:

The rain fell on the pastures at the end of the cattle drive,
The cows lowed, the bulls tore the ground.
All Ulster shouted to urge the beasts over the river —
The Champion's shouts, the heart's sound.

He rode in his Chariot, his eyes started from his head,
The Grey Horse struck who ran.
He thrust with his spear, they fell before him —
Hero of Ulster, the greatest man.

Blood was on Gold and on silver and on enamel,
The mud dried on his face:
Thirsty with death he looked for water and saw
A pool in a reedy place.

The Champion left his chariot and bent to drink:
Beneath his hands, water is red.
The reeds rustled, he threw his spear and saw
The otter shield on the face of the dead.

Three women cooked over a fire by dry thorns.
They told him, 'Take, eat!'
True to his Gesa, he gnawed the bone, and asked:
'Dog,' they said, 'this day is sweet.'

At the ford, the last of the cattle are crossing,
Erc says, 'Give me thy spear.'
True to his Gesa, the Champion hurls it.
When did Erc know fear?

On foot to the standing stone is the road of the Champion.
His own spear pierces his shield.
With a prince's belt he ties himself to the pillar.
Standing he cannot yield.

The hosts of Callum urge the cattle over the river:
Conchobar's chariots mass beyond the ford.
The host of Connaught dare not cross to meet them —
The Champion holds his sword.

Lugaid goes forward, brave, to deal the last stroke.
The Champion's head on the sand.
The sword falls from his shoulder — beneath the pillar
Earth receives Lugaid's hand.

The Hosts of Maeve roll forward into the river,
At her pole, a head.
The Champion's hand they throw in the face of all Ulster —
Emain knows Cuchullain is dead.

There was a long silence. When we looked again, Cathbad was gone. I pulled myself together. Who was dead, was dead, I told Gwawl, as harshly as I could:

'If you cannot pay your debts, King, then you must play again.'

And this time, we sat down to the Fichel of fifty-one moves, the Game of Champions, the longest that is commonly played. It must be obvious to you, now, that the more moves the less chance there is that the king will live. Yet it is possible to play the game of the fifty-ones moves, if you play well, and not to lose, if you hold the king, and if you are wise and cautious and at the same time bold. And play well I did that evening, with the circle of savage warriors to watch us, breathing over me and watching my style with interest, because there was not a man of them but was fair mad on the game.

After twenty-three moves, I killed one of Gwawl's men, though now he had played me once before it was harder to catch him. After forty-seven moves, I killed another.

And at the fifty-first move, when he thought he had me, I wafted the king gently out of his grasp, and that was the end, and all the Leinstermen who stood behind me saw it.

'Pay your debts, King Gwawl. Let us both, my man and I, go to Tara, and let us stay there in the Plain and be fed by the people of the village till there come an Eagle to feed us.'

'Aye, and it is a long time that it is that you will be waiting,' Gwawl sneered at us, laughed at us. 'What makes you think that the Eagles will ever come now?'

'Now?' I echoed.

'Aye, now. Do you think that you are the only one to know that the Eagles follow trade? The nightmare it is that follows all the Kings of Ireland, and not the High King only, through all their waking watchful nights. That is our terror, the thought of a Roman in every village of Ireland, stealing all our poor pennies to send back to enrich your incense-filled temples in Rome. No that shall never be while there is an Irish King alive.

'It was only by chance that I heard of it. If Cuchullain will go to Eboracum and to Londinium, to learn wisdom, I thought, why should I not go to Rome itself, and see for myself what made the oil-eaters so greedy? And so I did . . . And even there I should not have learnt what was going on if my Gesa had not driven me to gamble, and to meet that pretty fool with the Monopoly in his pocket. Ready he was to boast about it. I soon settled him. But you, Photinus, you were more trouble, and yet I would have done for you too, if not for Pryderi . . . If you had stayed in Londinium, I would have had you when the nights got dark. But I had no chance out there on the road, and in the Mere, with all *his* friends about you. Pryderi!' Gwawl spat. 'That two-and-a-half-obol king of a half-obol kingdom, and even that in pawn to the Roman, for all he is so proud of his crown and so careful of his people. Just because my young men have been raiding along the coasts of Dyfed, and how else shall they marry without heads to buy their brides with, and because the Romans have not been able to stop us as they promised, he takes it into his head to help any scheme that will bring down all the thrones of Ireland, and have us all in the same state that he is in. There was no hope of defeating him to get at you. But in spite of him, we knew all about you, we learned every detail of your plan and every change in your mind.'

'That cannot be,' I told him, and yet I knew it was true, that he did know everything, and I knew, and I *would* not know, and yet I did know, who it was that had told him, that had sat with Pryderi and me so long and so often by the fireside in the Mere, who knew all that Pryderi knew — and yet there were things she could not know, because I had not even told Pryderi.

'Rhiannon told us,' he shouted at me, in triumph. 'She sent us news of everything you said, by this messenger or that, men or birds or spirits, how should you know or how should you care? And when she knew the time, then she came to me, and I brought her off safely into this land of all her kinsman. And then, there was nothing to do, but to wait till you and Cuchullain came to waste both the armies of the North and of the West. When that was done, I could come out myself and become High King of Ireland, and who better for it than I who had saved the Island of the Blessed?'

'And what good will it do you?' I asked him. There was no harm in talking now, he knew enough. 'It is little comfort being the High King will be to you when the legions come. It happened to Vercingetorix after Alesia fell, and it will happen to you. A short walk in the Triumph, and then — into the Mamertine. Do you know it? A stone box, thirty feet square, with a spring in one corner, that keeps it always damp. But you will not feel rheumatism there, oh no, you won't stay long enough. Four men to hold you and one to twist the rope, slowly . . . slowly . . . and your eyes burst out . . . and the noise in your ears . . . and then, into the Great Sewer with what is left.'

He still laughed at me, strutting and threatening.

'And what makes *you* think that the legions will ever come? How do you think they will sail now? Aye, we knew that they would come soon, who wouldn't know, with the hammers and the axes going and the ships building in every creek? But the day that Cuchullain held the white mare for Conchobar to mount, that day Rhiannon did our business for us. That day she raised the Brigantes, that day she set all North Britain aflame from sea to sea. How can the Second and the Twentieth sail, if the Sixth is threatened?'

Aristarchos spoke for the first time.

'There are legions and to spare in Gaul and in Germany to hold down the Brigantes and let the others sail.'

Gwawl went on.

'Do you think we Barbarians are as disunited as politicians in Rome? On that same day, there was war from the mouth of the Rhine to the mouth of the Danube. That very day, the Marcomen sacked Vindabonum, and now they are pressing to Aquileia. There are no reinforcements for Britain.'

'Oh, my regiment!' said Aristarchos. 'Oh, my Rangers! To go to war, and I not there to lead you!'

'The regiment you raised among the Brigantes? How else do you think Vindabonum fell but when they deserted? Mutiny against Rome to them was loyalty to Rhiannon. They will pass across the land of the Chatti and through the Friesians across the North Sea, and will fight against the legions before the harvest.'

'I do not believe it,' said Aristarchos. 'It is not true. There is no rebellion. You are lying to make us despair.' He did not say 'Frighten us'; he did not know the word.

Someone stepped forward. I knew him, stout and middle-aged. He had been the other of the two men with the Mouse. Now he had a sword cut on the face, his ear was hanging by a strip of skin, and the unwashed blood was black. He held a bundle on his outstretched forearms, a scarlet Roman cloak folded under and up and over what might have been a great dish. The cloak was a fine one. It was not what the quartermaster issues, but made to measure of close-woven wool, light and warm together, fit for a tribune, or for a very senior centurion.

'This one died well. I killed him myself.'

He turned back the edges of the cloak. It covered a

337

shield, oblong and convex; the leather was hacked and gashed. In the hollow of the shield was a sword, legionary pattern, the edge gapped, the point turned. There was half of a staff of vine wood, snapped off. There was a bundle of Phalerae. I had seen them before. And black and woolly haired, the lips drawn back from the shining teeth in an awful grimace of rage and shame and pain, I saw the head of Caius Julius Africanus.

'It is true. When the Primus Pilus carries a shield and fights in the ranks, the legion is all but lost.' Aristarchos wrapped his cloak about his face, and wept. The middle-aged man went on.

'Now there is no one to stop us in the Island of Britain. We have burnt every ship on the Western Coast. The legions will not come.'

Now I knew why the army of Leinster had not come against us at Tara, why they had not been there to hold back the host of Callum the Hairy, so that their villages would not be burnt and their cattle not stolen. They had been at sea, saving Ireland, whatever the cost to Leinster, as Rhiannon had saved Ireland, whatever the cost to Britain.

I had no time to weep, not for the hand of Cuchullain in the dust, not for Africanus, fallen in the front rank. I had no time to weep for the treachery of Rhiannon. It is the surest mark of love, that it betrays, and how could I ever think otherwise? I could only face Gwawl and tell him:

'If you cannot pay your debts, King of Leinster, then you must play again.'

It was well dark when we played our third game of Fichel, the Game of Kings, the game of a hundred and nineteen moves. The Leinstermen stood round with their flaring torches, that brought smoke as well as light to the gaming board, and they counted the moves, shouting the numbers.

'Twenty-one!' and the king moved away in his constant circling.

338

'Twenty-two!' and one man came to back another that would have been killed otherwise.

The king turned and twisted, the eight men dodged and shuffled like wolves about an elk in winter, but I had too much of the wolf in my blood to die like an elk. Let me tell you this, it is easier to control one man on the board or on the battlefield than eight. It was late. Gwawl was tired from days of pursuit, by land and by sea, from battles and marches, from judgements and decisions. He played most of the time with half his men, he missed his chances.

'Seventy-eight!' and the men stood on three sides of the king.

'Seventy-nine!' and the king moved to threaten two men at once.

'Eighty!' and Gwawl saw the danger, but imperfectly, and moved one man back to where he was safe, when he should have brought a third man to guard them both.

'Eighty-one!' and the king struck, and a man rolled on the ground.

This reminded Gwawl that he had four men he had hardly used at all, and he began to move them to where he thought they might be of help in containing the king, and soon he lost another. But now my eyes were smarting from the smoke of the torches and the fire, and the sweat on my face had little to do with the heat of the logs and turf. My king dodged and feinted and moved spasmodically from edge to centre and back again to edge.

'A hundred and nine!' and I erred, and the king was stopped, trapped, if only Gwawl had wit to see it, he was dead next move, and I had lost, lost for myself, what was worse, lost for Aristarchos.

'A hundred and ten!' and he had learned his lesson too well, and he was more eager to guard his own piece than to attack mine.

'A hundred and eleven!' and the king was away, and safe for another move.

But there was still time. The six men pressed and pushed. The king was harried. Three moves left now, to each side,

339

and he was too near the edge of the board for comfort or confidence. Two moves each side, and he was pressed back towards the corner. One move each. Gwawl's last, and had he been more alert he would have seen his chance. But the very man he moved to block the king's way exposed another to vengeance.

'A hundred and nineteen,' cried all the Leinstermen together. The king, in his last move, struck, and struck true.

Gwawl sat rigid, looking at his board. Aristarchos sighed a long sigh. I could not move. We all three slept a little where we sat. I felt as empty as I had on the Night of the Thorn. The Leinstermen stood around us and watched, silent. Africanus stared at us from glazed, unclosing eyes. Suddenly, there was the sound of a cock crowing, the only cock left for miles uneaten, his neck unwrung. We all three blinked our eyes open into the new day. I said to Gwawl:

'Pay your debts, King of Leinster. Give us a boat, sound and dry, and food and drink, that we two may return to whence we came.'

'Go, then, to the Gods Below,' he answered. 'I give you the mercy you showed me at Rutupiae.'

But he was more merciful. They brought us down to the sea-beach where we ate a scanty meal of stale barley bread, and mouldy beef, and water from the river, muddied and fouled by the crossing of great armies high inland. The corpses of men and horses bobbed past us into the salt water. The Leinstermen ate no better than we two did.

They found us a big skin boat, and there was no saying it was not good enough, because it was in boats like this that the army of Leinster had crossed the sea to the Isle of Britain. More bread and meat they put in it, and a big jar of beer they found, the only beer for miles. They left us all we had, our weapons, and my bag with my spare eyes and my dice and other trifles. And then Gwawl came to me with my cloak, my sealskin, and he apologised that it was soiled, because he had had to kill the man who picked it up to get it back for me. And his own cloak, of

340

bearskin from the edge of the Summer Country, he gave to Aristarchos.

Gwawl and his men got into other boats. The middle-aged man took Africanus's white shield, and stood on the beach. The Irishmen paddled out to sea, towing us with them. Far out beyond the ninth wave they took us, till, low as we were in the water, we could no longer see the white shield on the shore. All the boats but one left us. Only Gwawl remained, and he leant over to me. He shouted against the south-west wind: 'One last thing. What was the answer to that riddle?'

'What riddle?'

'The one you asked me on the judgement mound of Arberth? What is both black and white and neither in earth or in sky?'

'Oh, that,' and I laughed, because it was such a little thing to remember through all the months of context and plotting and battle. 'You'll never be a Druid. Why, that was yourself, black hearted, white-clad, standing head in clouds on the mound above the Earth. And another thing, King of Leinster!'

'What?' He was drifting away now, towards the shore.

'Give up gambling — you haven't got the head for it.'

CHAPTER NINE

For seven days and nights we tossed on the seas, between
the Island of the Blessed and the Island of the Mighty. At
first we tried to head the boat eastward, across the south
wind. We paddled silently, our teeth clenched in the bitterness of defeat, saying nothing because neither of us would
admit defeat, neither of us would admit aloud what we
both knew, that we could no more paddle that boat to
Britain than we could fly.

And that boat *could* have flown. Light as a feather,
wicker-framed and leather-covered, it hopped and bobbed
across the wave tops in the hard wind. The seas broke
beneath us. We could not be swamped, but we were
covered in spray. Our clothes dried stiff and white. The
barley bread was soaked in salt water, the dried beef was
drenched in brine till it would have outlived a mummy.
We drank mouthfuls of the beer. It was a diuretic which
drained the water from our blood. Both Aristarchos and
I had thirsted before. We licked the rain water from the
bottom of the boat before the spray splashed in to pollute
it. For want of pebbles we sucked spare eyes from my
bag — he a ruby, I an amethyst, and that was a strange
precaution, for how were we to get drunk?

Only, before we shut our mouths against speech and
thirst, Aristarchos said:

'Already they sing their songs about Cuchullain: they
will sing none about us.'

'They will sing our deeds and give them to Cuchullain,'
I told him. 'Almost every Bard has made his own song,
and altered the plain truth of the deeds to fit his own metre.

342

Did you ever see the Setanta able to tell one horse from another? But a hero must have a horse that can be named. And each Bard makes his song fit what his Lord wants to hear, and there will in one generation be a hundred songs of Cuchullain. Yet each Bard will swear that he sings the true and authentic facts of the case, handed down word-perfect from eyewitnesses. At last, someone will write the song down, as Homer did, and write one particular Bard's song among many. And then there will be only one song about Cuchullain, and every other Bard will alter his own song to accord with the true, the written word. All the other tales will soon be forgotten, and we with them.'

'Forgotten and accursed, because defeated.'

'What kind of Briton are you dressed up to be? If you were really a native of the Island of the Mighty, then you would say that defeat is the surest sign of virtue and that failure shows how you enjoy the favour of the Gods. Gwawl has succeeded. He has challenged the might of Rome all across Europe, and he has saved his island, and there is little doubt that he will rule it when Maeve and Conchobar have torn out each others' throats. But no one in Ireland will remember him, and the Britons will know his name only as someone that Pryderi rolled in the mud, and they will invent reasons why that is how the game of the Badger in the Bag was first played. And Pryderi the King will be forgotten, except that as a king he wandered unknown through cities that did not know him, and that with some shadowy companion called Mannanan he cheated shoemakers and shield-makers. And there will be a shadowy memory that Madoc was a sea captain and that Heilyn once sailed in a ship, Caw will only be remembered as the father of his many sons. All will be forgotten, except that dying man bound to the standing stone.'

We spoke no more. By night we lashed ourselves to the single thwart by our belts, and clung on, besides, wakeful, lest we be overturned and drowned in our sleep. By day we took it in turns, one to sleep and one to beat off the birds who would have taken the bread from our mouths if we had had any bread, and the eyes from our heads if they had a chance. It was the salmon mallet we used for this.

We were drifted north by the winds and the tides. We passed close enough to some shore, to the eastward, to see great mountains, miles high. Another time we came near to a rocky coast with seals lying on the beaches, but the tide carried us off, and we watched it dwindle bluer and bluer through the day.

Then, on the eighth day, when we were very weak and not inclined to talk even had our lips been dry enough, I was awake and Aristarchos was asleep, and I realised that we had some peace. The gulls and the gannets had ceased to torment us: they no longer dived at our eyes. Instead, I could see them circling ahead of us, a tower of white feathers above some object moving across the water, as yet invisible from our little boat so close to the surface.

And then, as the seabirds came nearer, I began to see it all, lifting above the close horizon. First the tip of a mast, flying a pennant chequered with yellow and black. Then a great dark lug-sail, the sail of a ship on a broad reach, crossing us from starboard to port, and heading east across the north-west wind.

'A ship!' I shouted to Aristarchos. I shook him awake, I thrust the paddle into his hand. 'A ship! A ship, paddle to it, paddle to the ship!'

And paddle to it we did, and we shouted through our cracked dry throats, and now we could see the gunwales and heads above them, and she lost way and came round towards us into the wind, finer and finer as they made towards us as best they could. And what other ship would we see so far out at sea, and what other ship would we meet at such a time? A ship of the Venetii, a ship built long ago on the coasts of Gaul, a ship that Aristarchos knew as well as I. We shouted, we shouted, and we tried to believe we recognised the voices that shouted back to us.

We came alongside, under her lee, crossing her bow, and someone threw us a rope. I looked up into his face, and it was a face I had not expected to see on the salt water.

344

He no longer squinted, but it was the man I knew, from the inn at Bonnonia, who drew fish and made strange allusions. He helped us aboard, first Aristarchos, and I could hear his cracked cries of surprise and then the gurgling as he drank — he was never very dainty. Then I hauled myself up the side on a rope, and hands clutched me to help me over the bulwarks.

'Come on, boy,' said Madoc. 'Saved us a lot of trouble them birds have. Thought it was I did we'd have to go all down the coast of Ireland to find you.'

'Who shall drink of this water shall thirst again, but he who drinks of the cup of life shall never thirst,' said the man from Bonnonia. That, I thought, was a typical Brit saying, except that to my mild surprise he said it in Greek, a Greek with a Jewish accent, but the dialect of one of the smaller islands, Leros or Patmos or Cos. I snatched at the jug and half drained it before I saw whose hands had offered it.

'Not too greedy, now,' said Pryderi. 'It wouldn't be very dainty if we had you burst over the floor.'

'Not floor, deck,' I corrected him. I wasn't going to have him treat me as if I were a landsman. Now I was in my proper place, as he had been on the road. I looked around that lovely ship, lovely as a woman, I thought, lovely as Rhiannon. Oh, a splendid place to be, on the open sea, clear of all the plots and double dealing of the land. My spirits were rising again, as I drank, and cleaned a chicken leg and tore at a cake of oat bread. Now, I was in a ship, and I was my own master again, and among seamen. The only real landsman I could see was Aristarchos, and it was only for him that Pryderi would have to choose his words. I looked aft. Beside the steersman, in a short white tunic, unspotted, of course, by the marks of toil, stood Taliesin.

'What use is he?' I asked.

'Very useful he do be in recognising the stars,' Madoc assured me, but he went on, 'or at least he will be if ever we get a clear night and any stars to recognise.'

'And how many more have you got like this?' I asked testily. I felt I had a right to know. I had after all, been

345

promised the use of this ship for the summer's trade and I was at least entitled to have it for this return voyage.

'Only four men forward, like this one here,' said Madoc, waving at the man from Bonnonia, and speaking with the familiar tone of someone trying to delay the impact of bad news. 'And aft, there's five of us, and now you.' He hesitated, unsure of how to explain himself, and he was saved the trouble. Out of the cabin under the poop came Cicva.

'Well, at least we'll have some good food in this tub, as far as the cooking goes,' I admitted, grudgingly prepared to forgive the presence of a woman in a ship, seeing it was this sensible and competent queen. But then behind Cicva, yawning and stretching arms as if fresh from sleep, and shocking that was, too, being only a couple of hours before noon, why, who else would it be, with all those ghastly birds around us, but Rhiannon.

'If she's in this flaming ship,' I told them angrily, 'then it's me for the skin boat again. Hoist it out!'

'Shame on you!' scolded Cicva. 'And wasn't it Rhiannon herself who made us come out to sea again after we'd all got safe into the North among the Picts, out of reach of those filthy Romans with all their pillaging and atrocities that they're doing everywhere, delighted they are too that they've got an excuse. We took my little Mannanan up there to be fostered with his Aunty Bithig and home up there with my Grandfather Casnar I would have been pleased enough to stay, but no, out to sea she would go, and it was never letting her go by herself I could be, not with these old goats that call themselves sailors.'

Rhiannon came up to me, all smiling and shining, and looked at me in a proprietorial fashion, as if she had never done me a wrong. I glared at her.

'Why do you look at me like that, Mannanan, when I have saved your life a hundred times?' she asked. 'Did I not send all the birds of the sea to find you, and to hover above you like a tall mast with a fine flag on it, so that we could see you from afar and sail down to pick you out of the water? I belong to you, Mannanan, and after all I have suffered I still return to you when I could so easily be free of you for ever.'

'Traitor,' I told her. I was not angry, this was past the point of anger. 'You have betrayed me to my ruin, and may yet betray me to my death. And you have been the death of good men all up and down the edges of the Empire. What more trouble will you bring on me and on Caesar?'

'I might have been the death of one man at any time,' she answered, 'and saved all other blood. There was never a moment, Mannanan, from the day you saw me first in Londinium to the day you set sail for Ireland, when anything but my word stood between you and swift and silent death. There were men enough ready to kill you, Mannanan, eager to kill you. But I took an oath from Gwawl, and from all the men of the Brigantes, that there should not be a hair of your head touched. How do you think a one-eyed man lives in battle? You were safer facing the host of Gwawl than leading the host of Ulster.'

'And Maeve?'

'A hard woman she is, and cruel, and not one to give up her prey. But I made her swear, at the least, that if she had you in her power, she would keep you alive till I came, and then, we stand together, Mannanan — what can prince or queen or emperor do to harm us?'

I heard her voice and I looked into her eyes. I took her hand and I turned to my friends.

'Whither do we go now?'

'Not back to the Picts,' said Aristarchos. 'They will have my head, and I still have my own uses for it.'

'If we continue south,' Madoc declared, 'we will be on the shores that belong to Callum the Hairy, and it is already one ship of mine that he has trapped and looted, and I do not want to be in a second.'

'If we go south east,' Pryderi told us, 'then it is neither I nor Rhiannon nor Taliesin will live long, nor die slowly, if we meet the legions in the field.'

'And they are looking for me in Britain,' said the man from Bonnonia, to whom this conversation was of interest, 'for blasphemy and treason combined, in that I refused to burn incense before the statue of the Emperor.'

I ignored him. If a man could bring himself to do such a horrid and unprincipled thing as that, then what did he deserve but the punishment decreed by law, whatever that may be. I spoke only to the others.

'I have seen a map, and I have spoken to astronomers who know. Ireland lies half-way between Britain and Spain. Let us then sail west, passing north of Ireland, and in a few days we shall be in the harbour of Gades.'

I took the steering oar from Grathach's hand. They then trimmed the sail. I had the breeze on my right cheek.

'West, then,' I cried. 'West, due west, and home!'

THE END

Places mentioned in the text with their modern names

Bonnonia	Boulogne
Bordigala	Bordeaux
Calleva	Silchester
Corinium	Cirencester
Cunetio	Marlborough
Deva	Chester
Dubris	Dover
Durovernum	Canterbury
Eboracum	York
Glevum	Gloucester
Isca	Caerleon
Lindum	Lincoln
Londinium	London
Lugdunum	Lyons
Lutetia	Paris
Massilia	Marseilles
Noviomagus	Chichester
Pontes	Staines
Rutupiae	Richborough
Sulis	Bath
Venta	Caerwent

VOTAN
by John James

The setting for this brilliantly original fantasy is Germany in the second century. It is a tale set on the edges of the civilized world, a savage twilight of myth and superstition, untouched as yet by the great civilizations of the south.

Into this dark hinterland rides Photinus the Greek, priest of Apollo. He is journeying northward to Asgard in search of the source of Amber, the symbol of material wealth which is his highest aspiration. Chance (as he believes) heaps pain and misfortune upon him, until eventually the turning point comes. After being rescued by a wild Slavonic tribe who hail him as their promised god, he enters Asgard as Votan Aser, one of the Amber Lords.

This fascinating and accomplished novel is a mixture of magic and mythology, Norse Gods, and the splendour and barbarity of the Dark Ages.

'The best thing about the Dark Ages is that, where fiction is concerned, you can do what you like with them. There are legends and a few odd facts, but, for the rest, one man's imagination is as good as the next man's. And John James's is splendid'
Daily Telegraph

0 553 17358 8

BELOVED EXILE
by Parke Godwin

'It's enormously sensuous, violent, rowdy, and above all, it's solidly there; the characters get right up off the page and scream at you, across the centuries'
Marion Zimmer Bradley, author of The Mists of Avalon

Few legends have clung to our hearts as closely as that of the age of Camelot. It was a time when magical dreams were born. When kingdoms were made and broken. Now, this age is brought to fresh, stunning life in one of the most dramatic portraits of Guenevere ever created.

Guenevere: shrewd schemer, compassionate ruler, heartless tyrant, lover, warrior, slave — and always, always a queen.

'Godwin has created a Guenevere we have never seen before, someone fresh and new and totally believable . . . During the hours I spent captured by the spell of Godwin's storytelling, I believed every word and lived every scene'
Morgan Llywelyn, author of Lion of Ireland *and* The Horse Goddess

0 553 17181 X

A SELECTION OF SCIENCE FICTION AND FANTASY TITLES AVAILABLE FROM BANTAM BOOKS

☐ 17291 3	THE HEART OF THE COMET	Gregory Benford & David Brin	£2.95
☐ 17184 4	THE PRACTICE EFFECT	David Brin	£1.95
☐ 17170 4	STARTIDE RISING	David Brin	£3.50
☐ 17162 3	SUNDIVER	David Brin	£2.95
☐ 17193 3	THE POSTMAN	David Brin	£2.95
☐ 17398 7	RIVER OF TIME	David Brin	£2.50
☐ 17452 5	THE UPLIFT WAR	David Brin	£3.50
☐ 17250 6	RIDERS OF THE DIDHE	Kenneth C. Flint	£2.50
☐ 17256 5	CHAMPIONS OF THE SIDHE	Kenneth C. Flint	£2.50
☐ 17292 1	MASTER OF THE SIDHE	Kenneth C. Flint	£2.50
☐ 17384 7	CHALLENGE OF THE CLANS	Kenneth C. Flint	£2.95
☐ 17181 X	BELOVED EXILE	Parke Godwin	£2.95
☐ 17358 8	VOTAN	John James	£2.75
☐ 17188 7	THE BOOK OF KELLS	R. A. MacAvoy	£2.95
☐ 17154 2	DAMIANO	R. A. MacAvoy	£1.95
☐ 17156 9	RAPHAEL	R. A. MacAvoy	£1.95
☐ 17282 4	SONG OF SORCERY	Elizabeth Scarborough	£1.95
☐ 17283 2	THE UNICORN CREED	Elizabeth Scarborough	£2.95